The
True Natural

Tia C. Lynk

I want to thank my family and friends who helped and supported me. I love you all.

Contents

One They Meet ~ 1
Two The Lake ~ 16
Three The Legend ~ 27
Four Control ~ 41
Five Family History ~ 57
Six Protection ~ 73
Seven Attack ~ 89
Eight Special Gift ~ 108
Nine Celebration ~ 126
Ten First Lesson ~ 143
Eleven Visitor ~ 161
Twelve Another Ability ~ 179
Thirteen Reality ~ 195
Fourteen Revealed ~ 210
Fifteen Warning ~ 225
Sixteen Discovered ~ 241
Seventeen Home ~ 257
Eighteen The Past ~ 271
Nineteen Truth ~ 283
Twenty Betrayed ~ 297
Twenty One Souls ~ 307
Epilogue ~ 316

One
They Meet

I stopped walking; I didn't know where I was. Looking up all I could see was a white curtain all around me. The cold was bitter; I was too upset to feel it or even care. I was in a blizzard. I knew I needed to get home; though, I didn't know where I had come from or why I was upset for that matter. Turning around, I headed the way I thought was home. As I walked along, I heard a noise, like someone crunching snow on both sides of me. I knew I should protect myself; however, I couldn't risk it in case someone was close enough to see. I was starting to get scared. Suddenly, a shadowy figure appeared through the snow. I couldn't see who it was; though, I sensed I was in danger. The shadow drew closer; I could almost make out this persons features; a little closer...

I woke to a loud buzzing noise filling my ears. At first, I was confused and disoriented. I didn't understand what the noise was; then I realized that it was my alarm going off. I had been dreaming. It felt so real, like I was actually there. After a moment or two, I collected myself and got up. I pulled the curtain back to peek out my window to see what the weather was like this morning. The sun was just starting to come up; though, I could see it was going to be a typical blustery September morning in Colorado. At least the sun was rising hopefully it would stay a sunny day. This time of year, the weather was very unpredictable. I rummaged through my closet for a pair of jeans and a t-shirt. I put my shoes on and then brushed my teeth and blonde hair before heading downstairs.

I live in a two-story house, that was most likely built in the early nineteen hundreds or so, with my Aunt Marie Jackson, a young, kind faced woman with long, pretty, dark hair and blue eyes. I was just a baby when my parents died. Aunt Marie has been taking care of me ever since. I don't remember my parents; however, I think of them often. I wonder what they were like. Did they like the same things as me? Did they look me? Aunt Marie had no pictures left of my parents.

The kitchen walls were a light beige color and the tile floor was a few shades darker with intricate thick swirls. The cupboards were dark cherry and plenty of them. It's a good-sized room with a small breakfast nook big enough for a small table and four chairs to fit in. Aunt Marie was sitting at the table reading the newspaper and drinking coffee like she did every morning before work. She owns Sweet Retreat, the little bakery in town. People come from miles around just for her caramel éclairs. During the summer, I would help her out a couple days a week.

"Good Morning, Kendall!" she bubbled. She has always been a happy person, very friendly to everyone, yet also very cautious until she got to know you.

"Would you like me to make you breakfast this morning?" she asked.

"No thanks, I'll just grab a pop tart. I'm in a hurry anyway," I explained.

"It's only seven thirty," there was a puzzled look on her face. "School doesn't start until eight fifteen. What's your hurry?"

"I'm supposed to meet Sam. We want to go over a math test that Mr. Emerson is giving today."

That was partially true, we really did have a math test today;

however, I just wanted a few minutes alone before I faced the day, to get myself in order. That dream really shook me up. I didn't want to hurt her feelings though.

She smiled, "Okay honey, have a good day at school. I love you."

I knew she wouldn't push it any further. So I grabbed my coat and headed for the door

"I love you too," I called over my shoulder as I walked out.

The autumn wind was blowing my hair into my face, making it hard to see; however, I walked the path to the driveway thousands of times and could do it blind folded. I opened the driver's side door of my birthday present from last year, a midnight blue Jeep Cherokee that I absolutely love. I didn't ask for it, we were not what you would call rich, so it was a big surprise when I got home that day and saw it in the driveway. I had asked Aunt Marie how she had gotten the money for a vehicle like this. She brushed it off like she always did when I got something nice and said 'I have a secret stash.' I roll my eyes at her every time she says that.

I drove through the small town of Oak Creek to school. Aunt Marie and I moved here shortly after my parents died. Not much has changed since I can remember. We still have all the typical buildings of a small town, a market, gas station, doctor's office, a diner, and a few other small town stores along with my aunt's bakery. We even have one blinking red light in the center of town.

The high school in our town was a light-colored brick building with lots of windows in the front and sides. The lawn was as long as the school, with a sidewalk going up to the double doors in the middle and along the side of the building that leads to the student parking lot. It has the same teachers and almost the same students as last year. Though this year there had been a new addition, his name was Lucas O'Brien. We didn't get many new transfer students, so Lucas was the main topic at the beginning of the school year, well mainly the girls' topic; however, as time went by he was old news and the students found something else to talk about. I do have to agree with the rest of the girls though; he was kind of cute, with his tall, muscular stature and dark hair. He looked in-between a jock -although he doesn't play any sports- and the dark mysterious type; the kind of person that would not pay any attention to someone like me. We're not in the same social circle. I'm not sporty or the cheerleading type. I am just a regular, normal, average height sixteen-year-old girl. I do have about half of my classes with him though; we don't sit beside each other.

A few other students were already at school, but luckily, I found a decent spot to park. I gathered my books and walked across the parking lot into the side door of the building like I did everyday to meet Sam before first period. Sam Keeley has been my best friend since kindergarten. I knew she wasn't here yet, so I would wait for her inside in our usual meeting spot just around the corner of the front entrance. Being so early on a Monday, there were not that many other students here yet. I wasn't paying much attention and as I turned the corner, I bumped into someone. My books fell to the floor with several loud thuds. Great, the one-day I had to carry my books because I left my backpack in my locker last Friday.

"Oh!" I said. "I'm so sorry. I didn't see you. Are you okay?"

It shocked me as to who was standing there. Lucas O'Brien. I bent down to pick up my books hoping I could wipe the embarrassment off my face before I stood back up to face him.

"I'm fine," he chuckled as he bent down to help me. "Are you alright?"

When I looked up at him, he smiled. I was so stunned by the way he looked at me with his brown eyes that I dropped the books that I had already picked up. Karman walked by just then, of course.

"Nice one," she said.

I looked up in time to see her red curls bouncing behind her as she walked away laughing. We did not get along very well. Her parents Mr. and Mrs. Lambert have a lot of money. I like them; they are the type of people that don't throw it in everyone's faces. Karman on the other hand was the type to never let anyone forget it.

"I'm fine," I told him as we stood back up. I could feel my face getting redder every second with that stupid move. "Thank you."

"You're welcome," he was still holding my books as he reached out his hand. "I'm Lucas O'Brien."

"I know," I slowly took his hand and shook it gently. "I'm Kendall Monroe."

"I know," he grinned. "Can I help you get to your class?"

I was hesitant; Lucas was here, talking to me. Something I thought would never happen and he knew who I was. Would Sam be mad if I left? No, I couldn't leave her. I would wait.

"Umm actually I'm waiting for my friend Sam."

Just as I said her name, she came around the corner. Her dark brown hair was in a ponytail that swung behind her as she walked. There was a shocked smile on her thin face when she realized whom I was with.

"Hi," she said to the both of us, but held her gaze at me for a moment longer.

"Hello. You must be Sam."

"Yes I am, and you are Lucas," she stated the obvious with a giggle.

I rolled my eyes and shook my head at her.

After a few awkward moments of silence I said, "Well…we better get to class before the bell rings."

Lucas handed the books that he still had to Sam, and then turned to me with a smile. I really liked his smile. His brown eyes were warm and gentle and they held mine with ease.

"Let Sam help you carry your books to your locker. Okay?"

I returned his smile; I could still feel a trace of embarrassment on my face. "Alright; thanks again."

"I'll see you later," then he walked away while we just stared after him in a daze.

"What was that about?" Sam asked with a huge grin as we walked to our Spanish class.

I knew we wouldn't make it very far before she started asking me questions.

"I bumped into him or...he bumped into me, I'm not sure which and my books fell to the floor. He was just helping me pick them up."

She shook her head, "No, not that!"

"What then?" I was confused.

"The way he was looking at you...and you," there was amusement in her voice.

"What about me?"

"You like him don't you?" she grinned widely again.

"I don't know what you are talking about?" I said nonchalantly as we walked into Mrs. Garcia's class.

"Uh huh, okay," there was sarcasm in her voice.

I smiled and we both laughed as we took our seats.

After the bell rang for my last class of the day, I picked up my books and put them into my book bag. I didn't want a replay of this morning. One humbling a day is enough.

"So did you want to go see a movie this weekend? I was thinking we could have a girl's night out." Sam asked as we gathered our things.

I thought about the last time we had had one of those. I couldn't really remember so it must have been a while ago.

"Sure that sounds fun. Just let me run it across Aunt Marie though, okay?"

"Sure just let me know."

"Okay. I'll see you later."

Sam was headed back to Mrs. Ellis's room, our English teacher; it was one of only two classes we didn't have together. Usually we would walk out to the parking lot together; however, Sam had forgotten what her assignment was. We usually had the same assignments, but Sam had an extra one to catch up her grades.

I stepped out onto the sidewalk and froze. I had this feeling that someone was watching me. I looked around to see if anyone was out of place, when I saw a man standing a few feet from my Jeep. He was tall with dark hair and had clean clothes on so I could tell he wasn't a drifter. I felt a little nervous, all though I really didn't know why.

"Are you alright?" I heard a voice behind me say.
I just about jumped out of my skin. Heart racing, I turned around to see Lucas standing behind me.

"You scared me half to death!"

There was a hint of a smile playing on the corners of his mouth, "Sorry."

"It's okay. What are you doing?"

"I walked out to go home and saw you just standing there. You looked sort of freaked out."

"I saw..."
When I turned back to look at the man next to my Jeep he was gone.

"Saw what?"

"Never mind," I was a little bemused.
Where did he go? I looked around, but didn't see him anywhere.

Lucas eyed me suspiciously, "Are you sure you're alright?"

"Yes. I'm fine," I smiled uncertain.
There was a moment of silence as we looked at each other. I quickly found that I could look into his eyes forever, until he smiles of course, and then I look away because it's too much for my shyness.

"Come on, I'll walk you to your car," he said, pulling me out of our gaze.

"You sure have been nice to me today. I didn't think you noticed that I existed," I said jokingly.

"I've noticed," he whispered so low that I don't think he meant for me to hear.

We stopped in front of my Jeep. I was just about to thank him, but he spoke first.

"Sorry for scaring you back there."

"It's fine. Really," I told him.

"You looked like you were upset or something."

"Yeah, something," I thought about how I felt. I wasn't really scared; however, I couldn't put my finger on the exact feeling. "Thanks for walking me to my car."

"You're welcome," he smiled. "Anytime," his voice was gravelly and soothing at the same time.

I smiled back, "I'll see you later."

He chuckled, "See you tomorrow."

I got in my Jeep still thinking about that feeling. Not knowing what it was exactly, I locked the doors. Something I never do in this small town. I backed out of the parking space and headed for home.

I pulled into my driveway in front of my house and sat there for a few minutes thinking of the day I had just had. Lucas was paying attention to me for some reason. Not that I'm complaining, he was pretty cute, it's just that it was very different from any other day. I walked into the house with a smile on my face. I hung my coat up and was headed for the stairs when Aunt Marie came from the living room. She must have seen the expression on my face because she smiled.

"You seem to be in a good mood," she said.

I shrugged my shoulders, "Good day is all."

"I see. Got a lot of homework?"

"Not really," I said indifferently. "I'm headed upstairs to start on it now," I was still smiling.

She eyed me suspiciously, "Alright, I'll call you when dinner is ready."

My room was fairly big, big enough for a full bed with a matching dresser, a vanity set, and a computer desk. My room was on the corner of the house so I had extra windows that let in a lot of natural light. I dropped my book bag by the door and lay on my bed. My head was too full to do homework right now. I was still thinking about what had happened this morning with Lucas and the strange man near my Jeep. There was something about that man. I just couldn't figure it out.

I heard a knock on my bedroom door. I sat up quickly realizing that I had fallen to sleep. I got up and staggered to my door. It was Aunt Marie.

"Didn't you hear me?" she asked with a slight annoyance to her voice.

"No, I didn't. Sorry. I fell asleep."

"Well, dinner is ready."

"What are we having?" I asked curiously, as I followed her down the stairs. "It smells really good!"

"Chicken Di' Van; your favorite."

She was right, it is. Aunt Marie loves to cook; so do I, I must get that from her. I dished up both of our plates and brought them over to the kitchen table. We only used the dining table when guests were here.

"This is really good," I told her.

"Thanks, I slaved all day," she grinned.

"You did not you liar!" We both laughed.

After we finished and I was clearing the table, I asked, "I was wondering if it would be okay if I went to Steamboat Springs to watch a movie with Sam on Saturday. She wants to have a girl's night out."

"A girl's night out huh?" She thought about it for a moment, "Yeah I think it will be alright."

"Thanks," I said with a smile.

Once the dishes were done, I went back to my room to start on my homework. I knew I wouldn't be able to get it all done tonight if I wanted to get to sleep at a decent time. I would read the chapters for English tonight and do my U.S. Government assignment in study hall tomorrow.

The next day Sam was waiting for me in our usual meeting spot. The first words out of her mouth were not any sort of greeting instead it was a question.

"Did you know that everybody is talking about you and Lucas?" she said excitedly.

"No. What do you mean?"

"Every girl is jealous of you right now."

"What? Why would they be jealous of me?" I didn't understand because I didn't consider myself popular.

"Because," her eyes became unfocused and dreamy, "you were like the damsel in distress and Lucas came to the rescue," she sighed and came back to reality.

I laughed aloud, "That is the dumbest thing I have ever heard. Embarrassment does not qualify a girl as a damsel in distress!"

She laughed too, "Yeah I guess your right. Klutziness doesn't either!"

That made me laugh even harder.

Just then, we heard a voice behind us, "What's so funny?" We turned around and saw Lucas. I was surprised. Even though he said he would see me tomorrow, I didn't really believe it. Sam and I just looked at each other and giggled some more.

"It's nothing really, just girl stuff," I told him.

"Oh," he smiled, "Hi Sam."

"Hi Lucas," she could barely hold a straight face.

He turned his attention back to me, "Well, I'll let you get back to the girl talk. I just wanted to say good morning."

"Good morning."

He chuckled, "I'll see you in English."

"Okay. See you," I turned back to Sam with a grin.

"Boy, the girls are really going to hate you now!" Sam said with a smirk.

I chuckled, "Shut up! Let's go before we're late."

After Biology, I said goodbye to Sam until lunch and hurried on my way to study hall. This was my favorite class. I think it's everyone's favorite, although our reasons were different. I actually liked to do my homework here while the rest of the students liked to goof off, until the teacher catches them. I still had those few pages to read for Mrs. Blake's class in U.S. Government.

Just like in English, my heart accelerated as I reached for the handle to open the door. This was one of the two classes I had with Lucas without Sam. I was nervous because he was talking to me and because of what Sam had said. Also, just like in English, he looked up as I entered the room and smiled a half smile. He was sitting in his usual spot reading a book. I smiled back at him before taking my seat.

I finished the assignment at the end of the period. It took me longer because I couldn't concentrate. I felt like Lucas was watching my every move. I snorted; I was over reacting as I sometimes did when I was feeling self-conscious. When Lucas passed without looking at me, it made me feel silly for feeling like that.

I woke up Saturday morning feeling very refreshed. I lay there thinking about the week that had passed. It was not a normal week. First, Lucas had said hi to me everyday before class, something he never did until I accidentally bumped into him. Secondly, there was this feeling of something not being quite right. After thinking about it for a few more minutes and not coming up with any answers, I went downstairs for breakfast.

The kitchen was empty, which was very unusual. Aunt Marie was not at the table in her usual chair, reading her morning paper and drinking her coffee. I shrugged it off and grabbed a bowl of cereal. As I sat down, I noticed a piece of paper with my aunt's neat cursive handwriting lying on the table. The note explained where she had gone.

Kendall,
Went to Steamboat Springs, be back later this afternoon.
Love, Aunt Marie

After breakfast, I went to the living room to watch television. After flipping through the channels for a third time, I was frustrated and headed for my room to check my email. There was only a bunch of junk mail. I deleted the contents of my mailbox and shut the monitor off. Well, that took a whole five minutes. I had only been up an hour and I was already bored. All of my homework was already done. I did most of it yesterday in study hall. I was surprised that I got that much done though with Lucas in the same class. I couldn't help but watch him from the corner of my eye. Sometimes during the Study Hall period, I even caught him looking at me. That made it harder to concentrate.

Sitting in my computer chair, I gazed out my bedroom window. It gave me an idea. I threw on a pair of shorts, a t-shirt and put my running shoes on. I grabbed my iPod, stuck the earpieces in and went downstairs. It was a cooler day, the wind was minimal, and the sun was out, a good day for running. I turned my iPod to my favorite song and then jogged left out of my driveway.

It was actually relaxing just to run with no one around and no time limit. It felt good. I run sometimes as it helps me relax and clear my head. I decided to run around the block a couple of times. I turned right onto Sharp Ave. and was about halfway to the next corner when I got that strange feeling again, the feeling that somebody was watching me. I looked around; however, I didn't see anyone. I turned right onto the next street and stopped. About two hundred yards in front of me, I saw him. It was him; the same man I saw at school the other day. I just stared; there was something familiar about him. I have never seen him before, other than Monday, though it was as if I knew him. Neither of us said anything, he just looked at me for as long as I looked at him.

A loud honk made me jump and snap out of it. I didn't realize I was standing in the middle of the road. I moved to the sidewalk and looked back to where the man was, but he was gone. He bemused me. I wasn't sure which way he had gone, yet I knew he hadn't come past me. I turned around and headed back the way I had come.

At home, I was so thirsty I downed a glass of water before heading upstairs to take a shower. The hot water felt good, it helped relax my nerves. Twenty minutes later, I got out of the shower, wrapped a towel around me and went back downstairs to get another glass of water. I heard someone in the living room. I thought about the man from earlier, and started to get nervous.

"Aunt Marie?" I asked a little leery.
I realized then, that if there was someone in the house I should remain quiet. It was too late now.

"In here," I heard her say.
I relaxed and felt a little foolish as I walked in the living room. I saw the evidence of the shopping trip on the couch.

"Did you just get back?" I was sure she wasn't here when I got home.

"Yes. You were in the shower. I didn't want to open the door and scare you."

I thought about the man again, "Yeah, thanks for that."
I hoped she didn't hear the slight nervousness in my voice.

She looked up, her eyebrows pushed together. She had heard.

"I'm fine," I told her. Then I quickly changed the subject, "What did you go to Steamboat Springs for?"

She was the one who looked nervous now. She quickly looked away and started to pick the bags up from the couch.

"Just to get a few things we needed," she said.

I could tell she was hiding something from me. I knew right away, what she was doing; my birthday was getting close.

"Just a few things huh?" I asked her.

"Yep," she still wasn't looking at me.

"Alright," I said with a little bit of sarcasm. "Just no cars this year okay?"

I was still smirking when she looked up at me. There was shock on her face, and then it turned into a sheepish grin because she knew she had been caught. I laughed at her expression as I went to the kitchen.

I grabbed my coat and said goodbye to my aunt. It was time to go pick up Sam for our girl's night out. She lived just a few blocks from me, so I was there in a few minutes time. Sam was waiting outside for me. I pulled up by the curb instead of pulling in the driveway. She got in and slammed the door shut.

"What's wrong?" I asked. I could tell she was upset.

"I just had a fight with Jordan over the phone."

Jordan was Sam's boyfriend. They have been going out for a few months now.

"He doesn't want to go to the lake this year. There is a concert in Boulder that he wants to go to instead."

We had planned a few weeks ago to go to Steamboat Lake for the weekend. A tradition we do every year.

"He has known for how long now that I wanted us to go; now he is trying to back out of it. Boys!" she said exasperatedly.

For the rest of the ride to the theater we listened to music and bashed on the boys in our school.

We got to the theater and picked a chick flick. When the movie was over, we were starving. We went to the drive thru and then I dropped Sam off before returning home. The lights were still on when I pulled into the driveway; Aunt Marie was waiting up for me. She was curled up on the couch with a blanket over her watching television.

"Did you have a good time?" she asked as she yawned.

"I did, it was so much fun. I really needed that. Thanks again for letting me go."

"Your welcome, I'm glad you had fun," she yawned again. "Well, I'm beat I'm going to bed. See you in the morning."

"Yeah me too," I followed her up the stairs. "Goodnight."
It was a chilly night. I put on a long sleeved shirt and my comfy pants, and then got under my blankets to await sleep.

Two
The Lake

Friday was finally here. Even though I barely had any homework, the week still went by slowly. Every morning Lucas would greet Sam and me before class. We would talk sometimes on the way to lunch, but we never sat at the same table. When we were together for those few minutes standing in line for lunch, every girl would give me a dirty look. It made me a little uncomfortable. As Sam would put it, I was still the envy of every girl in this school. I didn't get it though.

I was still getting this feeling like something was off; however, I could never figure it out. I just brushed it aside and went about the school days.

After Lucas had left when the first bell rang, Sam and I hurried to get to class.

"Are you excited about this weekend? I can't wait to get away from school stress; how about you?"
Sam has asked me that everyday for the past week.

I rolled my eyes at her, "You know my answer. It hasn't changed from yesterday or the day before that, or the day before that."
She pouted. I sighed at her expression.

"Yes I am excited to go camping," I finally answered her. I grabbed her by her jacket. "Come on, we're gonna be late for class."

After third period, Sam and I parted ways to head for different classes. It was study hall for me next. I wanted to get as much homework done as I could so I didn't have a lot to do on Sunday when I got home from my weekend of fun. I sat in my usual seat and started the homework I had already accumulated. I didn't look up once. I was so into my reading that I didn't even hear the bell ring.

I felt something shake my arm. Startled, I looked up to find Lucas looking down at me, smirking.

"Are you going to lunch or are you going to just sit here until your next class?"

I looked around and saw that everyone else had left, "How long have I been sitting here?" I felt a little silly.

"Not long," he replied.

I put my book back into my bag and stood up. It felt good. I felt like I had sat there all day.

"Hey thanks for snapping me out of it," I said as we walked to lunch together.

"Anytime."

We walked in a comfortable silence as I thought about this weekend and I wondered if Lucas was going.

"Are you camping at the lake tomorrow?" I was secretly hoping he was. I was also hoping he didn't see that on my face.

"Yes. I heard some kids were going. Some of my friends are and they wanted me to go," he looked at me and smiled. I shyly looked away, "Are you?"

"Yes. Sam and I are leaving around twelve thirty."

We had paid for our lunch and was about to separate to sit with our friends before either of us spoke again.

"I'll see you tomorrow. I'm leaving right after fifth period," he told me.

"You're leaving?" I was a bit disappointed.

I tried to hide it, but I had a feeling it showed on my face.

He chuckled at my obvious question, "Yes I am taking a

half day."

"Oh."

He smiled at my one word response, "I'll see you tomorrow then."

"Okay," I replied.

He chuckled again. We went our separate ways to eat at separate tables, like we did everyday.

Everyone at our table was talking about going to the lake. A couple of them invited a friend or two. When I sat down, Sam was talking to Nadia, a dark skinned girl with long braided hair.

Sam looked up at me, "I saw you come in with Lucas. What took you so long?" she was grinning.

"Yeah," I started to explain. "I was doing homework and must have been really into it because I didn't even hear the bell ring. Lucas snapped me out of it."

I looked a few tables away from us and saw that Lucas was watching me. He smiled. I returned the smile and then turned back to my food.

Usually I'm pretty good at the activities Mr. Redley has us do; however, gym was a nightmare today. We were playing volleyball and it started out to be a fun game. Normally my and Sam's team does pretty well; however, Karman was on the same team as us and she didn't care about any thing that might break her nails. So, basically our team was one short.

The ball was coming right for me.

"I got it," I yelled.

Karman pushed me out of the way and hit it knocking me down. I scraped my elbow as I landed on the gym floor. Karman turned around to face me. I was shocked. At first, I thought she was going to help me up; however, she just looked at me, smiled deviously, and walked away. I looked at Sam. She usually knew all the gossip going around the school, but she just shrugged her shoulders. She knocked me down a couple more times until I had enough. It wasn't like her to participate. I walked over to where she was and as always, she was standing with her group of friends.

"What is your problem?" I asked her.

She shrugged her shoulders, "You were just too slow." She and her friends laughed and walked away.

I was so angry with her, like she cared if our team won or not. Usually she would stand on the sidelines talking to boys or playing with her hair or some other stupid thing like that. She was just being mean, as usual. My body was starting to feel a little strange, like heat from the anger was rising from somewhere deep inside of me. Sam came over and just like that, the strange feeling vanished as quickly as it came; nevertheless, the anger was still there.

"Don't let her get to you like that. She is just jealous."

"Jealous?" I said it with annoyance. "What does she have to be jealous of me for? She's the popular one," my face was still hot with anger.

"Yes, she is," Sam then grinned. "But, Lucas doesn't talk to *her* everyday."

I relaxed a little bit at the thought of Lucas and smiled back at her. I had to admit, that did make me feel better.

It was Saturday morning. That strange feeling that something wasn't right, or off in a way, was stronger today than any other day. Ignoring it, I got up and started packing my backpack. I grabbed my sleeping bag, pillow, and my bag off the bed; I took everything down stairs, and threw them on the couch. Aunt Marie was putting on her sweater, getting ready to leave for the bakery.

"Make sure you call me when you get to Steamboat Springs," she said.

I have to call her about halfway there because there was no cell service where we camp.

"Have fun and be careful."

"I will," I told her.

She kissed me on the forehead and walked out the door. I ate my breakfast, and then took a shower while I waited for Sam to get here. I was putting my stuff in the backseat, when a car pulled up in front of my house. It was Sam. She reached in the back to grab her stuff, and then said goodbye to her mom.

"Hi," she said as she tossed her stuff in the back seat.

"Hey. We just need to get the camping gear," I pointed to the garage.

After we loaded the back of the Jeep and I locked the front door, we started our hour and fifteen-minute drive to the lake.

We arrived late in the afternoon because we stopped in Steamboat Springs for lunch and a quick call back home. My friends and I had camped here every summer with our families ever since we were practically born. Now that we were old enough, we would come here without them.

Our usual camping spot was away from any tourist area. There was a small stoned beach and a big wooden dock on the edge of the lake. The markings of a fire pit was thirty or forty feet in from the beach, with a big circular clearing around it. Half of us unloaded the vehicles and sat the tables up, while the other half went to get enough firewood to last until the morning. Afterwards, everybody started to pitch their tents. Sam and I were sharing one. We finished setting ours up and then we unloaded my Jeep with our bags and blankets.

It was cooler this morning; however, it turned abnormally hot for the end of September. Sam and I walked the length of the dock and stuck our feet into the water; it was warmer than I thought it was going to be, but it was still too cold to swim. We sat there peacefully for a little while. It was relaxing, the feel of the cool water flowing over my toes with the beautiful scenery of the lake, hills, and pines.

"So," Sam said excitedly. "What are we doing for your

birthday?"

I shrugged my shoulders, "I don't know, I was thinking about a party, but__."

"A party sounds perfect," She cut me off mid sentence. "Where would you like to have it?"

I rolled my eyes and shook my head. There was no sense of arguing with her because I knew she was going to get what she wanted anyway. It would just be easier to give in now.

I finally sighed, "I don't know. What do you think?"

"Yay; well I was thinking we could have it at the lodge, I know my Dad would let us use the space."

Sam's mom and dad owned the lodge in town. It's big enough to fit a nice size crowd.

"I know Jordan would DJ it for us. We could get a huge cake and lots of decorations."

She kept on talking, though I didn't really hear her because that's when Lucas showed up with his football friends. Even though Lucas didn't play, he still hung out with them. He held all of my attention as I watched them set up their tent.

"Kendall?" I heard Sam say and I snapped out of it. "Didn't you hear me calling you?" she sounded a little annoyed.

I look back at her, "No, I'm sorry I didn't."

She looked in the direction I was just looking in and realized what held my attention. She sighed and smiled.

"Why don't you just ask him out?"

I looked away from her and out to the lake, "I don't know what you are talking about?"

I knew she had seen right through me; however, she only chuckled, "What ever you say."

I didn't know if I did like him or not. I did like the way he looked at me sometimes, like I was important.

"Let's go eat, I'm starving," she said. I had to agree, I was hungry too.

I got up to follow her when I felt something tug on my ankle. I tried to kick it away, though it wouldn't let go. It kept tugging while I kept pulling away trying to get loose, but it was no use.

"Kendall, what's wrong?" Sam asked worriedly.

"I don't know. Something has my ankle."

That's when it pulled me off the dock and into the lake. Fully submerged, the water was freezing. I kicked at what had my ankle, but it didn't let go. I broke the surface just long enough to let out a scream. I was panicking. I tried to tell myself that you drown faster that way, so I tried to calm down and get loose from what ever had my ankle. It was no use though and I was quickly running out of air. All of a sudden, I felt something pulling me the other way. There were two? I struggled against both of them trying to break free from their hold. Finally, the one that had my ankle let go; I was being pulled the other way when I lost consciousness.

The next thing I remember, I was coughing and spitting up water. I heard many different voices; however, they sounded muffled and distant. Someone asked if I was all right, though it wasn't to me. They sounded panicky. It was Sam I was sure. Then I heard another voice, it was deeper, gravelly, a mans voice.

"I think she will be fine, her lungs are clear of the water now."

I opened my eyes and the first face I saw was Lucas's; he looked upset and anxious. The fear in his eyes confused me a little; I liked looking in them anyway. It took me a minute to realize everyone else surrounded us.

"Are you alright? Did you bump your head?" his voice matched his expression.

I thought about that for a minute then looked down at my ankle. There were a few scratches; other than that, I was okay.

"I'm fine," my voice was shaky. "A little light headed and embarrassed though."

He smiled as he relaxed a little, "I thought I had lost you." Lost me? I was confused. What did he mean? He barely knew me. I'm sure he saw the confusion on my face and changed the subject.

"Good thing I know CPR."

I sat up, still feeling a little light headed, "Yeah good thing."

He helped me up, watching my every move, making sure I wasn't going to faint or something.

"Come on; let's get you into some dry clothes."

I let him lead me to my tent. I was cold from the water and probably in shock. The warmth coming from his body was comforting.

"What pulled me into the lake?" I was still shaken up. I could have died.

He quickly looked at the ground before he spoke, "It looked to me like you tangled yourself in some seaweed."

"How could seaweed grab my ankle and hold on like that?"

He didn't look back up to answer me, "Maybe it was tangled before you stood up?"

I was a little bit annoyed. "I didn't feel it there before and besides, my feet were not that far in the water."

He shrugged his shoulders, "I don't know."

I eyed him suspiciously. I had a funny feeling he was keeping something from me. But what? He barely knew me. I pushed it aside for now so I could change.

"I'll wait right here," he said as I zipped the tent.

I stripped from my wet clothes right at the door, not wanting to drip across our blankets. I put on a pair of jeans and a sweatshirt; they immediately started to warm me up. I stepped back outside where Lucas was waiting for me. I grabbed my wet clothes to lie out to dry and zipped the tent back up so bugs wouldn't get in. Then he and I walked to the campfire that someone had started while all the commotion was going on.

By the time I got changed and back over to the fire pit everyone was eating. There were hot dogs, which they cooked their own over the fire, and all kinds of chips and drinks to go with it. Lucas helped me to a log and made a plate for the both of us, and then he sat next to me while we ate.

I was the main topic of conversation for a while. Only after everyone had a chance to ask if I were all right, did it fade out. No one could explain what had really happened. They just chocked it up to an unfortunate event.

Lucas threw his plate in the fire and turned to me with a smirk, "Aren't you tired of being the Damsel in distress?"
I sighed and put my hand over my face. I knew exactly to what he was referring.

"You heard about that huh?" there was embarrassment in my voice.

"Yes. I hear the gossip around school too."
He pulled my hand away from my face and made me look at him. His eyes were burning into mine. Every time he looked at me like that, I felt an intense feeling between the two of us, a connection.

"There is nothing to be embarrassed about," then he smiled. "I would save you any day."
I smiled and shyly looked away from him as my heart fluttered. I noticed that everyone was glancing our way, especially Karman, she did not look happy.

"Thank you," I said, still embarrassed by the intensity in his eyes. "For saving me."

"You are very welcome…just promise me one thing."

I looked up at him, "And what's that?"
I was very curious by what he wanted me to promise him.

"No more swimming okay?" he smiled again and I felt a twinge in my stomach.

I sighed playfully, "Okay, no more swimming."

He laughed at my whininess.

It was almost dark and the fire was blazing warm and beautiful. Everyone was talking excitedly and roasting marshmallows. I was enjoying myself, sitting on a log by the fire with Sam. On the other side of her was Jordan. They were turned into each other, talking and giggling. They had made up the day after their fight. Sam always gets what she wants, mainly because he always gave it to her.

Karman was to my left in a lawn chair sitting on a towel. She was the type of girl that didn't like to get dirty. Lucas was by the food table, looking for another bag of marshmallows. I couldn't help but keep looking his way. He caught me a few times and I just smiled; it meant that Lucas was looking at me too. I could see Karman watching me every so often from the corner of my eye and I was sure she caught me watching Lucas. With no warning, she got up and walked to where he was. She was smiling and brushing her hair over one shoulder as she talked, glancing my way every so often, she was flirting with him. I could feel the heat boiling in my face, I was so angry with her.

After a few minutes, I had enough; I needed to clear my head. I got up from the log and walked towards the woods, grumbling to myself. Before I even made it to the tree line, I heard somebody come up behind me. I glanced back and saw Lucas walking toward me.

"What are you doing? Go back to the party."
I couldn't help but be angry with him too, even though he didn't do anything wrong.

"No. I came to make sure you were all right," he said it like he was really worried about me.

"I'm fine, I just needed to get away from Karman and clear my head," I kept on walking. We were out of site of the other campers now.

"I don't believe you," he said grabbing my hand and

spinning me around to face him.

I wasn't expecting him to do that. I lost my footing and spun right into him. He caught me before I landed on the forest floor and helped me back up.

"I'm sorry," he said.

When I looked up at his face, he had an apologetic smile. I followed his smile right up to his eyes, and then looked away because I felt my eyes begin to water. I didn't want him to see me cry.

"Why do I let her get to me like that?" I said angrily.

He was still holding me, the tears were coming whether I wanted them to or not, so I buried my face into his chest and let the anger out. His body was tense, but he rubbed my back as I cried.

After a few tears, I dried my eyes and looked up at him. He released me from his chest, yet he still held me close. Probably making sure I could stand on my own.

"Are you alright now?" he asked.

I studied his face; I could still see a trace of worry in it. "Yes, I feel much better. I'm sorry about that."

He half smiled, "It's alright."

"I'm not ready to go back yet. Do you want to walk with me for a little while?" I was hoping he wouldn't say no.

"Sure," he smiled and released me completely.

Three
The Legend

We walked in what seemed to be an endless forest. The only civilization around was the ranger station a few miles away. It was quiet and dark, yet every occasionally the moon would come out and peek through the thick blanket of leaves above us. Only our footsteps and our voices broke through the quietness. We talked about different things, like how beautiful it was here and how warm it was today. Now we were on the subject of school and the students in it.

"Will you tell me something?"

"It depends on what it is." I said playfully.

Really, I was worried it would be an embarrassing question; one that I didn't want to answer.

He was quiet for a few moments before he spoke, "Well, I was wondering what Karman did to upset you?"

I groaned in my head, it was one of them. That's what I was afraid of. What did I care if Karman had flirted with him and was probably going to ask him out? It's not like I had any claim on him. Before I could playfully tell him to mind his own business, something shining on the forest floor caught my eye.

"What is that?" I asked.

Lucas bent down and touched the shiny liquid stuff with his fingers.

"It looks like blood," he put it up to his nose to smell it. "It is blood."

"What do you think it came from?"
I was worried that whatever had spilt it was close by.

He stood up quickly, "I don't know, but I need to get you back to camp. It's not safe out here," his voice had an alerted edge to it.
He was acting so strange, so protective.

"What do you mean it's not safe?" I was very curious by what he meant by that.

"I don't have time to explain it right now," he grabbed my arm and started to drag me along with him.

I yanked my arm free from his grip, "Stop that! I know how to walk on my own!" I was annoyed that he wouldn't tell me anything.
He turned and looked at me. I could see the annoyance on his face, though danger or not, I stood my ground. He studied my face for a few moments and must have realized that I wouldn't budge without something, because his voice was calmer when he spoke.

"Look," his face relaxed a bit. "I will explain everything as soon as we get back, I promise, but right now we have to leave."
I saw something on his face close to how he looked earlier when he saved me from drowning. That look puzzled me. What could it mean? I dismissed it for now and let him have his way.

Neither of us spoke as we walked back to camp, more quickly than before. He was busy looking around, like he was searching for something or someone. All of a sudden he stopped.

"What are you doing? I thought we had to_."

"Shh!" he cut me off. "We need to walk as quickly and as quietly as possible."
He was looking to the right of us, I saw nothing, but I obeyed

him. Then I saw a movement in the shadows, a dark mass that made me stop. As it was getting closer, I could make out that it was actually a bunch of people. There were about a few dozen and they were spreading out to surround us. Lucas took my hand and looked at me with worry in his eyes. Even though I felt danger coming, I still felt that twinge in my stomach as he held it tight.

"What are you doing in these parts of the woods?" one of them asked.

He was the only one who spoke and was standing the closest, so I assumed he was the leader. He was too far away and it was too dark to make out the detailed features of him; however, I could tell he was tall and muscular.

"We weren't supposed to meet for two more weeks. What are *you* doing here?" Lucas spoke with accusation in his voice.

He knew these men?

"We were hunting," the leader spoke aggressively. "But, since we are here…you are looking for the half?"

"Yes," Lucas answered.

His voice wasn't the least bit shaky with no hint of fear in it. I on the other hand, was terrified.

"I was told you have it."

"Yes, that is true, though how can we be sure that you are not lying to us?" the leader asked with accusation.

Lucas spoke more calmly, "Because, there is nothing else you have that is worth value to us, we have nothing to gain if we take anything but the other half."

We were outnumbered and some of these men were bigger than we were. The leader stared at the both of us for a few moments, searching for something. I'm not sure what he found on our faces, if he could really see them at all; however, he relaxed his stance.

"Very well," he said and walked towards us. "You may leave with it."

I could see his face more clearly now. He had long hair that was tied behind his head and dirty clothes. He handed Lucas an old, tattered, piece of folded paper.

He turned to his men, "Let them through."

Lucas put it in his pocket, "Thank you."

"Hold on a minute," another voice said.

It was another man that was toward the front. Probably the leaders second in command. He was taller and stockier with mangled hair.

"Aren't you the ones they are looking for?"

I could feel Lucas stiffen as he pulled me closer to his side. It scared me. We started edging out the path they had made for us.

"No. No we are not," answered Lucas.

"I think you are. You are Lucas O'Brien, are you not?"

I was confused. What did he mean by the 'ones'?

I didn't have time to worry about that now because the second man was moving the same direction as we were.

"Stop them!"

They started to close in on us and that's when it happened. Something just took over my body, like an instinct, a reaction I had no control over. That same strange feeling I had in the gym only stronger. My mind didn't have to think about what I was doing. I felt the warmth flow through, reaching every part of my body.

I held my hand up and felt the warmth leave through my finger tips as I spoke, "Back off!"

The men in front of us flew in the air and fell hard on the ground about fifty feet back. I looked at Lucas in shock; however, he didn't see me. Lucas was fighting the men off with the same unexplainable force that I had just used, until they were all lying on the ground and we had our chance to run. We stopped running when we were almost back to camp and away from the group of men.

I was shaking when we slowed to a walk. I asked the

questions I wanted to ask the moment I felt the heat rising in my body. I meant to ask them one at a time but I blurted them out in a rush.

"What just happened? How did I do that? How did you do that? Who were they? What is going on Lucas?" I was feeling lightheaded and I needed to sit down.
We found a log lying on its side. Lucas sat down pulling me with him.

"Shh," he said trying to calm me down. "We're safe now."

After a moment or two, Lucas spoke again, "You were great out there." There was a hint of a smile in his voice.

"What is going on Lucas?" I demanded. He seemed to know a lot more than me.

He sighed and looked into my eyes, "You are a Natural, The True Natural. Other people might call you a witch. The word Natural means 'being something by nature'." He wore a look of perception on his face, "They had their suspicions when you were born, that you might be the one, the one with the powers to bring down Malik D'Viak and his people."

I looked at him with confusion. "What are you talking about?" I said disbelievingly.

"The legend says, when a True Natural dies, a new one will be born in exactly nine months. Born with special powers that you will fully reach at age seventeen, powers that match Malik's," he paused and looked at the ground as he spoke the next words. "You were the only baby born right after the last True Natural died."

"Who is Malik D'Viak?"

"He is our enemy and very dangerous."

"Why?"

"Even though he is very powerful, he seeks more and will do anything to get it."

"Why?"

"Well, no one really knows," he ran his fingers through his hair. "Some people are just born with the hunger for power."

I was still confused. I didn't understand any of this, "How did I know what to do without knowing I could do it?"

He half smiled at me, "You were born with the knowledge you need, sort of brought down from generation to generation, from Natural to Natural. Although, you shouldn't be able to until you come into your powers."

I thought about what Lucas had said, trying to make sense of it all. I searched his face trying to read it, before looking into his eyes. I saw the depth of truthfulness in them and I could tell that he wasn't lying to me. I was still confused, yet somehow I trusted him.

"Why didn't anyone tell me this before now?"

"Because they weren't sure you were the one. They didn't want to put that pressure on you until they were certain. I knew all along you were though."

I thought about the last thing he said and tried to figure out what he meant by 'all along'.

"What is your part in all this, why are you here?" I asked him.

He looked up from the ground and into my eyes. I felt that twinge again.

He slightly puffed up his chest and straightened his shoulders, "I am your Protector. I am here to keep you safe. I too have powers, as you saw tonight. They match yours in ways; however, I have things you don't. Powers that are very useful."

I wanted to ask about his powers; however, I had other questions I needed answers to first.

"How did you know what I was?" I asked him.

He tore his eyes away from mine. I thought I saw a hint of awkwardness.

"I am drawn to the True Natural. So I knew instantly, the moment I laid eyes on you what you were," he looked up quickly and gave me an apologetic smile.

"Then, you were there for the last True Natural." It wasn't a question, I already knew, but he answered anyway.

"Yes. His name was Isaac Norwood. He was very powerful and very gifted. He lived with his powers for a hundred and twenty years."

"A hundred and twenty years?" I said in a voice of disbelief. I did the math quickly in my head. "He was one hundred and thirty seven years old?"

He sighed again, not in annoyance, but in sadness.

"You stop aging in your early twenties and become an Immortal...just like me," his voice was hard yet his eyes showed sadness in them.

Immortal? I didn't have a reaction for that. I had never known of anything like this before, powers and immortality; a life being lived for hundreds of years, with all the possibilities and sadness, seeing life and death pass by.

"If it's true about the knowledge being born in me, then I should be able to do everything Isaac could do; right?"

"Not necessarily. Everybody doesn't think and feel the same way, so it may be different for you than it was for Isaac. You will need to practice your abilities__"

I cut him off, "Abilities?"

I was amazed that I could do...whatever I was able to do, before, and now I find out that I might be able to do more. I didn't know what to think. This was happening so fast.

I took a deep breath, "What else can I do?"

He looked back up into my eyes and smiled a little, there was that feeling in my stomach again.

"You might have many different powers, like the ability of knowing. It's not something you can't predict, you'll just...know."

"I can already do that," I told him.

"Really; how and for how long?" there was shock and confusion on his face. I didn't understand it.

"For as long as I can remember. I could always tell when

something bad was about to happen. For instance, I can remember when my aunt and I got into a car accident, the day before I felt like…something was off. Why; is that bad?" I was worried that there might be something wrong with me. Was this normal for a Natural?

"No, it's not bad, it's just that usually you don't start coming into your powers until a few days before your birthday. Though, I can see from earlier that's not the case with you."

He was silent for a few moments, no doubt thinking about what I had said.

I was getting cold and starting to shiver. Lucas noticed and gave me his jacket. I admired his chivalry. I put my arms through the sleeves and wrapped the coat around me. I was still confused and scared, but the warmth helped relax me.

"Thank you, for everything tonight," I said with sincerity as I looked back up at him. I was grateful; he had saved my life twice in one day.

"You're welcome," he smiled and again it sent butterflies in my stomach.

I felt connected to him somehow. It made me wonder about Isaac, if he had the same connection I felt.

"Were you and Isaac close?" I remembered the sadness in his eyes the last time we talked about him.

He didn't answer for a few moments. I didn't think he heard me at first, but then he sighed and began to talk.

"I met Isaac when we were in our teens. He delivered horseshoes for his father, who was a blacksmith and we quickly became friends." There was sadness in his voice, "It was 1872 when we came into our powers. Ulysses S. Grant was president. By some miracle neither of us was drafted into the civil war." He stared straight ahead but kept on going, "Because I was a little older, I was first to get my powers. I felt the need to protect him, the urge was so strong." He smiled a little, "He thought I was crazy at first, but when he came into his powers a few days later he then understood why I was acting so strange." Lucas glanced up at me, "That's how I knew you were the new True Natural. A Protector is drawn to the one he needs to protect. We are also born with the knowledge we need to know."

I rethought everything Lucas had told me about the legend, my powers Isaac and Malik D'Viak.

"So, Malik is after me?" I didn't like the idea of being hunted like an animal.

He looked into my eyes, "I will protect you."
He held my gaze; I saw strength, bravery, and truth in his eyes. I knew that at least I wasn't alone.

"We should get moving. We don't want to run into them again." He smiled a little, "Besides, Sam is probably worried about you."
I nodded in agreement, Sam would be worried and I didn't want her out here looking for me while those men were still in the woods.

Light flickered and dance through the trees. As we got closer, I realized it was the fire from camp. We made it out of the woods and back into the clearing where the tents stood. Sam immediately saw us and rushed over to where we were.

"Where have you been? I have been worried sick about you," she was upset.
I looked at Lucas as he looked at me. I had a feeling this was not something I could share. Not even with my best friend. So, I lied.

"We got lost," I told her, trying to sound convincing.
I knew these woods well enough not to get lost. So did she; however, the lie sounded more real than the truth.

She looked back and forth between the two of us a few times. Then a slow smile spreads across her face, "Lost huh?"
I knew what she was thinking, that we had secretly met in the woods. I nodded as I didn't trust my voice at the moment to

lie any further about what really happened in the woods.

"Well I'm glad you're back," she took my hand and pulled me forward, "You're missing all the fun."
I went along with her, but I had enough fun for one night. Lucas tagged quietly behind us.

I stayed up not wanting to hurt Sam's feelings; there was no need to spoil her night. We played our traditional game called Question and told ghost stories. I was barely listening to Jordan tell the beginnings of a story. All I could think about was what happened in the woods and the subsequent conversation with Lucas. I still had questions I needed answers for, though I couldn't very well ask them now. So, I just sat there pretending to listen to the ghost stories, waiting for a chance to get Lucas alone again.

It was getting really late. I wasn't sure if I could sleep, yet I decided to try.

"I think I'm going to bed," I said during Jordan's pause. I stood up and brushed myself off.

Sam looked up with confusion on her face, "You're going to bed? But, you're gonna miss the ending!"

"I know I'm really tired though." I turned and smiled at Jordan, "Besides, I heard this one before, I know how it ends."

He brushed his blond hair out of his eyes and grinned, "Night Kendall."

Sam let out a gust of air, "Alright I'll see you in the morning." She had her bottom lip playfully sticking out.

I chuckled at her expression, "Night everyone."
I walked around the campfire and was almost out of the circle when Lucas stood up.

"I'll walk you to your tent," he said.
I heard gasps and stifled giggles as we walked away from the fire. My tent was just a little ways from our group of friends. I turned around and opened my mouth to speak, but Lucas cut me off.

"I know we have more to talk about; however, now is not the time," he smiled and lowered his voice to a whisper. He nodded towards the campfire, "They are listening to everything we say."

"Okay," I said disappointedly.

I thought about the men from earlier tonight and I started to panic. Lucas must have seen it on my face.

"Don't worry," he whispered. "You'll be safe tonight, they're not coming back."

I was skeptical, "Are you sure?"

"I'm positive," he said reassuringly.

I don't think I want to know how he knows. I was still a little bit worried; however, I felt safe and I believed him.

"Okay."

I turned to go into the tent when he grabbed my arm and turned me back around.

"Kendall, relax I won't let anything happen to you. I promise."

I looked over at the circle of campers. Every head quickly turned away from our direction and back to the fire.

I looked back at him with annoyance and took a deep breath, "Alright, I'll see you in the morning then."

He half smiled, "Goodnight."

I stepped inside the tent and zipped it up.

I woke up the next morning feeling exhausted from the night before. I couldn't make my head shut up long enough to sleep well. I looked at my cell phone for the time. It was ten minutes to eight. I knew I wouldn't be able to go back to sleep. I put on my pants and sweat shirt from yesterday. The only clothes I had dry, thanks to almost drowning. I slid my feet into my untied boots, stepped over Sam as she slept and unzipped the tent.

The sun was just starting to come up. It was chilly, yet the fresh air felt good. I was groggy and wanted coffee. The fire was still going, barely. I put a few pieces of wood on it to bring it back to life. It made me wonder when the last few people went to bed. I grabbed a jug of water that someone had brought and dumped it into a kettle to put over the fire. I dug through the plastic bin that we all helped fill, until I found the instant coffee packs. Since there was no electricity out here, instant would have to do. After I poured the coffee, powdered creamer, and sugar in my cup I went to sit near the fire to wait for the water to get hot.

After a while, some of the others started to emerge from their tents. Sam staggered over to me and sat down. She looked barely awake.

"Late night? I asked smiling.

"Yeah, there were a couple of people still sitting around the campfire when we went to bed at four in the morning," she replied. "You should've stayed up with us, it was so much fun."

"I'm sure it was, but one o'clock was late enough."
Sam got up, poured the dry ingredients for coffee in a cup, and came back. There was enough water in the kettle for both of us to share.

"I never did get a chance to ask why you really left last night," she said curiously.

I sighed, "Karman was just being her normal self and I couldn't take it any longer. I had to clear my head. Lucas followed me to make sure I was alright."

She smiled widely, "Good thing he was here then."

"Yeah if not, I might be fish food right about now."
We both laughed, but mine wasn't as easy and light as Sam's was. Mine had a little fear mixed with it. Luckily, Sam didn't appear to notice.

Lucas was walking from his tent, with his friends, to where we were, "Morning."

"Morning," Sam and I said together.

"Did you sleep well?" his eyes lingered on mine for a few

moments longer. I knew it was because of what happened last night.

"Not really," we synchronized again.
Although our reasons were different, we looked at each other and giggled.

It had warmed up by the time we started to pack up. Sam and I were loading our gear in the Jeep when Jordan called Sam to his tent. I was just starting to take ours down when she came back.

"Hey, Jordan wants us to meet them in Steamboat Springs to spend the day on our way back home. Do you want to stop?" she asked hopeful.
Them? I looked up to see a dark haired boy with baggy clothes and a baseball cap, helping Jordan with the tent. Sean was Jordan's friend and he hung out with us sometimes. I hesitated. I had a long day yesterday and I really just wanted to go home.

"It's okay if you don't," she said, though I could see a trace of disappointment on her face.

"No, I just want to get home, but you should ride with them so you can go."

Her face lit up, then quickly fell, "No, it's a long ride back by yourself."

I smiled at her loyalty, "It's okay really. I insist, go have fun."

"Really?" she asked happily.
I nodded.

She smiled and turned to Jordan and Sean, "I'm coming with you, just let me get my things."

"You can leave them in the Jeep and get them later if you want," I told her.

"Okay. I'll help you with the tent at least."

"I can help her," we heard a voice say.
I didn't have to look up to know it was Lucas. I could

recognize his voice anywhere. He shifted his eyes to me and smiled. My stomach did a flip.

"Really? Thank you," she said and then turned back to me. "Are you sure you don't mind?" She still looked somewhat hesitant.

"Yes I'm sure. Now get going before they leave you," I smiled reassuringly at her.

She grinned back at me, "Thanks, you're the best." Then she was gone.

Four
Control

Lucas and I worked quickly together to get the tent down. My heart started racing and my stomach flipped as our arms brushed together. We both paused for a moment and I caught my breath. Did he feel what I felt when we touched? I looked up into his eyes to see that they were troubled. I wanted to ask, but I was too afraid to hear his answer. Then he smiled, making the trouble in his eyes disappear. I couldn't help but look shyly away; his smile made me feel weak in the knees.

"Thanks for helping me," I said not meeting his eyes, while trying to collect myself.

"You're welcome."

That's when I noticed my appearance. My clothes were dirty from the ash and the logs I sat on and they smelled like smoke.

"I cannot wait to take a shower." I tried to brush some of it off me.

"Speaking of going home," Lucas said. "Sam is right; it is a long way to drive by yourself. I could ride with you."

I yawned widely.

"Or maybe drive?" he chuckled.

Perfect, we were going to be alone. It made me glad because I would get my answers, yet I was nervous because we were going to be alone. Then I thought of how he got here and I felt disappointed.

"What about your friends?"

"They won't mind. Besides, it will give us a chance to talk."

We finished packing the Jeep and then said goodbye to everyone. I was still groggy and knew I shouldn't be behind the wheel, so I handed him the keys.

"Ready?" he asked as he shut his door.

I nodded as he started the engine and put it in drive.

We followed the trail we had made after all these years to the main road. It took us a little while to get off the trail. When we were safely on Highway 129 South, it was awhile before I asked any more questions. I had a hard time deciding which one I would ask first. Finally, I just picked.

"Who were those men last night? Are they Naturals too?"

Lucas grinned, "I was wondering when you would start asking questions." His grin faded and his expression became serious, "No, they're not Naturals, they are wanderers, nomads like. They are thieves and they are very dangerous."

Again, I wondered how he knew them. Did he hang around with people like that? He answered my thoughts as if he read my mind.

"I ran across them a few years ago, saved their lives. The leader said he would repay the favor," his facial expression did not change.

I thought about that favor, "That piece of paper?"

"Yes."

He lifted off the seat, pulled it out of his back pocket, and then handed it to me. There was writing on it, but nothing I could understand.

"What is it exactly?"

"It is half of an incantation that only you will be able to use. It will help defeat Malik."

Only me? I have to do this by myself?

"It was torn into two pieces long ago and sold. To whom I

don't know."

"Tell me about Malik."

"He is a Natural as well, one of the oldest. The older you are the more powerful your powers will be. He wants more and he will do anything to get them."

"What?" I was shocked and a little frightened at the thought, "If he is a Natural and older than me, then how am I suppose to beat him?" I was starting to panic. My breathing and heartbeat was rapid. "I don't know if I can do this alone."

"Don't worry so much. You'll have help. I'll be right there with you the whole way," he looked at me quickly again and then back at the road.

His eyes seemed to be full of honesty and I couldn't help but feel better when he looked at me that way.

"And besides, there are others out there like us."

"Us?" I asked curiously.

He half smiled, "Naturals I mean."

Oh, of course, "How many are there?"

"Hundreds, maybe thousands; each one has a special gift. Some of them have the same kind of power though."

I was intrigued at that thought; then I thought about Malik taking their powers away.

"When you said Malik will do anything to get more power, what did you mean exactly?" I was almost afraid to hear the answer.

"Besides time, the only other way, is to kill other Naturals and steal theirs."

"That's horrible!"

I felt this terrible pain and sickness in the pit of my stomach. How could someone be so cruel and heartless? How could someone take another's life so easily? I thought about how hard it would be to take Malik down.

"Isn't Malik stronger than me?"

"He will be at first, but you will be more powerful than any other Natural, once properly trained."

"I don't understand. If there are other Naturals, then why does all this belong to me? Why not one of the other Naturals or all of them?"

I was bewildered. A group of Naturals sounds more logical than one.

"Because, there can only be one True Natural, a leader, so to speak. The rest of them only have some of the powers you will have once you come into them," he glanced at me. "Malik wants your powers the most."

I understood the reason why Malik wanted me and I started to panic again. I could feel my heart beating practically out of my chest. He must have seen the distress on my face, because he took my hand. It only made my heart beat faster.

"It's going to be alright, I *won't* let anything happen to you!" There was a fierceness to his words.

After a while, I calmed down some. My heart rate had slowed, as well as my breathing. I picked back up with the questions. I needed to learn as much as I could if I was going to succeed.

"I thought Immortals couldn't die?"

I thought about all the myths and legends of Immortals. Beheading and burning came to mind.

Lucas fell silent and I didn't think I was going to get an answer, but then he took a deep breath and started to speak quietly. "Legend says that Immortals can't die of old age, sickness, or any other thing that affects humans and that is true. We can go through and feel it all, get hurt and heal like a normal human would. We can live through almost anything. There is only one way an Immortal can die," he sighed. "Their soul has to be destroyed."

We were almost to Steamboat Springs when my stomach growled. I haven't eaten since last night. Lucas heard it rumble and chuckled, lightening up the atmosphere.

"Is drive thru alright? You said earlier you wanted to get home."

"Yes, that's perfect," I replied.

We ordered our food and pulled up to the window. I reached for my wallet to pay for my half.

Lucas looked at me with a strange expression, "What are you doing?"

"Getting my money."

He shook his head, "I got this one."

"Are you sure? Because you don't have to do that."

He smiled, "I'm sure."

Once we got our food, we headed back on the road. As I picked off some of the lettuce, I thought about the lake and the seaweed.

"What was really trying to drown me? And don't tell me it was seaweed."

He smiled at my rebuke, yet then once again, it quickly faded, "No it wasn't seaweed. I think it was one of Malik's people, someone who could hold their breath for long periods of time, a Natural no doubt."

Great, it was already happening.

We made it back to Oak Creek in the mid afternoon. The sun was behind a blanket of graying clouds. It was chilly and looked like it was about to storm any minute. It was still too warm to snow though.

"Do you mind if I get dropped off at my house?" he asked me.

"No I don't mind," I was curious as to where he lived anyway.

We turned onto County Route 25 and drove a few miles south, then took a left into a hidden driveway. Sitting off the road a few hundred feet was a walkway leading up to a little, ground level house with a two-car garage. It was gray with white trim and had a flowerbed in front of the porch.

He pulled up in front of the house and shut the engine off.

"This is where I live. It's not much but it's a roof over our heads"

Our heads? "Your family, is still alive?"

"No, they died a long time ago. I live here with some friends," his eyes showed the slightest bit of sadness in them.

"Oh. I'm sorry, I didn't think," I was embarrassed and felt stupid.

He half smiled, "It's alright, the pain of their loss has passed, but I think of them often."

I looked back at the house; this time I saw a man standing on the porch. It was him, the man I saw at the school and on my run.

"I know him!"
I said. I was confused. How did this connect?

"You do?" he asked.
He looked surprised and nervous. There was something strange about his expression. I didn't understand it.

"Yes I have seen him recently, a couple of times."

"Oh," he quickly looked away.
I wondered what that was about, I didn't ask.

"He is one of my roommates." He looked awkward, "He has been looking out for you when I haven't been able to."
There was that connection.

"You've been watching me?" I started to feel the heat of embarrassment on my face.

He looked back at me, "Not *every* move. We just keep watch of the surroundings you are in, making sure you are safe."
That made me feel a little better. I could feel the heat in my cheeks recede a little.

"I keep watch in school and between Matt," he looked on the porch, "his wife Sara and myself, we divvy up nights to watch around your house." He looked back at me and smiled.

"How long has this been going on?" I was a little upset, even though I knew it was to keep me safe.

"This much? Only the last couple of months," seeing the

expression on my face, he put his hands up in defense. "Honest," he couldn't keep the grin off his face. "Do you want to meet them?"

I thought about that for a minute. I looked up to the man on the porch and back to Lucas.

"Just watching out for me?" It felt okay though I wasn't completely sure.

"Yes. I promise," he said then he smiled.

I couldn't help that flutter feeling in my chest, "Okay. I trust you."

We got out and walked across the lawn up to the porch. The man smiled at me, but looked a little leery at Lucas.

"It's okay," he said, "She knows."

The man's eyes flickered to mine for a moment.

"She was attacked at the lake."

"What! Are you alright?" the man asked. He relaxed his body; however, his expression was still shocked and confused.

"Yes, I'm fine," I looked into his dark blue eyes. They looked so familiar.

"This is Kendall," Lucas said.

The man held out his hand and I shook it.

"Nice to meet you Kendall, I'm Mathew," he said politely.

"Hello."

"Where is Sara?" Lucas asked. "I wanted her to meet Kendall."

"She went into town. I'm not sure when she will be back." Matthew said.

"Oh, maybe next time then," there was disappointment in his voice.

It started to sprinkle just then, "Well I better get home before my aunt starts to worry." I had called her when we were in Steamboat Springs. I looked at Matthew, "It was nice to meet you."

"Nice to meet you too; come back anytime you wish."

I smiled, "Thanks, I will."

Lucas walked me back to the Jeep, "Here is my cell phone number in case you need me."

"Thanks," I put the number in my cell, and then called him. I let it ring once and then hung up, "And here is mine...in case you need me."

Lucas chuckled at me, but then his smile faded a little, "Call me as soon as you get home okay."

"Okay, I will," I got into my Jeep, waved at them, and then drove back to town.

When I pulled into my driveway, the first thing I did was call Lucas. It rang two times and on the third ring, I heard him pick up.

"*Hello?*" Lucas answered.

"Hi. I'm sitting in my driveway as we speak."

"*Good. Now try to get some sleep tonight. You'll have nothing to worry about; someone will be watching the house.*"

I felt that paranoia of being watched and looked around, even though I probably wouldn't see anyone.

"Okay. I'll see you at school tomorrow."

"*Alright; goodnight,*" he replied. Then I hung up.

I looked in the rearview mirror at the camping stuff in the back. I decided I wasn't going to unload anything except my bag and pillow.

I opened the door with a relief of being home. I dropped my stuff off at the foot of the stairs and called for Aunt Marie. She came in from the kitchen and rushed over to hug me.

"You're home. What took you so long?" she asked.

"Sorry, I dropped someone off and met their family."

"Was Sam with you?"

"No, she and Jordan wanted to meet some friends in Steamboat Springs to hang out for the day. I was too tired," I explained.

"Oh. Did you have a nice time?"

"It was okay."

She chuckled, "Well it looks like you did. You're filthy."
I wasn't sure if I could tell her anything so I half told the truth.

"I, uh, fell in the lake."

"What!" her eyes were wide with shock. "Were you hurt?"

"I lost consciousness for a few moments. Someone luckily saved me before I drowned."

"Let me look at you," she placed her hands on my shoulders and looked in my eyes.

"I'm fine, really. I just need to clean up."

She eyed me for a few more moments and then dropped her hands, "Alright; make sure you thank them for me alright?"

I half smiled at her, "I will."

I grabbed my stuff and went upstairs to take a shower. After I was done, I wrapped a towel around myself and went to my room. I started to unwrap the towel to change when I remembered that someone was going to be watching the house. I didn't know when, so I walked to the window and closed the curtains. I put on some sweat pants and a t-shirt and then went back downstairs. Aunt Marie was folding laundry in the living room.

"I'm just gonna grab something quick and turn in early. I'm beat," I told her.

"Alright sweetie; there is some left over mac and cheese in the fridge."

I warmed up a plate and grabbed a drink. I peeked in the living room, said goodnight and then went to my room. I surfed the Internet while I ate my dinner. Afterwards, I lay down on the bed. My last thought before I feel asleep was of Lucas.

I awoke the next morning ten minutes before the alarm was due to go off feeling rejuvenated. After I changed and brushed my hair, I went downstairs. Aunt Marie of course, was already up and eating breakfast. I poured a bowl of cereal and ate it at the kitchen sink.

"I forgot to ask about my birthday last night. Is it okay if we have a party at the lodge on Saturday?" I gave her an amused look.

"Sam?" she asked.

I smirked and nodded.

She chuckled, "Its fine with me. I'll just make a bigger cake than planned."

"Thanks, I'll see you after school."

I looked around for any sign of someone watching me as I walked across the parking lot. There was no one, just the normal kids arriving for school. Sam pulled in so I waited for her.

In our normal meeting spot, leaning against the wall was Lucas. I was happy to see him.

"Good morning," he said with a smile.

"Hey," I smiled back.

"Did you sleep well?"

"Actually, better than I thought I would." I thought I would have nightmares of some sort.

"Good, you needed it." He smiled as the bell rang, "I'll see you in English."

"Alright," then Sam and I rushed off to class.

We entered the classroom to find that it wasn't Mrs. Garcia sitting in her chair. It was a balding thin man with glasses. He glanced up as we walked in, and then returned his attention back to the class.

We took our seats as he spoke in a scruffy voice. "My name is Mr. Pierce. Mrs. Garcia will be out for awhile, so I will be your substitute teacher," he smiled kindly. "I'm not sure where she left off, so I decided to give you a free period today."

I heard soft, excited murmurs all around me.

"On one condition," he said.

Sam and I looked at each other and smiled. Although, I really liked Mrs. Garcia, I was happy to have a free period.

"You have to stay in this classroom, but feel free to move around and talk quietly."

The room burst out with hushed voices. I pulled out my notebook and started to doodle.

Sam leaned towards me, "So tell me, how was the ride home yesterday?"

I knew it wouldn't be long before she asked her twenty questions. Normally I didn't mind; however, I couldn't tell her what happened, so I had to lie. I don't like to lie so it irritated me a little. I decided on telling her as much of the truth as possible.

"It was fun. We were starving so we got fast food through drive thru in Steamboat Springs before coming home." There, that was the truth.

"What did you guys talk about?"

This was the part that I had to lie about, "Nothing really." She scowled. I could tell she wanted more details.

"I met part of his family when he drove to his house though."

"He drove?" she asked.

That seemed to satisfy her curiosity.

"Yeah, I was too tired to get behind the wheel, so I asked him."

Her eyes were wide with excitement, "I have seen his family before, but I have never met them. What are they like?"

"Well I only met the guy, Matthew. He seemed really nice. He invited me back."

"Really? Are you going to go back?" her eyes popped with excitement again.

I shrugged my shoulders, "I don't know. It depends on if

Lucas invites me or not."

"Do you think he will?"

I nodded and smiled, "Yes I do."

She giggled, "Do you think he likes you?"

I didn't have to think about that. I already knew the answer, "I think he likes me well enough to look out for me."
I knew what question was coming next. I didn't really know that answer for sure. I was leaning towards liking him that way; however, if he was going to protect me, there's no way we would ever get serious. I wasn't ready to share my answer yet so I quickly changed the subject.

"Aunt Marie agreed to the party at the lodge. You want to start planning it?"
It worked. I dodged the question and we never got back to the subject of Lucas and me. For the rest of the period we talked about this coming Saturday. We had almost every detail worked out, right down to the karaoke machine. The next thing we had to do was invitations. Sam was coming over to my house tonight to get them printed, so we could hand them out tomorrow.

When I arrived to English, I handed in my homework. Lucas was smiling at me and I felt my heart skip a beat. I quickly returned the smile hoping Lucas didn't see my expression.

"Good news everyone!" the teacher said. "Pop quiz."
I sighed in my head, great.

All I could think about was this past weekend and the information I received. I couldn't concentrate at all during the English pop quiz; most of my answers were random markings. Then in Biology, we dissected a rat, gross.

When the bell finally rang, I told Sam I'd see her at lunch and rushed out the door. I was really looking forward to study hall. I had homework that I could start, though I was not in the mood. I entered the classroom, immediately I noticed that Lucas wasn't here, I wondered why. I sat in my normal seat, pulled out my notebook and started right where I left off from Spanish. Karman was sitting a few seats away from me and I noticed her looking my way occasionally. I tried to ignore her; however, I could feel her stare beat down on me. As soon as the bell rang, I gathered my belongings to put them in my bag, thinking this day couldn't get any worse. Then I heard someone call my name. I looked in the direction where Karman was sitting and saw her still in her seat, smiling. Great, whenever she smiles at me I know something mean is about to come out of her mouth. I looked up at the teacher's desk, but he wasn't there. I put my things away trying to ignore her.

"Where is your boyfriend?" she asked. "I see Lucas isn't here."

I was starting to get mad. After the kind of day I'd had this didn't make it any better. Why couldn't she just leave me alone for one freaking day?

"He's not my boyfriend," I said it plain and simple; nevertheless, she ignored me and kept on talking.

"What did he do, ditch you so he didn't have to be seen with you anymore?" she giggled.

That did it. I was so angry I threw my bag in my seat and stared at her through narrowed eyes.

"I am so sick of you taunting me and thinking that you are better than everyone else!"

I was breathing hard and fast and I felt the warmth flow through my body as I did in the woods, but I didn't care. All I seen was Karman's face and the devilish grin she wore. The heat was spreading at a tremendous speed. Then I heard the windows rattling behind me, and I snapped out of it. I couldn't let this happen here. I closed my eyes and took deep breaths trying to ease my anger. It seemed to help. The windows stopped shaking as I calmed down. Just then, the teacher spoke and I reopened them.

"What is going on in here?" he looked at the both of us.

"Nothing Sir, just a friendly chat," Karman said in her fake cheery voice.

I really hate it when she does that.

He narrowed his eyes suspiciously, "Get a move on then, or you'll be late for lunch."

Karman smiled at me deviously and walked out first. I hung back, pretending to tie my shoe, so I didn't have to walk with her. I fixed my pants leg and zipped my book bag. She had to be far enough ahead by now. I slung my bag over my shoulder and walked out the door. I was still angry and mumbling under my breath when I stepped into the hall.

"Hi," a voice said.

I looked up to see Lucas leaning against the wall, like he was waiting for something, or rather someone.

"Hi," I said grumpily then looked back at the floor and kept on walking.

He walked with me, "Are you alright?"

"Peachy," I replied sourly.

"Do you want to talk about it?"

"Not really."

"Okay," he said.

We were almost to the cafeteria. I didn't realize I was hungry until I smelled the food. We were waiting in line when I finally gave in.

"Karman and I got into an argument," I said.

"I see. I was wondering what set it off."

I looked at him, "How do you know what I did?"

The words came out a bit harshly. I was still upset and I didn't mean to take it out on him.

"I didn't really. I only guessed. I heard the windows."

"Oh," I shyly said looking back at the floor. "I was so mad at her. I felt like I did in the woods the other night. I think that if I hadn't calmed down, I might have hurt her."

Although she may deserve it, no need to say that out loud though. I looked back up at his face with regret. He was looking at me with empathy.

"Yes, you could have. I'm sorry I forgot to mention that part. It's been a long time since someone..." he looked around, "Well you know what I mean." He leaned in closer to me as we stood in line and spoke just above a whisper, "Until you are trained, you can trigger your powers with feelings, like anger or fear, or any other emotion. It has to be strong though."

"Right; stay away from strong emotions," I said half jokingly half irritated.

He chuckled at me, "I am surprised at how well you handled your first time."

"Don't you mean second?" I asked, remembering the night in the woods.

He smiled, "Right, second, but still, that was amazing; especially since you aren't suppose to do magic until after your birthday."

We filled our trays and stepped up to pay, Lucas was in the front.

"I got both trays," he said.

I shook my head at him, "No. It's alright; I'll pay for my own."

He didn't listen to me and handed the lunch lady a twenty. He looked over at me and grinned. I rolled my eyes at him. He took his change and moved forward so we were side by side. I was very aware at how close we were. I could smell his cologne; I took in his scent as an idea popped in my head.

"Lucas, did you want to sit with us today?"

I said us instead of me, hoping it didn't sound too obvious that I wanted him to be close to me. I knew he was my Protector; however, I barely knew him so it made it awkward to be around him at times.

He smiled, "Sure."

We walked to where Sam was sitting and put our trays on the table. She smiled happily while some of our other friends stared at us. Jordan's friend Sean got up, mumbled something, and then left the cafeteria. I wondered what that was about. I put it out of my mind and sat next to Lucas. This was much better than this morning. All of our friends welcomed Lucas and talked with him, everyone but Sean, only because he wasn't here. I saw Karman watching from the corner of my eye, I looked up at her that one and only time during lunch. I saw the expression on her face; it was a mixture of irritation and annoyance. I grinned, that made me feel even better.

Five
Family History

Between Lucas and Sam, school got better and better as the day went on. Sam was her usual silly self, which always made me smile. Lucas walked me to my last class and then to my Jeep. I didn't know if he was trying to make me feel better or if he was worried about this morning, how I almost lost control. Either way it worked because at the end of the day I was completely out of my bad mood. Karman didn't speak to me for the rest of it, which helped; nevertheless, I still felt annoyed with her.

Sam had followed me home to eat dinner with Aunt Marie and me and to help with my birthday invitations. I went to the kitchen to grab a couple of sodas before going to my room. I saw a note from Aunt Marie with a twenty-dollar bill, explaining that she had to work late and just to order a pizza. I put the money in my pocket and then we headed up the stairs. I opened the door to my recently cleaned room. This morning before school, I had hung up the clothes I had tried on but didn't wear and made the bed. I brought my vanity chair over to the desk for Sam and handed her a note pad to start on the wording while I looked for designs.

We had conversations, mainly about what we had come up with; however, the one we are having now is shocking me a little bit in some parts.

"Did you know that Sean likes you?" she asked.
That took me by surprise. I stopped what I was doing and looked at her.

"No, since when?"

"For awhile now; he told me not to tell you."

"How long is a while?" I was curious.

"Since about the beginning of summer," she looked up at me. "He was hoping you would want to stop in Steamboat Springs on the way home Sunday."

"Oh," I felt a twinge of guilt. "But, I don't like him that way, I think of him as a friend."

She shrugged her shoulder, "That's what I told him. That's also why he left the table at lunch today. You came walking over with Lucas and he got mad."
I thought about earlier and the expression on Seans face. It fit right in with what Sam was telling me.

"Should I explain to him that I only like him as a friend?"
I didn't want him to think that I was leading him on or anything. Sometimes the smallest gesture can make someone think that.

"No, you can't tell him! I told him I wouldn't say anything!" There was a hint of hysteria in her voice.
I almost smiled, but I stopped myself so I didn't hurt her feelings.

"Calm down. I won't say anything, I swear," I reassured her.
She stared at me for a few moments to make sure I wasn't lying. When she was convinced that I was telling the truth, she went back to work.

Another few minutes of silence went by before she spoke again, "Has Lucas asked you out yet?"
I should have known that was coming; however, I didn't see it.

"No," was all I said.

"Do you think he will?"

"Probably not."

She perked up and smiled, "Don't worry. I think he will." I looked at her but I didn't say anything. The relationship that was starting between Lucas and I was nowhere near boyfriend and girlfriend, even if I was beginning to want it to be.

It didn't take us long to get the invitations picked out. We set the amount we wanted and hit the print button, and then we went downstairs to order the pizza. We went into the living room to find a movie to watch while we waited for the pizza to arrive. We finally settled on a newer one that neither of us had seen. The movie was about half over with when the doorbell rang. I hurried to answer the door and pay for our dinner so I didn't miss too much of it. I gave the delivery boy the twenty, told him to keep the change and came back to watch the rest. After we finished eating and the movie was over, we went back upstairs to cut and fold the invitations in half.

It was getting late by the time we were done. It seemed like it took forever, yet we had fun doing it together. Sam had put half of the pile in her book bag to help hand them out, then I followed her downstairs to walk her out. I wrapped my arms around myself. It wasn't really cold outside, yet I shivered involuntary. I helped her get her camping things from my Jeep.

"Thanks for coming over tonight and helping me," I said as we put her things in the back seat of her car.

"No problem, it was fun," she replied. "I'll see you tomorrow at school."

"Alright, call me when you get home."

"Okay," she got in her car and drove off.

I shivered again and I turned back around to go inside. I had just taken a few steps when I heard something in the bushes to my left. It was too dark to see anything that the porch light didn't touch. I picked up my pace; not daring to run to spook whatever was in there. My heart started to beat faster as panic began to set in. I could think of nothing but Malik and how he wanted my powers most of all, even though I haven't come into them yet. It sounded like it was coming closer; I could see a shadow now. I was almost to the door when something grabbed my arm from the other side of me. I let out a scream and turned around. I realized at once, what it was -or who it was I should say- that had a hold of me.

"Matthew! You scared me to death!" My heart was pounding and my breathing was heavy. "What are you doing here?"

"I was keeping an eye out around your house when something grabbed me from behind and hit me over the head," he was rubbing the back of it as he spoke.

I glanced back at the bushes, yet there was nothing there.

"Lucas is on his way. Are you alright?" There was tension and worry in his voice.

"I'm fine," I wasn't worried about me; I was worried about his head. "Come inside and sit down. I think you might have a concussion."

He nodded in agreement and let me help him through the door.

I locked the door behind us and then helped Matthew to one of the kitchen chairs while I went to the freezer and grabbed a bag of frozen veggies.

"Here this will help."

He took the bag from my hand. "Thank you," he winced as he put them on the back of his head.

Before we could say anything else, there was a knock on the front door. I looked at Matthew as he was getting up.

"You should sit, I'll get the door," I told him and tried to push him back in the chair.

"No. If it's someone Malik sent I'll be the one to open the door, so you have a chance to run."

I didn't have a chance to argue because he walked past me

and stepped up to the door. There was another knock and someone calling from the other side.

"Let me in, it's Lucas," he said.

He unlocked and opened the door. Lucas barged in, walking right passed Matthew and over to where I was.

"Are you alright?" he asked in a rush. He was upset.

I nodded, "Besides being scared almost to death, I'm fine."

He turned to Matthew, "Are you alright?"

Matthew didn't say anything he only nodded.

"Damn it!" Lucas yelled. "I should have been here!"

"What's going on Lucas?" I demanded.

He looked at me, there was anger in his eyes, yet I could tell it wasn't towards me.

"One of Malik's men was here."

"What!" I was shocked. "Is that what was in the bushes?"

Lucas's face changed from anger to horror and then curiosity, "Where in the bushes?"

"Outside to the right," I told them.

Lucas and Matthew looked at each other, and then back at me.

"What happened? What were you doing outside?" he didn't say it accusingly.

"I was walking Sam out to her car, she left, and then I was going back inside when I heard something. I didn't dare run in case it was an animal. I was almost to the porch when Matthew grabbed my arm and scared me. I screamed before I realized who it was, and then we went inside."

"There must have been two," Lucas said.

"An ambush," Matthew replied. "That close and they didn't attack her? Why?"

All of a sudden, magically or not, I knew why, "Because, Sam was with me and we were surrounded by houses and people. They could have easily grabbed me if there were two; however, Matthew showed up and I screamed, drawing attention to the situation."

Before anyone had a chance to comment, the phone rang. I picked it up on the second ring.

"Hello?"

"Hi, I made it home," Sam said cheerily on the other line.

"Okay," I quickly said.

"Kendall? Are you alright?"

"I'm fine. I'll see you tomorrow."

"Alright; night."

I hung up and turned back to the room. A car pulling into the driveway interrupted us again. It was Aunt Marie coming home from work.

I looked at Lucas with wide eyes and a racing heart. "Should you be here?"

He looked at Matthew. They were silently communicating.

"I think it's time," Matthew said.

Lucas nodded in agreement.

I was confused, "Time for what?"

We were standing in the kitchen when Aunt Marie came through the door still confused by what they meant.

"Kendall?" she called out to me.

"I'm in the kitchen," I replied.

She walked in with a tired expression on her face; however, that quickly changed when she saw I had company. She looked at all of us, worry creasing her forehead, then her eyes settled on me. She rushed to me and hugged me.

"Are you alright?" she asked.

"I'm fine."

"What happened?"

I was confused by her actions and the scared look on her face.

"It's starting," Lucas answered her.

I looked at Lucas in shock. What was he doing? Would she believe the story or would she insist that I have nothing to do with them again? She looked down at my confused face, hers was full of worry and fear, and then she looked back up.

"He was here?" she asked.
I still didn't understand.

"No, but we think he sent two," Matthew answered back.

I pulled away from Aunt Marie's arms, "What is going on?" I demanded.

She looked at me with saddened eyes, "Come and sit with me Kendall. I need to explain a few things."

I looked at her face and saw a mixture of emotions, regret, anguish, sadness; I was beginning to understand now…she knew.

I followed her to the living room; Matthew went out the door, while Lucas followed behind us. We sat down on the couch; she took a deep breath and then looked at me. I looked back into her eyes, waiting for her to begin.

"How much does she know?" she asked Lucas, glancing at him briefly.

"Only her part," I heard him say.
I didn't look away from Aunt Marie to see his expression.

"Okay. First of all let me say, I love you and all I wanted to do was protect you."

I nodded, "I love you too."

She took a deep breath and began, "You are a Natural, handed down from your parents."
I heard Lucas clear his throat, though I didn't look up. Aunt Marie paused for a short moment and then began again.

"It is genetic. Sometimes it skips a generation or two; I was hoping it would skip you; however, I was told otherwise," she glanced towards Lucas once again.

"I'm sorry for keeping this from you; I thought it was the right thing to do. I wasn't sure you were going to come into your powers, but if you started to…if I saw a trace of it, I was going to tell you then."

I was shocked, confused, and worried at the same time, "How do you know all of this? And how do you know them?" I glanced over to Lucas.

She closed her eyes and took a deep breath, before opening them, "Because I am a Natural, and so are Matt and Sara. We have known each other for a long time now."

I felt the creases on my forehead as I thought about it. Before I could ask my next question, Matthew came back inside and sat in a chair by the fireplace looking exhausted.

"Sara is on her way. She'll be here in five minutes."

I turned to Lucas, "So, before when you told me about all of this you mentioned 'they' both of them," I pointed to Matthew and Aunt Marie, "and Sara are who you meant?"

"Yes," he answered.

I thought about everything for a moment or two and then turned back to Aunt Marie, "I don't understand. You're older than Lucas is. I thought you become an Immortal and stop aging in your early twenties?"

She relaxed her face and smiled, probably at my reaction, that I wasn't angry that she kept this from me all these years; shocked maybe and a little confused, but not angry.

"Yes you are correct; we don't age, though only if you keep practicing your magic. We don't age as fast as normal people when we don't use it, but we do age," she smiled and put her hand on mine.

"I think it's time we start practicing more. What do you think Marie?" Matthew asked.

"Yes I think it's time," she answered back.

Just then, there was a knock on the door. Aunt Marie got up and answered it. She came back with a blonde woman with blue eyes and a kind face. I stared at her just the same as I did with Matthew. There was something familiar about her too.

Matthew walked over to the woman; he smiled at her and brought her closer to me.

"Kendall, this is my Sara."

I stood up to greet her, "Hi."

"Hello," she smiled at me.

She glanced at Matthew and her smile grew. I just stared at her. I knew the features on her face, her eyes, the shape of her mouth; however, I didn't know from where.

Everybody sat down and started talking. I was quiet for a while, just listening to them replay what had happened tonight to Sara and how to prevent it from happening again. I thought about how different my life would have been if I had known. Would I be prepared? Or, would I not want it at all. The first question I really didn't have an answer; as for the second, it's not an option, not anymore.

I started to pay attention again when I heard my name. They were talking about keeping me safe.

Matthew sat up as he said, "I think she should stay home from school."

Aunt Marie nodded in agreement, "Keep her out of sight." I thought about earlier tonight. How they wouldn't attack with Sam around.

"I disagree," I spoke up.

Everyone turned to look at me as I continued.

"Think about earlier. They didn't attack because I was with someone out of the loop, not until I was alone. I think I will be safest around people."

Aunt Marie, of course, disagreed, "I don't want to take the chance of losing you."

"I agree with Marie," Sara said. "We have to keep you as safe as possible."

Lucas sat up, he looked at me, and smiled, "Actually I think Kendall is right. They won't approach her while there are witnesses around, especially a school full. We found that out earlier today when I patrolled the school grounds with Matt during study hall."

So, that's where Lucas was earlier today.

He stood up and started pacing, "The things that I am worried about now, are to and from school and while you," he looked at Marie, "are at work."

"I'll come home early everyday; make sure I am here when she gets out of school."

I was starting to get annoyed; they were acting as if I wasn't even in the room or wasn't capable of taking care of myself.

"You can't close the bakery early everyday; look how much money we would be losing!" I protested.

"Your safety is more important than money!"

"I know but_" I started to say; however, I was cut off by Lucas.

"I'll be with her until you get home. In fact, I think I should take you to and from school as well. I don't want you out of my site as much as possible."

There was an authority to his voice that nobody argued with.

He turned and looked at me, "What do you think?"

Someone was actually going to let me have an opinion for myself?

I smiled, "I think I can handle you being my Chauffer for the week."

Lucas laughed and the others either laughed along with him or grinned.

After that, the tension eased and everyone relaxed a little. Matthew suggested that he should stay here for the night to give Lucas his turn to rest. Everyone agreed, except for Lucas. He had a hard time with it. He wanted to be the one who stayed, especially after what happened tonight; however, he finally agreed. It made me feel happy that he wanted to be here. They knew Malik wouldn't send someone to try again tonight; nevertheless, it was just a precaution that made Aunt Marie, and Sara for that matter, feel better.

There was going to be even stricter round-the-clock watch for the house and school grounds. Lucas would be inside, while someone watched the outer perimeter.

It was almost midnight when I had finally crawled into bed after Sara and Lucas left. I lay there before I drifted off to sleep, thinking of tomorrow and the week ahead of me, not knowing what to expect.

I woke up the next morning feeling exhausted from the night before. I didn't fall asleep as quickly as I would have liked to. I was worried about what was hiding in the bushes, Matthew's head, my birthday party, after my birthday, and anything else in between. I finally dragged myself out of bed the second time my alarm rang. I got ready for school and put the rest of the invitations in my bag that Sam and I had finished last night, before I was almost attacked, kidnapped or whatever Malik had wanted done.

I got downstairs to find Lucas waiting for me in the living room. Plans were made last night for Lucas to pick me up this morning for school. Aunt Marie wouldn't leave for work until he got here. I was shocked that he was here already.

He stood up as I entered the room, "Morning."

"Hi," I said and walked to the kitchen, Lucas following right behind. "Where are Aunt Marie and Matthew?"

"They left already," he chuckled quietly, "I had to basically push your aunt out the door."

He was smiling when I turned around. It looked like he wasn't angry any longer from last night.

"Did you want some breakfast?"

"No thanks, I already ate."

I ate a muffin that Aunt Marie had made the day before and drank a glass of juice before grabbing my bag and heading out the door.

There on the side of the curb was a big, shiny, black, newer Dodge Ram pick up.

I smiled and looked at Lucas, "Nice truck!"

He chuckled, "Thanks."

I had to step up to get into the cab, which I liked. The seats were gray and it still had that new car smell to it. He got into the drivers side and turned the key. I smiled as it roared to life. I have always had a fascination with vehicles, trucks especially.

"Nice. Is it four wheel drive?"

He looked at me and chuckled, "Yes it is." He wore an amused expression on his face.

"What's so funny?"

"Well," he was still smiling, "you don't meet very many girls that likes trucks."

I chuckled, "Nobody said I was normal."

He laughed aloud, "You got that right!"

He put the truck in gear and we were off to school.

"Are you feeling better?" I asked after a few moments. "You were quite angry for awhile last night."

"A little bit," he answered. "Now that I am with you," he half smiled.

I felt the butterflies fluttering lightly in my stomach. Then his face became serious.

"I wasn't mad at *you* last night," he looked at me.

Even though it was only a glance, I could see worry in his eyes.

"You know that right?"

I pulled one corner of my mouth up into a half smile, "Yes I know."

I looked straight ahead before I spoke again because I didn't think I would be able to say it if I were looking at him.

"With all the other times you've helped and saved me, it wasn't until last night that I realized how much you really care about my safety."

I didn't look back at him to see the expression on his face. He was quiet and just kept driving.

We were almost to school before he spoke again. "I won't let anything happen to you. I won't be reckless again." Then he took a deep breath.

I felt guilty and wished I didn't say anything about last night.

"Did I bring back the bad mood?" I asked, hoping I didn't.

He shook his head, "No, I'm good."

His jaw tightened slightly and his words didn't sound convincing. He glanced at me just as I nodded. He let out a breath and his expression softened.

"Really, I'm good," he smiled at me crookedly, making my heart skip a beat.

The atmosphere was better when we pulled into the school parking lot. We were early, though some of the other students were arriving.

"How is Matthews head?" I asked. He had seemed okay, though I was still worried.

"He had a headache for a short time last night; however, he is fine now. Let's get inside where it is safe," he had his hand on the handle of the door.

"Wait!" I said.

He looked back with confusion.

"What are we going to tell everyone that asks why we are together so much this week? I mean I hate to lie, but we can't go telling them the truth either. They would have me committed."

He relaxed, his expression turned to amusement, "I asked that same question last night."

"And?" I was curious of his answer.

He smiled at my eagerness, "Your Jeep wouldn't start this morning, so you called me."

I shook my head, "Sam won't believe that. She will ask why I didn't call her." I sat there in thought for a few moments. "How about, my Jeep wouldn't start, so I got out to go call Sam when you saw me in the yard. You stopped to see what was wrong and if I needed a ride to school. Then tomorrow if they ask..." I shook my head as I let the words trail off because there was no doubt in my mind I would be asked. "I mean *when* they ask, we'll tell them it's being fixed." I shrugged my shoulders, "Maybe we can even hide it at your house to say it's in the shop."

He just looked at me with a smile with amusement still on his face.

"What?" I was curious with what I did to put that expression on his face again.

He raised one eyebrow, "You know, for someone that doesn't like to lie, you came up with a good one in just a few moments."

I smiled, "Not all of it, it was half yours."

I opened the door of the truck and got out. Lucas met me in front of the truck and ushered me towards the door, with me being very aware of his hand on my back. His touch made me tingle all over. As we walked across the parking lot a few people stared at us; however, I didn't pay any attention to them. I was just trying to make it inside. We were almost to the side door when my pocket was playing music, one of my favorite songs. I pulled my phone out of my jeans and flipped it open, a text message.

"Sam is going to be late this morning," I said to Lucas.

"That reminds me; make sure you keep your phone with you at all times today."

I looked up at him with alarm.

"Don't worry," he half smiled, "It's just a precaution."

I put my phone on vibrate and put it back in my pocket.

Lucas relaxed a little bit once we got inside. He decided it was best to walk me to every class, at least until my birthday. Then maybe I'll be strong enough to handle what ever comes. Right now though, my powers are not even half of what they should be, so I'm told.

I turned to him before I opened the door to Spanish class, "I'll see you in a little while."

He smiled, "Forty-five minutes."

Mr. Pierce had us do work sheets through the whole class, very different from Mrs. Garcia. I wondered when she would be back. I was anxious to get this class over with; however, it dragged on. Once it was over, I hurried to put my book in my bag so I could wait for Lucas, when I saw colored paper. The invitations, I forgot. I handed a few of them out to the students that were left in the room. I would hand out the rest during lunch.

I only stood in the hall for half of a minute when I saw Lucas coming through the crowd with one corner of his mouth pulled up.

"What are you smiling at?"

He shook his head as we walked to our next class together, "Rumors."

I was almost too scared to hear what it was; nevertheless, I asked anyway, "What rumors?"

Lucas opened his mouth to speak, but was quickly silenced by someone calling my name.

"Kendall, wait!" we heard her say.

Lucas's smile quickly faded as he pulled me closer to him and got ready to fight.

"Lucas, it's only Sam stop!" I whispered urgently.

It only took a moment for my words to sink in. When he realized what I had said, he relaxed and let go of me. Nobody seemed to notice his reaction, which was a good thing. We didn't need any more attention.

"I'm sorry," he looked down at my face, with a softened expression, yet with firm eyes. "I'm not taking any chances though."

I half smiled, glad that we were this close, "I know, its okay."

He let go of me just before Sam finally pushed through the crowd to where we were.

"Hi!" she said.

"Hi Sam," Lucas said.

"Hi! What took you so long?" I asked playfully, trying to cover up the slight tremble in my voice. My heart was still pounding by Lucas's reaction to a potential attack and to his closeness.

"I over slept. I forgot I had an English paper due today. Jordan came over last night to help me with it. I never got to sleep until twelve thirty."

"Yeah me either," I meant to say to myself, but Sam heard me.

"Really? Why?"

I didn't look at Lucas; I thought that maybe she would guess that I was with him if I did.

"I just couldn't fall asleep."

The bell rang saving me from another lie.

"Oh, well I'll see you in Biology."

"Alright," I replied. Then we separated and Lucas and I walked to our class.

We made it as the last bell rang. I went to sit in my normal seat; however, Lucas grabbed my hand, which caused butterflies in my stomach, and pulled me along with him.

"What are you doing? I whispered as we walked to the back.

He smiled, "Precaution."

I smiled to myself as I sat down. The teacher didn't seem to care so I pulled out my homework and laid it on the desk for her to collect.

Six
Protection

After English was over, Lucas again walked me to my next class. Sam caught up and walked with us. I could tell there was something wrong with her because she was quiet. She pushed passed me and into the classroom without a word. Lucas winked at me before I closed the door. I was on cloud nine thinking about the events of the day so far, until I looked at Sam. She was sulking. I sighed, I felt guilty for forgetting that there was something wrong with her.

"What's the matter?" I whispered when the teacher wasn't paying attention.

She looked at me with hurt in her eyes, "Why didn't you tell me?"

I pushed my eyebrows together and tried to think of what she was talking about, "Tell you what?"

"That you and Lucas are dating?" she pouted.

"What!" I said a little too loudly.

The teacher didn't look up; however, he cleared his throat. I remembered the looks Lucas and I were getting when we came to school together and remembered what he had said about rumors.

I chuckled softly, "Sam, were not dating."

She looked a little confused, "You're not?"

"No."

"Then why did you ride to school together?" she asked, still with confusion on her face.

I shook my head in disbelief, "Wow, word does travel fast; all because my Jeep wouldn't start. Lucas drove by as I was about to call you to come get me."
I really hated to lie to her. She is my best friend after all. I should be able to tell her anything.

"I'm glad I didn't or I would have been late too," I smirked to try to cover up the guilty feeling.

"Oh," was all that she said.

"And besides, if I was going out with him or anybody else for that matter, don't you think I would tell my best friend?" This part was the truth.

She smiled sheepishly, "I was hoping."

When the bell rang, I grabbed my bag and waited in the hall for Lucas again. Sam and I had parted ways at the door. I could finally see his face through the crowd; however, it wasn't the happy expression as when he had left me. He had his forehead crinkled up and he looked like he was deep in thought.

I met him halfway, "What's wrong?"
I was envisioning the worst, something like Malik or his people breaking into the school.

"Why didn't you tell me you were planning a birthday party?" he demanded.
This was not what I was thinking of. It annoyed me actually. I thought something bad had happened.

"Because with everything that went on last night, a party was the last thing on my mind!" I snapped back. I crossed my arms and glared at him.

His expression relaxed and then it turned to amusement, "I'm sorry."
I couldn't help but smile back with the annoyance fading quickly.

"I'm sorry too. Are you mad?"

He shook his head, "It just makes it easier for me to protect you if you tell me these kinds of things."

Lucas and I caught up with Sam and Jordan and walked to lunch together. I was starving. We got our food, paid, and then went to find everyone else.

"Aren't you going to sit with your friends?" I asked. Looking around and not seeing them.

He shook his head and opened his mouth to speak, but I cut him off.

"I know, I know, precaution," I said. "I'm glad."

I looked up into his eyes. They were so beautiful. I gazed into them, seeing the darker flecks of brown in them. Then he smiled which made me shyly look away. Every time he smiles, it catches me off guard, even though I know its coming. It seemed while all that was happening that we were there for a long time; however, in reality only a few moments had passed because Sam and Jordan were just sitting down at the table. Time seems to stand still when we share a moment like that; I sighed and followed Sam and Jordan's lead.

Sam pulled out the invitations. I saw, without surprise, she didn't have very many left. She handed them out to the ones at the table she didn't get to this morning.

"What did you do, hand one out to everyone in the school?" I jokingly asked her.

"Not everyone," she said smiling. "How many did you hand out?"

I smiled sheepishly, "Umm, like three or four."

She sighed, put out her hand, palm up and waved them forward. I grabbed a handful of the invitations, handing most of them to her.

"*I'll* make sure people get these," she huffed and put them in her backpack.

I was grinning at her when Lucas leaned into me and whispered in my ear, "Am I invited?"

He was so close to me. I could feel his warm breath brush my ear. My heart started racing and I had to breathe in and out deeply, yet quietly, to control my breathing.

"I don't know," I said tying to sound calm. "Are you going to bring me a present?"

He chuckled, "Anything you want."

Anything? I smiled as my thoughts went to Lucas kissing me.

"Alright, you can come, but surprise me on the gift."
I reluctantly turned my attention back to the table; I noticed Sean was glaring at us. Feeling uncomfortable, I looked away and back at my lunch.

The last few days had been great. I rode to and from school with Lucas everyday as planned. During these times, we would talk about all sorts of things, from our favorite color, to skiing, and even how we liked our eggs in the morning. I was really starting to get to know him. There are only two more days until my birthday. We haven't seen any sign of Malik's people since Monday night; nevertheless, Lucas was not letting me go anywhere without him, which was fine by me.

It was a windy Thursday morning. The sky was full of dark rainy clouds that threaten to let loose at any moment. I stretched and pulled a pair of jeans from a folded pile of clothes on the hamper that I haven't taken care of yet, and put them on. I dug through my closet for a shirt and settled on a gray long-sleeved one, it matched the clouds outside. Then I went downstairs for breakfast. Lucas of course, was waiting patiently for me in the living room.

Hi," he said.
He walked up to me, stopping about a foot from me.

"Hi," I smiled. I just couldn't help but smile when I'm around him. "Would you like some breakfast today?"
There was something different about his eyes. They were set

in a way that made my stomach flutter with butterflies.

"Yes, please."

He led the way to the kitchen; however, as he passed me, his skin brushed lightly against mine. This made the butterflies go crazy.

"What would you like?"

"Whatever you're having is fine," he replied.

I went to the cupboard and pulled out the box of pop tarts. After putting his in the toaster, I grab two plates from the cupboard. From the corner of my eye, I saw Lucas watching me intently. I grinned at him. He returned the smile with an expression on his face I didn't recognize, yet made my stomach feel fluttery again. My eyes followed him as he made his way to where I was and stopped in front of me. He was so close. He put his left hand on the counter behind me and looked into my eyes as if he was seeing into my soul. Then he leaned closer to me. If I stood on my tip toes just a half of an inch, our foreheads or maybe our lips would be touching. I started to lose control of my breathing my heart was pounding so hard that I thought it was going to beat right out of my chest. Just then, the toaster popped up making me jump. Lucas sighed lightly and reached behind me for a plate. He grabbed his food and went to sit at the table. I just stood there dazed and confused for a few moments. Snapping out of it, I put my breakfast in the toaster. I poured two glasses of juice and took them to the table. I grabbed a plate as the toaster popped up and sat down at the table. I ate in silence without looking at him.

After the awkward breakfast, I went upstairs to brush my teeth. I looked in the mirror at myself. My reflection looked as confused as I felt. What was that? Was I imaging things? He was so close, was he about to kiss me? No. He's my Protector. I must have imagined it he was just reaching for a plate. I splashed my face with water to help erase the nerves and then brushed my teeth. I grabbed my backpack from my room and went downstairs.

Lucas was pacing in the living room. He looked up as I walked in. I thought I caught a glimpse of worry in his eyes before he smoothed his expression.

"Are you ready?" he asked.
I nodded without speaking and followed him to the truck.

It started to rain and the wind was stronger. We drove in silence the whole way to school. When we pulled in, Sam was getting out of her car. She saw us and waved, and then she pointed to the building to wait inside because of the rain. Something was off, I felt...uneasy. My almost imaginary kiss was sure to be the problem. Putting my feelings aside, we ran across the parking lot and into the school.

Lucas walked Sam and me to Spanish, I was about to say goodbye to him until second period, but he cut me off with a question.

"Are you alright?" he looked at me with an odd expression on his face, there was worry mixed up in it.
It's as if he could see right through me, as if he could see what I was feeling. Not wanting to confess that I thought it was the almost kiss from earlier I lied.

"I'm fine," I pulled up one corner of my mouth in a half smile, hoping that helped cover up the lie.

He didn't look convinced but he nodded anyway, "Alright, I'll see you in a little while."

Lucas watched me through the morning as he walked me to the classes we didn't have together. The classes we did have together, we sat next to each other and I could see him watching me every so often. Just as I predicted, I was asked the next day why I was still riding with Lucas. I answered with the story we concocted. Thankfully, everybody seemed to buy it.

I didn't get any homework done in study hall. I didn't even pull it out of my bag. I just sat there next to Lucas, staring at nothing. I couldn't escape the feeling I had and I began to think that it had nothing to do with the incident this morning.

Throughout the day, the feeling had gotten stronger and stronger. Not knowing what it was, I began to fret over it a little. I knew Lucas could see it in my face. Not being able to stand it any longer, he asked me the same question as earlier.

"Kendall, what's wrong? Talk to me, please," he begged.

I couldn't hide it any longer. I took a deep breath and shook my head.

"I don't know. Something is just…different or wrong."

He looked at me for only a fraction of a second before making his decision.

"I'm calling Matt," he reached in his pocket for his phone.

I put my hand on his to stop him, "Wait until after class, it's almost over."

I glanced up at the teacher; he wasn't paying attention. Lucas sighed and nodded. I still had my hand over his; he looked at them, and then he flipped his over and entwined his fingers with mine. His hand was warm and rough with calluses from his training; however, his fingertips were soft and my skin tingled where they touched. When he looked at me, I liked what I saw in his eyes. There was a yearning and a connection between us. I still felt as if something was wrong, though he made me feel relaxed and safe.

When the bell rang all too quickly and pulled us out of the moment, we stood up and picked up our bags, never letting go of our hands. Lucas pulled me out of the classroom and out into the hall toward a door that led outside. We had to dodge kids going in the opposite direction to lunch. The rain had finally stopped, though the sun was still behind dark gray clouds.

Lucas let go of my hand, pulled out his phone and called Matthew.

"I need you to check the perimeter." He listened for a

response. "Kendall doesn't feel right," he looked at me as he spoke. "Alright," then he closed the phone. "Let's go inside while we wait. It'll be safer until we can leave."

"Leave?" I asked as we went back inside.

"Yes, we need to get some place safe where the three of us can protect you while we figure out what's wrong," he kept his eyes out the window while he answered me. "We can't do that here, in front of all these people if something should happen."

"You think someone will come here, at school?" I was starting to get scared now; I could even hear it in my voice.

Lucas could too, "No, but I think, if they are desperate enough, they might try as soon as school is out, when we leave to go home; which is why we are leaving now."

"Where?" I asked.

"My house; it's more secluded than yours."

Lucas's phone rang just then. He listened for a couple of moments before he spoke, "Okay." Then he hung up.

"What did he say?" I asked.

He took my hand and led me in the other direction.

"He and Sara are on their way to escort us home."

We waited inside for Matthew and Sara by the door that led to the parking lot. When they pulled up in a white Explorer, we stepped outside. Matthew stayed in the running vehicle while Sara met us at the door.

"Did you see anything?" Lucas asked.

"Nothing out of the ordinary," Sara replied.

The three of us rushed down the walkway and through the parking lot to the truck. Lucas led me to the driver's side and helped me in. Sara went to the other side. She was riding with us in case Lucas was right.

Lucas slid in after me and started the engine, "How are you feeling?"

"Scared," I replied.

Sara rubbed my arm in comfort, "It's going to be alright.

We won't let anything happen to you."

Lucas put the truck in gear and pulled out of the parking space, following Matthew as he led the way. Lucas took his hand off the steering wheel and put it over my balled up fist; I didn't realize I was clenching it. I relaxed my hand, flipping it over to entwine our fingers once again. Sara looked at them and then up at Lucas, but she didn't say anything.

We were just about out of town when Lucas spoke to Sara, "Call Matt, there has been an SUV following us for the last minute. Sara pulled her cell phone out of her pocket, pushing the send button twice. She was talking when Lucas let go of my hand to put it back on the wheel as he sped up.

"Hang on; they are speeding up with us," he glanced down at me. In just that quick glance, I could tell he looked uneasy.

I saw a big, dark SUV behind us with tinted windows so dark I couldn't make out the driver. The vehicle got so close it looked like we were towing it. It hit the back of the truck flinging us forward. I saw another identical vehicle come around the first and pass us. The one behind us hit the back of the truck again while the one in front was trying to run Matthew off the road. Sara rolled down her window, unbuckled her seat belt, and hung herself halfway out the window.

"Sara, be careful," I yelled.

I heard her mumble something and saw the SUV in the front go off the side of the road. The driver quickly regained control, came back and hit Matthew again.

"Lucas, try to keep it straight. I am having a hard time hitting him," Sara yelled in the truck.

"A lot easier said than done Sara," he replied.

I looked back at the vehicle behind us and saw it coming just before it hit us again. I was getting angry. Why couldn't they just leave us alone? I knew why, because Malik wanted my powers. They were still annoying though.

"This is getting ridiculous," I said as it hit us again.
I could feel the heat starting to rise in the pit of my stomach. I knew what was coming and I was ready for it this time.

I opened the back window and put my hand out like the last time, "Leave us alone!"
The heat left my body and was replaced with coolness as the SUV behind us lost control and flipped a couple of times. It landed upside down on the edge of the road.

"Whoa!" Sara yelled.
She got the other one very easily now that we weren't being hit in the backend every ten seconds.

By the time it was over, we were on County Route 25, almost to their house. When we pulled into the driveway, no one got out but Matthew; he went inside the house.

"Why aren't we getting out?" I asked.

"We are waiting for Matt to come back out to give us the all clear," Sara answered.
There was a worried look on her face. I didn't blame her. If the one I loved went in alone with no back up, I would be just as worried.

No one moved or spoke for the few minutes Matthew was in the house. He reappeared on the porch and nodded. Understanding the message, Sara and Lucas opened their doors and got out. Lucas held out his hand to help me out and the three of us headed for the door. We made it safely inside. I followed Lucas into a room I was sure was the living room. It was smaller than the one at my house; however, it had a warm, cozy feeling to it. I felt very comfortable here. All of a sudden, I was very tired. I sat down on the couch and put my head back to rest.

"Ouch!" My neck really hurt.
Lucas rushed over to the couch and sat next to me.

"Are you alright? What's wrong?" he asked anxiously.

"My neck hurts a little bit."

Sara sat on the other side of me, "Can you move it from side to side?"

I tried it and found that I could, it was just sore to do so.

"I think you'll be fine. Sounds like whip lash," she said. Then she got up and laid a throw pillow at the end of the couch, "Here, come lay down for awhile to rest your neck. I'll get you some aspirin."

Lucas got up to make room for my feet and sat in the chair near the pillow. I lay down and eased my neck down on the pillow. Immediately the tension started to ease.

Sara came back with a glass of water and the pills, "Here you go honey." She half smiled, "You are safe here; rest now."

I took the pills and closed my eyes, and then I reopened them quickly.

"I need to call my aunt. She will be worried if she gets home and I'm not there."

"Don't worry. I'm on my way now to do it. You need to relax for awhile," Sara said.

I did what she told me and closed my eyes.

I was riding in the truck. The radio was playing music in the background; however, I didn't notice it too much because I was sitting right beside Lucas in the middle seat. My hand was in his and my head was lying on his shoulder. I was very happy, just him and I in this moment. All of a sudden, something hit the side of the truck pushing us off the side of the road. I grabbed the dashboard for support as we went over a small bank. I screamed as we flipped over three times. When we stopped, we were upside down. It was cold. I could feel the blood rushing to my head and I could feel pain as it throbbed. When I finally got the seatbelt unbuckled, I crawled out into the snow. There was a sharp pain in my leg; nevertheless, I stood and limped to the driver's side to help Lucas. The truck was empty.

"Lucas?" I called for him. I couldn't find him anywhere, "Lucas, where are you?"

I awoke to people arguing softly in the other room. I was shaken. It felt so real, but it was just a dream.

"You are her Protector Lucas!" I heard a woman say. It sounded like Sara.

"I know." It was a mans voice. I could tell it was Lucas. He sounded sad.

I got up from the couch and stretched. Ow, I remembered that my neck hurt. It did feel better though. I looked around the room. The sun was shining in the windows casting a warm glow. It was a deep yellow, low in the sky, telling me it was late in the afternoon and the rain had finally stopped.

I walked out to the dining room to find Lucas sitting alone in one of the chairs at a huge table, with his head in his hands.

"Hi," I said.

He looked up from his hands, "Hi."

"Is my aunt here yet?" I sat down in one of the chairs opposite of him.

"She will be arriving in a little while," he half smiled at me. "How are you feeling?"

"Better, I'm not so tired anymore."

"Good and your neck?"

"That's better too, a little stiff though."

He smiled; however, it didn't reach his eyes, he looked troubled.

"Is everything alright? I heard you and Sara arguing just before I came out."

He straightened up a little too fast, "What did you hear?" I was taken aback by his sudden interest.

"Nothing really except Sara say "you are her Protector" and you said, "I know", that's it."

He smiled; however, again it wasn't a true smile. I knew something was bothering him.

"It's nothing important at the moment."

I heard my stomach growl. I was starving. I hadn't eaten

anything but a pop tart all day. Just then, Sara came in to the dining room.

"Marie will be here in ten minutes, she is stopping by your house to grab a change of clothes and your tooth brush," she said.

I was confused, "I'm not going home?"

"We think it would be better if you stayed here until your birthday," Lucas answered.

"But, I thought I was safer around a bunch of people?" I asked.

"Well you are, though we won't be able to fight them with magic. We need to be around in case something happens between now and Saturday morning. We can't do that around people," Sara replied.
I understood.

My stomach growled again, but this time it was loud enough that Lucas and Sara could hear it too. The amusement of my loud stomach made the atmosphere a little lighter.

"Would you like to help me make dinner?" Sara asked me with a smile.

"Sure."
I stood up and followed her out to the kitchen, not before glancing back at Lucas though. He still had that troubled look on his face, but he smiled.

The kitchen was beautiful. It had an Italian theme to it. Stone covered the wall behind the stove and a stone archway over top. It had dark cherry cabinets with tan colored walls and tiled floor. There was an island in the middle with two stools on the side closest to the dinning room and a stool on each end.

"I absolutely love your kitchen," I told her.

"Me too, it's my favorite room in the house."

"It definitely would be mine too!"

There was a confused yet happy, loving expression on her face, "You like to cook?"

I grinned and nodded my head, "I love to."

Aunt Marie came into the kitchen just as we were putting the pasta for spaghetti in the boiling water.
"Is everyone alright?" She rushed up and hugged me.
I winced in pain, "Ow."
She quickly let go of me. Her eyes were full of fear, "You are hurt."
"Just a little, my neck is stiff."
She hugged me again, just a little more carefully this time.
Lucas walked in the kitchen, "Are you okay?"
I gave him a quick, half smile, "I'm fine."
He looked at me for a couple of moments before he turned to Sara.
"How long until dinner? Matt and I want to check the perimeter, make sure no one has gotten through," Lucas said. Through? Through what? Before I could ask, Sara answered him.
"It'll be ready in about fifteen minutes, you have time."
Lucas nodded and looked back at me before leaving the kitchen. His expression was of worry and concern, yet also something that made my heart flutter. Sara and Aunt Marie noticed it too and shared a look. I cleared my throat, grabbed the plates from the counter, and walked out to the dining room to set the table.

I came back in to mix up the salad, to see Sara and Aunt Marie whispering. I couldn't make out what they were saying, because they stopped as soon as they saw me. I had a feeling it was about me. I pushed their suspicious action out of my mind and helped them with the rest of dinner.

Matthew was at the head of the table and Lucas was on his right, by the windows. They were talking as we entered the dining room with dinner. I sat the salad down and took a seat next to Lucas.

The conversation was about earlier this afternoon. Mainly

explaining to Aunt Marie what had happened. They had just started the conversation; they were at the part of me not feeling right.

"When did you start feeling like that?" Matthew had asked.

I looked up at him as I answered, "I was making Lucas and me breakfast, so just after," I paused.

Lucas didn't look at me, though I could feel him tense next to me. I was about to say, 'when I thought Lucas was about to kiss me' but I quickly changed my mind. Hoping nobody noticed.

"Breakfast," I finished.

I looked down at my plate, hoping no one had noticed my reaction, and finished my spaghetti.

They were going over some different strategies when a few questions had occurred to me.

"What did you mean earlier when you said you were going to check to see if they got through? Got through what?"

"While you were sleeping I put wards up around our property. They are enchantments to keep everything out," Sara answered.

"Unless you know the password, so to speak, you won't be able to get through," Aunt Marie spoke up.

"Is there a certain password for it?" I was worried that anyone could look it up.

"No, it's whatever word or set of words you want to use."

"Can every Natural do that?" It sounded pretty cool.

Sara smiled, "No, there isn't very many of us that can do that."

"Oh," I wondered idly if Malik was one of the few.

"Why was I so tired after we got here?" That was very strange.

Lucas turned to face me. There was a grin on his face that I didn't understand. "Because, you did magic way beyond what you should be able to do right now. When you are not trained properly it will tire you more easily."

I pushed my eyebrows together and thought about what he had said.

"So, what does that mean?"

He smiled widely, "It means you are going to be more powerful than we thought."

"Which is why Malik wants her so badly," Matthew said.

Lucas stopped smiling and looked down, "I know."

I could see the distress on his face and decided I didn't like it, so I changed the subject.

"How much damage was there to the explorer Matthew?" I asked.

He smiled, "Please call me Matt." I smiled and nodded. "The mirror is broken and there are a few scratches to the side, nothing too major."

"What about the truck?" I asked Lucas.

He grinned, "The bumper is in pretty bad shape. It needs to be replaced."

I felt my eyes widen with shock. Lucas laughed at my expression. I noticed everyone looking at him with curiosity.

He turned to them still smiling, "This is the only girl that I have met that is more worried about the vehicles than herself."

Everyone understood Lucas's laughter and joined in, including me.

Seven
Attack

After dinner, I started to gather the plates from the table. Sara stood and began to help.

"I got this," I told her.

"Are you sure?"

I smiled as I grabbed the rest of them, "I'm positive. It's the least I can do."

I stacked the plates Sara had on top of mine and took them to the kitchen. Lucas followed me in with the rest of the dishes that were left. I laughed softly while unloading my hands.

"What?" he asked in a curious tone.

"Are you afraid to leave me in a room by myself?"

He grinned, "No. Actually I came out to help you." He set the dirty dishes on the counter and began taking care of the leftovers, "And to see how you are doing?"

"I'm okay; just worrying." Something just dawned on me, "Oh no."

"What! What's wrong?" there was panic in his voice.

I turned to face him, "Sam. She is probably worried sick about me. I have to call her."

I headed for the living room where I left my cell phone. She is going to be so angry.

He grabbed my arm to stop me, "Relax. Marie called her before she left to let her know you are sick and that you would not be going to school tomorrow."

I shook my head and looked at the floor. I quietly laughed at myself and took a deep breath. I needed to relax I was worrying too much. Lucas chuckled at my reaction. I looked up at him and when our eyes met, they locked. He lifted his hand from my arm to move a strand of hair that was hanging loosely in front of my eyes, and then he caressed my cheek. We just stood there, neither of us moving, not even when Matt called in from the other room.

"Lucas, you in the kitchen?"

"Yes," he called back, never removing his eyes from mine.

"Let's go check the perimeter."

"Be right there," he smiled and released my face. "I'll return in a little while," his voice was calm and soothing.

I stood there for a moment dazed. I was not imagining things earlier; he was close to kissing me this morning and I bet we were close just now. I smiled turning half of my attention back to the dishes, while the other half was still on Lucas and the lingering feeling he left on my cheek.

It didn't take me very long to finish up in the kitchen. After I was done, I went to the living room and sat on the couch. The television was on, though no one was really watching it. The guys were not back yet and Aunt Marie and Sara were catching up with some of the things they didn't get a chance to talk about the other night.

I text Sam to let her know that I was all right and asked if she could text me the homework assignments for today and tomorrow, when she gets them. She sent one back letting me know that she would and if I thought I would be well enough for Saturday. Oh no, I forgot!

"What about my party at the lodge?" I asked Aunt Marie. She looked at Sara, but before they had a chance to answer Matt and Lucas walked in. They both had seen my expression.

"What's wrong?" Matt asked.

"I forgot about my birthday party on Saturday."
I was a little panicky. What if I couldn't go? I...well Sam practically invited the whole school and who knows whom else.
The four of them looked at each other. It looked like a silent conversation was going on.

"We think it will be safe enough. Once you are in your full power it will be harder for someone to get to you. You will need training; however, you will be able to fight if you have to. Plus you will be in a large crowd," answered Matt.
I smiled. Good, I was looking forward to some normalcy after the last few days; besides there was no way Sam would let me skip out, even if I was supposedly sick. I let Sam know it was still a go and asked her who was coming. I was right; practically everyone in town was supposed to show up at some point or another.

Aunt Marie was staying at their house as well. It didn't shock me all that much. She called her assistant to make sure he could open for her tomorrow and agreed to take his Saturday shift. Nobody was leaving the house until Saturday morning when it was safe for me to leave, well, safer than it is now. I would never really be safe until Malik was dead. He wanted my powers more than anyone else's. Lucas told me over dinner that Malik could take my powers from me at anytime; however, the best time to abstract them was just a few minutes after midnight, when they were fresh and new. So, for now, I am to stay in the safe environment they have made for me. I glanced at Lucas beside me on the couch. It wouldn't be too hard to find something to distract me. Other than the obvious, there was the television and a game console with about fifty games. I also have my ipod and if all else fails I can start on my homework.

I looked at the clock as I yawned; it was just past eleven.

"I agree," Matt said, "It's getting late. We will need our strength through out the night and tomorrow."

"I'll take the first shift," Lucas said.

"And I'll check the perimeter before I head to bed," Matt said. He stood up from the chair and stretched.

"I'll come with you," Sara stood up too. "You have everything you need for bed?" she asked me.

She had pulled out some bedding for me while I was doing the dishes and laid them on the arm of the couch.

"Yes, thank you."

She smiled weakly, "Sorry about the couch."

"It's fine really," I assured her.

She hugged me then walked out the door with Matt.

"I'm going to bed too," Aunt Marie stood up and hugged me as well, "See you in the morning."

"Night," I called back as she headed for the guest bedroom.

I got up and dug through my overnight bag for my pajamas; however, I couldn't find them. I pulled everything out, yet they weren't there.

"Do you need something?" Lucas asked.

"Aunt Marie forgot to pack some pajamas for me."

He chuckled as he got up and held out his hand to me, "Come on. I've got something you can wear."

I took his hand and let him pull me up.

We went down the hall to the second door on the left. He opened the door and flipped the light on to a small, neat, organized room. The bed was in the middle of the room with a nightstand beside it, a tall dresser was in one corner, and the closest in the other. There were shelves that lined the wall with books and music on either side of the window.

He dug through his dresser, pulled out a T-shirt, and a pair of jogging pants, "Will this work?"

I nodded, "Thanks."

I took them from him and went to the bathroom to change. I

could smell him on the clothes that he gave me. They were a little big; however, the pants had a drawstring, so I cinched them until they fit. I washed my face and then went back to the living room to make my bed on the couch. Lucas looked up as I walked in. Something flashed across his face; however, he composed himself before I could tell what it was exactly.

"What?" I asked in confusion.

I looked down to make sure I had everything on. It would be embarrassing if I had come out without something, like pants.

He tore his eyes away, "Nothing."

I didn't understand his behavior, though for some reason it made me smile.

I made my bed and then got under the covers. I looked at Lucas, he was staring at the television, but I don't think he was really watching it. His mind was probably where mine was.

"Do you think they will be able to break through the shield?" I asked pulling my knees up and resting my chin on them.

I was worried what would happen if Malik's people did break through, abduct me, and...I didn't want to imagine anything else. I would probably have nightmares as it was tonight without adding to them.

He looked at me and shook his head, "Not without the key words. Unless Malik himself comes, he might be the only one to break it."

Malik, the most powerful Natural. My heart started to pound in my chest. I could feel the terror that colored my face, because I knew the only way for him to get my powers was to kill me. Lucas, seeing the expression on my face, got up from his chair and sat next to me on the couch. He put his arm around my shoulders to comfort me.

"Don't worry. As I said before I won't let anything

happen to you."

I sighed, "It's not only me I am concerned about."

"The rest of us will be fine."

We sat there in silence for a couple of minutes while I let him comfort me. I didn't want anyone to get hurt because of me, or worse.

"Why don't you try to get some sleep now?" he suggested. He got up and sat in a chair near the fireplace so I could lie down. "Goodnight Kendall."

"Night."

I had a sudden case of déjà vu. I was riding in the middle seat of the truck beside Lucas. We were holding hands and my head was lying against his arm as he drove. I was very happy in this moment; however, something felt…off. I looked up just in time to see a vehicle smash into the side of the truck. We rolled over a bank; when we finally stopped, we were upside down. I unbuckled my seat belt and crawled out. I could feel pain; however, all I cared about was seeing if Lucas was all right.

"Lucas," I called out.

There was snow on the ground and it was cold. I went to the other side of the truck to help him out, but he was not there.

"Lucas?"

I was being shaken. I opened my eyes to a face over mine. I flinched in fear and gasped loudly.

"Kendall, shh it's alright. It's Matt."

I sat up, blinking my eyes in the dark, "Matt?"

"Yes it's me. Are you all right? You were calling for Lucas."

I thought about my dream, "Is he all right?" I could hear the panic in my voice.

"Yes he's fine, he's asleep," he assured me.

"What time is it?" It was still dark so I knew it was sometime in the middle of the night.

"It's just after four in the morning. Everything is all right.

Try to go back to sleep."

He stood and left my side as I lay back down. I kept thinking about the dream. It was so vivid and seemed so real. It was the same one from this afternoon. It was strange for me to dream it twice. With difficulty, I pushed it out of my head and fell off to sleep once again.

I awoke to the sound of banging pots and pans. I sat up blinking a couple of times; it was bright inside the living room. I could see the sun peeking through the curtains. I got up, stretched and then I folded the blankets. I laid the blankets on the floor next to the couch out of the way; I would need them for one more night. I went to see who was making all the noise in the kitchen; it was Sara.

"Morning," I said to her.

She turned away from the bowl of contents she was mixing to come over and hug me.

"Good morning! How did you sleep?"

I kept tossing and turning and along with my dream, not very well.

"Fine," I lied. "Can I help you with breakfast?"

"Sure, but let's wait for the others before we cook it."

I grabbed my bag and after Sara told me where the towels were, I shut the bathroom door. When I was showered and dressed, I went back out to the kitchen to see if Sara had started breakfast yet, some of the others must be up by now. I was right; Lucas and Aunt Marie were sitting on each end of the island drinking coffee.

"Morning Sweetie," Aunt Marie said.

"Morning."

Lucas looked up from his cup and smiled, "Hi."

The butterflies went wild. I sighed inside, "Hi."

"Would you like some coffee?" Sara asked me.

I tore my eyes away from Lucas to look at her, "Yes, thank you."

She poured coffee into a cup and handed it to me; I fixed it the way I liked it and then sat next to Aunt Marie.

Everyone was quiet as we sipped our coffee, just taking in the peaceful morning; kind of like the calm before the storm. It made me weary to think that the day was only going to get worse.

Aunt Marie looked up from her coffee cup, "What time did Matt go to bed?"

"We switched shifts at seven," Sara answered. "Is anyone hungry yet?"

Lucas answered with a smile, "I am."

"You're always hungry!" She got up and pulled the eggs and the bowl of contents she was mixing earlier from the fridge.

She looked at me with a smile, "I'll do the eggs while you do the pancakes?"

"Yeah, sure."

I thought of another question as we ate. Actually, it had been on my mind since last night; nevertheless, I didn't want to know the answer until now, when I absolutely needed to.

"What will happen if Malik does get my power?"

Everyone looked up at me.

"Sweetie, we won't let that happen," Sara replied.

I smiled weakly, "I know, what I really meant was, what if he had the kind of power he wants from me?"

Aunt Marie spoke this time, "It could mean the end of all of us."

I was right to wait; I was terrified. I looked at Lucas, there was worry and fear in his eyes; it was a mirror image of the way I felt.

After breakfast, I helped Sara and Aunt Marie clean up the kitchen while Lucas showered. Afterwards I checked my phone. Sam was suppose to text me, though I wasn't sure when. I pulled my phone out and saw that she had sent me a message; she sent the first half of today's homework. I still hadn't done yesterdays. I thanked her and then took out my books from my bag.

I had just started my homework when Lucas walked in the room, "Is that today's or yesterdays?

"Yesterdays," I replied.

He grabbed his book bag and sat on the couch next to me. We did all of yesterday's homework together, and then started on today's. After a couple of hours, I threw my books down.

"I need a break."

I reached forward and stretched. I could feel Lucas watching me.

"What do you want to do then?"

I shrugged my shoulders, "Anything."

I searched the room; my eyes ran across the game console.

"How about a video game?"

After about an hour of Lucas kicking my butt with a fighting game, Aunt Marie came in from the dining room.

"Sara and I are going to check the perimeter."

We paused the game to look at her.

"When we get back we'll have lunch," she turned to head back in to the dining room, but then quickly turned back. "Oh, Lucas; Sara wants you to wake Matt."

"Alright," he answered back.

I handed the controller to Lucas and stood up to stretch. He turned the console off and disappeared down the hall. Sara and Aunt Marie came from the dinning room.

"We'll be back soon," Aunt Marie said just before she closed the front door.

I sat on the couch and looked at my homework. Not that I really wanted to, I decided to do some more of it while I waited for Lucas and Matt to come out. Only a couple of minutes went by when I heard doors shutting. Lucas walked back into the room and up to me, holding out his hand. I looked up into his smiling face, before taking his hand and following him to the kitchen.

I sat on the stool while Lucas made a fresh pot of coffee and then he came to sit next to me while we waited for everyone. No sooner had he sat down when we heard the front door open and close. Sara and Aunt Marie walked in the kitchen with panicked expressions on their faces.

"What's wrong?" Lucas asked.

"We saw a glimpse of someone or something moving in the woods, just outside of the perimeter," Sara answered.

Lucas stood up and looked at me briefly before leaving the room without a word. Aunt Marie and Sara came over and put their arms around me.

"They're coming?" I asked.

"Not necessarily," Aunt Marie answered.

Lucas was gone and back in less than one minute, with Matt on his heels.

"We are going to check if we can see anything else," Lucas said. He then turned to me with concern in his eyes, "You'll be safe with them."

I opened my mouth to say something but he lifted his hand and cut me off.

"I'll be right back."

I sighed, but didn't argue. He turned away from me and then he and Matt walked out the door.

"Kendall, do you feel anything?" Aunt Marie asked immediately.

I shrugged my shoulders, "I don't feel that much different from yesterday. That feeling never really went away, just eased up a little."

She didn't seem to relax any. She stood up, "Come on, let's go wait in the other room."

We left the kitchen and went into the living room.

We sat in silence waiting for Matt and Lucas to return, not wanting to make a sound to cover any cry for help. After a while, Sara began to pace. This made me more nervous. I looked up at the clock above the television; it was quarter past three. I couldn't stand this waiting.

"It's been over an hour. Where are they?"

Aunt Marie put her arm around me, moved the hair from my face, and looked up at Sara.

"They are fine," Aunt Marie said reassuringly to both of us.

The front door suddenly opened making us all jump. Sara turned ready to defend. To my relief Lucas and Matt walked in. Sara relaxed and I let out a breath of air.

"We've seen them too. There are two of them, maybe three. We think they have been out there since last night," Matt said.

"They can't get in. They have figured that out," Lucas added. He sat next to me, "But, I think they are really going to try to get through once it gets closer to midnight."

My body became rigid with fear. Even though I knew it was coming, I was shocked it was so soon.

Matt nodded, "I think you are right Lucas, but to be on the safe side one of us needs to stay with Kendall at all times," he looked at me, "Even to go to the bathroom."

I couldn't find my voice so I just nodded.

I could smell dinner coming from the kitchen. Sara and Aunt Marie prepared dinner insisting I stay in the living room away from any windows. We would all be eating in the living room tonight.

"When do you think they'll attack exactly?" I asked Lucas. I was as prepared as I was going to be; nevertheless, it would make me feel better if we could estimate the time.

"If our theory is right then it will be just before midnight." My body became rigid again and I balled my hands into fists. Lucas reached over, unclenched my fist, and laced his fingers with mine.

"Relax. They will have to get past the four of us before they can get to you, something they won't be able to do," he looked up at my face. "Each of our powers are different from each others."

The others entered the living room with dinner. With a sigh, Lucas let go of my hand. We took our plates as he continued.

"You've seen Sara's power and parts of mine; we can do what you have done so far. It's called Telekinesis."

"In other words," Sara said as she settled in a chair. "We have the ability to move objects with our minds. I can also cast spells, like with the protection wards outside."

"Is that something I'll be able to do?" I asked her.

"It's hard to know what other powers you will have. You have to have an affinity for it, like with Telekinesis."

"And I," Matt spoke up then, "have Night Vision."

"And if any of us are hurt I can heal them," Aunt Marie added.

I felt my eyes widen with shock and confusion, "You're a Healer?"

I didn't know that was possible. Of course, I didn't know real magic existed until recently either. Her smile confirmed it as much.

Matt stopped eating and looked at me, "Can you ever remember being any sicker than the beginning stages?"

I thought about my childhood, as far back as I could remember. Not once could I remember having a serious cold, the flu or even the chicken pox even though almost everyone had it in grade school. I looked back at Aunt Marie in disbelief.

"You were doing magic all this time?" A feeling of astonishment washed over me.

She was smiling sheepishly, "Just a little, only to make you better when you were…well…getting sick, or cut yourself, or fell and bruised yourself."

Matt laughed, "See what I mean?"

"That's why she looks younger than she should," Sara added.

"How old are you really?" I asked Aunt Marie.

She smiled nostalgically, "I was born in the fifties."

"As was I," Sara added.

"How about you?" I asked Matt.

"I'm a little older. I was born in the forties."

"Wow you guys are old," I said jokingly.

Everyone laughed.

The air seemed lighter in the room it helped me relax a little. I looked at the clock again. It was almost eight, just a few more hours until my birthday. I was not looking forward to it.

I heard music playing from my bag, a text message. It was from Sam, she texted me the rest of the homework assignments for today and to ask how I was feeling. I sent back my thanks and told her I was feeling much better. Sam sent me another text asking if I could meet her tomorrow at noon to help her set up the lodge. The party doesn't start until seven; however, knowing Sam, she just wants to make sure everything is perfect.

"Do you think it will be safe enough to meet Sam at the lodge at noon tomorrow to help her set up?"

I was mainly asking Aunt Marie, though I knew I had to clear it with the others for safety reasons. She looked at the others. By their at-eased expression, she had their answer.

"If tonight goes smoothly, I think it will be safe enough, as long as one of us goes with you," she said.

"I agree," Lucas added.

Sara spoke up, "I can go with you, if that's alright of course?" She looked at me with hopeful blue eyes.

I smiled, not only because she was looking at me like that, but also because I really wanted to get to know her. There was something about her.

"I would love for you to help," I answered.

A thought fluttered to the front of my head. I forgot to officially invite Matt and Sara to my party.

"You are coming to my birthday party, aren't you? I hope you are."

Matt took Sara's hand and they smiled at each other, then he said, "We wouldn't miss it for the world."

I was relieved and felt a feeling of significance, even though Aunt Marie has raised me from a baby, and even though I had just met them, their presence mattered as much to me as Aunt Marie's did. I texted Sam back to let her know I would meet her at the lodge at noon and that I was bringing someone to help.

Sara and Matt had left to check the perimeter. They decided it would be best to do so every hour. Lucas had not left my side all evening; neither had Aunt Marie really, although she would get me whatever I needed then hurry back into the room. I felt a little guilty that Aunt Marie and Lucas were staying with me, knowing Sara and Matt might need them if there were trouble outside.

Lucas seemed to have sensed my stress because he looked at me and asked, "How are you holding up?"

"Okay, just worried and scared."

"We won't let anything happen to you."

"I know, what I meant was, I'm worried about what is going to happen to me, when I come into my powers."

"Oh," realization flashed in his eyes. "I see. Well, it's one of the best feelings in the world," he smirked, "Almost."

Aunt Marie cleared her throat advising Lucas to stay on track.

Lucas continued, "It's a sensation that runs through your whole body at once. You'll start to feel it almost immediately."

Aunt Marie spoke up, "Don't be scared when it happens, you'll feel whole, like you don't know how you ever survived without it, like Lucas said, it's one of the best feelings in the world."

I smiled and relaxed a bit, their explanation made me feel

better; nevertheless, I was still nervous.

I yawned and stretched out my arms. Just sitting and waiting was very tiring. The anticipation itself could make a person go crazy.

"Why don't you rest? We'll wake you if anything happens," Lucas said.

I shook my head no, "I'm okay."

"Kendall, you'll need your rest for later," he used his no-nonsense voice.

"Lucas is right, you should rest," Aunt Marie added.

I looked at them both. I was a little annoyed that they were ganging up on me. I was tired though, so I decided to give in to their request.

"Maybe for a few minutes."

I lay my head on the arm of the couch and curled up in a ball. I yawned as I closed my eyes waiting for sleep to come and take me away from the stress of the night for a little while.

I never truly fell asleep. I just lay there, sometimes with my eyes open. I was too anxious to get any further than that. After awhile Sara and Matt came back inside with news. I sat up to hear what they had to report.

"There are about six or seven people now, just circling the perimeter," Matt said, pacing in front of the fireplace.

"Do you think Malik has shown them a way in?" I asked. I began to feel very worried again.

"Maybe," Sara answered. "We put another enchantment around the inside of the first. If they are trying to get through the first, it will take them just as long to penetrate the second."

That was reassuring. At least we would have a head start.

I looked at the clock again; it was ten thirty now. My stomach was tied in knots. I hated the anticipation. I expected Malik and his people to try to break through the enchantments any time. Silence fell over the room and everyone took turns pacing. Matt, with his night vision, watched through the window into the dark. I felt like a caged animal in the zoo, like someone was watching every move that I made. Whatever happened, I was ready for this night to be over.

I lay my head back on the arm of the sofa and thought about tomorrow, knowing this night would be behind me, but also knowing what lies ahead. What kind of training I would be doing, what kind of powers I would have. A loud noise arose from outside, pulling me from my thoughts. It sounded like thunder only not quite as loud.

"What was that?" I asked.

Lucas rushed in front of me and stood in a protective stance.

"They are trying to break through the barrier," Sara answered.

"It sounds like they are desperate to get through," Aunt Marie said as she looked at me with worry.

I looked at the clock; twenty more minutes left until midnight and this anxious feeling.

The thunderous sound kept coming, now along with cries of pain.

"It hurts them but they won't stop," Lucas said now sitting on the couch next to me.

"They fear for their lives if they go back empty handed," Aunt Marie added.

I just looked at her confused, "Go back? Isn't Malik here with them?"

"I don't think so," Matt answered. "If Malik was here, then he would likely already be through the first barrier."

"Why do you think he isn't here himself?" I asked.

He shook his head, "We're not sure. They only thing we can guess is that you have enough protection to stop a small human army and because of that, he doesn't want to take a chance of injury."

I turned my attention to Lucas. He was already looking at me with concern. He put his arm around me the same moment I leaned into him for comfort.

The thunderous sounds stopped, only to be replaced with loud blasts. Everyone went from window to window to see what was happening. Everyone except Lucas and me, only because he pulled me back down as I tried to go.

Matt turned from the window, "They are using their powers to try to break through. You would think they would have tried that first, before hurting themselves."

I hated that the clock had a hold of me; nevertheless, I kept watching it anyway. The time ticked by, faster and faster. There were only ten minutes left now.

"Get ready, a few of them got through," Matt called out.

"What!" I said as Matt and Sara rushed out the front door. This was it, the moment we had been fearing for two days. My heart started to beat rapidly and I was losing control of my breathing. Aunt Marie rushed to me to help protect me. I could see the fear and worry on her face. We could hear fighting outside, blast after blast; however, we couldn't see what was happening, or if anyone was hurt. I was going crazy not knowing. I wanted to be out there fighting too, doing anything I could; however, I knew I needed to remain safe.

There was five minutes left before midnight. I felt a change coming over me. It began in the pit of my stomach much like when the first time I used my magic only this was different. Warmth like summer sunshine beating down on you on a cold winter's day slowly spread to the rest of my body. As I was changing, the front door flew open and slammed against the wall, breaking the mirror that hung on the wall next to it. Glass shattered and fell on to the floor as someone walked in; I was too focused on what was happening with me to tell anything other than in was a man. Lucas stood protectively in front of us as the man ran forward.

"Stop!" Lucas shouted and threw out his hand.
He hit the man, but just barely. The man darted around the room in front of us trying to get to me. This mans speed was unreal; I realized speed must be his ability. He charged again and this time Lucas struck him with magic. The man flew backwards against an end table, knocking it and the lamp to the floor. The man quickly got back on his feet and, not wasting any time, he thrust forward again. The man got close this time; he had Lucas's shirt in his grasp, though luckily not tight enough. Lucas knocked him down again. The man was struggling to get up, but it was like Lucas was some how holding him there.

"Marie!" he yelled over his shoulder.
Aunt Marie left my side and knelt over the man lying on the floor. She didn't say a word as she sat there with both hands on his chest. A moment later, she stood back up and faced us. There was an appalling look on her face. I knew from her expression that he was dead.

We heard someone just outside the door. Lucas threw his hand out again without thinking and blasted the door back against the wall. The rest of the glass from the mirror fell from its frame and landed onto the floor.

"It's only us!" Matt exclaimed and slowly came through the door, Sara right behind him.
Just then the clock on the wall chimed, it was midnight. Something wonderful completely took over my body and I forgot about everything else. The warmth intensified, yet it didn't burn, it was more like I thawed out, or woke up. I felt so many different emotions all at once. I closed my eyes, smiling, letting them flow through me. Energy coursed through my veins, I felt stronger and more alive than ever. They were right. I have never felt anything as wonderful as this.

I opened my eyes to see everyone staring at me. I felt amazing, alive with energy.

Aunt Marie rushed over to me with tears in her eyes and hugged me, "Happy birthday!"

When she let go of me I was right back into another hug, first by Sara then by Matt. They both wished me happy birthday. Sara had tears in her eyes as well. Lucas was next; he wrapped his arms around me and pulled me into a hug. I could feel the warmth of his neck where my fingers touched. Our hug was longer than the rest; it felt very nice and comforting. I pulled back away from him just enough to look at his face. He looked into my eyes; he had that same look as he did that day I thought he was going to kiss me. His smile made my heart flutter and my knees weaken, even though I felt as strong as steel.

"Happy birthday," he whispered.

"Just as soon as we make sure everyone is over the perimeter we'll come back to celebrate," Matt said.

Even though I didn't want to, and I'm pretty sure Lucas didn't want to either, we let go of each other. Matt, Sara, and Aunt Marie picked up the man that was lying dead on the floor and carried him out the door leaving Lucas and me alone.

Eight
Special Gift

Lucas closed the door behind them and we started to clean the mess up. I wondered if there would be another attack again tonight; however, this new feeling inside me dominated any negative feelings I might have had.

"You were right you know," I said.

"About what?"

"I have never felt anything like this before. I wish I could feel this way all the time."

He smiled and chuckled at me.

As we were finishing with the cleaning, the others returned. They looked weary, yet there was another expression on their face. It was a mixture of confusion, fear, and relief.

"What is it?" Lucas asked.

"Everyone is gone," Matt answered, "Even their dead."

Lucas and I looked at each other, then back to the others.

"Isn't that good?" I was confused.

"Well, it is good that they're gone, but why? Why pull back when they were right here?" Matt asked.

"That is strange," Lucas said.

What could it possibly mean? Were they planning another attack on us or did they just simply give up? My intuition told me that they don't just give up. I had a feeling that Malik doesn't do something just because, that there was a motive behind everything he did including this hasty retreat.

"Well it's over for now, so let's try not to worry too much. Right now let's celebrate Kendall's birthday like we promised with some ice cream," Sara said.

"I agree," added Aunt Marie. "But, I think we should keep watch and check the perimeter every hour to be on the safe side."

Aunt Marie and Sara took my hand; I looked back at Lucas as they led me to the kitchen.

We were all laughing and having a great time by the time our bowls were empty. Matt and Lucas had a race to see who could finish theirs first. Lucas won, though not by much. They both complained of a brain-freeze. Aunt Marie wouldn't heal their foolishness, which made us laugh even more.

We were up late talking about the coming days, how I would need to practice my powers to see what exactly I could do. Although I was very interested with what they were saying, I was so tired. I had my head lying on my arm, drifting in and out of sleep.

"I think we all should get some sleep. Its one thirty and we have a party to get ready for," Matt said. "Although I think Kendall may already be sleeping."

I opened my eyes and smiled, "Not yet, but close."

I heard Lucas chuckling at me, and then get up off his stool, "I'll take first shift again tonight."

I saw Sara and Aunt Marie glance at each other, but they didn't say anything.

Sara hugged me, "Goodnight."

"Goodnight," I replied.

Aunt Marie hugged me as well, "Night Sweetie."

"Goodnight."

She turned her head towards Lucas while she still had me in her embrace, "Goodnight Lucas."

I thought I heard something in her voice, maybe something along the lines of disapproval or wariness.

"Goodnight," Lucas replied politely.

She released me and went to her room. I looked at Lucas maybe he heard it too. I couldn't tell though from his smiling face. Dismissing my thoughts, I went to make my bed.

"I'm going to check the perimeter before I go lay down," Matt said and then walked out the door.

After the couch was made into a bed, I changed into the clothes Lucas let me borrow the previous night. When I returned to the living room, Lucas was sitting on the end of the couch. I dropped my bag on the floor and curled up on the middle cushion facing Lucas. He was smiling at me. Every time he looked at me that way, I couldn't help but feel an assortment of emotions; dizzy, happy, lucky, confused, along with countless others; however, most of all I felt safe.

"What are you smiling about?" I asked.

He shook his head, "Nothing really, just happy."

My stomach was doing flips inside, "Happy about what?"

"Well, for one thing you are sitting here with me, alive."

I nodded my head, "Yeah I'm happy about that too!"

He chuckled at me, "And two, that you are the True Natural."

I pressed my lips together in a thin line and frowned with one side of my mouth.

"Oh, I don't really like the idea of someone chasing me for the rest of my life," I looked down as I spoke.

"Don't think of it that way. There is so much more to this life than you think."

I looked back up at him, "Really? Like what?"

"Well there are the powers of course. Even though they are a lot of work to learn how to control them, they are very useful and sometimes you can have a lot of fun with them."

I smiled. I was looking forward to that part.

"Plus, you will get to meet a lot of new people."

I pushed my eyebrows close together in confusion, "What do you mean?"

He grinned, "Every other Natural felt you transform into the True Natural and most will want to meet you."

"Oh!" I exclaimed. "What else?" I was eager for more.

He chuckled at me, "How about we put this conversation on hold until we are not so tired?"

He laughed at my pouty expression. Then he reached out and took my hand pulling me closer to him. I shifted myself to fit inside his arms and snuggled up to his warm body, wrapping my arm around his waist. It felt so natural, like I was meant to fit here; like he was meant only for me.

He kissed the top of my head, "Sleep now."

Sleep in his arms? I melted and felt my heart going wild. I sighed and closed my eyes. Even in all this mess, my last thought was of happiness.

I opened my eyes to a brightly lit living room. I felt so happy and complete; I was alive and I could feel the power inside me.

"Happy birthday!" I heard a voice say.

Suddenly remembering I had fallen to sleep in Lucas's arms, I looked up to see him smiling at me. All the emotions I felt last night in his arms came flooding back to me. It made me smile.

"Did you sleep well?"

I nodded then sat up as I yawned and stretched, "Like a baby. Not a single nightmare this time."

He looked at me in confusion, "This time?"

I forgot he didn't know about the dream I had twice in a row.

"Yeah, I dreamt the same dream a couple of times, its nothing."

He looked at me suspiciously, but let it go. Good, I didn't want him to worry anymore than he already was. I wanted to change the subject.

"How did you sleep?"

"Pretty good, considering I slept half sitting up with someone on top of me the whole night," he smiled playfully at me.

I shyly looked away, "I'm sorry; I didn't mean to stay there."

He put one hand under my chin to make me look at him. The smile was gone; in its place was a look that made me feel weak in the knees. His eyes held mine intensively.

"Don't be sorry, if I wanted to move I would have," he said.

The butterflies were going wild along with my heart.

He held his gaze for a few moments longer, and then he smiled, "So, what would you like me to make you for your birthday breakfast?"

I shrugged my shoulders, "What is everyone else having?"

His expression was like I was missing something, "We are the only ones here right now. Matt and Sara are checking the perimeter, then they are going into town and Marie left for work already."

"Already?" I looked up at the clock on the wall, it was quarter to ten, it was later than I thought. I looked back at him, "Did you just wake up too?"

He shook his head, "No, I woke up about nine."

I smiled, I was glad he had waited for me to wake up before he moved. He stood and grabbed my hand pulling me up.

"Come on, I'm gonna make you breakfast."

He made me sit at the island while he cooked eggs, bacon, and hash browns for the two of us; however, I was allowed to get my coffee. Occasionally, he would look at me and smile; last night made him just as happy as it did me. Lucas brought our plates to the island, and then sat next to me.

"This looks great!" I told him.

"Thank you."

Not only did it look good, it was good. I ate everything he made for me.

After breakfast, we cleaned up the kitchen and picked up my blankets. I was getting all of my stuff together to leave when Lucas got a text message.

"Sara is gonna meet you at the lodge. Do you mind if I drop you off instead?"

I shook my head, "I just need to go home first."

Lucas carried both of my bags, leading the way to his truck. It was colder today than it has been all school year. Even though the sun was shining, the wind coming over the mountains was chilly. It finally felt like an October day. I wrapped my free arm around myself, rubbing my hand up and down my arm causing friction to warm me. The other was in Lucas's hand. Lucas opened the door for me as usual, and then shut it when I climbed in. From the moment we pulled out of the driveway, he was very alert and kept watch in the rearview mirror for signs of trouble.

We pulled into the driveway of my house and together we walked to the porch. I fished the keys from one of the front pockets of my book bag and unlocked the door. Lucas went in first to check the house to make sure there wasn't anyone there that wasn't suppose to be. I followed close behind him as he checked each room. The last room was mine. He opened the door and checked every inch analyzing more than just the potential danger.

"Nice room," he dropped my bags on the floor by my bed.

"Thanks."

I took my toothbrush from my bag and got some fresh clothes from a folded pile I had put on my hamper a couple of days ago before school.

"I'll be ready to leave in a few minutes," I said and left for the bathroom.

When I came back in, Lucas was sitting on the edge of my bed reading one of my old magazines.

"I'm ready."
I put the dirty clothes in my hamper and grabbed my keys off the desk where I sat them when I entered my room. After I locked the front door, we got in the truck and left to meet Sara and Sam.

We arrived right on time. The lodge looked like a large log cabin building with a neon light in one of the front windows. I saw dirty blond skater-boy hair behind a green Ford Ranger as we were pulling in. Jordan was pulling some of his equipment from the bed of his truck; he waved and smiled at me. As we were getting out, Matt and Sara pulled in and parked beside us. We met them in the front of our vehicles. They both had a couple of bags in each hand.

"What's all this?" Lucas asked as he took the bags from Sara; always a gentleman.

"Well, since Kendall has been stuck in the house for two days and couldn't get anywhere, I decided to buy some things for her party." Sara smiled at me, "Marie said you hadn't bought anything for it. I hope that was okay?" She looked a little worried.

I hugged her, "Of course it is thank you."

We walked inside into a large room. There was a bar to the left of the building and a small stage in the right front corner. The kitchen door was on the far back wall. Sam spotted me instantly and ran up to me. She just about knocked me over when she lunged to hug me.

"Happy birthday! I have missed you so much, don't you ever get sick on me again!" The words rushed out of Sam with a bit of whininess to her voice.

"Hi…Sam…I can't…Breathe."
Everyone laughed. She let go of me so I could breathe, a bit of red colored her cheeks.

"I have only been out of school for a day and a half," I told her.
Her face fell a little and she stuck out her bottom lip. I

chuckled softly; her pouty face always made me laugh.

"I missed you too!"

She grinned happily.

"Sam, I want you to meet some friends of mine," I turned around to introduce everyone.

"This is Matthew and Sara," I pointed my finger at them as I said their names. "This is my best friend Sam."

After they greeted each other, Sara spoke to Sam, "I bought a few things for the party. I hope that's okay."

Sam smiled like I did, "Yeah, that's great." She looked at me and narrowed her eyes playfully, "I didn't get a lot, because somebody was sick and couldn't go with me last night to get some decorations."

I rolled my eyes at her. Lucas was watching the two of us with a grin. Jordan called Sam for help; his hands were overloaded and he was about to drop some of his equipment.

She looked at Matt, "It was nice to meet you."

"Nice to meet you too."

Then Sam looked at Lucas and smiled, "See you later?"

He smiled back politely, "Yes."

Then she rushed off.

Sara turned to Matt and Lucas, "You two need to leave now, we have work to do."

Lucas looked at me with a hint of worry in his brown eyes. Before I could say anything, Sara beat me to it.

"She'll be fine with me Lucas." There was a trace of annoyance in her voice.

He relaxed his expression, only a little, "I know."

I gave him a reassuring smile as Sara kissed Matt, then she practically pushed them both out the door.

She turned back to me with a smile and grabbed my hand, "Come on; let me show you what I bought."

We went to the table where the guys had put the bags down. She pulled out blue, silver, and white balloons along with blue and white crepe paper, blue and silver curling ribbon, dark blue and white table clothes, and a helium tank. I was speechless; I stared at all the stuff she had bought with wide eyes.

I looked up at her, "You didn't have to do all this."

She was wearing a confused expression, "Blue isn't your favorite color?"

I smiled widely. "Yes it is, but__"

She lifted her hand to cut me off and then she smiled, "Then yes I did."

I hugged her tightly, "Thank you so much!"

"Your welcome."

"But really, you have to let me pay for some of this. This must have cost you a fortune."

She shrugged her shoulders, opening some of the decorations, "Not really, besides, I have a secret stash."
My smile faded. A secret stash? I pushed my eyebrows together as I thought. After a few moments, I shrugged my shoulders. She must have gotten it from Aunt Marie. I called Sam over asking her to bring her decorations with her to the table.

We started decorating by hanging the crepe paper up, put the tablecloths on, and then hung long curling ribbon from the ceiling above the dance floor. We were almost done when Aunt Marie walked in with a small round cake. When I looked closely at it, my eyes lit up. It was decorated with double heart patterns on the edge of the top and halfway down the sides of the cake. Cornelli lace filled the insides of the double hearts. There were hundreds of light and dark blue sweet pea flowers in a thick S shape with some of them hanging down the front side of the cake.

"Oh my God, that is so beautiful! But, with as many people as Sam has invited, I don't think it's going to feed everyone," I was a little worried.
She smiled as two more people came through the door, holding identical cakes as the first, only each one a bit bigger

than the one ahead of it.

"I think I got it covered."

I smiled widely, "Do you need help putting it together?"

"No that's okay. I'm not putting it together for a few more hours," she said as she disappeared into the kitchen.

It was twenty after three when we had finished decorating. I went to see if Aunt Marie and Sara were done helping Sam and Jordan set up the DJ and karaoke equipment.

"What else is there left to do?" I asked Jordan.

He poked his head around a speaker that he was hooking up, "After I hook up these babies, the only thing I have left to do is the lighting." He pointed to some party lights and a disco ball, "Sean is coming to help me with those though."

I smiled, "Alright."

"Speaking of Sean," Jordan said.

I followed his gaze to the door and saw Sean walking in with a ladder.

"Hey man, sorry I'm late," he called.

"It's okay. We only have the lights left, but that is going to take us awhile anyway," Jordan replied.

Sean looked at me and smiled just before tripping over his untied shoelaces. The ladder he was carrying hit the floor with a loud clatter. Sam let out a small giggle; however, I bit down on my lower lip to keep myself from smiling.

"Ah! Sorry guys," Sean said with a beet red face.

Just then, a man with dark thinning hair came from the kitchen. Mr. Keeley, Sam's Dad.

"What happened?" he asked through his mustache.

"Sean stepped on his shoelace and dropped the ladder," Sam giggled as she spoke.

"Oh, I see. Well, if you tie your shoelaces you wouldn't trip over them."

"Yes Sir," Sean replied. Immediately he bent down to tie

them.

"How are you guys coming? It looks pretty good!"

"We're almost done Dad," Sam answered him.

Mr. Keeley nodded and turned to go back into the kitchen. "Gotta get back to the truck; by the way, happy birthday Kendall!" he said not looking back.

"Thanks," I called back; however, he was already gone. Sean had finished tying his shoe and was setting the ladder up.

"Are you ready to go home?" Aunt Marie asked as she and Sara headed for the door.

"Yes, I'm starving!" I turned to Sam, "I'll see you around seven."

"Alright and don't be late!"

I smiled. "Yes mother!" I said with a bit of sarcasm in my voice.

I was almost to the door when I heard someone running behind me.

"Kendall, wait up a second!" Sean was jogging up to me.

"Hey, what's up?" I said with a half smile.

He stopped beside me, "I um…I uh…I was just wondering who you were coming to the party with?" he quickly looked down at his fumbling hands.

After what Sam told me about him, I kind of had a feeling something like this was going to happen.

"Oh, I'm coming with my aunt."

"Oh, okay."

"Who are you coming with?" I asked uneasily.

"I told my Mom I would let her know if I was coming back with her and Dad or if I was driving myself," he paused and looked back up at me with hope in his eyes. After a couple of moments, he spoke again, "I think I'll ride with them."

I half smiled at him again, "Okay, I'll see you later then."

He smiled back, "Yeah, okay."

I felt a little guilty; I knew he was trying to get the nerve to ask me to go with him, yet I was also relieved. I don't like *him* that way.

Sara and Aunt Marie were in their cars when I came out of the lodge. Aunt Marie was parked in the spot Lucas was in. I opened the passenger door of Aunt Marie's Dodge Durango.

"I'll see you in a little while," Sara called out her window. I paused long enough to say "okay" before getting in. Then we followed her out of the parking lot.

"I'm a little confused about something," I said to Aunt Marie.

"What's that?" she asked casually.

"We'll, I was going to ask Lucas, but seeing that it's your power, I thought you could tell me."
She paid more attention to me now.

"I thought the only way an Immortal could die was with the incantation?"

She shook her head understanding my question before I really asked it "No you misunderstood. The only way is for the soul to be destroyed. It doesn't mean there is only one way it can be done."

I understood then, but I still asked my question, "So, that is how you killed that man last night?"

She looked ashamed, "Yes. I don't like killing, but when my family is in danger…"
She didn't finish her sentence. There was a fury in her that I had never seen before. After a few minutes, she calmed herself and it diminished.

"I'm sorry you had to see that last night." She shook her head regretfully.

"I understand," I replied.
She smiled at me wistfully.

"If that power destroys Immortals, then why can't it kill Malik?"

Her smile faded and her expression turned sad, "Sweetie,

it has been tried many times, he is just too powerful."

"Oh. Of course it wouldn't work," sarcasm filled my words.

"It's going to be okay."

I nodded. I wasn't so sure, but I had no choice.

"There is something else I am wondering about. It may be a dumb question, but why did everything happen at midnight like a fairytale?"

It reminded me of Cinderella, only magic began for me instead of ended.

Aunt Marie smiled kindly, "Because you were born at midnight."

When we got home, I went to the living room while Aunt Marie went to the kitchen. I was still a little tired from the previous night. I lay on the couch and turned on the television, channel surfing. I thought about my powers again, wondering what other ones I might have. I sat up and tried to see what I could do; however, I couldn't bring that feeling at will. I still didn't know how. Disappointed, I laid back on the couch.

"What would you like for your birthday dinner?" Aunt Marie called out from the kitchen.

"Um, how about lasagna?"

Lasagna is one of my top ten favorite foods, along with ice cream and salty snacks.

"Alright, that sounds good."

I got up from the couch and went to the kitchen. "Would you like any help?"

"No it's your birthday. Besides, Sara will be here in a few minutes to help me."

I was a little confused, yet excited, "Sara?"

"I invited them over for your birthday."

I smiled widely. I controlled the expression on my face long enough so Aunt Marie couldn't see how excited I was to see them, well Lucas, a few hours earlier than planned. I kind of got the feeling that there was something she wanted to say every time Lucas and I held hands, or when he put his arm around me to comfort me. She never said anything; however, I could see it on her face.

"I should probably take a shower before dinner," I said, then hurried up the stairs with the same wide grin as before.

After I showered, I put on a t-shirt and a pair of sweat pants until it was time to change for the party. I looked through the dresses in my closet, which was not very many. I couldn't find anything so I looked in Aunt Marie's closet. Way in the back was three dresses that looked like they were my style and would fit me. There was a blue spaghetti-strap one with a bubble hem, a white spaghetti-strap V-neck with black flowers above a thick black hem on the bottom, and the last one I pulled from her closet was a little black chiffon dress. It gathered in the middle just under the bust line, with wide shoulder straps. I took all three downstairs to ask if I could wear one tonight.

Halfway down the stairs I could smell the lasagna cooking, it smelled good. Aunt Marie and Sara were in the kitchen prepping the salad.

"Hi Sara!"

"Hi sweetie."

"Um, Aunt Marie, can I wear one of these tonight?"

She looked up to see the dresses I had in my hand, "I forgot I had those."

She and Sara came over to look at them. I thought I saw a wistful expression on Sara's face.

"So, would it be alright if I wear one?" I asked.

Aunt Marie smiled. "Of course you can, it's your birthday."

"Thanks!"

I heard the front door open and close and then saw Matt and Lucas walk in the kitchen.

"Something smells good!" Matt said. "Hey sweet pea," he

said to me as he kissed my forehead making his way further into the kitchen.

I smiled. It made me feel very warm inside, "Hi guys."
Lucas was leaning against the doorframe of the kitchen with his arms folded across his chest. We both smiled at the same time, which of course, sent butterflies to my stomach.

"Which one were you thinking of wearing?" Aunt Marie asked.

I turned my attention back to the dresses, "I'm not really sure. I like them all for different reasons; nevertheless, it will depend on how they fit or if they fit me at all."

"Well, take them upstairs and try them on, dinner won't be ready for another half hour."
I scooped up the dresses and headed for the hall to the stairs, though not before stealing a glance at Lucas. He winked at me as I passed which made me smile, sending the butterflies in flight once again.

I tried on all three dresses; however, I liked the black one the most. I laid it out on the bed separate from the others and then went to my closet to get my strapped heels and my black dressy light jacket that would match well with the style of the dress. I put the shoes and jacket with the dress I was going to wear and then hung the others back in Aunt Marie's closet.

By the time I got back downstairs there were only twenty minutes left until dinner. I went to the kitchen to help, though Aunt Marie and Sara wouldn't let me do a thing. They told me it was my birthday and I wasn't allowed to do any work, so I went to find the guys instead. I found Lucas and Matt sitting in the living room, they looked up from their conversation and smiled, then continued as I sat in an empty chair; they were talking about fixing their vehicles.

I sat there thinking about everything that had happened last night; how close Malik's men came to succeeding and how I could've helped them.

"When can I try my powers?"

They both looked up at me with an apologetic look on their faces.

"When you are with one of us," Matt replied.

"And away from people and breakable objects," Lucas said with a smile.

He was probably thinking about the incident with Karman, as I was.

"I know you're dying to get started; however, we have a party to go to later," Matt said.

I looked down at my hands, I was disappointed, even though I knew the answer was to wait, I was still hopeful.

Matt saw the disappointment on my face, "I promise if you come over to the house tomorrow we'll get started then. Plus you can pick up your Jeep."

I looked back up at him with a smile, "Okay."

We laughed all through dinner as they talked about old times. I found myself interested in the places Lucas has been. He has lived in every state at some point, including Hawaii, when it wasn't a state. It was six o'clock when we finished dinner. I took my dishes to the kitchen and started to take care of the leftovers. Aunt Marie and Sara came from the dining room with a handful of dishes and caught me.

"What are you doing?" Aunt Marie asked.

I smirked, "Taking care of the food."

"Well that is the only thing you are allowed to do. Besides you need to get ready for your party."

I went through the living room to get to the stairs.

"They kicked you out again huh?" Lucas asked with a smile.

"Yes, they used the excuse that it was time to get ready for the party this time."

He and Matt laughed.

"I'll be back down in a few minutes."

I closed the door to my room, turned the stereo on, and

then sat down at my vanity. I brushed my hair as it was tangled from letting it dry without brushing it first. I twisted it up in the back, and then grabbed my clip off the side of the mirror to hold it in place, pulling a couple strands down in the front to frame my face. Then I hair sprayed my head. The song ended and one of my favorites that I liked to sing along with came on. I was really into the song as I put my make up on.

"I didn't know you could sing like that?" Someone said behind me.

I jumped and whipped around to see Sara standing by the door with an apologetic smile on her face.

"Sara, you scared me to death!"

"I know. I'm sorry. I did knock, but you must not have heard me."

She walked over and sat on the edge of my bed closest to me.

"It's okay, still a little jumpy I guess."

She smiled kindly, "Where did you learn to sing like that?"

I shrugged my shoulders, "I don't know. It's just something I've picked up."

"Well you're really good."

"Thanks," I said while I put on my mascara.

"You know there is going to be karaoke tonight, you should sing."

I shrugged my shoulders again, "You think I'm that good?"

She smiled, "Yes I do."

I couldn't help but stare at her in moments like this. She was so familiar to me. I just couldn't put my finger on where I knew her.

"We are leaving in a few minutes; I wanted to give you my present before we left."

I didn't notice until now she had a little black box in her hand.

She handed it to me. "Happy birthday!

I took the lid off the box, there lying across the bottom was a necklace with blue and white stones; a blue teardrop pendent hung off the chain. There was a pair of dangle earrings that matched. I stared at them with my mouth open for a few moments.

"Sara, they are beautiful!"

"You like them?" she asked.

"Yes, very much!"

"They were your mothers," she softly whispered.

I looked up at her in shock and surprise, "My mothers?" The only thing I had of my mom's was a jean jacket that Aunt Marie had given me a few years ago.

I stood up and hugged her, "This means so much to me. Thank you!"

"You are very welcome. I thought with this being a special birthday you needed something special. Plus, I thought they would look good with that black dress."

I looked at her with a puzzled expression, "How did you know I would pick that one?"

"Because, that dress also belonged to your mother. Here let me help you."

She took the necklace from the box; I turned around so she could clasp it for me.

"You knew my mother well?" I asked.

She sighed, "Yes, very well."

I turned back around to face her, "I wish I could remember them."

She smiled, though her eyes were sad, "They are always with you," then she hugged me. "I'll let you get dressed now," she shut the door behind her.

Nine
Celebration

I was putting my mother's earrings in as I descended the stairs. I saw everyone by the front door. They looked up at me with different expressions on each of their faces. Matt was smiling up at me, Sara and Aunt Marie had tears in their eyes, and Lucas had his mouth open with an expression I couldn't quite explain, yet one I really liked. It put a big smile on my face.

"How do I look?" I asked.

"Wonderful!" Aunt Marie answered.

"You look beautiful," Sara agreed.

Matt still had a smile on his face, "You look like your mother."

Lucas didn't say anything. He just stared at me with that same expression.

"You two better get going so you can change and get to the party," Matt said.

They decided that Matt should stay with me. Lucas didn't like the idea of someone else protecting me; nevertheless, he agreed to let him do it.

"Alright, we'll see you there," Sara answered.

She hugged me, and then Matt walked her out the door while Aunt Marie went upstairs to change, I'd guessed, leaving Lucas and I alone. We just stared at each other as we stood in the foyer for those few awkward moments. Finally I smiled, which broke the silence.

"I..." he paused, "I guess I'll see you in a little while," he stammered.

My smile faded a little. That was not what I expected; however, I answered him anyway.

"Okay."

He walked out the door; before he had shut it all the way, he looked back and smiled.

I went back up to my room to grab my things and caught my reflection in the floor length mirror. I liked who was staring back at me. Matt's words played in my head.

"You look like your mother."

Did I really? I tried to remember what she looked like, tried to remember anything about her; however, nothing came. Feeling a little sad, I dabbed a little perfume on my neck and wrist, grabbed my wallet and jacket, and then went to find Aunt Marie.

She was in her bathroom recurling her hair, "I'll be ready in ten minutes."

I sat in a chair in her room to wait for her. On her bed, I saw that she had laid a pair of black dress pants and a light blue blouse; it was one of my favorites on her. It complimented her eyes and went well with her tanned skin and dark hair.

Aunt Marie locked the front door, and then the three of us left for the party. I was still thinking about what Matt had said about my mother.

"Do I really look like my mom?"

Aunt Marie glanced at me as she drove. She smiled sympathetically, "More than you realize."

I smiled, but then it quickly vanished, "I wish she was here."

She placed her hand over mine and squeezed, "She is."

We pulled into the parking lot of the lodge. There were already a lot of cars here. I recognized a few of the cars from school. I could hear the music playing long before we reached the lodge doors. Once we were inside, Aunt Marie went straight to the kitchen while Matt started to scan the room for uninvited guests. I looked around until I found Sam. I didn't have to look far; she was walking my way with a grin on her face. I met her halfway.

"Wow, you look awesome!" she said.

"Thanks, so do you!"

She was wearing a light purple dress with spaghetti straps and her hair was down in curls.

"It looks great in here with the party lights and the disco ball," she said.

"Yeah they really make the silver ribbon hanging from the ceiling pop out," I said in agreement.

Jordan and Sean joined us a moment later.

"You look great!" Sean said with a smile.

"Thanks you too."

I turned back to Sam, "I'm going to get a drink, then mingle my way back to your table."

"Okay."

"Hi Jordan!"

"Hey!" Jordan replied then he and Sam left, leaving Sean behind.

"I'll come with you. I need one too," Sean said.

"Happy birthday!" Mrs. Keeley said.

She was behind the bar tending it for the night. She was as tall as her husband was with dark straight hair that was cut into a bob. She was thin and pretty, Sam looked a lot like her.

"Thanks," I replied with a smile.

"What can I get you two?"

"I'll have a Coke please," I answered.

"For me too," Sean said. He pulled out his wallet, "I got

both of these."

I shook my head, "I'll get my own."

He started to protest but was cut off by Mrs. Keeley, "The birthday girl doesn't have to pay for anything tonight." She smiled and winked at me as she handed me my drink.

I thanked her and started to mingle my way to my friends table. Sean went ahead of me after the third person. I guess he was bored.

By the time I made it back to the table, it was twenty after seven. Even more people had arrived. I sat down next to Sam, saving a space between Sean and me for Lucas; however, Sean moved over a seat to sit next to me.

"I saw that you came with your aunt," he said.

I smiled half-heartedly, "Yeah, I told you I was."

He shrugged his shoulders, "I know, but I still thought you would come with…"

He didn't get to finish and I didn't get a chance to ask him what he was going to say because Sam grabbed my arm.

"Come on, dance with me," she said, "I love this song."

We made our way to the dance floor without difficulty, there were only a few people there, and stopped right under the disco ball.

I was having so much fun. After another song, I glanced around the room. I looked for a moment at Sean and Jordan; they were at the DJ stand talking. I turned my attention back to Sam and the dancing group of kids. When the song ended, a slow one started. Jordan came up and asked Sam if she would like to dance. I looked around; the one I wanted to dance with wasn't here yet. I sighed and edged my way to the side of the dance floor to go back to the table.

Sean stepped in front of me smiling, "Would you like to dance with me?"

I hesitated. I didn't really want to, though I also didn't want to be rude, so I smiled and answered, "Sure."

Sean took my hand and led me back on the dance floor. He

put his hands on my waist and I put mine on his shoulders, not wanting to give the wrong impression if I put them around his neck. I could tell he didn't know how to dance, because we pretty much just swayed back and forth to the music in the same spot.

"I forgot to say it earlier, so happy birthday.
I smiled, "Thanks."
"So, are you having a good time so far?" he asked me.
I nodded, "Are you?"
He smiled, his hazel eyes shining brightly, "I am now."
I felt a little guilty because of the way he was looking at me. I knew he liked me; however, I didn't feel the same way. I hoped I wasn't leading him on. I didn't want to be rude, so I smiled half-heartedly back at him.

I was glad when the song ended and a fast one began. I immediately dropped my hands from his shoulders; however, he didn't let go of my waist.

"Sean, the song is over."

He smiled at me, "I know. I was hoping I could get another one?"

"Maybe later, right now I need to sit down."
That wasn't true, I just felt uncomfortable. He let go of me, but then took my hand and led me to the table. He pulled the chair out for me as I sat down, and then sat next to me on my left.

We sat there in silence. I felt awkward sitting there with him by myself. I looked toward the door; however, there were so many people here I couldn't see ten feet away from me. I looked back to the table at my glass; it was almost gone. I turned to Sean and opened my mouth to tell him I was getting a refill, when I heard another voice speak first.

"Looks like you could use another drink."
My heart started to race. I didn't even have to turn around to know who was speaking. I turned and looked up to see Lucas looking down at me with a smile.

"Yes I could," I said and stood up, the chair sliding across the wooden floor.

Sean stood up too, "I can get it for you."

I turned back to him with an apologetic smile, "Its okay, I can get it."

I took my glass off the table and walked away with Lucas by my side. I glanced back at the table, Sean looked really mad. I felt that twinge of guilt again.

We walked to the bar and ordered our drinks, and then we stood along the wall to talk. Lucas looked really good. He had on khaki pants and a black long sleeved shirt, which was un-tucked and the sleeves rolled up to his elbows revealing the muscles in his forearm.

"When did you get here?" I asked.

"Only a few minutes before I rescued you."

"Oh, yeah thanks for that," I said.

He smiled, "Your welcome. It looked like you needed it."

I nodded in agreement.

Lucas walked with me as I mingled; he stood by my side and never left it as I talked to everyone who stopped me. Everyone was wondering when cake and presents were, so I made my way to the kitchen to check in with Aunt Marie. When we entered, she was putting the smallest of the three cakes on the top of the garden tiered shelves. The cake was even more beautiful put together than when it was separated.

"This is gorgeous," I commented.

"You are very talented Marie," Lucas added.

"Thank you both."

"Everyone is wondering when cake and presents are going to start," I said.

She looked at her watch, "It's almost eight now so, probably quarter after we'll do the cake then presents."

"Alright, I'll have Jordan announce it over the mic."

Lucas took my hand and led me out of the kitchen to find Jordan. We spotted him standing on stage with the karaoke equipment. Lucas got his attention and asked him to announce the time of the activities. Jordan did; however, he also added that there would be karaoke following after. I thought of what Sara had said earlier to me about singing. I quickly decided that I was too chicken to do it.

"Is Sara here?" I asked Lucas as we walked to where the cake was to be brought out. He looked down at me with a half smile, "Yes, kind of."

I looked at him with confusion, "What do you mean, kind of?"

"She and Matt are checking the perimeter."
I felt the color instantly leave my face.

He noticed and quickly changed his tone from nonchalant to reassurance, "It's okay; it's just a precaution."
I felt better; however, I was still a little worried. Sara and Matt came into view then. Sara was smiling so I figured everything was fine.

"Its all clear," Matt said quietly to Lucas as the music stopped.
Lucas nodded and faced the kitchen. I followed his gaze to see Aunt Marie pushing a cart forward with lit candles on the top of the cake. The cake was gorgeous all put together, the S pattern of the flowers aligned so they looked like they weaved down the separated cakes. Everyone broke out with the "Happy Birthday" song.

"Blow out the candles and make a wish!" Aunt Marie called out after they stopped singing.
I stood on the left side of the cake; I closed my eyes as I thought of a wish. It only took me a couple moments to come up with the perfect one. I opened my eyes and flashed them to Lucas. I took in a gust of air and blew out the candles. I looked at Lucas again with a grin on my face as everyone applauded around me. He tilted his head a little bit. There was a half smile on his face, yet he looked suspicious as well; he must have guessed my wish was about him.

I grinned as I looked at all the happy smiling faces of my friends and family. They wished me happy birthday as Aunt Marie and Sara cut the cake. As tradition, I got the first piece. When Lucas got his, we squeezed our way out of the crowd and found our table. We had just started eating when Sam and Jordan joined us.

"This is really good," Jordan said.

"I know. Chocolate cake with peanut butter filling or frosting is my favorite," I replied.

"Well I think it is my new favorite too."

The three of us laughed at him.

After everyone that wanted cake had a piece, Aunt Marie came to get me, "Do you want to open presents now?"

"Yeah sure," I stood up and followed her; the rest of the table did the same.

She made me sit in a chair next to a table with dozens of gifts on it. After she got everyone's attention she handed me the first present, it was from Sam. I looked at her and smiled as I tore the paper off. Sam had gotten me a couple of CD's and a gift card to my favorite clothing store in Steamboat Springs.

I opened a few more presents before she handed me an envelope. A piece of paper fell into my lap as I pulled the card out to read it. It was from Aunt Marie, Sara, Matt, and Lucas. I read the card as it wished me happy birthday and then I picked up the paper and read it. I smiled widely as I realized what it was.

"Oh my God, thank you so much!" I looked at each of them.

"What is it?" Sam asked.

"It's a season pass for skiing," I replied.

Sam had a surprised look on her face, and then she smiled.

"It was Lucas's idea," Aunt Marie said.

I thought about one of the conversations Lucas and I had on the way to school last week about how much I loved to ski.

I looked at him in surprise, "You remembered!"

He was grinning, "Of course I did."

After another half hour, I finished opening my gifts. I got more CD's, gift cards, money, and two movie vouchers.

"Thank you so much everyone, I love everything!"
I stood up as everyone separated and went in different directions. I gathered all of my presents; Lucas and Sam helped me take them out to the vehicle. When we got out to the Durango, I could properly thank them for the gifts. I opened the back, emptied my arms, and then helped Sam with her armful.

"Thank you for the gifts," I said to her.

"Your welcome. I can't believe how many people showed up."

"Well you did invite the whole town, remember?"

She smiled, "Not the whole town, just the parents of most of the kids at school."
I chuckled as she went back inside to grab the rest. Lucas chuckled as well.

I turned to him, "And as for you, I love my gift." I hugged him tightly, not only because of the gift but because it felt really good. I just used the gift as an excuse, "I can't believe you remembered."

"I remember everything about you," he replied.
I smiled shyly. I felt my stomach fluttering again.

Sam came back out while we were still hugging. "Oh! Sorry!"
I let go of him and looked at Sam, she was grinning at us.

"This is the last of the presents," she handed them to me and turned, still smiling, to leave, "Oh by the way Kendall, Sara is looking for you. She say's they are about to start karaoke."

I felt my ears and cheeks get red, "All right I'll be right there."

"Karaoke?" Lucas asked with a puzzled tone as I put the bags in the back and closed it.

I looked up to see the same look as his tone, "Yeah, Sara heard me singing earlier and wants me to sing tonight."

He smiled widely, "Really, are you going to?"

I shook my head, "No way!"

"Why not?" There was a hint of disappointment on his face.

"Because I am too chicken."

He snorted, "Hardly." There was disbelief in his voice.

"What do you mean?" I was confused.

"After what I have seen you do before you got your full powers, there's no doubt in my mind that you are not a chicken."

We went back inside, got a drink, and then went to find a table to listen to people sing karaoke. Jordan sang first, a popular rock song, he actually didn't do too bad; however, it got worse from there until he sang another.

Sara, Matt, and Aunt Marie came to sit with us as Karman began her song by Madonna. She was good; however, she was acting very slutty.

"Of course she would be good, she's good at everything," I said with annoyance.

"She may be good, but you are better!" Aunt Marie said.

I just snorted.

"You are! Won't you sing? I know you can, I heard you," Sara asked. "Go show her up! Please?"

She was looking at me with puppy dog eyes. I looked at my aunt for support; however, she had the same expression on her face. I looked at Matt and Lucas. They both were half smiling. Lucas shrugged his shoulders.

I sighed heavily, "Okay fine! When you two look at me that way, how can I say no?" I turned to Lucas and narrowed my eyes. "You are in trouble for not sticking up for me," I said with as much evil as I could. "You're supposed to be my Protector, well protect me from them!"

He only grinned at me, the tone in my voice didn't faze him

one bit. I went to give my request to Jordan, and then came back to the table.

"How many are in front of you?" Matt asked.

"I'm up right after Karman," I said in a huff.

When her song ended, everyone clapped. Jordan called me up. I was nervous. I got up and so did everyone else at the table, following me to the stage.

"You'll do great," Aunt Marie said to me.

Karman stepped off the stage as I stepped up. "Don't suck," she whispered as we passed.

I ignored her and took the mic from Jordan. I picked a song that I knew by heart.

"Are you ready?" he asked.

"As ready as I'll ever be."

He smiled then looked to the crowd that gathered after he said my name, "Kendall is a bit nervous; can we give her a round of applause?"

Everyone cheered and clapped for me, that almost made it worse. Being the birthday girl, of course I would get a bigger audience. Then the song began to play. Not needing the words, I stared out above the crowd of people focusing on one point and began right on cue. I saw the surprised look on Matt and Lucas's face. It actually made me feel better. I was completely relaxed by the middle of the song and when it was closing to an end, I didn't want it to. I wanted to feel this feeling forever.

Everybody broke out in whistles and cheers when the last bit of music was playing. Jordan was staring at me in amused shock when I handed him the mic. I smiled back and walked to the edge of the stage.

Lucas was there to help me down, "You were amazing!"

"See I told you, you were good," Sara said.

"I keep telling her that, but she doesn't ever believe me," Aunt Marie said with a smile.

Sam came up then. "Where did that come from?" she

asked excitedly.

I shrugged my shoulders, "I'm wondering that myself." I grabbed Sam's arm this time, "Come on, I'm feeling good, come dance with me."

We danced about four fast songs. When the fifth started, I had to sit down. Sam wasn't ready to sit yet, leaving her on the dance floor, I walked to the table. Aunt Marie and Sara were the only ones there.

"Where are the guys?" I asked as I caught my breath.

"Outside, checking," Sara looked at me as she said that.

"Any reason to be afraid?" I asked a little leery.

She smiled and shook her head, "Just making sure."
I didn't return the smile I only nodded.

The fast song ended and a slow one began. No one left the dance floor instead, they paired up and kept on dancing. It made me think of Lucas and I wished he were inside. Then, he appeared beside me; wish granted.

"May I have this dance?" he asked, holding out his hand with a slight bow. He looked very old fashioned.
I took his hand with a smile on my face. He led me out on the dance floor stopping somewhere in the middle. He pulled me close to him and wrapped his arm around my waist. Then he took my other hand with his and we started dancing the way they use to in the era Lucas grew up in. It was so much different from dancing with Sean. Lucas knew how to dance.

We spun around slowly a couple of times before either of us spoke. I was just enjoying being this close to him. Although our bodies weren't touching, I could still feel his warmth against mine.

He looked down at me, his eyes dark and mysterious. "Did I mention how beautiful you look tonight?" he asked.

I smiled, "No. You think I'm beautiful?"

He half smiled as his eyes stared into mine, "Very much so. I can barely keep my eyes off you tonight."

I shyly looked down at his chest and grinned. My heart was

beating rapidly. I couldn't believe what I was hearing.

"I saw you dancing with Sean earlier," he said.

I looked up to see a smirk on his face. I couldn't help but smile back at him, even though he had to bring that up.

"Yeah you did. Why, were you jealous?"

His smile faded as he looked away from my eyes. He was jealous! I had to admit, that made me feel good, because it meant that he did feel something for me.

I put my hand on his face to make him look into my eyes, "Don't be jealous of him." Worrying about his reaction, I looked down as I said the next words, "You already have me."

He let go of my hand and put his under my chin to make me look at him this time. He looked deeply into my eyes, like he was searching for something. He must have found what he was searching for because he bent down slowly, staring into my eyes as long as he could before our lips touched. His lips were so soft and warm against mine. I closed my eyes as he moved his hand from under my chin and placed it on my face and neck as we kissed. My heart was beating so hard.

I could hear something rattling in the background, along with breaking glass. After a few more moments, he pulled me closer to him. I wrapped my arms around his neck as his lips moved with mine. It was a variety of kisses, soft and slow, hard and fast. His lips parted now and then, making mine part with his; I could feel his warm breath in my mouth. My heart was pounding wildly as the sound of the rattling got louder.

The kiss lasted for about thirty seconds or so, not nearly long enough for me when he pulled away. We looked into each other's eyes and smiled. We were both breathing hard trying to catch our breath.

"Did you hear that?" he asked after a moment.

"The rattling sound or my heart?"

He chuckled, "The rattling."

"I vaguely remember hearing it," I said with a smile.
He didn't say anything; he just smiled widely like I was missing something obvious.
"What?"
"Remember what I said about your emotions getting in the way of your powers?"
At first, I didn't remember and I just looked at him with confusion, then it came back.

"You can trigger your powers with feelings, like anger or fear, or any other emotion, it has to be strong though."

The feeling I have now is very strong, "I did that with the glass?"
He nodded and grinned. I smiled in amazement and lay my head on his shoulder.
"Will you tell me what you wished for?" Lucas asked after a few more turns. We weren't really dancing now, more like swaying to the music.
I lifted my head and looking into his eyes, I grinned, "You just granted it."
He smiled and slowly bent down to kiss me once more, pulling back only after a few moments. I smiled widely and lay my head back on his chest. I didn't notice anyone else for the rest of the song, just Lucas with his arms around me.

When the song ended, instead of going back to our table, we went outside. The night air was chilly, yet it felt good on my hot skin. It wasn't only the dancing that raised my body temperature. We weren't the only ones with this idea, Sam and Jordan followed us out. Sam smiled widely at me. I was sure by the smile she had seen the kiss Lucas and I shared.

Lucas and Jordan started talking about the football team. They seemed to get along really well with each other. It's not crucial that they get along it just makes it easier, especially now that there was something more happening between

Lucas and me.

Sam and I were talking about the party when Nadia, the girl Sam was talking to the other day at lunch, walked out with her parents.

"There you are," Nadia said to me. "I wanted to say goodbye and thanks for inviting us before we left."

I hugged her, "You're welcome. I'm glad you came. Thank you so much for the tickets," I said to her and her parents.

She started talking to Sam and me, though I didn't follow, I was too distracted by Lucas. Apparently, he had that same problem; he was staring back at me with a smile.

Nadia touched my arm and brought my focus back to the conversation, "I'll see you at school on Monday."

I nodded, "Thanks again."

I started to get cold; I wrapped my arms around myself to try to keep warm. Lucas noticed immediately and put his arm around me.

"Come on, lets get you inside, you're freezing!"

We met a few more people at the door that were leaving. After we said goodbye and I thanked them, we went to find our families.

Matt and Sara had their coats on when we found them. Their expressions had changed. Nothing drastic, yet I could see it.

"It's eleven o'clock, are you ready to leave?" Sara asked Lucas.

He glanced at me before he spoke, "No. I think we are going to stay a little while longer."

She looked at him for another moment before turning to me with a smile, "Happy birthday, Kendall! The party turned out great," she hugged me goodbye.

"Thank you so much for the gift and the decorations!"

She let go of me, "You're welcome!"

"Thank you!" I said to Matt.

"You're welcome, I hope you enjoyed it. Happy

birthday!" he said and bent down to kissed my forehead. Then he and Sara walked out the door together.

I turned back to Lucas, "Didn't you ride with them?"

"No. I brought my truck in case…"

I grinned at him, "In case what?"

I knew he was going to say, in case something happened between us.

He smiled back, "In case you wanted me to drive you home."

On our way to find Aunt Marie, a few more people said their goodbyes.

"Let's try the kitchen," Lucas suggested.

He was right; she was taking care of left over cake.

"Do you want some help?" I asked.

"No, I'm almost done I just have a few more pieces to take care of."

"Why don't you leave them out? Maybe someone will eat them before they leave," I said.

"Alright. Are you ready to leave?" she asked.

She had the same expression on her face as Matt and Sara. Their expressions were subtle, yet still noticeable. I wondered if Lucas noticed too.

"No, Lucas said he would give me a ride home, if you were ready to leave."

She eyed the two of us for a moment, "Alright, but don't stay out too late and don't worry about cleaning up tonight. I already talked to Mick; we'll come back in the morning and do it."

Mick was Sam's Dad.

"Okay," I replied.

She hugged me goodbye, "Happy birthday sweetie! I love you!"

"Thanks, I love you too!"

She grabbed her coat from the hook by the door, "Goodnight!"

"Goodnight," Lucas and I said together.

"Come dance with me," I took his hand and led him out to the dance floor.

Sam and a few of our other friends were still dancing.

I was having such a good time dancing and talking with friends, that I didn't notice that almost everyone had left until Sam said that it was time to close up. I thanked her and Jordan for everything and made plans to meet them around ten tomorrow morning to clean up. After we grabbed our coats and Jordan shut the music off, the four of us walked out together.

Ten
First Lesson

The night air was cool and the sky was bright with the moon. Lucas led me to the driver's side of the truck. I slid across the seat as he climbed in behind me.

"Shall I take you home?" he asked.

"I don't want this night to end," I replied.

He leaned over the middle of the seat and pulled me close to him. Then he kissed me softly on the lips. My heart beat rapidly again. Before I lost control of my breathing, he pulled away.

He chuckled at me as I sighed, "Neither do I, but we promised Marie that we wouldn't stay out too long."

I looked at the clock when he started his truck. It was one in the morning. It was later than I thought. To my dismay, he leaned back and put the truck in gear.

I noticed the Explorer on the curb in front of my house as we pulled up.

"Why are Matt and Sara here?" I asked.

We parked in my parking spot; my Jeep was still at Lucas's pretending to be broken down. He shut the truck off, but didn't get out. It was bright enough to see the shape of his face, there was a puzzled look upon it.

"What is it?" I asked.

"Didn't Marie tell you that we are spending the night?"

My stomach was doing flips, "Why?" I smiled widely, "Not that I'm complaining."

He chuckled at me, "Well, being the first night into your powers, we're not sure what will happen."

I was about to ask what he meant, but he spoke again.

"I am here just in case."

I wondered if he was worried about Malik and his people coming after me again or about me and what I might do now that I can use my powers at full strength; not that I knew what or if I will even have any others besides Telekinesis.

"Did you have a good birthday?" he asked oblivious to my thoughts.

I smiled, forgetting about my worries, "Better than I could have ever imagined." I shyly looked down, "You were my first kiss."

I looked back up, his expression was calm, yet his eyes held a bit of anxiousness in them.

"How was it?" he asked.

I smiled, "Like a fairytale, a dream or a wish come true."

He smiled back, "I've wanted to do that for quite a while now. I'm glad it was special for you too."

Without another word, he got out and went around the front of the truck to open my door for me. We walked hand and hand up the walkway and onto the porch. I thought it would be completely dark inside the house; however, as soon as I opened the door, I could see the kitchen light was on.

"Someone's up," I whispered to Lucas.

He closed the door behind us and followed me to the kitchen. Matt looked up from his coffee cup as we came into view. He looked tired and worn out.

"What's up?" Lucas asked with as much confusion in his voice as I felt.

He looked between the two of us before he spoke, "Nothing we need to discuss tonight. We'll talk about it tomorrow."

"Goodnight!" I said.
Then we both turned away from Matt and started to walk back into the hall.

"Can I have a word with you Lucas?" Matt asked.

I turned around to look at Lucas. The light coming from the kitchen made it difficult to see his face; however, I knew he could see mine because the light was shinning in my eyes.

"I'll wait up for you," I whispered.

He nodded and turned back into the kitchen. I walked slowly to and up the stairs hoping to hear something, yet all I could make out were whispers.

The rest of the house was quiet. Only the soft ruffle sounds of my dress made any noise. I tip toed through the hall towards my room, closing the door before turning on the light. I took off my heels and got ready for bed. Then I sat on my bed while I waited for Lucas. I could have told him goodnight downstairs; however, I wanted to tell him when we were alone.

Exactly five minutes and twenty seconds later, I heard a soft knock on my door. I opened it to see Lucas standing there. He wore the same tormented expression as the day I saw him sitting at the table after he and Sara had argued.

"Are you okay?" I asked after he came in.

I flipped the switch on the wall down, not wanting to disturb anyone with the light, though I left the door open. Besides, I didn't want to get caught with the door closed with a boy in my room.

"I'm fine," he said as he sat on the edge of my bed.

"What did Matt want?"

He hesitated and cleared his throat, "He wanted to tell me to get some sleep. The other three are going to keep an eye on things tonight."

That didn't really make any sense. Why couldn't he have said that in front of me? I pushed it out of my mind and turned my attention back to Lucas. I sat down next to him.

"Are you tired?" he asked.

"A little. Are you?"

Being this close to him, it was bright enough to see his face.

He smiled, "A little." He scooted himself to the top of the bed and propped himself up with a couple of pillows, "Come here."

I crawled up onto the bed where he lay. I took my hair clip out and let my hair fall loosely around my face.

I noticed he was watching me, "What?"

He didn't answer right away. It made me feel self-conscious.

"I didn't think you could be anymore beautiful than you already are, but I was wrong. The moon light glowing on your skin…" he didn't finish, instead he pulled me close to him.

I laid my head on his chest as he wrapped his arms around me.

"Sleep now," he whispered and then kissed the top of my head.

I always felt very safe and relaxed in his arms, so it was no surprise that within a couple of minutes my eyes were heavy.

"Goodnight," I said as I closed them drifting off to sleep.

Some kind of light was flashing across my eyelids. Like tree tops blowing back and forth from a gentle summers breeze. I opened them to see that it was the ceiling fan moving the curtain slightly, letting the sunshine through. I lay there thinking about last night and how wonderful it was, the kiss especially. It was like a dream, almost too good to be real. I remembered that I had fallen asleep in Lucas's arms again last night. A blanket that usually lies at the bottom of my bed fell down in my lap as I sat up. I looked around my room for him, but he wasn't there. I really liked waking up in his arms and was a little disappointed. He must have left as soon as I had fallen asleep. At least I would see him downstairs in a few minutes, I was happy about that.

I'm glad I woke up now; I had to be at the lodge in an hour to help clean up my birthday party. I pulled the blanket off me and headed for the shower. After I got dressed, not bothering to fold the blanket up, I went down stairs. On the way to the kitchen, I saw that someone had brought in my presents. Aunt Marie and Sara were sitting at the kitchen table. I didn't see Matt or Lucas.

"Hi," I said.

"Morning!" they both answered me not looking up from their paper.

I poured myself a bowl of cereal and sat down next to Aunt Marie.

"Where are the guys?" I asked.

Sara looked from behind the paper she was reading, "They went home already."

"Oh," I tried not to sound as disappointed as I felt.

Not seeing Lucas this morning almost made last night seem like a dream. I saw from the corner of my eye that they were both staring at me. I pretended not to notice though.

After a few minutes of glances and awkward silence, Aunt Marie spoke, "I have to go into work for a few hours. Sara is going to take you to the lodge then to her house afterward."

"Why do you have to work today?"

I didn't want her to miss my first lesson.

She must have read my thoughts because she smiled and said, "Don't worry; I only work until one this afternoon. By the time you are done cleaning and get to Matt and Sara's it will be time for me to get out of work."

I sighed, "Okay."

I finished my cereal and then took my bowl to the sink to rinse it out. I was already missing Lucas. After this past week and then last night, I have already begun to build a strong connection with him.

"Are you ready to leave now?" Sara asked me; bringing me back from my thoughts.

"Yes," I kissed Aunt Marie on the cheek.

"Make sure you grab your jacket, it's a bit chilly this morning."

I listened to her and put my mom's jean jacket on before closing the door. I stepped onto the porch, immediately I felt the sting of the chilly morning hit my cheeks. I was glad I listened to Aunt Marie. It was late this year, but I could tell that fall was finally here. The leaves had changed from green to their bright red, yellow, and orange colors. This was my favorite time of year, when everything changes to get ready for something new.

"So how was your birthday?" Sara asked as we drove into town. "Did you have a good time?"

I smiled, thinking about one thing in particular, "Yes, it was the best birthday I have ever had."

I had a feeling she wanted to say something else; however, she didn't.

We were the first to arrive at the lodge. The only other people I knew that were coming were Sam, Jordan, and Sean. We only waited a few minutes before Sam and her Mom pulled in. Jordan and Sean were right behind them. I waved at them, they all waved back with the exception of Sean; he didn't acknowledge me. As soon as Mrs. Keeley unlocked the doors, Sean went straight to the equipment and started to tear down.

"What's up with Sean?" I whispered.

"He uh…" Jordan started to say as he rubbed the back of his neck in hesitation.

Sam looked at him then to me, "He isn't in a very good mood today."

She gave me a look like there was more to it than that; I got the meaning and knew that she would tell me all about it later.

The only thing left to do was sweep and mop. Mrs. Keeley

said we didn't have to mop, though since they let us use the lodge for free, I figured I owed them that much. Sara served up some left over cake as I finished sweeping. Sara and Mrs. Keeley were at the bar while the rest of us pulled a couple of tables together.

"So, Kendall, a few of us are meeting at my house later for a study group. Do you want to come over?" Sam looked hopeful.

I really should, I still had some homework left that I needed to finish; however, it was my first day to start training my power. Sean's face was blank, yet I saw hope in his eyes.

"Yeah I do, but, I have to pick up my Jeep today after my aunt gets out of work."

Sam's face fell a little, as I knew it would. I would have to make it up to her later.

I gave her an apologetic smile, "Sorry."

"That's okay. I understand. It's just with you being sick these past couple of days, I've missed you."

I chuckled at her neediness and finished my cake.

Sam yawned and giggled. I looked up to see that she was smiling at Jordan.

"What time did you get to sleep last night?" I asked her.

Her cheeks flushed red and she looked away from Jordan, "About two thirty, I think."

If I had to guess, she and Jordan didn't go right home after they had left the party.

"What time did you get to sleep?" she asked me in return.

"Actually, not long after Lucas took me home," I smiled as I thought about the night before.

Sean stood up so fast that he tipped his chair backward, bringing me back from my dream world. He picked up his plate and fork and stomped to the kitchen, slamming the swinging door open, as much as a swinging door can slam that is. Jordan gave me an apologetic smile and then he too went to the kitchen taking all of our plates with him.

"He's mad at me, isn't he?" I felt a little guilty.

"Um a little, but mainly he is mad at Lucas."

I was confused, "Why would he be mad at him? I'm the one who left him at the table last night."

"Yeah, but Lucas is the one who took you away from him and the one who kissed you."

She leaned in a little closer to me, "Speaking of kissing! How was it?"

Forgetting all about my guilt for the moment, I smiled widely and said, "It was magical." In more ways than one. "I couldn't have asked for a better first kiss."

"Then what happened?" she wore a huge devilish smile on her face.

"Nothing, we said goodnight and then I fell asleep."
I realized I made a mistake in my wording. I should have only said, 'then we said goodnight'. I looked back at her. Even though it was a small mistake, I wasn't sure if she would notice it or not.

"Oh," was all she said.

"What happened after *you* left the party?" Now it was my turn to wear the devilish smile.
As far as I knew she was still a virgin, we both were. We had decided a few years ago that we would wait for the 'one'.

She shook her head, "Nothing too bad. On our way home, we stopped at the park for a few minutes. It was romantic, we kissed for awhile in the moonlight, and then he took me home."

We both sat there in a daze thinking about our perfect night, until Mrs. Keeley snuck up behind us and made us jump when she spoke.

"Are you done cleaning?" Mrs. Keeley asked.

"Almost Mom," Sam answered her clutching her chest.

"I just have to mop then we are done," I added.

"Alright, Jordan is doing that now," Sam's mom said before turning around and walking back to the kitchen.

"I can finish that," I called to Jordan.

He didn't look up from the floor when answering me, "Don't worry about it, besides I didn't get you a present so, happy birthday!"

Both Sam and I laughed at him, "Thanks!"

"Are you ready?" Sara asked.

"Yep, just let me grab my stuff."

Jordan put the mop bucket away and then followed us out. I turned to face my friends to say goodbye. Sean immediately got in Jordan's Ranger. I waved at him; however, he didn't wave back. I would have to try to fix the tension between us, try to explain that I only like him as a friend.

I got into Sara's car feeling relieved that that was over, "Thanks for helping us today."

She smiled, "You're welcome sweetie, anytime. I'm glad we got to spend some time together."

I smiled, "Me too."

I was glad. I liked hanging out with her, she reminded me of someone, though I still couldn't figure out whom.

My Jeep was parked in front of the garage in her driveway. It looked even shinier than when I had left it. I must have missed it more than I thought.

Sara caught me looking at it and smiled, "I bet it will be nice to have your Jeep back huh?"

"Yeah," I smiled. "But, I didn't mind the company I rode with."

We didn't go inside; instead, I followed her through the garage and out a door that led to the back yard. During my stay here for those couple of days, I was worried about other things like my life that kept me from going into the backyard, or outside at all. It was very pretty, though cluttered, not what I would expect it would look like. There was a small man-made pond with rocks going all the way around it, with plants and flowers behind and on the sides of it. There were flowerbeds all around the yard with roses, columbines of all sorts, and other plants and flowers that I didn't know the names to. There was also a wooden shed in the left corner of the yard. Then there were things that looked like they didn't belong; some rocks and leaves in separate piles and a piece of plywood sitting on top of two sawhorses with different objects lined up on it. The line up looked like it was set up for target practice.

"What's all this?" I asked.

Sara smiled, "Its part of your training."

Matt and Lucas came out from the woods straight ahead of us. The moment I saw him that ache in my chest immediately lifted.

"Hi guys!" Sara said.

"Hi Hun," Matt replied. "Did you have fun?"

She glanced at me and smiled, "Yes. What were you two doing?"

"Checking the woods, we're good to go," Lucas answered.

"Good to go?" I was confused with what he meant. I knew it had to do with me learning my powers, but what was he looking for? "I thought we didn't have to worry about Malik right now?"

Matt shook his head, "We always have to worry, but we were checking to make sure there were no campers around."

Lucas stopped in front of me with a grin on his face, "You could get loud."

He never took his eyes off me while everyone chuckled at him.

"Hi," he said.

"Hi," I smiled and shyly looked at the ground.

"Shall we get started?" Matt asked interrupting our flirtatious conversation.

"Don't worry sweetie, they are good teachers." Sara added.

Lucas took my hand and together we followed Matt to the middle of the yard.

"First thing you need to learn is control. Let's start on gliding. Lucas," Matt pointed to the objects on the board.

Lucas winked at me before letting go of my hand and taking a few steps forward away from us. He held out his hand, palm facing up and began to raise it; the watering can rose along with his hand. I moved around so I could see his face. He was grinning. He made it look easy like he wasn't concentrating at all. I remembered the last two times I did magic before I came into my powers, it made me really tired. The first time wasn't so bad; however, the second made me so tired I had to sleep for a while.

I looked back and forth from Lucas's hand to the watering can, studying his every move. Turning his hand around, the can turned with it in mid air. When he straightened his hand out and slowly pulled his arm towards him, the can moved in his direction. When his hand reached his body, he grabbed the watering can with his other. He faced me and laughed, I knew he was laughing at me. I felt my mouth open and quickly closed it.

"It's very easy," he said.

"For you maybe."

He chuckled again.

"Okay Kendall, you try," Matt said and came to stand next to me, "Don't be nervous, you already know what to do. Just let it flow through you."

I took a deep breath and held out my hand. I focused on a soda can, bringing my hand up like I saw Lucas do. The can rose along with my hand. I giggled and lost my focus sending the can back down on the board with a clatter.

I looked at Matt, "That was awesome."

"Yes, it was very good for your first try; however, you need to try and stay focused."

Trying to stay focused was a lot easier said than done, when I'm not provoked. Let's say like when I'm being chased. Having to do it and trying to do it was completely different.

"You can do better than that," Lucas taunted me with a grin.

What was I just saying about being provoked? I playfully narrowed my eyes at him. Something just clicked inside. I knew exactly what I was going to do next and how to do it. I turned back to Matt.

"I'm ready," I said.

"Okay, this time try and bring it to you."

I nodded. Focusing on the can, I held out my hand again. With my palm up, I started very slowly brining it back towards me. When my hand hit my body, I grabbed the can with my other. Everyone applauded, though I wasn't done yet.

"That was very good," Aunt Marie said behind me.

I turned around to see my aunt sitting on the porch steps with Sara. She must have arrived while I was concentrating.

"Do you want to see something else?" I asked.

They looked at me curiously. I dropped the can on the ground, and then grinned at Lucas. I made the can rise again. With my palm facing up, I slowly began to close it. I could hear and see the can start to crunch and bend. When my hand was fully closed into a ball, the can was smashed flat. Then as easily as before, I reversed my actions, opening my hand, the can did the same. When my hand became fully open and flat, the can looked like it did before I crushed it.

I looked at Lucas arrogantly with a smile, "How was that?"

I knew I could do even better than that.

"Or how about this?" I asked before he had a chance to answer.

I raised both hands up this time. Everything off the board, the watering can Lucas put back, a couple of glass jars, a small garden shovel and a couple more soda cans, rose in the air. I turned my palms inward so they faced each other, forming an invisible circle. All the objects were now in the form of a circle as well. Keeping the form, I tilted my circle sideways to the right, watching the circle of objects roll to the right. Then I straightened my hands and did the same thing to the left. Again, the circle of objects obeyed my command. Grinning, I separated my hands and placed them palms up, while the objects lined up side by side in the air. I spread my hands even farther apart, putting more distance between them than before. I turned both of my hands outward, watching the left half of the objects spin one way, while the right spun the other.

After a few minutes, I decided that was enough showing off. I lowered my hands back down until everything was back on the board. I took a deep breath; feeling exhausted; however, satisfied I turned to face everyone. Their faces were just as I suspected, shocked and amazed. I was amazed with what I had just done, though in that moment I knew exactly what I needed to do, it felt so wonderful. Their expressions slowly turned into smiles.

"Show off," Lucas whispered with a grin.

I laughed at him.

"That was very good!" Sara said.

"Yes it was, but I think she needs a break for a few minutes," Aunt Marie said.

She sounded worried. She must have seen the exhaustion on my face. She and Matt helped me to the steps to sit down. Now that I was relaxed, I instantly started to feel better. I was worn down, yet surprisingly not drained.

"You are more controlled than you should be," Matt said, explaining why I'm not drained. "I should have seen this coming, knowing what you could do before you came into your powers." He was talking more to himself than to me. "I am very curious as to what else you can do!"

"Yeah, you and me both," I said.

Everyone chuckled at my reply.

I relaxed on the steps for a while longer, but the curiosity got to me. I was anxious to see what else I was able to do or needed to learn. Fearing for my life fueled some of that anxiousness.

"What's next?" I asked, not wanting to think about my fear any longer.

"Well, let's see how well you are at blocking," Matt replied.

I followed him to the middle of the yard again.

Matt pulled something from his hip, "I'm gonna throw a knife at you, try to stop it before it gets to you, okay?"

I was nervous even more than before, "I can do this." I thought to myself.

Lucas looked just as nervous as I did. That didn't help calm my nerves at all. He jumped up from the steps and stood in front of me.

"I don't think that's such a good idea Matt," his voice was serious and authoritative; it didn't match the face I saw a moment ago.

Matt opened his mouth to protest; however, Sara cut him off.

"Maybe I should go first," she took my place in front of Matt.

Lucas and I moved to the side out of the way. He looked calmer now. Matt and Sara looked the same, like they were unconcerned that in just a few moments there would be a knife thrown at Sara.

"Are you ready?" Matt asked.

She nodded without another word.

It all happened so quickly. I saw Matt pull the knife back behind his head and extend his arm as the knife flew towards Sara. I panicked; I didn't think it would stop in time. I threw out my hand and pushed the knife away from the center before Sara had the chance to stop it herself. It fell to the ground just off to the right of its path.

Sara smiled. It annoyed me because she acted like it wasn't serious, "I'll be fine. We can't die, remember?"

I was starting to get upset, "Yes, but you can still get stabbed. You heal like a normal person would, it will still hurt!"

I was almost shouting now. I couldn't believe they weren't taking this seriously.

"Kendall," Lucas called to me. It still sent butterflies in my stomach every time he said my name. I looked up at him. "She'll be fine."

"But I_" I started to protest.

He shook his head and looked into my eyes, "Do you trust me?"

I did trust him one hundred percent. I still couldn't help this feeling though. When his eyes stared into mine, I couldn't help but give in.

After a few moments I sighed, "Yes, I do."

He saw the defeat in my eyes and smiled; "Besides, if anything happens to her, Marie can heal her in no time."

I looked at my aunt; she was still sitting on the steps. She gave me a smile of reassurance.

"Okay," I finally said.

"Let's try again then," Matt said.

Lucas took my hand while we stepped back, probably to keep me from acting on instinct again. This time we watched, only. Matt threw the knife, and again I wanted to stop it; however, I didn't have to. The knife stopped in midstream. I looked at Sara, her arm out stretched in front of her. As she dropped her arm, the knife fell to the ground. Then they both turned to face me.

"You see what she just did; it's very similar to gliding, though instead of moving the object, you stop it."

"It sounds easier said than done," I replied.

"You'll be fine; just when you go to stop it don't push."

I let go of Lucas's hand, taking Sara's spot in front of Matt. Aunt Marie walked over and stood by Sara and Lucas, probably just in case she was needed.

"Get ready, remember to relax."

Matt pulled the knife behind his head again, and then threw out his arm, releasing the knife. It only took me half of a second to act. I pushed the heat out from my hand and quickly regretted it. The knife didn't stop; it flew backwards towards Matt. I couldn't tell if it missed him or not.

"Oh my God!" I was panicking, my heart starting to beat rapidly.

Everyone started laughing, except for Matt; he just looked at me with wide eyes and a smile.

I didn't think it was funny, "I am so sorry! Are you okay?" I was starting to shake. I had come so close to really hurting him, even if he couldn't die it was still scary.

"I'm fine, a little scratch, you mainly tore my shirt."

Everyone burst out with laughter again as he turned around to show us his shirt and the blood that was on it. It looked like a lot. I groaned. I felt very nauseous, not because of the blood, I was never squeamish at the sight of it, but because I could have hurt him far worse than that.

"Relax. I'm fine, really, see," he showed me his arm after he wiped the blood off with his sleeve.

It looked a little deeper than a normal cat scratch. I felt better after seeing it; however, I was still freaking out a little.

"See, just a scratch. Are you ready to try again?" he asked.

"What? After what I just did, you want me to try it again?"

He half smiled, "Yes."

I chuckled humorlessly, "Okay, it's your body."

He chuckled and stood back in his place.

"Ready?"

Not really, yet I nodded.

"Only this time don't push it, kind of pick it up and drop it."

He threw the knife just as before, and just as before, I put my hand out, only I was very careful not to push it this time, but pick it up as instructed. It worked. It stopped in midstream and fell to the ground.

"Very good!" Matt said. "Your control is incredible. I've never seen a Natural this good in the beginning."

"That's a good thing right?" I asked.

"Yes very good."

I smiled. It made me feel like I was doing something right.

"Can we take a break? I'm starving," I asked.

Plus, my nerves couldn't take anymore of the knife at the moment.

"I don't think we will have to go over anything but the blocking." Matt said as we made our way towards the porch. "We will be using that quite a bit through your training. You are the best student I have ever had."

What did he mean by that? Sara and Aunt Marie went inside while Matt, Lucas, and I sat down at the patio table.

"You have taught others?"

"Yes. I used to be a teacher, one of very few. I used to do the same as I am doing now with you. I would help others train their powers, although you are completely different from them. They have only one, in some cases two powers to train. As for you, you may have many, we have only seen two."

"Why did you stop teaching?" I asked.

"Because you were more important. We didn't need any unwanted attention here so we lost contact a few years ago when we moved here."

Sara and Aunt Marie brought out some sandwiches and ice tea.

"So on a scale from one to ten, how advanced am I?" I asked.

"Well for your first practice, I would say an eight or a nine; however, if you were already trained, I would say a six or a seven," Matt replied.

"You are more advanced than Isaac was for his first

lesson," Lucas added, "And I have never seen anyone more powerful than him, except for Malik, which wasn't by much."

"So that means?" I already knew the answer. I just wanted it confirmed.

"So that means you should be able to kill Malik," Matt replied.

Even though I knew that was what he was going to say, I was still terrified.

I was silent for the rest of lunch. I could tell that Lucas knew I was panicked because he kept glancing at me. I would look up at him every so often and give him a half smile, trying to reassure him that I was okay. I was only worried about my future and what I was meant to do.

Eleven
Visitor

After lunch, Lucas and I went to practice what I had learned so far, while the others cleaned up and evaluated my lesson.

"You are doing exceptionally well you know?" Lucas said. We were gliding the water can back and forth.

I didn't respond to his statement. I had something else I was worried about, "Is it true? What you said about Isaac?"

He pushed the can back to me, "Yes."

"Did Malik go after him like he is me?" I wasn't hesitant on asking the questions. I needed to know.

He stopped and sighed, "No, not at first."

"How long was it before Malik started to hunt him down?"

He looked at me understanding what I was really asking, "A couple of years after he came into his powers, two maybe three."

Two or three? He was already hunting me down. I must be more powerful than Isaac was. They kept telling me that, though I never really believed them. That means he's not going to stop until he kills me or I him. Lucas saw the distress on my face, he walked the few feet that were between us and put his arms around me.

"I'll be right here with you," he said.

"I know," I hugged him tighter. "I don't think I could do this without you."

I looked up into his eyes; they were full of worry and pain. He bent down, there was an inch left between us. I closed my eyes waiting for our lips to touch, waiting for him to release the anticipation I felt. Yet, it never came, as someone cleared their throat. I opened my eyes as Lucas pulled back and away from me. It was Matt.

"Are you ready to start on another lesson?" his eyes were slightly narrowed as he looked at Lucas, then normal when he looked at me.

I sighed and glanced at Lucas, "Yes."

"Matt! Can you come in here please?" Sara called out from the back door.

I followed Matt's gaze to the porch. Sara was smiling; however, there was distress in her eyes. I got the feeling that she was hiding something.

"Lucas, why don't you show her some of the things you can do. I'll be right back."

I have been waiting to see what he could do since the day I found out about the legend and my destiny.

Lucas smiled, "Well, I can manipulate all the elements, earth, wind, fire, and water. For example, I can't create rain; I can only shape it to my will, watch."

He turned to the small pond in the yard and held out his hand; as he raised it, the water rose out of the pond. He turned his hand and the water twisted into a waterspout. He held it there as it spun for a few moments and then he turned his hand back and slowly dropped it. The water fell back into the pond and went still, not one drop fell out onto the ground around it.

"That was amazing, but isn't it just like Telekinesis, what I have been doing with the gliding?"

"Sort of, except with Telekinesis the objects have to be solid. Do you want to try?"

"Yes."

"Okay, just focus only on the water, because if you don't you will be lifting other things around it."

I did what he told me to do; however, I didn't feel anything like before, there was no heat this time. I focused even harder, yet nothing.

I stopped and turned back to him, "I must not be able to do it."

"Maybe, we'll come back to it some other time."

"What else can you do?" I asked.

"Well I am a Marksman, kind of like a sharpshooter, but without the gun."

"Have you ever missed?"

He smiled, "Not once, not even when I had my first lesson." There was a pride sense of joy as he talked about his abilities.

"Must be nice."

He shook his head; he knew exactly what I was talking about, "I like you, had trouble blocking my first time."

I smiled. It made me feel less like an imbecile.

"Is there anything else besides Telekinesis, Elements, and a Marksman?"

He smiled, "I can fight really well; being a Protector, it comes in handy."

"That's a super ability?" I wasn't really convinced.

He smiled at my suspicion, "Some say it is. I was never taught how to fight; however, the moment I needed it, it revealed itself to me."

"Show me," I insisted.

He smiled again, though with more attraction, "With you?"

"How about with me instead?"

We both turned around to see a tall dark-skinned man walking towards us with Matt. I moved closer to Lucas just in case anything should happen.

"Graham?" Lucas said.

"Yes it's me."

Lucas looked down at me, "It's alright, he is a friend."

I relaxed a little; however, I stayed behind him as we moved closer.

"I had a feeling you would show up sooner or later," Lucas said.

"Yes," he glanced at me before he spoke again. "I felt the change."

Lucas turned to me, "I want you to meet a very old and special friend of mine. This is Graham." Lucas looked at me and smiled, "And this is Kendall."

"How do you do?" Graham said in a deep voice; he took my hand and kissed it.

"Fine thanks. It's nice to meet you."

"As is you my dear."

Graham's eyes were grey and mysterious. He looked around the age of thirty or so; however, he seemed much, much older than that.

"Graham was my mentor. Everything I know is because of him," Lucas said.

Graham laughed in a deep voice at Lucas, "Thank you, but you surpassed me in many ways."

Lucas was smiling, he looked really happy. He caught me looking at him and his smile grew even bigger. Of course, that made me look away shyly.

"How is Kendall doing?" Graham asked.

"Great, she is more advanced than she should be," Matt answered with a smile.

Graham nodded, "That is good."

"She is even more advanced than Isaac was," Lucas added.

"Really?" he sounded impressed. His hand was on his chin, he looked like he was in thought, "I wonder if Malik knows."

"He does," I answered him.

There was a trace of fear and worry on his face.

"We think he knew before we did just how advanced she would be," Matt added. "He sent his people here three times before she came into her powers; however, as soon as she did, they backed off."

"She could do magic before her birthday as well," Lucas added.

"Hmm," Graham was scratching his chin; he still had that same look on his face, like he was deep in thought.

"I know that look, what are you thinking?" Lucas asked.

He seemed concerned with Graham's reactions to the information.

"Let's go inside for a cup of coffee and I'll tell you what I think might be happening."

"What's going on?" I whispered as we made our way to the house.

"Graham has a theory about Malik."

Lucas and I went straight to the dining table and sat down beside each other; everyone else followed except for Sara and Aunt Marie. Sara brought out mugs and a pot of coffee while Aunt Marie brought out the creamer, sugar, and a plate full of muffins she probably baked this morning.

As Sara poured the coffee, Lucas started the conversation.

"What are you thinking?"

Everyone, including me looked at Graham in anticipation of his answer.

"First, let me gather all the facts," he looked at me first. "You could do magic before your birthday?"

"Yes. I could tell when something bad was about to happen, I pushed a group of men away from me and I flipped an SUV over."

"Really? That is something."

Lucas glanced at me and winked.

Lucas was next. "She is more advanced than Isaac, yes?"

Graham asked.

"That's right," Lucas answered.

Then Graham looked at Matt, "They were after her before her birthday?"

Matt nodded, "After she came into her powers, they backed off."

Graham looked back at me, "Have you seen or felt anything since your birthday?"

I didn't say anything I just shook my head.

"Very interesting; everything is adding up."

"What is adding up?" Aunt Marie asked. I heard anxiety in her voice.

"Well, somehow Malik knew how advanced Kendall was going to be. As powerful as Isaac was, Malik never started to hunt him down until a few years after he came into his powers. So that tells us for sure that Kendall is going to be as, if not more powerful than Isaac."

Lucas took my hand reassuringly; he didn't look at me, yet somehow he knew I was scared.

"Why did they back off then, when they were so close?" Sara asked.

"I think his people were sent here to try to kidnap, not kill her. I think Malik is waiting for her to train her powers now," Graham answered.

I looked up at Lucas; there was a mixed expression of fear and understanding on his face, like something had just dawned on him.

Lucas glanced down at me and back to Graham, "Coming from the True Natural, her powers will be worth more once she trains them herself."

Lucas squeezed my hand, then stood up and started pacing.

"That's my theory," Graham said.

"You're right," Matt looked back up at Graham. "It does add up. I knew there was something odd that night when they backed off."

Perfect, "It's never going to stop, not until he_" I didn't even finish.

Lucas sat next to me again putting his hand under my chin to make me look at him; there was fear in his eyes.

"Don't think that way. Nothing is going to happen to you, I won't let it," Lucas released my face as I leaned into him for comfort. "I would die before I let anything happen to you," he whispered to me.

I noticed Graham watching us; there was a comprehensive expression on his face.

"What can we do?" Aunt Marie asked.

"Just what you have been doing," he looked at me. "Keep practicing and even though you are able to take care of yourself, still keep your Protector or someone able to fight with you at all times."

I nodded. I didn't say anything. I didn't know what to say. Everything Graham had just said seemed to make sense. I was terrified. From the looks on the faces around me, I wasn't the only one.

"We do have half of the incantation," Lucas said.

"Really?" Graham asked.

Lucas nodded.

"I can't read it though. It's in some other language," I added.

"May I see it?"

Lucas left the table and headed down the hall. Within seconds, he was back in the dining room with the incantation in hand. He handed it to Graham before taking his seat next to me.

Graham unfolded the paper and looked it over, "I see why you can't read it, it is written in Medieval Latin."

"What does it say?" I asked.

"Well this half of it say's 'Your death'."

"Do you know where the other half is?" Lucas asked.

"I'm afraid I don't," Graham replied. He folded the paper

back up and handed it back to Lucas, "The last time I knew, it was making its way from Australia to the States. Virginia area I think. This was a few years ago though, it could be anywhere now."

The room fell completely silent; everyone was probably thinking about the same things I was, Graham's conclusion and wondering where the other half of the incantation could be. I wondered what the other half said and how it worked.

Matt broke the silence with a not so unexpected question to Graham. "Would you like to stay for dinner?"

He smiled kindly, "Sure you have enough?"

"Of course," Sara replied. "Did you and Kendall want to stay for dinner too?" she asked Aunt Marie.
I pulled away from Lucas's arms and sat up with a smile.

"Well, I guess that answers your question," she said.
Everyone laughed at my reaction.

"By the way, these muffins are fantastic," Graham commented.

"Thank you," Aunt Marie replied.

I tried to help with dinner; however, Aunt Marie and Sara insisted that I continue with training and told me that if I wanted to help I could do the dishes later. Graham wanted to watch me train to see for himself just how advanced I was. It's not that he didn't believe Matt and Lucas. He said he just wanted to see first hand.

I showed Graham everything I had done so far, I was even better at blocking this time. Graham seemed to be impressed, though he didn't say anything as I practiced. His presence actually made me a little nervous.

"I want to see you do something now," I said to Lucas.

"What would you like to see?"

I shrugged my shoulders, "Anything you want to show me."
He smiled and turned to the right corner of the yard. The

ground slightly shook as he raised his hand and a pile of dirt and rocks began to form higher and higher. I knew I could do this too. Without waiting for him to stop, I joined in. I did the same thing only I lowered my hand to shrink the pile back down to its original form. We didn't stop there. Next, we moved over to the pile of rocks. I wanted to see his reflexes, to see if they were as good as he said they were. I threw a rock at him; before it got close to him, he raised his hand and blew the rock into tiny pebbles. I smiled. Lucas threw a rock back to me; before it got to me, I squeezed my fist crushing the rock to sand. We kept hurling the rocks back and forth, one right after another. Each time he would stop the rock coming at him by blocking or breaking it and each time moving a little closer to me.

By the sixth or seventh rock, Lucas was standing right in front of me. He grabbed my hands and held them together, not letting me move.

"I win," he said intimately, just inches from my face.

"Only because you cheated," I replied.

"Now that is what I am talking about," Matt said, interrupting us.

"You were right, she is really good," Graham said. "I see why Malik is interested in you."

"Time to eat!" Aunt Marie called from the back porch.

During dinner, Lucas and Graham caught up some. I listened to their stories from years ago, some exciting and some hilarious. They have known each other since Lucas came into his powers. They separated soon after Isaac died and haven't seen each other since then.

"How long are you in town for?" Lucas asked Graham.

"I'm not sure."

"Well, do you have a place to stay?" Sara asked.

"Not yet. Is there a hotel in town?"

"No," Matt glanced at Sara and Lucas; they nodded. I didn't understand the exchange.

"But, you should stay here," Matt said.

That would be great. I could tell that Lucas was happy. He seemed different since Graham showed up. Not in a bad way, just more relaxed.

"I wouldn't want to impose."

"Nonsense; we have a spare room and we would love for you to stay."

"Matt's right, besides it will give you a chance to get to know Kendall," Sara added. It was settled.

I was taking care of what was left of my aunt's famous cheesecake when she and Sara came in to help me.

"What do you think of Graham?" Aunt Marie asked me.

"I like him. How long is he staying for?"

"I'm not sure," Sara answered. "But, he is a friend of Lucas's, so as long as he likes."

I was happy. I knew it would make Lucas happy too.

It was time to leave, it was getting late and I still had some homework left. There was one good thing about leaving; Lucas was coming with us. I told him he didn't have to, but he insisted. I felt guilty because he had to leave Graham, yet I also felt happy because he was going to be with me. I said my goodbyes and made plans to come back tomorrow to practice.

Lucas and I followed Aunt Marie home. Aunt Marie unlocked the door and let Lucas go first to let him check the house. There was nothing out of the ordinary so we headed to my room to do the rest of our homework.

"Don't stay up too late you guys," Aunt Marie called from the hall as she headed to her room.

"We won't, goodnight."

By the time we were finished it was almost eleven. Usually I'm not this slow with my homework, but I couldn't really concentrate, I kept thinking about everything that happened today and last night.

I looked behind me at Lucas; he was propped up against my headboard reading an old magazine I had. Apparently, it was his favorite pastime. He finished his homework about a half hour ago. I rolled over on my side propping my head on my hand and just stared at him as he read.

"Find anything interesting to look at?" he asked me without looking up from the magazine.

I smiled, "Yes."

He dropped the magazine on his lap, put his hands behind his head, and looked at me.

"Very," I looked away as he smiled.

My smile faded as I sighed.

"What's on your mind?" he asked. He sounded concerned.

"I was just thinking about Graham and how you had to sacrifice your time with him tonight."

He sat up and turned himself around to lie at the end of the bed with me, propping his head in his hand like mine. He moved a strand of hair away from my face, and then caressed my shoulder all the way to my elbow and back, his eyes following his hand as he did it.

"It's not a sacrifice when it's about you."

I smiled as he leaned in and kissed me. I closed my eyes and wrapped my arms around him, pulling him closer to me, not caring if we were caught. We weren't going any further. I wasn't ready to give myself away; however, Aunt Marie wouldn't know that.

I felt his warm breath on my lips as he kissed me. My heart rate had risen and my breathing became heavy, yet I didn't care, I didn't want to stop; however, just like before, he pulled away. This kiss lasted longer than our first; however, not nearly long enough for me. I smiled and sighed. I opened my eyes to see that Lucas was grinning.

"Like I said, it's not a sacrifice."

We lay there not really carrying on a conversation. The

silence wasn't uncomfortable or awkward, more like relaxing. We weren't there very long when Lucas sat up pulling me with him.

"I think we should get some sleep."

I walked him to the hall.

He turned and kissed my forehead, "I'll see you in the morning."

I started to close my door, but he put his hand on it to stop it.

"Do me a favor and leave your door open."

I looked at him with confusion.

"So I can hear you…just in case."

I shut my light off and walked back into the room. I changed into my pajama bottoms and got under the blankets. I lay there before I drifted off to sleep, thinking about how I felt about Lucas. I could see us going somewhere; however, I didn't want to look into the future, there were things that I didn't want to face right now; fearful things. I just wanted to live in the moment and handle whatever came next when it arrived; so, I decided that was just what I was going to do.

I woke up feeling very groggy the next morning. I must have overworked myself yesterday, even though it didn't feel like work. I looked at the clock; it was only six forty three. I sighed and got up, knowing I wouldn't be able to get back to sleep. I needed some coffee before I started the day, and so I went down stairs to make a pot.

Aunt Marie was already up standing over the coffee pot pouring herself a cup.

"Morning; I was just coming to do that."

"Morning sweetie," she looked at me and frowned, "Are you sick?"

She handed me her cup and felt my forehead.

"No, I'm just tired. I think I overworked myself yesterday."

"Yeah I guess so. Would you like to stay home today?"

she asked as she poured herself another cup.

"No I already missed a day and a half. I need to turn in my homework."

Just because I had powers and was the key to end Malik, didn't mean I wanted to let my grades slip.

"Alright; I'll see you tonight then."

"You're leaving already?"

Usually I leave before she does.

"Yes. I have a big order this afternoon."

"Okay, have a good day."

It was ten after seven. I poured Lucas a cup of coffee. I didn't know how he drank his, so I fixed it the way I liked, hoping that he liked it that way too. I knocked on the bedroom door that he slept in last night. I was surprised that it was shut. He answered quicker than I thought. When he opened the door, I couldn't help but stare; his hair was wet and he was in nothing but a towel. When I realized what I was doing, I quickly put my head down and covered my eyes.

"Oh! I uh…um…sorry."

It was the first time I had seen him with his shirt off; he was built exceptionally well, his chest and stomach muscles stood out. I couldn't help but peek at him again.

"Here," I handed him the cup and turned to leave; however, he grabbed my arm and made me turn back to him.

He kissed my forehead, "Good morning."

I moved my hand away and looked up at him; he was smirking.

"Good morning."

I felt awkward standing so close to his half-naked body. I quickly looked down at my hands.

"Thank you for the coffee," he said and then took a sip.

"I didn't know how you liked it, so I made it the way I drink it."

"It's perfect."

I looked up, my eyes following the hard lines of his muscles from his navel up to his smiling face, "I'll let you get dressed now."

I left him at the door and went to shower.

It was cold out this morning, I'm glad I dressed warmly. I turned the heater on as soon as we got in my Jeep and then I put in one of the CDs Sam had gotten me for my birthday. It was nice having my Jeep back. The freedom that goes with owning your own vehicle and actually being able to drive it was a great feeling.

I pulled into the parking space next to Sam. She smiled as she saw Lucas get out of the passenger seat. I was panicking a little because we never discussed why we would be together. Lucas saw my expression and steered me away from Sam.

"Are you okay?" he looked calm; however, his voice had that concerned edge to it.

I nodded, "I'm fine we just never talked about why we are still riding together after I got my Jeep back."

He stared at me for a few moments, his eyes searching mine, as if he was trying to see into my soul, until a slow smile spread across his face.

"It should be obvious."

I couldn't help but smile. He didn't say we were together; however, he implied it.

Once Sam and I were alone, she bombarded me with questions, one in particular.

"So, are you and Lucas dating?" her face was full of excitement and she was grinning.

"It's not official, but it's close."

"Awe; I told you, you guys would wind up together."

As I turned in most of my homework this morning, I was loaded down with more. The day was only half over with and I already had as much homework as I normally get in one day. I assume the teachers were preparing us for the first marking period.

Lucas and I walked to lunch together. After paying for our food, we headed towards my friends. I felt a little guilty for taking Lucas away from his.

I had to ask, "What about your friends?"
When I looked around the cafeteria, I saw the guys he used to hang out with sitting at their normal table.

"They weren't exactly my friends."
I looked at him in confusion.

He grinned, "Do you know how cute you look when you're confused?"
I smiled and sighed.

"I had to look like I had friends."

He confused me even more, "So what, they were like paid actors?"

He chuckled, "Exactly."

I shook my head, "You know that sort of made you look desperate."
He was the confused one now.

"You paid a bunch of guys you didn't even know to hang out with them, just to get close to a girl."

He laughed out loud this time, "I see your point."
I couldn't help but laugh too. I sat down across from Sam who was bouncing in her seat.

"Do you know that everybody is talking about your party Saturday?" she asked.

"Really? What are they saying?" I smiled.
It was pretty good. So many people showed up. When you have a best friend whose dad owns a large enough space and an aunt who owns a bakery, why go with a typical party?

"Just that it was the best party they had gone to this year." She turned to Lucas, "We couldn't have done it without Sara. Please make sure you tell her I said thank you again."

"I will."

The first bell rang as we gathered our books and lunch

trays. We were in line for the garbage and it was our turn next. Sean squeezed between Lucas and me, slamming Lucas in the chest with his shoulder, almost knocking the trays to the floor.

Sean put his tray away and turned back with a sneer, "Sorry."

Although he apologized, it didn't sound sincere. It looked to me like he had done it on purpose.

"Are you okay?" I asked Lucas.

"I'm fine, he is just mad at me, so rumor has it," he watched Sean with narrowed eyes until he walked through the cafeteria doors.

I thought back to Saturday night, I knew the reason, though I wanted to hear what Lucas had to say about it.

"Why?"

Lucas looked back at me with a calmer face and a half smile, "Because I have you and he doesn't."

My heart fluttered at his words. I still felt a little guilty, I didn't want to hurt or make Sean angry, but I couldn't stop smiling from the words Lucas had just said.

After school we went back to Lucas's house to train some more. Graham and Matt were in the back yard, sitting at the porch table.

"Hey! Graham was just telling me stories of you two up in the New England area."

"Good ones I hope," Lucas replied.

Graham chuckled, "Hello Kendall."

"Hi." I looked at Matt, "Hi Matt."

"Hi sweet pea. Was it nice to have your Jeep back?"

I smiled and nodded, "Where is Sara?"

"She was on guard duty and then she has to stop in to see your aunt," Matt replied.

"Graham and I are going to check the woods before we start. We didn't get a chance to earlier; we were checking the town and just got back."

They were keeping an extra watch while I trained my powers. Malik could show up at any time. They want me as safe as possible. I'm glad.

"Shall we get some of our homework out of the way while we wait?" I asked Lucas.

"Sure."

I received a little more homework the second half of the day. It equaled out to be almost double with what I normally get. It's going to take me all night to do if I don't do some of it now.

Matt and Graham returned just after Sara pulled in; I took a break and helped her put the groceries away.

"You look tired," Sara remarked.

"I am a little bit; it was a long day and night," I answered. My thoughts wandered to the memory of last night, the kiss Lucas and I shared. I tried to hide my smile, but it escaped; Sara saw it. I quickly pulled out of my thoughts and took care of the rest of the things I had in my hands.

Training today went pretty well. I had no trouble blocking. Actually, I am excelling at it. Matt was a really good teacher and according to him, my reflexes were right where they should be for an experienced Natural. Again, I impressed everyone with how far I have come in just two training sessions. Having nothing to compare it with I had no clue as to how good I was. What I did know was that I was almost as good as Lucas.

Aunt Marie had to deliver her big order she had today, to a few towns south of us. She wouldn't be back until later this evening, so Sara was feeding me.

Sara did the dishes as well so that I could get some more of my homework done while it was still early, knowing I was tired. It was eight thirty when I closed my books. I still had a couple of chapters to read for US Government, though I would do that in study hall tomorrow. Lucas of course, was already done. I guess when you have been around as long as he has you would know a few things. I was still jealous though. I stood and stretched, lying on the floor had stiffened my body.

"Are you ready to leave?" Lucas asked.

I shrugged my shoulders and yawned, "I'm in no hurry."

He chuckled, "I think you should get some sleep tonight."

"I agree," Sara replied.

She looked at Lucas with an odd expression. I had a funny feeling a conversation was being held without words. I noticed it with Aunt Marie and sometimes Matt, yet I couldn't figure out what was wrong or what they were not telling me.

We said goodnight to the others and walked out into the night. It was foggy and the air was chilly, I wrapped my arms around myself. Being as tired as I was and with the weather, I shouldn't be behind the wheel, so I handed Lucas the keys.

Twelve
Another Ability

The rest of the week flew by and it was now Friday evening. Sam was a little upset with me by Thursday. We haven't hung out since my birthday. I missed her too, but between training lessons and homework, there wasn't much time to do anything else. After talking to Lucas, I suggested to Sam that we double date and go to the movies. Plus, it would give me a chance to use my movie vouchers. She was ecstatic; however, she had to see if Jordan wanted to go. She was supposed to let me know tonight.

We had been eating at Matt and Sara's every night this week, except tonight, Aunt Marie invited the crew over to our house for dinner. It was a nice change being home for the night. I finished most of my homework after I had one of my last few days of training. Matt and Lucas said I wouldn't need much more, Graham agreed. I was just as good as Lucas was with my reflexes and blocking.

Lucas and I got a little bit closer in our relationship. He hasn't kissed me since Sunday night, except on the cheek or forehead. I was waiting patiently for the next one. We have unofficially been seeing each other for almost a week now. We hadn't declared what exactly we were and I wondered if he has thought about what I'm thinking now. He placed his hand over mine. The warmth of it radiated through my whole body.

"What are you thinking about?" Lucas asked.

I smiled as he brought me out of my daze, "Nothing really."

I swear that man is a mind reader. He stared at me unconvinced, but didn't push it any further, I was glad.

We were all sitting around the dining room table talking about what Malik was up to and where he might be. I had become tired of listening to it. We weren't gaining anything by talking except more concerned. Lucas stopped talking mid sentence when I got up from my chair. I could feel the eyes of everyone on me as I walked into the living room. A few minutes later Lucas walked in to the room to find me lying on the couch.

"What's wrong?" his voice was gentle, yet filled with concern.

I brought my feet up to make room for him, "Nothing, I'm just tired and I don't want to talk about Malik anymore tonight."

He smiled half-heartedly, "Okay, what do you want to talk about then?"

My recent thoughts came to mind; however, I didn't say anything. Besides, we weren't technically boyfriend and girlfriend yet; I don't think.

I sat up, turned around, and laid my head in his lap, "Anything."

"Well, did you know it is supposed to snow Sunday night?" he asked as he played with my hair, trying to distract me from my bad mood.

"No," I was shocked.

It was getting colder, though I didn't realize it was cold enough for snow already.

"Yep, it's not supposed to stick though."

His charm worked once again, he got my mind off my troubles and worries. In just a few minutes time I was laughing at one of his jokes and cheering up.

After awhile we heard laughter coming from the dining room. I lifted my head a little to listen. I reminded myself of a cat or dog perking its ears up at an unfamiliar noise in the distance.

"Would you like to go back and join the party?"
I smiled. He seemed to always know what I wanted.

For the rest of the evening we talked about things, other than Malik. Mainly we -well they- talked about old times. I was leaning on Lucas's arm, having a good time, when the next thing I know, I was being gently shaken awake. I blinked a few times clearing the blurriness from my eyes. Everyone but Lucas and I were standing; the others were getting ready to leave.

"How long have I been asleep?" I stood, straightening out the muscles in my legs.

"It's been about a half hour or so."

I looked at his arm as he stretched it out in front of him, "Are you stiff?"

"Not too."

"Sorry."
He looked up at me with a grin.

I was riding in the middle seat next to Lucas, my head was resting on his arm and we were holding hands just listening to the music as Lucas drove. I didn't know where we were going and I didn't care, I was happy in this moment. Then I realized something familiar was happening. I remembered from some time before, looking out my window. I sat up and peeked out the window just in time to see a dark vehicle with tinted windows smash into us.

I sat up, the sweat pouring off me. That dream! I remembered having it twice before. I remembered what happened in the end; Lucas was missing. Even though it was just a dream, I was scared. It was just after four in the morning. I got up and walked out of my room to the door down the hall where Lucas was supposed to be sleeping. I knocked lightly on the half-opened door, hoping that Aunt Marie didn't hear me. She would not approve with what I was about to do. I didn't give him time to answer before I pushed the door open and peeked inside. Sitting in the middle of the bed was the silhouette of Lucas.

"Kendall, what's wrong? Are you okay?"
Even though he had been asleep, his voice still had an alert edge to it.

"I had a bad dream," Wow, that sounded childish. "I mean, I have had this recurring dream three times now. It always ends the same way and it scares me."

"What is it about?" he asked.
I sat on the edge of his bed as I broke my dream down to the basic parts.

"You're safe now."
He gently touched my shoulder. At once, I started to calm down. His touch had a way of easing my worries. I didn't want to feel that anxiety of my dream again, the panic and fear of not being able to find Lucas. I thought of a solution, one that might get me into trouble.

"Can I sleep in here with you?"
He didn't answer right away. It was too dark to see his expression, but when he answered, he sounded conflicted.

"I don't think Marie will approve of that."

"Please, I don't feel safe right now. I need you."
My words were more real than I imagined they would be. I heard him sigh, but he scooted himself over to make room for me. I crawled under the blankets and faced him. Now that we were closer, I could see his face more clearly; the shape of his nose, his jaw line, and the shape of his eyes. I couldn't see their color as I looked into them, but I imagined the liquid brown with the dark brown flecks in them.

"Are you feeling better...now that you got your way?" I could see him smile.

He gave in easier than I thought he would. Falling asleep in Lucas's arms in a matter of protection or where someone could see was a bit different than me coming to his bed in the middle of the night.

"A little bit."

I turned away from him and snuggled up to his body to warm up. He wrapped his arm tightly around me, took a deep breath and let it out slowly. I could feel his breath moving loose strands of my hair.

"This could get us into trouble you know, if Marie walked in right now."

I was a little disappointed; however, he was right, "Do you want me to leave?"

"No!" he answered quickly and slightly tightened his arm around me.

I smiled at his reaction. It made me feel better knowing that he didn't want me to leave.

"Then I don't care."

I thought about the way the others acted and whispered when they thought I couldn't hear them. I now realized what they were whispering about.

"They don't like us being together do they? The others I mean."

"They have no choice, I am your Protector."

I shook my head, "That's not what I meant."

"I know," he took a deep breath and let it out slowly. "They say if we become_" he paused.

He loosened his arm when he realized I was trying to turn around to face him, "What? If we become what?"

He half smiled, "If we formally become boyfriend and girlfriend, they think I won't be able to do my job right, which is to protect you no matter what."

I searched his face trying to see any flicker of doubt, hoping he didn't believe it too. I didn't see it, though I wasn't sure.

"What do you think?" I asked nervously.

He didn't answer right away, which made me even more nervous.

"I think...they are wrong."

I smiled inside, my heart started to beat faster and the butterflies took flight once again.

"I have never felt this way for anyone, or anything for that matter, in all the years I have lived," he caressed my face. "I don't want to give it up."

This is what I have been waiting for since the day I had met him. I felt a few tears escape from my eyes; he saw them too and wiped them away with his finger.

"Why are you crying?" his voice held a trace of fear.

"Because, I feel the exact same way about you, but I didn't want to say anything. I didn't know if you felt as strongly for me as I do for you."

Lucas relaxed his face and smiled. He kissed me tenderly on the lips, caressing my face as he did. He pulled back after that one sweet kiss. I opened my eyes to see him still smiling.

"Close your eyes now and sleep," he said.

I woke up still in Lucas's arms, we hadn't moved an inch the rest of the night. He was still asleep. I lay there watching him, thinking of our exchanged feelings last night and how much I needed him. I touched his forehead and slowly moved down across his cheek. His eyes were still closed, so I kept going. I stopped at his lips tracing them with my fingertips feeling how soft they were. Then he smiled. Startled, I pulled my hand back and looked up; his eyes were open.

"I'm sorry I woke you."

"I'm glad. How did you sleep?" he asked.

"Comfortably. You?"

"The same."

Aunt Marie's bedroom door closed. We sat up quickly and listened. When I heard the stairs squeak, I thought she was heading downstairs. Lucas jumped out of bed wearing nothing but his boxers, peeked out the door and then stepped out closing it behind him. I waited anxiously for his return. My heart was beating so fast. Aunt Marie was pretty easy going; however, I knew I would be grounded for life if she knew I snuck in here last night. Lucas opened the door scaring me half to death, until it sunk in that it was him and not Aunt Marie.

He smiled at my reaction, "I thought you didn't care?"

"I don't, but I would rather not get grounded for it."
He came back to bed and propped himself on one hand. I tried not to stare, but I couldn't help it. My heart pounded in my chest. He caught me staring at him; I looked away deciding it was a good time to go get dressed for the day.

I leaned towards him and kissed him on the cheek, "I'll see you downstairs."
I was so happy I couldn't stop smiling. I felt like I was walking on a cloud of happiness that wrapped it's self around every piece of me.

After breakfast, I called Sam. She was supposed to have let me know last night if she and Jordan wanted to go to the movies. On the third ring, someone picked up.

"Hello?"

I immediately recognized Sam's voice. "Hey Sam!"

"Kendall, hi! Sorry I didn't get a hold of you last night. My parents made us have a family night, no electronics. My Mom took all of our cell phones including my Dad's and never gave them back until this morning, ugh!" She said all of that in one breath.

"Sam, breathe," I told her.

She giggled, *"Sorry."*

"So, did you talk to Jordan about tonight?" I asked.

"Yes, I asked him right after school yesterday, he said yes, but can we ride with you?"

After Sam explained that her mother borrowed her car for the day because hers was in the shop, we made plans for everyone to meet at her house at six. I hung up the phone and went to find Aunt Marie and Lucas. They both looked up as I walked into the kitchen. They were doing the dishes. It made me grin.

"We have to take my Jeep tonight and meet Sam and Jordan at her house at six."

"It's still okay if we go isn't it?" I was hoping Aunt Marie hadn't changed her mind.

"Of course it is your Protector will be with you." She emphasized a little on the word 'Protector'. "Why didn't Sam call you last night?" she asked.

"Family night."

Training went really well today, I did everything perfect, so Matt says. I have been teaming up with Sara against Lucas and Graham to battle with our Telekinesis. Every day I would get better; however, we still lost, except today. Today we kicked their butts. I high five Sara as we both laughed.

"You have surpassed all of the students I have ever taught," Matt said as we walked across the yard to the back porch.

He would watch the battles and guide me, sort of like a coach. I sat next to Lucas on the steps as Aunt Marie brought out a tray of glasses and a pitcher of tea. I helped her pass out the filled glasses. I handed one to Graham, and then one to Lucas. Lucas took the glass from me and winked, which made me smile and blush a little. I don't usually blush that much at anything; however, our conversation this morning kept the butterflies going all day. Graham saw our exchange. Actually, he catches us a lot with the little things; like when every time Lucas looks at me I smile or when he stands next to me he puts his hand on my lower back or how we always sit next to each other; things that the others don't always see.

It was four o'clock by the time we finished for the day. I wasn't tired like I was after each training lesson in the beginning; each time it got easier on me. We sat on the back porch talking about how this weekend will be my last training session; I was happy and sad. Happy because I felt equal to the rest of group, yet sad because my powers would be fully developed; meaning, Malik would soon be after me again. I'll try not to worry about it until the time comes. I remembered the bargain I made with myself to take and handle whatever may come.

"We better get going so were not late for our date," Lucas said pulling me from my thoughts.

"Date!" Matt exclaimed. There was a disapproving look on his face.

My thoughts drifted back to last night about how the others don't approve of Lucas and me.

"Yes, date," Lucas replied boldly, yet politely. "Sam wanted to hangout with Kendall, so we thought we would do something as a group."

"It was my idea," I added, trying to take some of the pressure off Lucas.

"Well, I don't like it," he responded.

"They'll be fine Matt," Sara attempted to reassure him.

"She's trained and they know to keep an eye out," Aunt Marie added.

Matt didn't budge though. After a few moments of silence, Lucas sighed and stood up.

"Come on Kendall," he held out his hand and helped me up.

"Wait," Matt sighed in defeat. "Lucas, before you go can I have a quick word with you?"

Lucas glanced at me, then let go of my hand and walked inside with Matt. I looked at Aunt Marie and Sara with concern; they both grimaced at me, which made my stomach tighten.

"Come walk with me while we wait," Graham suggested to me.

We walked a little ways into the back yard before he asked, "How are you coping with everything, it must be a lot to take in."

"A little worried and scared, but okay. If it wasn't for Lucas I don't know what I would do," I looked up to see that he was looking at me with comprehension on his face.

"Yes, you are very safe with him. You have nothing to worry about when he is around. He is very good at what he does." He smiled at me, "I can tell he worries and cares about you very much. I see it in the way he looks at you. It is a good thing what you two have. Don't let it go."

I smiled at Graham's reassurance. It's almost as if he overheard our conversation earlier this morning. I'm glad that someone understands.

By the time we walked around the yard once, Matt and Lucas emerged from the house; they both looked calmer and their expressions were lighter.

"Are you ready to go?" Lucas asked with a half smile.

I turned to Graham, "Thank you for the advice."

"You are quite welcome young lady."

I hugged Aunt Marie and Sara goodbye. Sara's smile made me feel better. She and I have become pretty close in this short time we have known each other. It's as if I already knew her but forgot. She and Matt were like family now. Matt walked us to my Jeep.

"I apologize for my outburst earlier. It's just, well, you are_" he paused a moment and then changed his words. "I just worry about you is all."

I smiled kindly. "I know, but I am safe with Lucas," I said quoting Graham.

Matt returned the same kind of smile, "I know." He looked at Lucas and nodded, "Go, have a good time and be careful."

I hugged him goodbye.

"Have fun sweet pea," he said and kissed the top of my

head.

I smiled once more at him, and then got into the passenger seat.

I looked at Lucas before we pulled out, "That went well." He grinned.

"Did you get a change of clothes?"

He nodded, "I got them earlier while you were training with Matt."

I used Aunt Marie's shower so we didn't have to wait for one another. I was already running late and I was having a hard time deciding what to wear, this being our first date and all. I decided jeans was the way to go, though I dressed them up with a nice blouse and my favorite heeled boots. I grabbed the movie vouchers and after I locked the door, we headed to Sam's house. Jordan wasn't there when we arrived. We didn't have to wait but only a few minutes. It was long enough for me to introduce Lucas to Mr. and Mrs. Keeley properly.

We were on the road by ten after six and I was already having a good time. Lucas drove while I talked with Sam. It was nice doing something with her. She's my best friend and I have missed her. We ate at a burger joint. It wasn't a romantic first date kind of place; however, it was the type of food we all liked. Lucas paid for my dinner like a gentleman; Jordan did the same for Sam. We decided on a scary movie, though it didn't start for another half an hour. We stood in line to exchange the vouchers for tickets. I handed them to Lucas when it was our turn. Lucas smiled politely and handed them to the girl in the ticket booth.

"I'd like one for me," he turned and smiled, "and one for my girlfriend."

I grinned happily, my heart pounded in my chest. I wanted to jump for joy. This day couldn't get any better than this. I looked at Sam behind us in line, she looked just as happy as I did.

Across the street from the theater was a lit up park. Sam

suggested we take a stroll around it while we waited for the movie to start. I'm glad she suggested it. The landscape was beautiful with its autumn colored trees and bushes shedding their leaves. There were ponds and benches lining the walkway that was lit with street lamps. In the middle of the park was a huge fountain that was lit up. I'm also glad I wore jeans and my heavy coat it was freezing tonight.

Lucas and I were a few feet behind Sam and Jordan; they were holding hands and leaning into each other.

"Did you know Sara has been on our side for awhile now?" Lucas asked casually.

On our side? It made it sound like we were at war with the others.

"No."

He looked at me and smiled, "The first time I met you in the hall, when we bumped into each other, I felt something then for you."

I remembered the day as if it were yesterday, how humiliated I felt.

He took my hand and entwined his fingers with mine, "I talked to Sara about it; she didn't think it was a good idea, so I did my best to hide my feelings from you." He looked at me again and smirked, "As you can tell I didn't do a good job for very long."

I chuckled softly, "I'm glad."

"I explained to Sara after awhile, how I was feeling; that day at the table, when you overheard us talking."

I nodded remembering that it was the day I thought he was going to kiss me.

"That night, after watching us, she finally understood. Matt of course didn't."

"What about Aunt Marie?" I asked.

"She is kind of stuck in the middle. She agrees with both sides to an extent, though mainly she agrees with Matt. That could change though."

I tilted my head sideways, "Why?"

"I explained the things to Matt that I did to Sara, I'm sure he will let Marie know."

"Which is?"

He chuckled at me, "Basically, that I have never felt this way before and I would die before I let anything happen to you and being *with* you will not affect my ability to protect you."

I smiled and leaned my head on his shoulder as we walked.

It was almost time for the movie; we still had to buy drinks and snacks. We caught up with Sam and Jordan and made our way back to the theater. The movie was great. It had the typical serial killer and the screaming actresses that always gave themselves away. Sam and I both turned into our dates during the gory parts. The first time I turned into Lucas I heard him chuckle. I looked up and saw a hint of satisfaction in his expression.

By the time we dropped Sam and Jordan off and said our goodbyes, it was after eleven.

"Do you think Marie is up?" Lucas asked as we made our way to the front door.

"My first real date, she's up."

He laughed as he opened the front door for me. Sure enough, we walked in and found her curled up on the couch watching television. She looked up as we walked in to the living room.

"Did you have fun?" she asked while pretending to be interested in the show that was playing.

I smiled, "Yes, we watched a scary movie."

"I'm glad you had a good time." She stood up, "I'm going to watch this upstairs. Goodnight."

"Night," Lucas and I said together.

We took off our coats and sat on the couch.

"Has our date ended?" he asked.

I looked up at him with a grin, "Nope!"

He chuckled at me as I moved closer to him and leaned my head on his shoulder. We were snuggled up together watching the same show Aunt Marie was watching. Graham popped in my head and I remembered our earlier discussion in the back yard.

"Graham and I talked earlier, while you and Matt were sorting things out," I said to him.

"What did you talk about?"

"You."

He looked down at me with a confused expression.

"He said he could see how much you care for me and that I am safe with you."

"He speaks the truth."

I half smiled, "Are we that obvious?"

He laughed like I was missing the joke.

"What?"

"Graham has another ability besides Telekinesis."

I crinkled my forehead into a puzzled look.

"He has the ability of Knowledge. He can tell almost anything about a person in just the few minutes within meeting them."

I was completely aware of where he was going next.

I finished his sentence for him, "And he has been around us for a week now."

He smiled, "I knew he would notice right away."

"Why didn't he ever say anything?"

"I don't know. Everyone else knows what he can do."

"Everyone but me, until now," I felt left out.

Lucas could see it on my face. He put his arm around me, "Graham does things at his own pace when he feels the time is right…hmm."

"What are you thinking?" I asked.

"Saying that makes me wonder why he has chosen now to come here."

We both sat there in thought as a few minutes had passed. I

yawned and snuggled into Lucas more not really caring at this point.

"Are you ready to sleep?" he asked.

"Yes."

I shut the television off and we walked upstairs together, pausing at my bedroom door.

"Is the date over now?"

I looked at him confusingly, "Yes. That's the second time you've asked me that. Are you in a hurry to get it over with?" I asked jokingly.

He smiled, "No, I was in a hurry to do this."

He bent down and kissed me softly on the lips. He touched my face and then tangled his fingers in my hair. As the kiss grew stronger, my heart beat faster. I wrapped my arms around his neck at the same time he wrapped his around my waist. I could feel the heat of his body as he pressed into mine. I could feel the warmth of his breath as he parted my lips. When our tongues touched, they danced together to their own beat. This kiss was different; there was passion.

After a couple of minutes, he pulled away and rested his forehead on mine. I was light headed and almost out of breath from the intensity of our kiss. Not to my surprise, Lucas was breathing rapidly as well. We stopped kissing; however, we were still wrapped in each other's arms.

"I had to stop," he said.

I knew why, it was the same reason that I didn't push to go further.

"If I didn't stop now, it would be that much harder to resist you. I don't think you are ready, and that's okay. I'm not in any hurry, if you decide you even want to. The decision is completely up to you. I'll be okay with whatever you choose."

I started to answer him, but he cut me off, "Shh." He kissed me tenderly once more and then pulled completely out of our embrace, "Goodnight."

I was dizzy over our kiss and our conversation, "Goodnight."

I lay in bed thinking about what had just happened and what it could have led to. I was shocked, yet happy he felt that way. Most guys try to pressure a girl into sex as soon as possible. Lucas was born in the 1850's, so it could be that era, the way he was brought up and lived; either way I felt lucky that by fate, I found someone like him.

Thirteen
Reality

Monday morning there was a blanket of white covering everything. It was so beautiful. There was something magical about the first fallen snow. The winter wonderland fit perfectly into the enchanted world I now knew.

I was feeling really happy. My training was complete and Lucas and I had officially declared ourselves boyfriend and girlfriend. That was the main reason for being happy. I didn't even care that I already accumulated a lot of homework and it was only lunchtime. Sam and I talked about the past weekend, she was happy for me. The only negative thing that had happened today, besides the mountain of homework, was the way Sean was watching us. There was a hint of anger and jealousy in his expression. I hated that he felt that way and I wanted to fix it; however, I promised Sam I wouldn't confront Sean. I'm going to have to talk to her about it again.

It was the end of the school day and as usual, Lucas and I rode together. We were walking through the parking lot when Karman approached us, her red hair blowing in the wind. She didn't even look at me, she acted like I wasn't even there; however, she definitely noticed Lucas by the smile on her face.

"So, Lucas," she said. "I was wondering, are you free

Friday night? My parents are having a small get together and I wanted to know if you would be my date."

I couldn't believe my ears. She was asking him out; right in front of me no less. I was uncontrollably angry with her. I could feel the heat in my face. I edged forward as Lucas grabbed my arm to stop me.

"I'm sorry Karman," he responded without smiling, "but, I will not join you." He glanced down at me, "I have a girlfriend."

His response to Karman sent my heart racing, more than it already was. She glanced down at me with disgust for a brief moment and then back at Lucas. She was almost the same height as him, so she didn't have to look up like I did.

She smiled and shrugged her shoulders, "Well, if you change your mind, it's at my house at seven and its semi-formal."

Without another word, she left with a smirk on her face. I stood there frozen with anger astonished at what she had just done.

Sam had caught up with us then. "What did Karman want? I saw that she…Kendall, what's wrong?" It took her only a second to put it together, "What has she done now?"

"She just asked Lucas out right in front of me, like I wasn't even here."

Sam opened her mouth in shock, "She didn't?"
I confirmed her question with a nod.

"And you didn't beat her to a pulp?"

"I was going to, but Lucas stopped me," I narrowed my eyes and scowled at him.

"She is such a cow. She must have heard that you two are an item now. She was just being mean."
I just stared at her with my mouth open in disbelief.

She shrugged her shoulders, "What? It was good news." She pushed her eyebrows together, looking worried, "I'm sorry. Are you mad at me?"

I wasn't mad at her, I was still angry with Karman. I didn't need to take it out on Sam.

"No, of course not, it is good news." Girl time would cheer me up, "Hey do you want to come over?"

She made an apologetic face, "I do, but I can't. I already told my mom I would help her at the lodge this afternoon. I'm sorry."

I shook my head and forced a smile for her benefit, "Its okay. I'll see you tomorrow."

"See you," she veered to the right and got in her car.

Too angry to drive, I handed Lucas the keys. There went my good mood.

The whole drive to my house, I stared out the window seeing nothing except the smirk on Karman's face. Lucas tried to apologize when we first got into the Jeep, though I told him it wasn't his fault. That was the last thing said for the rest of the ride.

When we pulled into the driveway, Lucas shut the engine off. Instead of getting out, he just sat there letting me fume in silence. After only a few minutes, he must have had enough of the silence between us.

"Are you mad at me?" There was sadness in his voice.

I was upset, hurt, and angry, though not with him. I looked at his face. His eyes held the sadness I heard in his voice.

I put my hand in his, "Of course not. I don't blame you for things that are out of your control."

His expression turned serious as he looked into my eyes, "I would *never* hurt you like that."

I felt relieved at those words. Even though we were together, I still couldn't help but think that maybe Karman could steal him away. Of course, he would always be my Protector; however, he doesn't have to be my boyfriend. Then he kissed my hand and made me smile. He got out of the Jeep, came around and opened my door for me.

We started on some of the homework we had while we

waited for Aunt Marie to come home; we were riding to Matt and Sara's together. She had called as soon as we walked in the door to let us know that Sara invited us to dinner again tonight.

My mood was a little better by the time we left the house and halfway through dinner, I was back to my old self. After dessert, Matt and Graham left to check things around town and around my house. Since Lucas has been staying with Aunt Marie and me, security around our house has been minimal. However, since we think Malik will send someone for me again, now that my powers were fully trained, the security will be tight again.

It was getting late and I was getting tired; plus I still had some homework left to do.

"Are you ready to leave?" I asked Aunt Marie.

"Almost; I want to stay with Sara until the guys get back."

"If you want to finish your homework, we can take my truck back to your house," Lucas suggested.

"Alright," I looked at Aunt Marie for her approval.

"Go ahead I'll be right behind you in a little while."

I turned to Sara, "You don't mind, do you?"

She smiled kindly, "Of course not."

The next morning I wasn't as tired as I thought I would be. We were up until eleven finishing homework. Well, I was doing homework while Lucas distracted me by playing with my hair, until I put it up, which made him laugh. My stomach was queasy. The only thing I had for breakfast was a glass of water. I didn't think I would keep anything else down. Aunt Marie already left for the bakery, so she couldn't heal me. I told myself I would be fine in a little while. It would go away soon.

It was freezing and had been snowing on and off since Sunday. We had nearly four inches now. Lucas started the truck a few minutes early so it was nice and toasty when we left for school. I liked his truck. I could sit in the middle close to him. I put my hand in his as we pulled away. Still not feeling well, I lay my head on his shoulder and closed my eyes. We were almost to school when my stomach twisted and clenched.

"Lucas pull over, I think I'm going to be sick."

He quickly pulled to the side of the road for me to get out. As the truck came to a stop, the sick feeling completely went away. I looked at him in confusion, and then I looked around at our surroundings, it seemed so familiar for some reason. Then it hit me, my dream! I looked ahead of us a few hundred yards just as a black SUV sped around the corner, at the exact point we would have been if we hadn't pulled over.

"Lucas go, go now!"

He looked at my face and saw the fear there. He put the truck in reverse and backed up as the SUV came closer. I had to hold on as he spun the truck around at full speed. He shifted into drive and squealing the tires, sped in the direction we had just come from. We passed the road to my house as we headed towards the side of town opposite from the school. He pulled his phone from his coat pocket and pushed the send button.

"Matt, they are after her. We are on our way now."

Without waiting for a response, he hung up and tossed his phone into the passenger seat. We didn't speak as he drove, I didn't want to distract him. I remembered what happened at the end of my dream and even though we were away from the place it happened, I didn't want to take that chance of it still happening.

The SUV sped up along the side of us and was trying to force us off the road. We were being hit too hard for me to steady myself to use my powers. Two more SUV's appeared, one in front and one behind us. Along with the one that was trying to ram us off the road there were now three. Lucas put the truck in four-wheel drive and accelerated even more. I was scared; we were heading straight for the vehicle in front of us.

"Hang on we're going around," Lucas said.

There was nowhere to go around except into a field to the right. We had just missed the SUV by inches when we pulled into the field. We were there for only a few moments before we slid back on to the road, with all three SUV's now chasing after us.

Matt, Sara, Graham, and Aunt Marie were in the front yard waiting for us. I was surprised to see Aunt Marie; I thought she was working. As we got out of the truck and was running towards the door, the three SUVs pulled into the front yard; a few men and women got out from each. A battle ensued around us as we ran. When we were safely behind our family, we would join; however, before we could safely get there I tripped over a producing tree root and fell flat on my stomach to the ground. I tried to push myself up; however, someone grabbed both of my ankles and was dragging me back towards the vehicles. I was trying to turn around to use my abilities to get rid of whoever had me, but they held a firm grip on me and I couldn't twist enough.

"Lucas! Lucas help me!"

Lucas turned around and saw me being dragged away. His expression contorted with terror as he ran back for me. He waved his arm forward; as he did, the person that was dragging me let go of my ankle and flew backwards into the trees.

Only a few moments had passed from when we pulled into the driveway until the time our family got to us. I stood and turned around looking behind me; I couldn't believe what I was seeing. There were eight maybe ten people using different abilities making their way towards us. I saw these people using Telekinesis and powers with the Elements; I also saw some of them carrying guns. These people were Naturals, yet they carried guns? As they started shooting at us, Sara fell to the ground. I tried to help her up when I noticed with dread that she was bleeding. Before I could do anything, Aunt Marie flew passed me and landed behind us on the ground. I looked back to see that she wasn't moving. I hoped she was knocked out and not dead. I heard shot after shot being fired around us. Graham fell to the ground and right behind him Matt fell where he stood. One by one they all were being shot.

"No!" I was horror struck. I refused to believe what I was seeing.

The only ones left to fight were Lucas and I and we were outnumbered. They were closing in on us. I was reminded of the group of men at the lake. The only difference with this group was that one of them was duplicating himself; his blond hair stuck out everywhere. Lucas and I kept throwing the men and woman backwards, but there were too many of them.

I could see my family and friends lying bloody on the ground. I stopped fighting and paused as a sudden, overwhelmingly strong feeling took over my whole body. It's nothing I have ever felt before. I looked up at Lucas; he looked back at me as he dodged out of the way of objects flying at him. There was fear in his eyes; he saw the terror and anger in mine. I walked through the shower of bullets, fierce winds, and anything else that was being used against us directly towards the group.

"Kendall, No, stop!" I heard Lucas yelling at me, but I didn't listen.

This feeling was so strong and my uncontrollable anger at what these people have done shook the ground.

"Stop!" I yelled just before they got a hold of me.

As the word left my mouth, all of the men fell to the ground at once. The blond haired man lost his concentration and unwillingly pulled himself back together as he fell to the ground.

"Leave, now!" I demanded. My voice was powerful and slightly amplified.

They gathered up their men that were still lying on the ground, got in their vehicles, and backed out of the driveway. As they left, the ground stopped shaking.

Lucas was suddenly standing right in front of me, "Kendall, are you alright?"

I don't immediately respond to him; I was watching the SUV's, until I couldn't see them anymore.

I looked at Lucas as I snapped out of my trace-like state, "I'm fine, let's help the others."

We went to Aunt Marie first; she would be able to help the others. She was already stirring as I knelt down beside her. Thank God she was still alive.

"Are you alright?" I asked her.

She had suffered a cut on the back of her head and some scratches on her arms. She wiped her arms with her hands, as if she was brushing off dirt; when she removed them, the scratches were gone.

"Yes, are you?" she asked in return.

"Now that I know you're okay," I hugged her tightly.

She held the back of her head healing it as Lucas and I helped her to her feet, "What happened to the others?"

"They were shot."

Sara was next; her eyes were closed, yet I could tell she was awake and in a lot of pain. Blood was smeared on her shirt and in her hair; Sara had been shot in the chest. Aunt Marie put both of her hands over the wound and closed her eyes. A few moments had passed when both Aunt Marie and Sara opened their eyes. Sara sat up and hugged us.

"Let's get you inside before they decide to come back," Sara said to me.

"But, what about Matt and Graham?" I asked as Lucas and Sara pushed me towards the house.

"I'll take care of them," Aunt Marie replied.

I pulled away from the direction I was being shoved and turned and faced Aunt Marie, "You can't be out here by yourself."

I turned to Lucas, "Will you stay here with her while she heals?"

He shook his head, "I can't leave you."

"We don't have time to argue Lucas. Someone must have heard the shots and called the police," Sara said urgently.

We didn't wait for Lucas to answer as Sara and I walked towards the house leaving him behind.

About a minute had passed by when Lucas and the others came into the house; by that time, Sara had changed from her bloody clothes and brought out a few guns.

"I figure we have about thirty seconds before the police show up. Go change quickly while I get things set up in the back yard," she said to the other three.

"What do you want me to do?" I asked her.

"You stay here with me," Lucas responded with authority, before Sara had a chance to answer.

Although I was upset, I listened to him. Like Sara said, now was not the time to argue.

By the time the sheriff's patrol car pulled in, everyone was changed, clean, and back in the living room.

"There are two of them, one is going around back," Matt whispered. "Just act as natural as you can," he headed for the door as one of the deputies knocked. He cleared his throat and opened the door, "Hello. What can I do you for Sir?" There was a pause before Matt spoke again, "Sure, come on in."

He and the deputy walked in the living room.

"This is Officer Riley," Matt said.

The deputy took off his hat flattening his brown hair to his head. He was Matt's height though a little heavier.

Sara moved forward holding her hand out, "Hello, I'm Sara."

She was polite, if I wasn't there, I would never have guessed that she had just been shot and healed.

"What brings you out here?" she asked.

The deputy looked around eyeing us all suspiciously; however, he lingered on me a moment longer before turning his attention back to Sara and Matt.

"There was a complaint of guns being fired," the deputy glanced back to me.

"Yes, we were sighting in our guns before hunting season," Matt said as he pointed to the rifles propped against the wall.

Graham looked agitated as he stared at the deputy. He noticed that Deputy Riley was very interested in me, more so than he should be perhaps. Graham gave Lucas a long meaningful look. Lucas immediately stiffened up. My heart started to race. Something in the way Lucas and Graham communicated made me even more nervous. There was another knock on the door.

"I'll get it," Graham said eagerly.

Graham returned with the other deputy following. Graham shook his head slightly at Lucas and I felt Lucas relax a little bit. Just as the first deputy, the second took his hat off as he entered the living room. The second deputy was thinner and shorter than the first, but with the same color hair.

"Howdy folks, I'm Officer Becker."

Officer Riley looked at me and Lucas, "Why aren't you two in school?"

"We are sick," Lucas answered.

He turned his attention back to Matt, "Do you mind if I take a look around the property?"

"I just did that. Everything seems fine," Officer Becker informed his partner.

"Well then, do you mind if I take a look around the house?"

Lucas started to get up; however, Graham cleared his throat

for Lucas to be patient. Lucas understood and leaned back against the couch pulling me closer to him; out of the two deputies, only Officer Riley saw the exchange.

"I see no reason to go any further, we can clearly see the evidence here, and there are targets in the back yard," Officer Becker said. His statement held an edge of annoyance towards his partner. "Sorry to waste your time and thank you for your cooperation," he put his hat back on. "You have a nice day now."

Matt and Sara followed them out.

As the door shut, Aunt Marie came and sat next to me. She and Lucas put their arms around me and exhaled. I didn't relax though; I was too worried about that deputy and the way Graham and Lucas were acting. I could hear the patrol car back out of the driveway as Matt and Sara walked back in the house.

"What was that all about?" I asked Graham.

I noticed that everyone else was looking at him as well. My mind played over the way Lucas and Graham acted, how they were on edge while Officer Riley was here, and then how they seemed to relax a little when Officer Becker walked in, I was also thinking of the looks I kept receiving from Officer Riley. Before Graham answered, I had put the pieces together.

"He was one of them? Here in the house?" I asked, my voice cracking at the end.

"Yes," Graham replied. "That's why I wanted to answer the door. I wanted to get a quick reading from his face. I knew then, only Officer Riley was one of them and wouldn't attack with his normal human partner here."

I don't remember seeing Officer Riley's face during the battle, but then again I didn't see much of anyone's features, except for the blond haired man.

"Just think, if Graham wasn't here we might have never known one of Malik's people is posing as an officer of the law," Sara said.

My phone vibrated and rang just then scaring me half to death. I stood up from the couch and pulled my phone out of my pocket. It was a text from Sam asking where I was. What was I suppose to tell her? I looked at Aunt Marie for help.

"It's Sam," I said.

"Just tell her you're sick again."

I sighed. I really hated lying to her. She was my best friend; I was supposed to be able to tell her everything. I sent a message telling her I was sick and sat back down between Aunt Marie and Lucas.

"Marie," Lucas spoke softly. There was a hint of regret in his voice. "Please know that I am truly sorry for my behavior. I do care what happens to you and I_"

Aunt Marie put her hand up to cut him off, "Lucas, stop."

I looked at his face; he did look torn up about it.

"I understand why you did what you did, I am not upset," she half smiled at him. "To tell you the truth, I'm glad Kendall has someone like you."

I looked from Aunt Marie to Lucas; they were both smiling at each other now. Lucas shifted his eyes to me and grinned; I knew exactly what he was thinking, Aunt Marie had changed her mind.

We relaxed a little bit; however, were still on guard for whatever could happen. I couldn't stop thinking about that man with the blond hair. If anyone would know what kind of power it was, it would be Matt.

"What is the name of the ability where the man kept duplicating himself?"

It made me very curious and I wondered what other kinds of power other Natural's had.

Matt was staring out the window. He closed the curtain and turned towards me. "It's called Duplication, kind of like Astral Projection except there is no limit in most as to how many multiples they can make of themselves."

"By the way, Kendall, that was some power you showed earlier," Graham added. "I thought you might have it."

"What was it exactly?" I asked, surprised and confused.

"Well it's a strong form of Telekinesis controlled by emotions, like a Latent Ability."

I immediately thought back to the glass breaking when Lucas kissed me the night of my birthday.

"Will my ability grow to become that way full time?" I hoped not, that was really strong. It scared me to think of what I could do.

He rubbed his hand on his chin, "It's hard to tell, my guess though, would be no. I think it will be one of those powers that will show itself when needed."

It was finally Friday, the last day of school before winter break. There has been no trouble with Malik since October; however, the conflict Sean had with Lucas, and Karman's goal in life to antagonize me was getting out of hand. Just today, I had to force myself from reaching across the table and smacking Karman at lunch. Since the day she had asked Lucas out, she sometimes invited herself to sit with my group of friends at lunch; she did this just to annoy me. Lucas tried to ignore her; however, she still asked him questions just to engage him in conversation with her. She was flirting with him.

I still felt a little guilty about Sean. I tried to hint to him that he was my friend; however, he wouldn't listen to me. Whenever I would try to talk to him, he would tell me he had to go. I was beginning to get annoyed with him. Sean and Lucas still didn't get along and there have been a couple of times when I thought they were going to fight.

Over Thanksgiving break, Matt and Graham traveled in search for the other half of the incantation. Graham was correct in the last place he had heard it was, somewhere in Northern Virginia. They were gone for three days, but they didn't come back empty handed. Matt and Graham found the man that bought it; however, he had sold it immediately after coming to America to a man from Texas. There were plans to go right after Christmas. Graham and Matt were driving this time. Sara and Lucas were staying with Aunt Marie and me again while they were gone. Actually, Sara would stay, since Lucas had practically moved in. From the outside world, it would cause gossip and suspicion if a teenager's boyfriend moved in. That's why the only one who knew about Lucas's living situation was Sam; I could never keep something like that away from her. As it was, it was killing me to keep my powers and who I really was a secret from her. I am having a hard time with the secrecy and I think very soon I will have to tell her, despite what everyone else thinks.

The weekend went great. With no homework to do for the entire break, we had to find something else to bide our time. On Saturday Sam stayed and of course Lucas. We stayed up late playing games. Sam and I camped in the living room while Lucas slept in the family room. I suggested he should go sleep in his bed; however, he refused and told me that he felt better if he was on the same floor as me while we slept. After we woke on Sunday morning, just before noon, Sam and I made brunch for everyone. Now we were up in my room hanging out and talking.

"You two are getting really serious aren't you?" Sam asked me while Lucas was showering.

I knew she would eventually ask me that, actually I was surprised she hadn't a few weeks ago.

"Besides him moving in?" Answering her question with a question.

"You said that's not permanent."

"It's not."

I didn't answer; she kept looking at me waiting for one. After a few moments, she raised her eyebrows impatiently.

"Yes," I finally answered as I looked up to see approval quickly replace impatience and annoyance on her grinning face.

Fourteen
Revealed

I could smell the scent of pine as we walked by to the department store. A burly, lumberjack looking man with thick whiskers and a plaid coat, was loading a Colorado Blue Spruce on the top of a vehicle. Each year Aunt Marie and I pick a tree from the local tree farm in town. This year Matt, Sara, and Lucas went with us. We picked out two trees, one for each house. After the guys set the trees up, we drank hot chocolate and listened to Christmas music while we decorated them, like one big happy family; it was nice.

Sam was the last person I had to buy a present for. Lucas was almost the last one. I didn't think I would be able to get him anything as he wouldn't leave my side long enough to shop for him; however, Aunt Marie and Sara finally convinced him to share me with the girls.

"What are you thinking about getting Sam?" Lucas asked.

"I'm not sure, maybe a gift card."

"Is she hard to buy for?"

"No, not at all," I giggled. "She just likes shopping."

The stores were crowded with last minute shoppers and the lines were a nightmare; however, we made it back home in time for dinner. All of my shopping was done, yet I still had some wrapping to do, which I would finish tonight. I decided Lucas was going to help me, he just didn't know it yet.

Either he has spent every night at my house or I would stay at his. Sara would try to take over a few nights a week; however, Lucas was so stubborn he wouldn't give in. It's not that he didn't trust her to protect me. He said he just didn't want to take the chance on leaving me just in case Malik sent someone or came himself.

It was the morning of Christmas Eve. I got up early hoping that Lucas and Aunt Marie were still asleep; I wanted to make breakfast this morning. As I walk in to the kitchen, Lucas was drinking coffee at the table. He chuckled at my surprised expression.

"You're up early for a vacation day," he said.

"I wanted to make breakfast this morning," I answered as I poured myself some coffee and sat next to him.

As he positioned himself to look at me, he smiled. The kind of smile that makes me go weak in the knees. Even when sitting down.

"Why are *you* up so early on a vacation day?" I asked with a grin.

"I couldn't sleep."

"Usually children cannot sleep Christmas Eve, not the night before."

He smiled, "You are comparing me to a child?"

I laughed as I got up and started breakfast.

Lucas and I spent the rest of the morning outside clearing the sidewalk and driveway. It would be so easy for Lucas to clear the snow with magic. When I suggested it, he frowned and handed me a shovel. I knew it was because we were on the street where people could see us; however, I teased that he just wanted me to suffer. By lunchtime, I was frozen; we came in and curled up on the sofa with a blanket and some hot chocolate to warm up.

Sam's parents, Mr. and Mrs. Keeley had invited us to their

annual Christmas party tonight. They had also invited Matt, Sara, and Graham, Lucas of course was my date. However, before we did anything else today, Aunt Marie, Sara, and I needed to bake pies and other goodies for tomorrow. One of my favorite things about the holidays was the bonding that goes with baking. I am happy to be able to have Sara here this year.

The phone on the wall rang. On the third ring, it stopped and Aunt Marie bustled into the living room a few moments later.

"They will be here in a few minutes," she said.
Lucas and I looked behind us as she spoke.

"We'll need to get started as soon as they get here. The Christmas party starts at seven," she rushed the words out and then turned and bustled back through the dining room to the kitchen.
I looked at Lucas and chuckled as I uncovered and pulled my feet from his lap.

"Is she always this rambunctious around the holidays?" Lucas asked with a grin.

"Not normally this much."

The aroma of apple, pumpkin, and pecan pie swirled around the kitchen. Every few minutes we would have to chase one or all of the guys out as they continued to try to sneak one of the goodies we had baked. Finally, after the fourth time they tried, Aunt Marie sent me out with a tray full of assorted cut out sugar cookies all frosted with homemade frosting. All three men smiled widely as I walked in the room holding the tray. Lucas took a cookie, and then pulled me down on the couch with him. I sat the tray on the coffee table and snuggled into him while I had a minute before they had noticed I was gone for too long. He winked at me as he bit into his cookie, making me smile.

Over the past few weeks, I had noticed a different kind of feeling come over me. I had never felt it before and I lack the words to describe it. I felt it sometimes when Lucas would simply look at me or touch me innocently. All I knew was that I really liked it and I didn't want to lose it.

"Kendall, these cookies won't frost themselves!" Aunt Marie hollered from the kitchen, popping my inner thought bubble.

I sighed heavily and rolled my eyes making Lucas laugh. I took a bite of his cookie before going back to the kitchen.

It was snowing lightly as Lucas and I walked up the Keeley's walkway. The multi-colored Christmas lights from the porch reflected off the falling snowflakes making it look like falling glitter. The wreath bounced against the wooden door as Lucas knocked. Mrs. Keeley opened the door with a smile.

"Kendall, Lucas, it's nice to see you again. Please come in. I'll take your coats for you."

Lucas helped me with my coat, and then handed both his and mine to Mrs. Keeley; she smiled approvingly at his manners.

"Merry Christmas," I said as she hugged me.

"To you both as well," her smile faded slightly and she looked a little confused. "Where are the others?"

"Aunt Marie will be here soon, she's waiting for the last pie to come out of the oven."

"And my relatives will be here shortly," Lucas added.

"Here, these are for you." I handed her a white box from Aunt Marie's bakery with a big red bow filled with the cookies we had just baked this afternoon.

She smiled widely; she knew exactly what the box contained, "Thank you so much. Her cookies are the best. They just melt in your mouth."

Lucas and I smiled at her as she described the cookies.

"Well, refreshments are in the dining room," she looked around, "and Sam is around here somewhere."

"Thank you, would you like me to take the box of cookies to the dining room?" I asked.

She pulled the cookies away from me. "No, these are mine," she said with a sheepish smile.

I laughed and looked at Lucas as she took our coats and her box of cookies to the other room; he was smiling too.

The Keeley's house was decorated from top to bottom. Garland wrapped around the cherry wood banister of the stairs. Velvety red bows and Poinsettias were placed all around their house as well. The living room was on the left side of the house opposite of the stairs. I peeked in to look for Sam. There was a warm fire burning in the fireplace straight ahead. Their tree was in the corner opposite of the fireplace. It was decorated with an array of mismatched ornaments they had collected throughout the years and its multi-colored lights twinkled and glowed similar to the ones on the porch.

After saying hello to the other guests, we made our way to the dining room. Sam found us just as we were getting ourselves drinks.

"Merry Christmas!" she said excitedly.

"Merry Christmas," we both replied.

"I'm so glad you're here!" she sighed. "It would be pretty boring if you didn't come."

I was about to ask why; however, just then Karman came in, walking right up to us. Her hair was pulled up into an elegant bun.

"Lucas you're here!" she exclaims and linked her arm through his. "Come on, I want to introduce you to my parents," she said and pulled on his arm in attempt to drag him along.

"Excuse me! Where do you think you are going with my date?" I demanded before she took three steps.

Lucas pulled his arm free from her iron grip.

"Your date?" she asked with false innocence as she smirked.

"You know damn well Lucas is my boyfriend Karman!" I felt my face heat up with anger.

We were a few inches away from each other's faces now. She was almost a head taller than I was and even though I was forced to look up, I didn't back down. I narrowed my eyes as we stared at each other. Mrs. Blair, Sam's neighbor walked into the room then. She was an old, widowed woman, with nothing better to do than gossip around town. We both looked at her briefly, and then back at each other.

"This is not over!" Karman whispered, so Mrs. Blair couldn't hear.

She then turned her nose slightly in the air and whipped around heading in the opposite direction. I looked at Mrs. Blair before I turned back to my friends; beady eyes were filled with suspicion and excitement, no doubt her next story already turning in her head.

"Come on," Sam said as she grabbed my arm and pulled me forward. "Let's go to my room for a minute."

We followed her up the stairs to the second floor. The carpet was the same beige color as the one downstairs and the walls were the same burgundy color. The upstairs was decorated with Christmas decoration just as much as the downstairs. Two doors down on the right from the top of the stairs was Sam's bedroom.

"Ugh!" I grunted as I paced around her small room.

Neither Sam nor Lucas spoke a word; they were quiet and let me vent the anger out of my system.

A minute or so went by when Lucas stepped in front of me and placed his hands on the tops of my arms, "Kendall, relax."

I glared at him; however, he kept his eyes focused, trying to communicate something to me. Then I understood. I must keep my emotions under control or who knows what could happen.

"Breathe," he said.

I listened to him and inhaled deeply then slowly let it out. After a couple breathing exercises, I felt my body relax and my anger ease.

"I'm sorry Kendall, my mom invited her parents," Sam said.

I looked at Sam, "Its okay." Then I looked back up at Lucas, "I'm fine now."

"Are you ready to go back to the party?" Sam asked.
I nodded and then we followed Sam back downstairs.

The rest of the evening went great; however, Karman would stare at us from across the room. Sam told me to ignore her, which I did. It turns out that Sam and I had gotten the same gift for each other. After eating as much holiday food as we possibly could, the party ended with some Christmas carols. Some guest listened while others sang along. Sam and I joined in the singing in an effort to help drown out the off-key voice of Linda Crosson, a pretty girl from school who always wore her light brown hair in a two-sided braid. Sam and I grinned at each other whenever she struck a high note.

I caught Lucas watching me out of the corner of my eye. He smiled when I turned to face him. There was that hard-to-describe feeling again. It was strong. Stronger than anything I had ever felt, including the night I changed.

Sean and his family were leaving the same time as we were. There were times throughout the night when I noticed Sean looking at me with a different expression on his face. His look made me think that he felt guilty about his recent actions. I was waiting in the foyer with Aunt Marie and Sara as the guys followed Mrs. Keeley to fetch our coats. I smiled politely at Sean, thinking that would be all that he would allow; however, to my surprise he smiled back and walked up to me.

"Hey Kendall," he said.

My smile quickly vanished and I narrowed my eyes, "Are

you speaking to me now?"

Since my birthday party, Sean and I had only exchanged a few words. I wondered if he had gotten over from being angry with me.

He smiled at me sheepishly, "Yeah, about that." He looked down at the floor, "I'm sorry. I've been acting like a jerk."

"It's okay. I forgive you," I told him.

He looked back up with a grin. His eyes flickered above my head then back to my face. He opened his mouth to say something; however, quickly changed his mind and closed it.

"What?" I asked.

"Well, I know you have a boyfriend, but you're standing under the Mistletoe."

I looked up, and sure enough, the green Christmas plant was hanging from the ceiling above my head.

"What do you say? As a friend I mean."

I thought about it for a moment and decided it was okay; however, instead of my lips, I held out my hand for him to kiss. He smiled and then pulled my hand up to his lips and kissed it. Just then, Lucas was at my side; there was a strange expression on his face.

"Merry Christmas Kendall," Sean said with a half smile.

"Lucas," he said as he nodded to say goodnight.

"Sean," Lucas replied.

Lucas turned to me, "I have your coat." His voice was stiff.

"Thanks."

He helped me put it on. I could tell he was agitated. Aunt Marie and Sara wore anxious looks on their faces, I didn't understand. We said goodnight to the Keeley's and some of the remaining guests and then walked out into the cold night air.

"I had a good time tonight, well after Karman's stunt."

I looked at Lucas; I could barely see his face from the light of the dashboard. He didn't look back at me, which I thought was odd.

"Did you have a good time?"

"Yes," he replied, still not looking at me.

There was something wrong; however, I didn't know what.

We pulled in the driveway just as Aunt Marie was getting out of her vehicle. I was worried and thought that maybe I had done something wrong. Lucas held the door for me as I stepped in to the house. I hung my coat on the rack and went to the kitchen. Aunt Marie was at work putting the cooled pies away.

"Hi sweetie," she said as I grabbed a soda from the fridge.

"Hey," I said glumly.

She noticed my tone and stopped what she was doing to turn and face me. There was concern in eyes.

"What's wrong?" she asked.

I shrugged my shoulders, "Lucas is upset, I think I did something wrong."

She hugged me, "Go talk to him. It'll work out."

I took Aunt Marie's advice and left the kitchen to go find Lucas. I found him sitting on the couch with the television on. I sat on the other end and tucked my feet underneath me.

"Lucas? Is something wrong?" I asked.

He looked at me; in his eye's I saw different emotions, fear, worry, sadness, and something else I didn't recognize.

"I'm fine," he answered.

After a few moments, I realized that that was the only answer I was going to get. I decided it was best to go to bed. Without another word spoken, I got up from the couch and headed for the stairs. I was almost out of site when Lucas spoke.

"Kendall?"

I turned to face him.

"Yes?" I asked hopeful.

He looked at me with anxious eyes, "I..." He closed his eyes and then reopened them with a sigh, "I'll see you in the morning."

My face fell a little bit. I thought that maybe he was going to tell me what was wrong.

"Goodnight."

I walked up the stairs and into my room, leaving the door open for Lucas.

I tossed and turned trying to get comfortable; however, nothing worked. All I could think about was the way Lucas acted and the way his eyes held all those different emotions. I replayed the night, going over every detail trying to come up with an explanation. Then, I thought of Sean. I remembered my birthday, how Lucas told me that he was jealous when I danced with Sean.

"Oh, no!" I said out loud.

The guilt immediately started to overflow in me. I had made amends with Sean; however, I had hurt Lucas in the process. I jumped out of bed. I didn't hear anyone ascend the stairs, though I looked in his room anyway; as I predicted he wasn't there. I rushed down the stairs to find, not Lucas, but Aunt Marie sitting on the couch.

"What's wrong?" she asked.

"I need to talk to Lucas."

"He went to check things out around the house before he turned in for the night."

My eyes widened, "Did either of you hear something?"

"No. It's just for precaution."

"Oh," I relaxed; however, I felt another wave of guilt pass through me. "Alright, I'll talk to him when he comes back in. Goodnight."

"Night sweetie."

I went back to my room to wait for Lucas. I lay my head on my pillow, thinking about what I was going to say. How much I was sorry that I had hurt him.

I opened my eyes to see my room bright with the morning

light. I lay there stretching and relaxing before the busy day got started when the memories of last night came flooding back. I quickly sat up and stumbled out of my blankets. I don't even remember getting under them. I rushed to Lucas's room, but he wasn't there. I felt panicky; I must have really upset him. I figured I would brush my teeth and hair before going downstairs.

I could hear voices as I descended the stairs. I walked through the living room to get to the kitchen. The tree caught my eye. The presents had tripled since I went to bed. I stared in amazement for just a moment and shook my head before entering the kitchen. I was surprised to see Matt, Sara, and Graham this early in the morning; they all smiled as I walked in.

"Merry Christmas," they all said.

"Merry Christmas," I replied with a smile at each of them, saving Lucas for last.

He was smiling at me, yet his eyes still looked troubled.

"Eat your breakfast, so we can open presents," Aunt Marie said excitedly.

I smiled at her excitement, "Alright, but first." I looked back at Lucas, "Can I talk to you for a minute?"

He nodded and followed me to the living room. I stopped by the couch, I sighed before turning around to look at him.

"I know you're upset with me. I didn't mean to hurt you, I told you I never would. Lucas I'm sorry!"

My eyes started to well up with tears and then overflow onto my cheeks. Lucas pushed his eyebrows together in confusion. He reached up and gently wiped the tears from my face.

"Kendall, I'm the one who should be sorry," he said in a gentle voice.

I looked at him through the tears, "What?"

"I'm not mad at you and you didn't hurt me."

"I didn't? But, last night, with Sean and the Mistletoe?"

"That wasn't your fault. I saw he was apologizing and

only kissed you on the hand," he looked down and away from my face.

"Then what's wrong?" I was confused.

"Well, I was worried more than anything," he looked back up at me. "That maybe…"

I couldn't stand this, "What? Talk to me."

"That maybe you might decide that Sean was better for you…" he looked back down.

"Instead of you?" I asked.

I let out a gust of air. I was relieved that I hadn't hurt Lucas; however, I knew the pain he suffered and the fear he felt about losing me to someone else.

He looked back up into my eyes, "I have confidence and strength, but with you, sometimes I don't know myself."

I reached up and touched his face, "Lucas. Please don't worry. He's not the one for me, you are."

He smiled slightly as I reassured him.

"I know what you mean though," I looked down this time. "I feel that way sometimes with you and Karman."

He put his hand under my chin and brought my head up to look at him. There was an intensity to his stare as he looked into my eyes.

"You don't have to feel that way anymore," he smiled. "She's not the one for me, you are." His smile faded slightly, "Although, I guess I was a little jealous last night."

"Why?"

"Because, Sean was the first one to kiss you under the Mistletoe," he looked over my head. "Hmm," he said to himself, as his grin got bigger.

"What are you thinking?" I asked, my spirits rising by the second, now that I understood.

He took my hand and pulled me along with him to the doorway between the living room and the foyer. He faced me, and then looked up at the ceiling. I followed his direction to see some Mistletoe above us. I don't remember that being there yesterday. We looked back at each other and smiled, I knew what was coming, and I was looking forward to it. Lucas brushed my hair back leaving his hand to linger on my face as he bent down to kiss me. I wrapped my arms around him and pulled him closer to me as he did the same. This time after only a few sweet moments, I pulled away from him. I didn't really want to; however, our family was waiting for us to start the Christmas morning. I lay my head against his chest and took in the moment. That new feeling was showing its self stronger than any other time; I understood what it was and I knew what was happening now, I was falling in love with my Protector. I didn't know if it was smart or the right thing to do; however, I couldn't help the way I felt.

We walked back to the kitchen, with me leading the way. I was smiling as I took the plate of French toast Aunt Marie had made me for breakfast. Everyone except Aunt Marie and I left the kitchen to settle themselves around the tree.

"Everything work out?" she asked.

"Yes."

She smiled, "I knew it would."

As I ate my breakfast, I thought about the conclusion I had come to, about falling in love with Lucas. It made me wonder if Aunt Marie would approve.

"Aunt Marie?"

"Yes?" she must have noticed a difference in the tone in my voice because she looked up from the food she was prepping for dinner.

I hesitated as I thought about how to ask her my question.

"Are you really okay with me and Lucas?"

I wanted to make sure, before I let this feeling go any further before it's too late; although, I had a feeling it might be already. If I had her blessing so to speak, it would make it that much easier.

She sighed and smiled, "Honey, when you asked me this

question a few weeks ago, I told you then that I was okay with it. I see how much he cares about you and I see_" She stopped in mid sentence. "I couldn't take that away from you, not when you have been so happy, considering what you have been through."

I smiled blissfully as I got up from the table, taking my empty plate with me, and hugged her.

"Thank you."

"You're welcome. Now come on, let's get in there, Sara had been waiting impatiently for you to get up. Actually she was just saying as you came down, that she was going to go wake you up."

I laughed as I felt a loving warmth wash over me.

Aunt Marie and Sara passed out the presents. Lucas and I sat beside Matt on the couch with Graham in the recliner. Each of us took turns opening a gift, except for me; I went two or three times to everyone else's one. My present from Sara was a cashmere sweater, light blue and so soft. Matt's present to me was a jewelry box with seven draws and on each side was a cabinet to hang necklaces. The doors to the cabinets were made of glass with intricate rose patterns etched in the glass; it was beautiful. Graham gave me a CD binder along with a few CD's and Aunt Marie gave me a new snowboard, binders, and snowboard boots; Lucas promised to help me mount them later. In return, I gave Aunt Marie a cashmere scarf that I purchased at a discounted price online. I had a difficult time trying to find something for Graham and Matt. After a few suggestions from Lucas, I found a nice shaving kit for Graham and a multi-tool for Matt. The Multi-tool was like a Swiss Army knife, only to me, it was much, much cooler. As for Sara, she was opening her gift now. It was a set of solar-powered flower pond lights.

"I know you can't use them now, but I_" I started to say; however, Sara cut me off.

"I love them," she said with a smile.

Lucas and I were left to exchanges gifts. I was excited to give him mine; I got him a silver pocket watch with a pattern of knots on the front. I saw him looking at it during one of our shopping trips. I bought it for him the day I went shopping with Aunt Marie and Sara. It was a bit pricy for me; however, it was worth it to see the look on his face when he opened it.

"This is amazing. I had one of these a long time ago."

"Do you like it?"

He looked up with the most meaningful look, "I love it. Thank you."

He showed me the design that was on it.

"You see this," he ran his fingers across it. "This is a Celtic knot."

"What does it mean?" I asked.

"Well, it means different things to different people, unity, uninterrupted life cycle, luck."

"What does it mean to you?"

"A little bit of each of them."

He smiled that half smile I liked so much and then handed me a package, my present from him. I tore the paper off to see a little box overlaid with velvet. I opened it and gasped. I could imagine the look on my face, by the way he was grinning, it must have been priceless.

"One carat, princess cut," he said.

I reached into the box and pulled out a pair of studded diamond earrings. The light reflecting off them made rainbow sparkles.

"They are beautiful!"

I immediately put them in.

"I'm glad you like them."

After we cleaned up the wrapping mess, Lucas helped me take all of my things to my room. While Aunt Marie and Sara tended to dinner, Lucas helped me attach the bindings to my snowboard just like he promised he would.

Fifteen
Warning

Christmas dinner was wonderful. Sara shared some of her secret family recipes that tasted a lot like Aunt Marie's. After dinner, we went to the living room and brought the pies in with us. I sat on the floor to make room for the others on the furniture. Matt cut me a piece of pumpkin pie and then he sat on the couch beside Sara; they shared a bite of their pie with each other. Sara laughed as she teased Matt with hers; they look so happy. It made me wonder what my parents were like and how different my life would have been if they were still alive. Graham caught me looking at them, I quickly looked away and down at my dessert. It was a private moment that I didn't want to share. I'm not angry with graham; it's not his fault he can read me.

Lucas spoke as he sat next to me on the floor, breaking Graham's silent gaze.

"So, when are you guys thinking of leaving for Texas?" he asked.

"In the next day or two," Matt answered.
I looked at Lucas's face; there was fascination there, yet also yearning. I sighed, as much as I didn't want him to go, I knew it would fulfill a part of him to go after the incantation.

"Lucas, why don't you go with them this time?"

He looked at me, "I can't leave you here."

"You're right," Graham agreed, "She should come too." The room went quiet and everyone looked at Graham.

"What?" Lucas sounded shocked.

"Well, when Matt and I went to Virginia, we had a hard time getting the information we needed."

"What do you say?" Graham asked, not only to me.

"I don't know if that's a good idea," Aunt Marie said. She looked very uncomfortable with the idea.

"I am worried too," Sara added.

"It might make it easier to get the information we need," Matt said. Sara looked at him horror-stricken. He put up his hand to show that he wasn't finished speaking, "However, I don't know if it's a good idea either. We might put her in danger."

I spoke up, "I'm already in danger."

I didn't know if I wanted to go; however. I felt like I needed to state the obvious. Lucas was being very quiet. It's not like him to not put his thoughts into a plan. He looked as though he was in thought, debating something.

"What do you think Lucas?" I finally asked him.

He looked at me with worry in his eyes, and then composed himself before turning to the others to speak, "I agree with Marie." He looked at Graham, "However, it makes me wonder why you think Kendall should go this time."

I remembered Lucas telling me that Graham does things for a reason, and now I wondered what this reason was.

"I truly believe that we need her this time," Graham said. Lucas thought about it for a moment before he answered.

"Kendall actually made my mind up for me," he looked at me, "However, I would like to know your thoughts on the subject."

After a quick decision, I decided I wanted to go. I looked at Graham and Lucas as I spoke; I didn't want to see the disapproving looks on the others faces that I knew would be there.

"Well, this is about me, so I think I should help as much as I can when I can."

"I think you should stay here, where it is safe," Matt said. There was an authority to his voice, like a father would have.

"But, it's not safe here. We're on the lookout every minute. Malik could show up tonight, tomorrow, who knows when."

Lucas took my hand and gave it a gentle squeeze. I was close to hyperventilating.

"Kendall is right; it really doesn't matter where she is, she will always be in danger," Lucas directed to the others.

It didn't make me feel any better that he agreed with me.

"If she gets out of town for a few days it may help not only to find the other part of the incantation, it might also help with her nerves," Lucas added.

I smiled inside. He takes good care of me.

"What if you're attacked?" Aunt Marie asked.

"Then we'll handle it like we do here," Graham replied to her.

I could tell we were winning the others over. Aunt Marie looked back and forth between Graham, Lucas, and I.

She hesitantly sighed, "Alright, you can go, but even though you are the True Natural, you listen to everything they tell you to do."

"Okay," I looked at Lucas. He smiled; however, he still had that concerned look in his eyes.

Matt, Sara, and Graham went home soon after dessert. It had been a long day and I was tired. I said goodnight to Aunt Marie and Lucas and then headed to my room. I was putting my gifts away when I heard a knock on my door. Lucas walked in and sat at my computer desk; he sat in silence watching me as I worked to finish clearing my bed off.

"When are we leaving?" I asked.

The others were making plans while I took the dessert plates to the kitchen so I didn't hear all of them.

"Early Sunday morning, before dawn," he replied.

"Why so early?"

He smiled at my tone of disgust for the early time.

"It takes about twelve hours to get there. We will return sometime Wednesday afternoon."

I was a little worried about my financial situation. I didn't let that slip my mind earlier. I had some birthday money left over; however, not enough for four days worth.

"What are you worried about?" he asked with concern, yet with a confused look.

He does this a lot. He always knows when I'm worried about something.

I smirked at him, "You tell me. You're the one reading my mind."

He chuckled at me; then his face became serious, "Are you worried that something will happen on our trip?"

I shook my head as I climbed on my bed, "That is something to be worried about, but no, not that."

He still looked confused. After a moment he said, "Tell me."

I looked down at my bedspread, "I don't have a lot money. I don't think I can go."

I looked up expecting to see disappointment on his face; however, instead I saw amusement.

"You're not upset?" I asked a little confused at his reaction.

He smiled, "No."

"Why?"

"Because you don't need any money to go."

He was confusing me even more.

"We are going to be gone for four days and Christmas just got over with, I need money," I replied sarcastically.

He just kept smiling at me. It was actually quite annoying.

"What? Are you going to pay for everything?"

"Yes," he simply replied.
I sighed loudly and flopped back on my pillows.

"Would you stop worrying?"

I pulled myself up and propped my hand under my head, "The only way I'll let you pay for everything is if you are rich!" I was a little smug, knowing that I had won.

He didn't respond. He just sat there, staring at me with a smirk. Again, it wasn't the reaction I thought I was going to get. I sat up as the question slowly came to the front of me head.

"Are you rich?"

He stared at me for a few moments before answering, "Yes."

I thought about all the times he had paid while we were together.

"Why didn't you tell me this before?" I asked slightly annoyed.

He shrugged his shoulders, "I don't like to brag about it."

I narrowed my eyes, "But, you could have told me." I said the words more slowly than normal.

He pushed his eyebrows together, got up, and sat on the bed facing me.

"Don't be upset. I didn't say anything because it doesn't matter."

I opened my mouth to argue, but he cut me off.

"Kendall, money doesn't make a person. I wanted you to know me as me, not someone who had money."

I couldn't argue with that. I would want that too. He took my hand and rubbed the back of it with his thumb.

After a minute of letting it sink in, he asked, "Are you still upset with me?"

I sighed, and shook my head, "I was more shocked that anything, but I wish you had told me before."

"I'm sorry," he was sincere.

I smiled a little putting my hand on his face; he closed his eyes.

"Tell me about it," I said as I removed my hand.

He opened his eyes and glanced at my bedside table, "I will soon, it's late. Besides, you don't want to sleep too late in the morning; we have a trip to get ready for."
He grinned at my surrender and then kissed my cheek before leaving my room.

The next morning I woke up exhausted. I kept dreaming that I was poor and living on the streets. Lucas, not knowing who I was, would walk by and completely ignore me, then I would wake up; it would repeat itself over and over. My subconscious was playing with my thoughts.

After I got ready for the day, I went downstairs. As usual, Aunt Marie was up at the crack of dawn sitting at the kitchen table, drinking coffee, and reading the morning paper.

"Morning," she said.

"Hi. You know, it's not very often I get up before you," I said teasingly.

"That's because I don't like to sleep all day, like someone else in this house," she peeked up from her paper grinning.

I chuckled, "Where is Lucas?"

"He is outside checking the Durango. You guys are taking that instead of the Blazer,"
I could still hear a trace of worry in her voice.

"That reminds me," she added. "Do you feel anything or have you had a dream about the coming trip?"
I could now see the worry on her face as I heard in her voice.

I shook my head, "No. I don't feel anything."
I saw her features relax a little.

"Aunt Marie, I'm gonna be fine," I tried reassuring her.

She smiled half-heartedly, "I do trust you and your powers, I'm just worried. I would feel better if I was going too."

"Why don't you then?" I asked; it would be good if she

came along.

She thought about it for a moment, "It would make me feel better, just in case I'm needed."

I smiled, "It's settled then."

I felt much better now that she was going too. I got up from the table to go find Lucas.

He was under the hood of the Durango. He heard me approach and looked up from the engine.

He grinned, "Hi sleepy head."

I couldn't help but smile back when he looked at me that way.

"Hi. What are you doing?"

"Checking the oil and other things before we head out in the morning."

He wiped a thin, long metal strip with a dirty rag, put it back in the engine, and then pulled it back out to look at it. I smiled as I watched him intently. I was mesmerized. There was something about the way he worked that held my attention. I was still staring at him when he looked back up.

"What?" he wore an amused expression on his face.

"Uh, nothing," I stammered out and pulled myself together.

He laughed, he saw right through me.

"So, I talked to Aunt Marie," I was trying to change the subject. "She is coming with us." I pushed my eyebrows together, "Actually, I'm surprised she didn't decide to go last night."

"I am as well," Lucas added.

Later that night, I went to bed around nine hoping to fall asleep early. Matt and Graham were meeting us here around three in the morning; of course, that didn't happen. I was nervous about the trip tomorrow and what we would or wouldn't find. I never fell asleep until after eleven.

I was walking in an unfamiliar place. The sun was shinning brightly above me. Below my feet was a thin layer of snow with clay showing through in most places. Even though the sun was shining, it was cold. The wind blew all around us making it feel even colder. Lucas and Aunt Marie were beside me, the others followed behind to help protect me.

"Where are they?" Aunt Marie asked.
Responding to her question, I looked around. There was nothing here but an open field, some telephone poles, and an empty road. There was an ominous feeling in the air.

"What do we do now?" I asked.

"We wait," Matt replied.

We didn't have to wait long. A car we didn't recognize pulled off the road beside ours. Three men and a woman exited the vehicle. The driver got out first and led the others as they made their way towards us; his hair was greasy and slicked back showing his receding hairline and shiny forehead. He looked at all of us, lingering on me for a moment.

"This is her?" he asked, looking around waiting for someone to answer him.

"Yes," Lucas answered him.
I started to feel uneasy.

"Ah, you're her Protector," the balding man said in a deep southern accent.
Lucas didn't answer him this time. I looked up to see the expression on his face. He looked impassive, yet cautious as well.

"I have what you are looking for," the man said. He looked at me and smirked, "Though, not for free."
The other group of people snickered with the driver.

"What do you want?" Lucas asked emotionless.

"Send the girl over," his eyes flickered to me, "and I'll give you what you want." He was still smirking.

"Not a chance," I could hear the anger in Lucas's voice now.

"I'll go," Aunt Marie said.

The mans smirked turned into a wide grin, "Fine."
As Aunt Marie walked slowly towards them, Matt moved beside me and Graham moved beside Lucas. My stomach knotted with

anxiety. As she stopped in front of the balding man, the man to the right of him moved forward.

"He is lying!" Graham exclaimed.
Before there was time to react, the second man reached out and touched her. Within just a few moments, she fell to the ground. I could see her eyes open, wide with fear. There was no doubt in my mind that she was dead.

My eyes flew open as I let out a blood-curdling scream. Before I had time to sit up, Lucas was in my room.

"Kendall, are you alright? What's wrong?"
I heard the light switch on the wall flick. The light from the ceiling fan blinding me. Aunt Marie sat on the opposite side of the bed her face mimicked Lucas's worried tone. Without answering Lucas, I bolted up and flung myself at Aunt Marie.

"You're alive, you're alive," I said sobbing.

"Shh, I'm right here," Aunt Marie whispered trying to calm me. "It was only a dream…" her last words trailed off and faded out. I felt her body tense as she realized what had happened.

"What happened in your dream?" Lucas asked me once I had calmed down enough to make sense.
It didn't surprise me that he knew that I dreamt a warning. I released Aunt Marie and wiped the tears from my face.

"We were in the middle of nowhere, four people met us there. They wanted me to take something that we wanted from them," I looked at Lucas. "But, you told them no." I looked to Aunt Marie now, "You went instead, and then you fell."

Aunt Marie looked at Lucas for a moment and then back to me, "It's going to be alright."

I shook my head vigorously, "You don't understand if you go with us you are going to die."

An hour and a half after waking hysterically from my dream, Matt and Graham arrived. I told them right away about my dream and that I think Aunt Marie should stay home. Both Matt and Graham agreed with me; however, of course, Aunt Marie disagreed. She was worried about me and that we might need her in case something should happen.

"Please Aunt Marie," I begged her for what seemed like the hundredth time as we loaded our things in the back of the vehicle. "Please stay here."

"What if you need me?" Her eyes were full of fear and worry.

"I'll be fine, we'll be fine, but you won't. Please do this for me."

She looked into my pleading eyes, searching. Finally, she sighed, "Are you sure your dream wasn't just a dream?" I could hear the sound of defeat in her voice.

"Yes. I'm positive, trust me."

She sighed again, "I do." Then she hugged me, "You be safe."

"I will," I sighed with relief.

She let go of me and looked at Lucas, "You keep her safe!" she demanded, and then hugged him as well.

"I give you my word."

I instantly felt better, the tension in my stomach eased, "Thank you," I hugged her again before I climbed in the backseat with Lucas. "I love you so much. I couldn't bear it if anything happened to you."

Her voice was weak, "I love you too."

With Matt driving, we backed out of the driveway. I looked back and waved to Aunt Marie and Sara as we drove out of sight.

It was daylight now. We had just passed Colorado Springs when I had fallen asleep. There were a few differences, Graham was driving and Matt and Lucas were asleep.

"Where are we?" I whispered to Graham trying not to wake the others.

"We are just inside Texas, a couple of hours from Amarillo," Graham replied. When he tried to whisper, it made his voice sound deeper.

That means in just a couple of hours we would begin our search for the other part of the incantation

A few moments had passed before I asked, "Do you think we'll find the other part of the incantation?"

I saw him press his lips in a hard thin line in the rear view mirror, "It changes hands very quickly. Most don't want it in their possession for too long." He looked in the mirror at my disappointed expression. "But, we should get a lead on it even if we don't find it."

Hoping that wasn't the best we could hope for, I sighed and lay my head against the headrest.

We pulled into the parking garage of our hotel a little after three in the afternoon. Like a gentleman, Lucas carried my suitcase for me. The hotel lobby was wide with marble flooring circling a sitting area with matching leather furniture and dark carpeting. Opposite the sitting area were the registration desks that lined the length of the wall. There was also a little souvenir shop that featured things from the Lone Star state. The entire front of the shop was glass; I could easily look inside and see all the different types of memorabilia on the shelves. Towels hung on the wall along with T-shirts and swimsuits. Lucas caught me looking in. I quickly turned away, no need to give him any ideas.

After Matt checked us in, we took the elevator to the sixth floor. Matt slid the key into the slot and opened the door. A short hall with a closet, led into the room. It was beautiful. The living area and kitchen was one big room separated by a small counter bar and three stools. There was a hall off the living room and on the opposite side of the room was a door. I sat my smaller bag on the emerald colored couch, that didn't look comfortable at all, to look in each room. Down the hall was a door to the left that led to a bathroom. It was beige with emerald green colored tiles. I was immediately aware of the color scheme of the room. Across the hall was a bedroom with two beds with white bedding; the carpet was white like the living room, and with not to my surprise, the curtains were the same color green as the couch and tiled floor. The room off the living room was another bedroom. It was almost identical as the first; however, this room had an adjoining bathroom.

"This hotel room is amazing," I exclaimed as I walked back out to the living area and to the window. The room looked over the city, "And this view is gorgeous. I bet it's even better at night."

They grinned at my reaction to the room.

"Lucas," Matt said. "Would you show her to her room?"

Lucas smiled picking up my suitcase, "This way Madame."

He held his hand out and gestures towards the room with the bathroom; I smiled and led the way. Lucas set my suitcase on the bed closest to the bathroom, and then set his on the other.

I looked at his bag, and then at him, "Matt doesn't object to this?" I asked.

Even though he is not related, he is like a father figure to me. Not only that, but it would get back to Aunt Marie.

"He does; however, I gave him my word that nothing would happen."

My thoughts immediately went to that night in October, the night where things almost went too far.

"And as you can see there are no alternatives, unless of course this is uncomfortable for you," he looked as if he wished he had thought of that first.

"No, of course not!" I blurted out.

He smiled at my reaction and then he gave me a quick hug before turning to his suitcase.

When I was settled in, I called Aunt Marie as promised to

let her know we had made it safely. Once I hung up, we headed out to find a restaurant; there was one in the hotel; however, I wanted to see some of the city. Amarillo looks like any other city to me, with its sky scrappers, warehouses, shopping districts, and traffic; however, there is something different about it; it has a certain charm.

We left the car parked and walked a few blocks. We found a restaurant called The Steak House Saloon. The inside was wooden from floor to ceiling. It was decorated with country and Texan memorabilia. Country music played in the background as the hostess showed us to a table. I ordered a meal that could feed three of me. When I couldn't eat anymore, I excused myself from the table to find the restrooms. I had to pass the restaurant bar to get to and from the restrooms. On my way back, I saw someone familiar. I could feel the color leave my face and my heart rate sped tremendously. The man saw me staring at him. He looked at me curiously for a moment, nodded once to say hello, and then turned away from me. All I could see of him now was his slick-back greasy hair.

I returned to the table wide-eyed and frantic. Lucas knew immediately that something was wrong and stood up.

"What's wrong?" he looked around to see if anyone was about to attack.

"Shh, sit down. Don't draw attention to us. There is a man at the bar, wearing a tan jacket facing away from us."
The three of them took turns glancing at the man inconspicuously like professionals would do.

"That is the man from my dream. The one who ordered the kill for Aunt Marie," I could hear the distress in my voice. The man got up from his barstool and headed for the door. Lucas rose from his seat as well.

"Where are you going?" I asked.
"I'm going to follow him."
"No!"

"Kendall, I'll be alright."

I grabbed his hand to stop him, "Lucas please!" I begged. He looked at my worried face, opened his mouth to say something, but was cut off by Graham.

"I'll follow him," Graham said. "Matt, give me your cell phone."

"Graham_" I tried to stop him from going after the man as well, but he cut me off.

"I'll call as soon as I can." Then as quickly as he made the decision, he got up from the table and walked out the door.

This is not what I wanted to happen; however, as guilty as I felt I was glad Lucas didn't go. Matt got up from the table as soon as Graham was out of sight.

"Where are you going?" I asked worriedly.

"I'm going to the bar to see if I can get any information on the guy."

I could see him talking to the bartender. He sat down on a stool and ordered a drink. A few minutes passed before he returned to the table.

"What did you find out?" Lucas asked.

"Well, the bad news is, the bartender doesn't know his name, the good news is, he'll be back tomorrow night to watch the game. Apparently he comes here every Monday."

"Well that's something at least. Let's call Graham."

Matt shook his head, "I think we should wait a little longer. If he doesn't call in a half hour then we will call him."

I agreed, though I didn't like it. I had seen what that man and his group could do.

There were ten minutes left before we could call Graham. Lucas would touch the top of my hand or my arm reassuring every couple of minutes to help me relax, not realizing I was fidgeting. We sat there drinking our beverages, waiting for either news from Graham or the end of the half hour. I could see that our server was getting a little annoyed that we were holding up one of her tables.

With only three minutes left, Graham walked through the door. I sighed with relief and relaxed, thanking God.

He shook his head as he walked to the table, "I lost him after a few blocks. I think he knew he was being tailed."

"What do we do now?" I asked as we were leaving the restaurant.

"We wait," Matt replied.

We stopped at a grocery store on the way back to the hotel. It would be cheaper to buy groceries and make our dinners at the hotel since we had a kitchen; however, the only thing we bought was drinks and snack food. I guess if you have money, it doesn't matter much.

I was sitting on one of the kitchen stools texting Sam. We were talking about Amarillo and what it was like here. I told her yesterday I was leaving town for a few days and I would see her when I returned. As if I knew she would, she asked me where I was going. I told her the truth, as much of it as I could anyway. I hated to lie to her, even more than I already had. I told her that I was going with the guys to find a friend in Texas, but asked her not to repeat what I had told her. Being my best friend, I knew, of course she would keep a promise to me, no matter how crazy it sounded. I could tell she was worried about it. Luckily, I evaded the rest of her questions that day. Lucas looked at me intently for a moment. I knew that look. He was up to something. When he grinned, it kind of made me nervous.

"What?" I asked.

"Well, since we have nothing to do until tomorrow, I thought we could go swimming."

I shook my head, "I didn't bring my swimming suit."
His grin got even bigger. He grabbed my hand, pulled me off the stool, and out the door.

We stopped in front of the souvenir shop. The displays in the window were brightly lit. I looked at him and opened my mouth about to protest.

"Don't," he said.

He knew I was going to say something about money.

"I told you I was paying for this trip," his grin was still in place.

I did know that, though I was thinking more along the lines of hotel and food.

"You know, by the time we get suits and get changed the pool will be closed."

"It's only eight thirty, the pool doesn't close until ten," he smiled smugly. "Now quit procrastinating and go pick a suit."

I sighed heavily and let him have his way. He laughed and followed me into the store.

I am glad we went swimming; the warm water helped me relax. We stayed at the pool until it closed and then returned to our room. I changed from my new white two-piece and into my pajamas. I flipped my hair over combing it with my fingers and then put it in a messy bun on the top of my head. I hung my suit over the shower rod to dry and left the bathroom. I remembered that I wanted to see the view at night. I looked out the big window in the living room. The city lights twinkled in the darkness. I was right, the view was better at night.

Sixteen
Discover

The morning was a dismal grey and snow replenished what had melted from the previous day. It was coming down so hard that I couldn't see anything out the window. No sky or streets, no traffic or bustling people going about their workday, I could barely make out the shapes of neighboring buildings. It's not much of a view to look at; nevertheless, I stared out the window anyway. I was worried about tonight, worried that my dream might come true. Only, it will be someone else that dies instead of Aunt Marie. It was a useless worry we knew what to avoid; however, it was still there, pulling on the memories of my dream.

Lost in thought, it startled me when Matt spoke beside me.

"Even though you can't see very clearly now, it is still beautiful."

I had a feeling he wasn't just talking about the view, but more of the bigger picture of what was happening. I looked up at his face; he wore a sad smile. Something was trying to break through the surface of my memories, something vital; I just couldn't grasp it.

"We're going to be alright," he said. He put his arm around my shoulder; it felt nice and comforting. "We won't let anything bad happen," his eyes shown an honesty I could believe. It even helped me relax.

The day dragged on in parts and it took all of my effort not to fidget during those times. Lucas would help me relax; however, even he couldn't hold it down for long. We spent most of the day in the hotel. We ate breakfast at the hotel restaurant, and then we went swimming. Now, I was playing with the remote, using my magic to make it float in the air and sometimes flip the channels; I was bored.

It was almost time to leave for the restaurant. Matt had left about an hour ago. We decided it was safer for him to sit at the bar, just in case the balding man recognized Graham from the other night. We got lucky and arrived at The Steakhouse Saloon a few minutes before the man. Just as we hoped, he arrived and headed straight for the bar. He wore his tan coat and his hair was slicked back just as before. We only ordered drinks, not knowing what was going to happen or how long we were going to be here.

"Remember, don't make eye contact with Matt, but keep watch for his signal," Graham reminded us.

We didn't want to draw attention to the fact that we knew each other and that we were conspiring. We laid out a plan last night and went over it this morning to make sure we were all on the same page. We were supposed to wait for a signal from Matt, and then Lucas and I were to get the car. Once we got the man into the car, we were going to get the information we needed from him.

Matt sat two stools away from the man, but ignored him, (all part of the plan). I couldn't see the television from where I was sitting, yet I assumed the game had started from the cheers coming from the bar. I sighed heavily in frustration and impatience.

Lucas put his hand over mine and squeezed, "Be patient, Matt will give us the signal soon."

"I just want this part to be over with."

"Soon," he replied.

The tension I felt was unbelievable. I was so nervous that something was going to go wrong. I didn't have a bad feeling when I woke up this morning. That at least, made me feel better. It was just the surrealism of my dream. The emotion I felt seeing a loved one dead on the ground that fueled my worries.

The man rose from the bar stool and headed towards the restroom. Matt glanced our way before following him. That was the signal.

"Meet us out back," Graham whispered, and then he followed Matt.

We paid our bill and hurried to the car. Not wanting to sit near the perilous stranger, I got in to the passenger seat and closed the door.

It seemed like hours that we sat waiting behind the building with the car running; however, in fact, it had only been a few minutes. It was dark outside now, though at least the snow had stopped falling. A dimly lit street lamp revealed a blue dumpster between two doors along the back wall of the building. I didn't know which one they would exit, so I watched them both. The pavement was uneven and filled with big potholes, making it look more ominous than it really was.

"Shouldn't they have come out by now?" I asked after another few minutes.

"They have to lure him out, otherwise it could cause a scene and he might get away," Lucas replied.

"I'm scared."

He sighed and took my hand, "I know you are. It will be over soon."

"Shouldn't bravery come with powers? Shouldn't I be fearless?"

He half smiled, "It should; however, we are human, even though we become immortal, we still feel all the human emotions."

Our conversation ended as the door on the right of the dumpster swung open. Matt and Graham were half dragging, half carrying the man to the car. I got out and opened the back passenger door for them. Matt got in first and together he and Graham got the man into the backseat. Once Graham got in, I shut the door and climbed back into the front seat.

"What happened?" I asked, "Is he…dead?"

"No just knocked out," Matt replied.

"What power did you use?" I asked curiously.

In each attack, I hadn't seen anything that knocked people out besides throwing them into something.

"The power was my fist," Matt answered with a grin.

It took me by surprise that they used physical force.

"Did anyone see you?" Lucas asked.

"Yes; however, we told them he had passed out and we were taking him home," Graham answered.

"Clever," I said. "What now?"

"Now we drive out to the middle of nowhere and wait for him to come to," Lucas answered.

Forty-five minutes later, I heard rustling sounds coming from the back. I looked in the backseat to see that the stranger was awake and that Matt and Graham were holding him down.

"You'll let me go if you know what's good for you," the man shouted as he tried to wrestle free.

"We know what you are. It's crucial for you to know that we are Naturals," Matt told the man.

The man settled down a bit after hearing Matt's words, "Where are you taking me?"

"Some place where we can get information out of you where no one will overhear us."

The man looked nervous. "I don't know anything," he rushed out.

"That right there tells me otherwise," Graham said.

Lucas drove about ten more minutes before pulling over in the middle of nowhere. Matt and Graham got out of the vehicle in reverse of how they got in, this time with the man awake and struggling to break free. I was in motion to follow them; however, Lucas grabbed my arm.

"Not yet. Wait for me to come get you."

"Why? That's not the plan," I said confused.

"I know, but I have an idea."

I trusted Lucas and sat back against the seat while he got out.

I gazed out the windows at the surroundings. As far as the headlights reached into the darkness, I could see that the terrain looked similar to that in my dream. It wasn't the exact same place though. Also, the events in my dream occurred during the day. Doing things differently and being prepared would change the circumstances and of course, there would be a different outcome. I took comfort in that.

I could see the others talking, though couldn't hear the conversation. Lucas looked back at me and the stranger's eyes followed. The stranger looked interested yet nervous at the same time.

It wasn't very long before Lucas came to get me. I stepped out into the chilly night air, the wind nipping at my exposed skin. I walked slowly to where the others stood, stopping short a few feet of them.

"Marvin is it? I would like you to meet the True Natural," Lucas introduced me.

The man's eyes widened and his jaw slightly dropped. He didn't speak; instead, he only stared at me wordlessly. I stared back at him with a feeling of disgust, knowing what kind of person he was.

"Now would you like to tell us what we need to know or would you like us to force it out of you?"

The man named Marvin refused to answer.

Lucas shrugged his shoulders, "Alright."

Holding on to Marvin firmly, Matt and Graham spread his

arms out to the side.

Lucas turned to me and winked, "Whenever you are ready."
This part was in the plan, to scare him into talking. Although, I didn't believe I was the best one to scare anyone, I quickly acted the part and stepped forward, smiling devilishly.

"Wait, wait, wait!" Marvin cried out. Whatever the others had told Marvin about me had made him frightened of me, "I don't have it!"

"Not good enough," I used as much force as possible in my voice in order to sound convincing. I took another step forward.

"But, I know who does," he quickly added.

"We're listening," I said.

"I gave it to a couple from Wyoming."

"Their names?" Matt asked.

"I don't know," Marvin lied. Lucas looked at me. "Cooper, their name is Cooper. Keep her away from me!"

I smiled sarcastically, "You know, without backup you are quite the coward."
He looked confused. I didn't explain my statement to clear up his confusion. Instead, I walked back to our vehicle.

After a few more minutes of interrogation, Matt and Graham dragged the man back to the Durango. To my surprise, he backed away.

"What are you doing?" Matt asked. "We are done, we have the information we need from you, we will take you back."

"No! I'm not getting in that vehicle with *her*."

I got out from the front seat, "Don't be ridiculous, it's freezing out here. Plus, we are in the middle of nowhere. Let us take you back."

He shook his head, "I'll take my chances." He looked around, "Out here in the cold."
I started to protest, after all, it was never our intention to hurt

him unless necessary; however, Lucas interrupted me and ushered me back to the passenger seat.

It wasn't until we were back into the city that anyone spoke. I wondered if they were thinking the same things that I was; wondering who this couple was, if they were dangerous, and if they still had the other half of the incantation. I also thought about Marvin.

"What did you say to Marvin to make him terrified of me?" I asked.

"Just that you are the most powerful, good Natural there is. To prove it, I told him you could do magic before you came into your powers," Lucas answered.

"Why didn't he fight back at all?"

"Because he is a normal human being, with no powers," Graham answered.

I was shocked that someone who was a normal human knew about us; however, I myself was having a hard time keeping my secret from Sam.

"How does he know about us and how could he get the incantation?"

"There are people out there who know about us, who don't have powers. Perhaps he is friends with a Natural. As far as the incantation, anyone can have it; however, only you can make it work," Graham continued.

I lay my head on my pillow with a sense of relief, knowing that nothing bad had happened tonight. We didn't get the other half of the incantation; however, as Graham foretold, we did get information as to where it might be. Wyoming. As Marvin told us where the couple was from, I thought I saw a flicker of emotion on Lucas's face. I couldn't put my attention to the matter at that particular moment. Now, as I lay awake, listening to Lucas's breathing, I realized what that emotion was, longing; the same emotion I felt sometimes for my parents. Yet, why would he long for

Wyoming? I looked over at Lucas as he slept. I could see his silhouette in the dim light coming through the curtains, his chest rising and falling, keeping pace with the sound of his breathing; my question would have to wait.

Tuesday was an eventful day. We ate breakfast at the hotel restaurant and then spent the rest of the day sight seeing in the city. With the stressful night behind us, it was easy to relax and have a good time. At times, I couldn't help but think of Marvin. The guys convinced me that we didn't just leave him out in the cold last night that it was his choice to decline the ride back and that he was fine. I also asked what they thought he would do when he made it back. Would he come looking for us with the rest of the people from my dream? Graham answered that question, he told Marvin that we were leaving last night and reassured me that we would be safe.

We checked out of the hotel at four o'clock Wednesday morning. Tired from getting to sleep late the previous night, I slept nearly half of the way home. The other half I was awake seemed longer than the ride to Amarillo. Even though I called Aunt Marie everyday, it was nice to see her face. Sara was at the house as well, which made me happy. I missed her just as much. I called Sam as soon as I was settled, knowing she would be waiting for my return. She didn't tell me she was coming; however, it didn't surprise me that she showed up. I asked her if I had missed anything in our sleepy town for the days that I had been gone. As I suspected, I hadn't. In return, she asked how Amarillo was and if the guys had found their friend. I told her they did, and that the trip was fun. Really, only the last day was, without worry and stress; however, I left that part out.

The rest of winter break was ordinary and relaxing, the way I wanted it to be. Sam and I had hung out every day, either at her house or at mine. Lucas of course didn't like me going to Sam's house alone. Yet, each time I headed for her house, he gave me no trouble about it, which gave me the suspicion that I actually wasn't going to be alone, that someone was going to keep an eye out.

Monday morning flew by. Being the first day back to school, I would assume that the teachers wouldn't hand out any homework, but I was wrong. At least it wasn't an overwhelming amount. The lunchroom was buzzing with the excitement of tales from winter break. Sean sat down at the end of the table opposite of me; he smiled and waved. I was happy that he had gotten over his anger at Lucas and I dating and that we were friends again. Well, as good of friends as we were before. I smiled and waved back at Sean before turning back to Sam and the conversation of our ski trip. We were planning to go this weekend. The weather was supposed to be perfect for skiing. Karman wasn't sitting with us today either. I am thankful for that.

By Friday, I was back to my routine. When I wasn't at school, doing homework or with Sam, I was with Lucas and our family gathering every bit of information we could find on the Coopers. After researching the Internet, Aunt Marie and Sara made some phone calls to every Cooper that lived in Wyoming; they narrowed the search down to two couples. One lived in Rock Springs. The other lived a few miles north in North Rock Springs. I saw that longing look on Lucas's face again. I didn't ask him about it then; however, I did make a mental note to ask him in the near future.

Lucas and I arrived to the cafeteria before Sam today. We had just sat down when I saw Sam rushing towards us. Her eyes were wide with shock and concern.

"What is it Sam?"

"I just overheard Karman saying that she is going to corner you after school," she sat her food tray down and took a few deep breaths to relax her lungs from running.

"What?" I asked. Lucas leaned in closer to hear her story.

"I guess she and her friends have been talking about it since my family's Christmas party."

"And *you* haven't heard anything about it until now?" I asked sarcastically.

"I'm serious Kendall! It has been on the down low until now. Karman are planning something and let's face it, she is bigger than you."

I bit my lip to keep myself from smiling at her usage of the words 'on the down low', "Okay, okay."

"What are you going to do?" she asked.
I could tell she was worried for my safety.

I shrugged my shoulders and simply said, "Nothing."
Lucas looked as though he approved of my answer. Sam was right, Karman was bigger than I was; however, I believe I have something that she doesn't, common sense. Besides, I could win a fight against her without even touching her. Of course, I wouldn't do that; use my powers to harm a defenseless normal human being, perhaps to scare though. If Karman challenges me, I will stand my ground.

Sam was worried for the rest of the school day and seemed annoyed that I wasn't. I didn't feel the need to be, I knew there wasn't going to be a fight.

The end of my last class had finally arrived. Lucas and I were holding hands as we walked the halls that led to the parking lot. Sam was with us. Without surprise, Sam was right about the gossip. Karman was waiting at the door that led out to the parking lot.

"Hey guys," she said in her fake cheery voice.
I nodded once to her in greeting.

"Um, Kendall, can I have a word with you for just a second?"
I looked to Sam and then to Lucas, each of them wore a worried expression on their faces, although their worry was for different reasons. Sam's was fear I'd get hurt, Lucas's was

fear I'd lose control; however, I was the exact opposite of his worry, I was in complete control.

"It's okay," I said to them.

I handed Lucas my bag and followed Karman through the exit. We rounded the corner of the school to an area of the building where there were no windows. It's a spot were some of the kids come to smoke and don't easily get caught. As I suspected, Karman's friends were waiting for us.

"Let's get this over with," I said to Karman.

She turned to face me with a look she gets when she thinks she has gotten away with something.

"Except, I have one request."

"What's that?" she asked with a smirk.

"It will be just you and me."

I had a plan I've been working on for most of the day. She thought about that for a moment before turning to her friends. She dismissed them as if they were her minions; they obeyed and left us alone.

"Are you ready to get what's coming to you?" she asked me, still with a smirk.

"I think you have that backwards."

There wasn't any anger in either of our voices, but the menace was there.

"Really?" she seemed intrigued by my revelation.

"Yes. You are nothing but a bully and I've had enough."

"I don't think so," Karman grabbed my jacket.

The heat rose immediately. I could feel it spreading through my entire body, yet I was still under control.

"Get your hands off me!" I demanded.

"Or what?" she looked amused.

I narrowed my eyes, "Or you'll regret it."

She laughed, "Bring it on! Your measly little threats don't scare me," she was still laughing when she released my jacket.

I smiled cunningly, "You asked for it."

I focused my thoughts as I raised my hand to use my power to lightly push her backwards, not to hurt her, to scare her. Karman lost her footing and stumbled backwards; confused, she stopped laughing and looked around her, searching for someone.

"There is no one there Karman."

She quickly turned back to me with a new look on her face, that of awareness. She understood that it was me that had pushed her. I pushed her backwards repeatedly until her back was pressed against the wall. I stood a foot in front of her now. She struggled against my force, yet I held her against the wall.

"Now," I looked her in the eyes. "You will leave me alone from now on, understood?"

She nodded, too afraid to speak.

"And you will leave my friends alone. Is that understood?"

She nodded again. She no longer struggled against me. Her eyes were wide with fear.

"You will stop bullying everyone and you will treat others with dignity and respect. Is that understood?"

She nodded one last time.

"Good. I'm going to release you now, but before I do I warn you, this is not all I can do!"

I released her; however, she didn't move, she was frozen with fear. I turned away from her and headed back to Sam and Lucas. Before I rounded the corner I turned back to Karman, she still hadn't moved a muscle.

"Oh yeah, one more thing; I will be watching you."

I was smiling when I returned to Sam and Lucas. Sam's face relieved when she saw that I was unharmed.

"So what happened?" she asked.

"She won't be bothering us anymore."

Sam smiled; however, Lucas looked concerned. I shook my head at him while Sam was distracted to let him know that I didn't hurt Karman. He would be disappointed at what I had done; nevertheless, I would still tell him regardless when we got home.

I was really looking forward to skiing tomorrow. I was also excited that Sam and Jordan were coming with us. 'Us' included everyone, except Aunt Marie and Sara; they decided to stay home for the afternoon. We planned to stay for the entire day and since Sam and Jordan were riding with us, they stayed the night at my house.

We left early the next morning; by ten thirty, we were on the chair lift for our first trip down Mount Werner. The view from the lift was gorgeous. The mountain was covered with pine trees and the snow on their branches sparkled like diamonds in the sun light. Lucas and I were in the front followed by Sam, Jordan, and Matt. Graham was waiting for us at the bottom, for precaution. I didn't feel like anything would happen here, I felt comfortable. Besides, open space, people, and my Protector surrounded me.

We finally reached our destination at the top of my favorite intermediate trail. I was anxious to start down the slopes. Aunt Marie had taught me how to ski when I was younger; however, as I got older, I had to take lessons to learn how to snowboard. I was surprised to find that Matt and Sara knew how to ski as well.

Sam and Jordan went down first. I fastened my feet onto my board, front foot first, then stood up and pulled my goggles down. Lucas was pulling his down when I looked up at him.

"I'll see you at the bottom," I said.
I didn't wait for his reply. I angled the nose of my board and started to glide down the mountain, picking up speed as I angled it towards the fall line. I smiled as I felt the rush of adrenaline run through me. It was similar to that of the feeling I felt on my birthday when I came into my powers. I

looked to my left and saw Lucas a few seconds behind me. I reached the bottom and slid to where the others were waiting. Lucas was slowing as he came closer to us. He bent down, grabbed the nose and tail of his board, and completed a 360-degree turn. Lucas rose just before he came to a complete stop covering us with shavings of snow laughing at the outcome of his stunt.

We went down a different trail before lunch. Once we had finished eating, we headed to the famous Mavricks Superpipe and Terrain Park. We couldn't wait to show off our tricks. Without waiting for Sam and I, Lucas and Jordan, with a "woo", took off. I watched Lucas do an air to fakie and then on the next kicker he did a back flip. I was impressed; I had no idea that he was that good. He never told me he was rich either. It made me wonder if he was hiding anything else.

Jordan was pretty good too; he has improved a lot since the last time I saw him on his board two seasons ago. He was doing tricks that involved grabbing the board while in the air as well as a few grinds. Sam and I looked at each other.

"Ready?" she asked with a grin.
I pulled my goggles down and followed her down. Sam was fairly new to snowboarding. This is her second season, last year she broke her ankle just before the season opened. Like me, she pulled some basic tricks.

The day had gone smoothly. We hadn't seen anything out of the ordinary. It was getting late; however, we had enough time for one more run down the mountain. Jordan was tired out so he and Matt would wait for us at our favorite restaurant. Graham, like Matt, had skis and was following us down this time. We took the appropriate lift to the Christmas Tree Bowl. My heart was racing and my stomach turned as I strapped my feet onto my board. I stood up and took a few deep breaths to ease my nervousness. The Christmas Tree Bowl was an expert trail.

"Are you alright?" Lucas whispered in my ear.

I smiled weakly, "I'm fine, it's just the trail."
Previous seasons when I would run this trail for the first time I would feel nervous; however, I don't remember it being this much.

"I'll go first," he said.

I looked at Sam, she looked just as nervous as I felt.

"You'll do fine," I said trying to conceal my nervousness from her.

Lucas heads down first, Sam and I followed him. Usually after a few seconds, I would start to relax and enjoy the run; however, it was different this time. The tension never let up. It took me a few moments to understand why I was feeling like this, something bad was about to happen.

I heard it first before I saw it. A thunderous roar issued behind us. I whipped my head around to see a cloud of white coming towards us at a tremendous speed. I realized it wasn't only a cloud; an avalanche was behind it. I looked ahead to find Sam, she was just a few yards ahead of me. I straightened the nose of my board a little more towards the fall line to pick up speed and race towards her. I knew we wouldn't be able to out run the rushing snow; we had approximately ten seconds before it closed in on us. I caught up with Sam and yanked her down to the ground as we slid to a stop.

"What are you doing?" she asked.

"Put your hands over your head and keep down."

She looked up the mountain and saw the avalanche, "But_"

"Just do it Sam, trust me."

There was no more time for Sam to argue with me, because the cloud was inches away. I fell to my knees behind her to protect her too. Lucas and Graham's faces flickered in my mind; nevertheless, I had to focus at the task at hand and concentrate so I pushed them back out. I held out both of my hands, palms forward to force the snow around us. If anyone could see, it would look like I was trying to push the snow back up the mountain. I watched the snow part around and above us. I was getting tired; however, I directed all of my energy and held my focus. I wasn't going to let us die like this.

Within a minute, the avalanche was past us. I relaxed my arms and immediately checked to make sure Sam was all right. She was lying on the ground, staring up in horror.

"Are you okay?" I asked as I helped her off the ground.

"What was that? How did you…the snow…" she started to panic.

"Sam, calm down. It's alright, it's over."

I know exactly what she is going through; she saw my power.

Seventeen
Home

The snow had come to a rest and was packed around us in a circle about eight feet high.

"We have got to try to climb out," I said to Sam. She was relatively stable. "Do you want to go first?"

She shook her head, "No you go."

I unbuckled my feet from my board and with Sam's help, on the second try I climbed up and over the packed snow. Once I was out, I looked around. I couldn't believe what I saw. Some of the trees were completely under the snow or just the treetops sticking out, while others were completely untouched. I saw no one, my thoughts flashed to Lucas and Graham; I hoped they were okay. I didn't dare to think about them any further; not knowing if they were all right was hard enough.

"Hand me the snowboards then I'll pull you out," I yelled down to Sam.

She passed the boards up and then reached and grabbed my hand. I pulled with all of my might; however, I was struggling. I just didn't have the strength to lift her out. A hand reached down grabbing Sam's wrist and helped pull her out. With great relief, I recognized Graham. I hugged him tightly once Sam was out.

"Are you okay?" I asked him.

He nodded, "Are you two all right?"

Sam nodded, yet she looked like she might be in shock.

"We're okay. Have you seen Lucas?" I asked.

"Not yet," he answered.

"How did this happen?" I asked.

Sam and I hurried to strap our feet back onto our boards. The three of us looked back up the mountain. Being on top of the avalanche, we could see the next trial over. It wasn't empty, there was a skier heading down the mountain.

I turned to Graham, "You don't think…"

Graham's eyes flicker to Sam so I didn't finish my sentence.

"I do," he said confirming my fear.

We slowly went down the trail looking for Lucas and anyone else who may have been ahead of us. I was starting to get nervous when we reached the bottom and didn't find him. Search and rescue teams were already in action. We passed a team with a German Shepard rescue dog heading up the trail we had just descended to look for survivors. It was crowded with panicked people and trained volunteers. I heard an argument in all the chaos near by. I recognized one of the voices. My heart started racing as I searched for the arguers.

"I'm sorry, but you can't go," someone said.

"My girlfriend is still up there!" the familiar voice shouted.

Just around a small group of people was a folded table with a volunteer behind it holding a clipboard. Standing in front of the table with his back to me was Lucas. I let out a breath I hadn't realize I was holding and ran to him.

"Lucas!" I cried out.

He turned around and immediately his face relaxed from anger to relief. He closed the short distance that was left between us and wrapped his arms tightly around me.

"Oh Lucas, I was so worried that you were crushed under the snow."

He pulled away enough to look at my face, "Kendall, I would have survived; however, Sam is mortal and to a degree you are too." He pulled me towards him and squeezed me, "I'm just happy you are alive."

He would have survived. I felt a little dumb for not remembering that. I was only thinking about losing him. Graham and Sam met up with us a moment later.

"Matt and Jordan are on their way," Graham reports.

He must have called them when we had made it safely down the trail. I glanced at Sam she didn't look very well.

"Lucas, Sam knows," I whispered to him. "We have to tell her now, I *want* to tell her."

He sighed and nodded, "We have no choice now."

I turned to her, "Sam, I know you are scared and confused, I will explain everything soon. But, right now you have to trust me, by not telling anyone what happened up there. Do you trust me?"

She looked at me with confusion on her face; however, she nodded. Matt and Jordan met up with us now. Jordan hugged Sam and Matt hugged me.

It was dark by the time we arrive back in Oak Creek. The ride home was long and quiet. No one had spoken a word since we left the scene of the avalanche. I was worried about Sam. What she was thinking? Is she afraid of me? Does she still want to be my friend? Or, would Sam accept me for what I was now? Whatever she chose, I would try to understand and accept it. She's my best friend and I may not like it; nevertheless, I will support whatever decision she chooses.

"I need to go to your house before you take me home," Sam said.

Good, she wants to talk. Does this mean she is okay with it? I was hoping for the best.

"Alright," I replied trying to hold the nervousness out of my voice.

I might have fooled Sam; however, I didn't Lucas; he grabbed my hand and gave it a squeeze.

We dropped Jordan off at his house, and then drove to mine. I wasn't surprised to see the Explorer parked in front of my house. Matt must have called Aunt Marie and Sara sometime during the chaos; we were barely out of the car when they rushed out of the house and hugged us asking if we were okay. When we entered the house, we went straight to the living room to talk. Good, let's get this over with. I sat next to Sam on the couch and took a few deep breaths to prepare myself for what was to come. No one spoke for a couple of minutes. I figured they were waiting for me to start. I took a deep breath and began.

"Sam," I said. This felt all too familiar, except now I was in Aunt Marie's position. "I want to explain what happened today and what I am. Then if you decide…if you don't want to…" I was unable to form a complete sentence.

"If I don't want to what?" she asked. Her tone was curious.

"If you don't want to be friends with me anymore."

Her expression turned to a mix of shock and confusion, "Is that what you think?"

I didn't answer her.

"No matter what, I'll always be your friend."

I smiled halfheartedly. I wanted to believe her, though we would see if she changed her mind once she has heard the whole story.

I told the story as it was told to me. I began with the legend and continued with the basics of what she needed to know. Who we were, that Lucas was my Protector, and about Malik. I would fill in the rest later, if I didn't scare her off before later came. She quietly listened without interrupting, though not expressionless. At first, there was confusion; however, as the story progressed, excitement, worry and fear, joined in. I remembered feeling the same way back when I had first heard the story.

Once I had finished, I sat there as patiently as possible while she thought, waiting for her questions to spill; I was shocked that they hadn't already. More and more time passed and I started to get nervous. All of a sudden, she flung herself towards me and hugged me. I hoped it wasn't for the last time.

"So, now that you know the basics," I paused for just a moment, my voice going softer, "did you change your mind?"

Sam looked as though I had offended her, "Of course not. I think this is the coolest thing ever. I mean of course, there is the bad guy. What was his name again?"

I smiled a little, "Malik."

"Right, Malik, there is him, but everything else is awesome. I have to admit, I was a little freaked out when you made the snow go over us, but afterwards I was very grateful."

I took a deep breath letting it out slowly to relax my nerves. I was happy now that everyone that I cared about knew my secret.

After we explained to Sam a little more about us, we described the avalanche in more detail to Sara and Aunt Marie. They both agreed with the rest of us, that one of Malik's people set off the avalanche. I was still amazed that I was able to manipulate the snow since I couldn't do it that day while training with Lucas. We assumed then that I didn't have any control over the water. Matt says that I may have more abilities that still haven't materialized yet. His revelation excited and frightened me.

Aunt Marie took Sam home. She was gone for over an hour; however, when she returned Sam was with her. After Sam's mom gushed over her like Aunt Marie and Sara did to me, ensuring she was all right, Sam was allowed to come back for the night. I was very surprised; Mrs. Keeley was the protective type and for her to let Sam leave after a near death experience, was unusual for her. I had a feeling Aunt Marie had something to do with that.

Sam, Lucas, and I stayed up well into the night. Lucas and I answered any questions that Sam had that she hadn't asked already; I even showed her some of my powers.

"So, let me get this straight. All of you have similar powers called Telekinesis?"

"Yes, for the most part, everyone except for Matt, he has night vision and Aunt Marie can heal."

Sam's jaw dropped and her eyes widened, "Your aunt can heal?"

I nodded. Her expression made me giggle.

"That has got to be the coolest thing ever. It must be nice not ever being sick," her face became somber and I could tell that she was putting some things together.

"What?" I asked her.

"If your aunt can heal, then why were you sick just before your birthday?"

I half smiled, "I wasn't sick. I was being protected from Malik and his people; he sent people to abduct me."

Her eyes widened with fear. Lucas and I told Sam about each time Malik sent someone for me, just to let her know how dangerous Malik really was.

Things have been moving quickly since winter break, first Christmas, our trip to Amarillo, and New Years Eve, which we spent quietly with our family. The last thing that had happened was the avalanche and the divulgence our or true selves to Sam. Now, two weeks later we were planning a weekend trip to Wyoming. Matt and Graham left the previous weekend to investigate the Coopers. There were two addresses in different towns of close proximity. They were seeking out the right one before the rest of us arrived.

It was Thursday, the lunchroom was loud, making it easy for Lucas, Sam, and I to have a quiet conversation at the end of our table about the coming weekend. Lucas and I were taking tomorrow off from school to get an early start. We told Sam the real reason we went to Amarillo. She was worried of course, now that she understood the danger of finding the incantation and what it meant. The more we told her about Malik, the more she feared him and wanted me to stay away from him; she knew that it was impossible though. Sam wanted Malik stopped as much as we did. Lucas assured her that this time it would be a little different. I found out what he meant later.

Sam came over after school to help me pack. Since the night we revealed the truth to her, she has spent almost every evening with us.

"What hotel are we staying at this time?" I asked Lucas.
We were up in my room filling my bag with a weekend supply of clothes and toiletries.

"We're not," he replied.

Sam and I looked at him at the same time, "Where are we staying then?"
He had that longing expression again. It brought back the questions that I had forgotten about.

"My home," he smiled.

I realized my mouth was open in surprise and quickly closed it, "When you say home?"

"I mean, where I grew up; on the horse farm." His smiled faded, "Or did you want to stay in the city? I mean you don't get to see it very often."

"No, your house will be great!" I smiled.
I really wanted to see where he grew up.

I was the first one up. I had showered, brought my bag downstairs, and eaten breakfast before anyone had their first cup of coffee.

"Are we in a hurry?" Aunt Marie asked smiling at me.

"Sort of. Is everyone awake?"

Sara had been staying with us since Matt and Graham left, mostly to help protect me; however, I think a little part was because she was lonely. Aunt Marie chuckled at my impatience.

During the six-hour ride, I tried to imagine what Lucas's home was like. He hasn't said much at all about his family, except that they used to train and board horses. Of course, they wouldn't be alive now. It made me wonder if it was too painful for him to talk about.

Lucas drove the last hour with me in the front seat with him. We turned east onto a dirt road. The land was flat with snow-covered mountains in the distance. After a few miles, we pulled into a long driveway with a wooden fence on each side. It led to an old styled, beautiful three-story farmhouse with a wrap around porch and shutters on the sides of each window. Behind to the right of the house, was a huge, two-story building with another wooden fence leading around a pasture. My jaw dropped immediately as I took in the image in front of me. I didn't know what I expected; however, it wasn't all of this.

Lucas saw my expression and laughed, "Do you like it?"

I nodded, "It's beautiful and so big."

We parked in front of the house. When we exited the vehicle, a dark-haired woman in a black cowboy hat and boots greeted us. She smiled as we approached her.

"Lucas!" she called out and wrapped her arms around him pulling him into a tight squeeze.

She had a very pretty face with lines that made her look experienced.

When she finally let go of him Lucas turned to me, "I would like you to meet someone. Kendall this is Sky, Sky, Kendall."

"It's nice to finally meet you Kendall," she hugged me, "Lucas has told me so much about you."

I looked at him a little surprised. He smiled sheepishly and shrugged his shoulders.

"It's nice to see you again Sara."

"Likewise. Do you remember Marie?"

"Of course, it's nice to see you again. How long has it been fifteen years?"

"Seventeen, too long."

"Yes," Sky agreed.

As we walked across the wooden porch and into the massive house, I wondered how Sky knew Aunt Marie.

The interior of the house was just as beautiful as the outside. There were so many rooms, a person could get lost in here. The foyer held an elegant staircase made of dark cherry wood. A sitting area was to the right of the foyer and an office opposite of that; I assumed the office was used to run the family business. Lucas hadn't talked very much about his home, yet it never dawned on me that it was still an active homestead. The dining room was big enough to feed an army. The kitchen was off from that. It had been modernized with new appliances yet it still held an old-styled charm. There was another set of stairs in the kitchen that led to the second floor; this set was plain, yet was still made with dark cherry wood.

"Your house is amazing," I said to Lucas.

We entered a family room with a television, where everyone else had gathered.

"Thank you, although I give all the credit to sky and Xavier for keeping it up and running."

Sky beamed at him, "Well, given the circumstances, I have been more that happy to do it all these years."

In that instant I knew that she knew who I was. Lucas knew exactly what I was thinking.

"Your thoughts are correct," he grinned at me. "Sky is actually a distant relative of mine."

I was astounded. Until now, I didn't think he had any relatives still alive. He chuckled at my expression and took my hand leading me to the mantle where an old black and white photograph sat. A beautiful antiquated silver frame held the picture of a family, a mother, father, and two boys. The younger boy I didn't recognize, the older boy I could tell was a younger Lucas.

"My father Devlin started this farm with my mother, Eleanor, before my brother and I were born. I was twelve when this picture was taken. Duncan," he pointed to the smaller boy, "was eight. Sky's great, great, grandfather."

It took me a moment to realize what he actually said, "Sky is your niece?"

Lucas nodded in agreement, although it was just a rhetorical question.

"We didn't have much when this picture was taken but we survived and so did the business; not without struggles of course. The depression was tough; however, soon we were back on our feet again. The horse industry has been doing great ever since. Again, thanks to Sky and her husband."

He stared at the picture for a couple moments longer. I could see the sadness in his eyes.

"You miss them."

"Very much."

I reached for his hand. The look in his eyes brought back my feelings of sadness I sometimes felt for the loss of my own parents. His mood changed suddenly and he smiled.

"Come on," he pulled my hand and we headed towards the back door.

"Where are we going?"

"I want to show you something."

We crossed the snow-covered yard and entered a huge white building. It was a stable full of horses. The air was filled with the scent of sawdust, hay, and general horse smell. The stable contained two rows of stalls that lined the length of both sides of the building. Toward the back, in the middle was a room with no door. Above the room was a landing. I couldn't see the stairs from where I was standing; they must be to the rear of the room. On the far end wall on each side of the center room, was a door. I could see light coming through the casing cracks and figured they must lead outside.

"This is amazing. Do you own all of them?"

Lucas gleamed at my reaction, "No."

We walked down the farther side row of stalls.

"Most of them belong to the farm, some are boarded here temporarily, and some of them are permanent, while others were rescued," his eyes narrowed slightly and his expression changed to disgusted, "from neglect."

We stopped in front of a white horse with a white main and tail. Lucas made a clicking noise with his mouth to call the horse to the stall door. The horse turned quickly and came to Lucas. When the horse was near, Lucas reached out and touched its head and neck.

The horse nuzzled its nose against Lucas, "I've missed you too." After a moment of quality time, Lucas spoke to me, "This is Ice, she is my horse."

I immediately pictured a prince riding along on a white horse like in a fairytale.

"You see her hooves," he continued, oblivious to my thoughts. "How they are a pinkish color? She has no pigment. She is called a Dominant White Horse, very rare."

"She's beautiful. May I?" I reached my hands out towards the beautiful creature.

Lucas looked into the horses eyes as if he was communicating with her.

"Go ahead, its okay."

I rubbed my hand the length of her face and neck. I could feel the muscles under her white coat.

"She likes you."

"I like her too!" I replied. "She seems so calm and gentle."

"Do you want to ride before dinner?" he asked.

I smiled, "Yes."

The horse Lucas picked out for me was called Dante. The gelding was a light chestnut color with a blond main and tail. Lucas led the two horses to the room with no door. He disappeared into the room for a few moments and then came back out with a couple of blankets; he placed them on the horses' backs and then went back into the room. This time he came back out with a saddle and placed it on the back of Ice. I sat on the edge of a bale of hay and watched him work as he fastened the belt of the saddle around the horse's stomach. There was an expression of pride and enjoyment on his face as he worked; it made me happy to see him this way. He put the saddle on the other horse and then one at a time, put something shiny in their mouths and pulled the head pieces up and over their ears.

"What are they for?" I asked.

"The leather head piece is called a bridle and the metal piece in the mouth is a bit; it directs the horse as to which way the rider wants to go."

When Lucas was finished, he helped me off the bale and onto Dante, "Here, put your left foot in the stirrup."

I held the saddle as I swung my right foot over the horses back and adjusted myself to the saddle; I felt very comfortable here. Lucas guided both horses out of the barn before mounting Ice. After showing me how to use the reins and my feet to direct the horse, we were off.

The sky was clear and the sun was just beginning to set in the west, the waning sun turned the horizon a purplish orange color. With the snow-covered mountains in the distance and the snow covering everything in site, the scenery looked like a postcard. The further we go the more beautiful it gets.

"How far are we from your property now?"

"We are still on it," Lucas replied.

I was surprised, it seemed like we have gone miles since we left the barn. Lucas laughed at my expression.

"How much land *do* you own?"

"Hundreds of acres close to a thousand. My land begun the second we turned down the dirt road." He pointed to the east, "During the summer months, the back part is crops."

I listened intently as he told me about his land and how it looked during each season; how the fields become covered in wild flowers in the spring and summer and what color the leaves turn in the fall.

It was dark by the time we brought the horses back to the stable. Once we put the tack away, brushed the horses off, and put them back in their stables we went into the house. Dinner had just been put on the table. Matt and Graham were back, sitting at the dining table with Aunt Marie, Sara, Sky, and a man I didn't recognize, yet I assumed was Sky's husband.

"You're back! I've missed you. Did you find anything out?" I said excitedly all in one breath.

Everyone chuckled.

"I missed you too and yes we have some information," Matt replied.

Lucas introduced me to the man sitting next to Sky. Xavier; his eyes matched his dark hair and his skin was leathery and tanned from working outside. The information the guys had come back with was of the Cooper's life pattern. Though it was never the same, they had watched them for days. They would follow the Coopers to and from work everyday; however, the evenings were different. Once, they had lost the Coopers; however, the next morning they were on their way to work, just as they did the morning before.

"What do you make of it?" Lucas asked.

"We're not sure." Graham answered. "However, I think we need to approach them soon."

After dinner, we moved to the family room with the television. They did a lot of catching up and I was reminded of when Graham had first arrived. It was getting very late and after a long day, I was exhausted.

Xavier stood up from the couch and stretched, "I'm hitting the hay. Morning chores come early."

Lucas took my hand and pulled me from the floor, "I'll show you to your room."

The hall was dark and I couldn't see well; my eyes hadn't adjusted to the darkness yet. Knowing his way without the need for light, Lucas moved forward taking me with him. I was blinded when he flipped a light switch on. When my eyes adjusted to the light, I saw that we were in a quaint little bedroom. My things were already brought up, lying on a blue comforter that was spread out across the bed.

"The bathroom is at the end of the hall. Matt and Sara are at the other end and Marie is right beside you," he bent down and kissed my cheek. "Get some sleep. If you need anything I'm just across the hall," he pointed to a door kiddy corner to mine. "Goodnight Kendall."

He started to pull his hand out of mine; however, I yanked him back. I didn't really make him move, yet there was enough force to make him stop and turn back towards me. I moved closer to him and wrapped my arms around him. He mimicked my actions and squeezed me tightly. I pulled back just enough so I could see his eyes. I could see the flecks of darker brown in them. I stood on my toes, closed my eyes, and pulled his face to mine. Our lips moved together, gently and smoothly. My heart raced and my breathing was quick.

When we pulled apart I smiled, "Goodnight."

He chuckled and kissed my lips once more before closing my door halfway. I heard a door open but not close, he was sleeping with his half open as well. Just like always.

Eighteen
The past

I rolled on my side and opened my eyes. I had to blink a few times as my eyes adjust to the light. My temporary room was bright with the morning light. I got up and peeked out the curtains; it was a beautiful sunny day. When I was ready for the day, I peeked in the room Lucas showed me was his; it was empty, he must already be downstairs.

The smell of bacon hit me as I walked down the stairs I thought would lead me to the right room. I reached the bottom and was relieved to find myself in the doorway of the kitchen. The window over the sink was wide, letting the natural light in easily. Cupboards lined every wall in this roomy kitchen, with the two beside the refrigerator going from floor to ceiling.

"Well good morning there!" Sky said. She held a frying pan full of scrambled eggs.

"Morning everyone," I sat down at the table next to Aunt Marie.

"Scrambled eggs?" Sky asked.

"Please."

She filled the plates in front of us before setting the pan back on the stove and sitting down at the kitchen table.

"Did you sleep well?" Sky asked as she poured herself a cup of coffee from the plastic pot on the table.

"Yes thank you," I took some bacon from the plate in the middle of the table. "Where are the others?"

"The guys are checking the land." Sky knew that I was aware of why the land had to be checked; however, she was surprised by the worry and fear on my face.

"Don't worry, everything is fine," Aunt Marie put her hand on my arm. "They're just making sure."

"Have you seen anything of Malik or his people at all?" All three of us looked at Sky.

She shook her head, "Not a thing."

I relaxed a little and finished my breakfast; however, not without thoughts of Malik and the safety of the guys.

Sky stood up from the table and took her plate to the sink, "Well, I better get to work; I've got to clean the rest of the stalls before lunch."

I loved horses and wanted to learn as much as I could about them.

"Can I help?"

"Sure. I could always use another pair of hands."

I put my empty dishes in the sink and followed her out the back door.

I hadn't notice the day before that there were a couple more rooms attached to the tack room. Each door was made from the same wood as the barn. When Sky entered the last room, I could see that it was for storage with lots of tools. She came back out with two shovels and a pitchfork.

"Okay we need to move the horses one at a time so we can muck out their stalls."

She walked to the stall next to me where a black horse was housed. Above the stall on the wall was a wooden plaque with the word Midnight etched in it.

"This big guy is first."

Sky leaned the tools against the wall, and then put something I thought was called a halter on the horse; she moved him to the empty stall on the end closest to us. She handed me the shovel with a grin.

We worked together in silence for a little while, only the sounds of our breathing broke it. It didn't last long though. I was glad; the silence was getting a little uncomfortable.

"How are you holding up honey?" she asked.

Even though I held a shovel in my hand, I knew she wasn't asking about the work.

"It's tough at times, worrisome at others, but I think I am handling it okay."

I checked the cement floor to make sure I got everything.

"I'm no Natural, yet I see a tremendous amount of strength in you."

The compassion on her face forces a smile from me.

"Mostly because of Lucas."

I've said this many times, yet I couldn't help saying it when it is so true.

She nodded, "Yes, you two are a perfect match." Her eyes sparkled.

I had the impression she meant more than just Natural and Protector. She confirmed my suspicion with a smile and a wink.

I thought about her words as we finished clearing out the stall. I knew how I felt about Lucas, and I knew how he felt about me, to a point. Did he really feel for me the way I did for him, was he falling in love with me too?

I leaned the shovel against the wall and watched Sky spray the stall. Like Lucas, there was pride on her face. She liked what she did.

"How long have you been running the farm?"

She stopped spraying and laid the hose over the rail, "Pretty much since you were born."

I rolled my eyes. Did everyone know about me?

She forked straw into the stall as she continued, "I was twelve when my parents told me about Lucas and the legend. So, when he told me about you and after I met you, he asked if I would take care of the place. I was happy to do it."

Excitement jolted through me, "So you must have known my parents and Isaac?"

She sighed, "Yes, I remember Isaac."

I didn't let it slip that she dodged my question about my parents. But, why would she not answer it? Sky forked another pile of straw and pitched it in the stall.

"What were they like?" I asked. I thought I saw a trace of panic in her eyes. "Lucas and Isaac I mean."

She relaxed her face and sighed, "Where there was one, there was the other. They were inseparable, as close as brothers would be. They would die for each other; they tried, only one succeeded."

I could see the same sadness in her eyes as Lucas held in his when he talked about Isaac.

"What happened?"

"Lucas didn't tell you?" she asked clearly confused.

I shook my head. I could see her debating with herself on whether she should tell me or not; however, when she sighed I knew she was going to tell me.

"Malik wanted Isaac's powers too, not as bad as yours I'm sure you know, yet bad enough that he sought him out. After years of trying to catch him with out succeeding, everyone thought he gave up. We never saw it coming. Somehow his people got a hold of Lucas and Isaac of course, went to save him." The sadness in her eyes spread to the rest of her face, "Isaac talked Malik into a trade, his life for Lucas's. As I take it, that's a hard thing to do with Malik. Bargain with him I mean. Lucas was not happy; he tried to persuade Malik not to take the trade, but of course, Malik agreed with Isaac. Malik knew what he was doing all along." She paused for a moment and took a deep breath, letting it out slowly, "Isaac died right in front of Lucas's eyes."

As the tears spill from my eyes, I saw Sky wipe a few of her own away.

"It took Lucas a long time to get over it. Eventually, he did get better, I think mainly because of you. He knew that you needed to be protected and has kept watch on you since you were born."

Then the barn door swung open, scaring us both. Lucas walked through the door smiling. It quickly faded when he saw me wipe away the rest of the tears. Something I was trying to hide. He looked at Sky with a disappointed expression; he knew what we were talking about.

He reached down for my hand. "Come on," his voice matched his expression.

I stood up and followed him out, glancing back at Sky just before we walked out the door. She was back to forking straw into the stall. I'm glad I found out what had happened, yet I am also a little nervous. I hope he isn't too upset with Sky for telling me about how Isaac died.

Lucas was quiet as we walked toward the pasture. We stopped at the wooden fence looking out over the field where a few horses were browsing. He looked down at me with a saddened expression.

"I'm sorry you found out that way. I should have told you. It's just...I don't like talking about it."

He searched my face for forgiveness.

"It's okay. I understand."

He sighed and wrapped his arms around me into a hug. I felt like I needed to comfort him, to take away his pain, yet here he was comforting me instead. I couldn't imagine losing Lucas, not only because we were together, more of the reason because we are Natural and Protector. In these short few months, I've come to realize that a bond between a Natural and their Protector is strong. So strong that I don't think even death can break it; that's why Lucas still has a hard time with Isaac's death. Within a few minutes, Lucas seemed to relax. I didn't realize he was staring at me as though he was deep in thought. I caught a glimpse of something in his eyes before he smiled and it vanished.

When we returned to the house, we found the others at the dining room table, their plate's half-empty. As I sat down, I tune in to their conversation. They were talking about this morning.

"Did you see anything?" I asked.

Lucas smiled, "Nothing that shouldn't be."

I'm glad he is in a better mood.

"I wonder why we haven't seen or heard form Malik or his people," Sara said.

"I've been asking myself that same question. It took me awhile; however, I think I know the answer now," Graham said.

"I think I do too," I added.

The others looked between Graham and me. Graham nodded and raised his hand for me to explain to them what we have come to realize.

"He's biding his time, waiting for the perfect moment," I looked at Lucas. "Waiting for us to be alone and away from each other."

"The perfect time to capture you," Lucas said.

Graham and I shook our heads in unison.

"The perfect time to ambush and capture you," I corrected him.

I heard gasps around me; however, I was focused on Lucas's face. First, he looked shocked as he quickly put the pieces together. Then anger flashed across his face followed by fear and concern. He wrapped his arm around me. I could see from my own mental images what was going through his mind; how Malik lured Isaac by capturing Lucas to give up his life and powers to save him.

"I knew I was missing something. I didn't put the pieces together until I read Sky and Kendall again," Graham said.

"It's so simple, we should have all known," Aunt Marie added, wrapping her arm around me as well.

We were all quiet for a few moments as the revelation sank in. It was terrible news; however, now that we know what to expect, we could do something about it.

"I think we should pay a visit to the Coopers now," I said. I was ready to end this. I am tired of living in fear, waiting for Malik to strike at any moment.

"With what you two have just brought to our attention, 'we' are not going anywhere," Lucas replied.

I stood up, "But, the incantation. Malik has to be stopped!"

I was annoyed that he was trying to keep me away from the one thing I needed to get to stop all of this. True, Malik was lying in wait; nevertheless, I still felt like I needed to do something.

"And he will, though right now I think we need to lay low until we figure out a plan."

I started to argue some more, but I was cut off by Matt.

"Kendall, I agree with Lucas."

"As do I," Graham added.

Aunt Marie and Sara nodded in agreement as well.

I was out numbered, "But…" I looked at all of their faces; each one wore the same expression of agreement. I could tell that I had lost this argument. "Fine!" I sat back in my chair and crossed my arms.

"I think we should leave this afternoon instead of tonight," Graham suggested.

"I agree," Aunt Marie said. "Sara and I can stay here with Kendall and Lucas just in case."

"I'll stay behind too," Sky added. "I may not be a Natural, but I do know how to use a shot gun."

Aunt Marie nodded and looked around the table, "The rest can go?"

Everyone agreed.

Plans were made and right after lunch, they left for North Rock Springs. Having two people to confront, they didn't know how long or how many people it would take should a fight occur. Of course, I was upset that I couldn't help; however, the feeling of worry overshadowed my distress. I hoped it would go as smoothly as they had planned.

I didn't like this. I hated this feeling of anticipation. Hours go by with no word from them at all. I was really starting to worry. I couldn't help but think the worst. When I voiced my fear, Sky tensed up. I could tell she was worried too. Xavier was there with no power only a gun. It wouldn't kill a Natural only slow them down. I didn't voice my concerns again. We sat in the living room waiting. Someone would get up and start pacing; not doing any good, they would sit back down. Sky turned on the television at an attempt to try to lighten the atmosphere, although it was no use.

I lay on the couch, closed my eyes, and propped my feet up on the armrest, trying to ease my stomach. My feelings of worry and fear kept getting worse by the minute. I couldn't take it any longer.

"I'm going to the bathroom," I looked at Lucas longer than necessary, trying to communicate with him. I didn't want to worry the others just yet.

Luckily, he caught on, "I'll go with you."
Lucas followed me out of the room and in to the bathroom, shutting the door behind him.

"What's wrong?" he asked, his eyes searching my face for the answer.

I shook my head, "I don't know. Something…is not right." I took a deep breath, "Lucas, what do we do?"

"I'm going to call them. We should have heard from them by now."
We stepped out of the bathroom and nearly ran into Sky. She was wide-eyed and pale.

"What's wrong?" Lucas asked.

"They ran into trouble. Xavier is hurt."

Lucas and I walked her back to the living room and on to the couch.

"It's going to be alright," Lucas tried to sooth her.

Approximately thirty minutes later, cutting through the darkness, a pair of headlights traveled down the long driveway. We knew that the guys were on their way back; however, we were still cautious. We didn't want to assume anything. Aunt Marie met them at the door. Matt and Graham were holding up Xavier. All of their shirts had bloodstains on them. Sky rushed to Xavier and the three of them helped him on the couch. Xavier looked badly wounded. Aunt Marie opened his shirt to reveal a bullet hole in the center of his chest. Each time he would cough, his blood would leak from the wound. She immediately placed her hands over the wound and closed her eyes. Within a few moments, Xavier settled down and opened his eyes. Aunt Marie put the bullet in a bowl someone had brought in. Xavier still looked weak and he still wore the blood; however, he swung his feet off the couch onto the floor and sat up, putting his head in his hands. Aunt Marie left for the kitchen. Sky took her place on the couch putting her arms around Xavier. Her face was still pale as she lightly sobbed.

"What happened?" Lucas looked between Matt and Graham.

"They knew we were coming, we were ambushed," Matt replied.

"There were a dozen at least, but the Coopers were nowhere to be seen. We barely made it out."

Everyone glanced at Xavier.

"I do have some news though. Whether it's good or bad, I'm not sure." Graham looked at me as he spoke, his face sullen, "I read a few of the men during the battle. Malik has the other half of the incantation. The Coopers gave it to him as soon as it was in their possession. They are with him."

What are we going to do now? How are we going to get it

when it is in Maliks hands? My stomach tightened at the thought.

"There was a very good chance that they might have taken you tonight," Graham added.

The five of them wore an expression of concern and fear. I looked at Lucas. I wasn't annoyed anymore that I didn't go with them, I was thankful, not only for my own sake, but for his too.

"Did anyone follow you?" Lucas looked out the window.

Matt shook his head, "No."

"The perimeter is still secure," Sara added.

"Somehow they knew we were coming; however, they didn't know that the two of you weren't," Matt expresses.

"What do you think Graham?" I was curious to see what his opinion was.

"Honestly, I don't know. I didn't read that from them. Maybe they didn't know. If I had to guess, I would say Marvin tipped them off."

They told us the details of the ambush and how Xavier was shot, and then we spent the next few hours trying to figure out a plan to stop Malik. Without coming up with anything logical, we went to bed hoping that maybe the morning light would bring clearer thoughts. Not only has it been a long night, we still had a long drive home tomorrow.

The next morning I was still plagued with thoughts of Malik and how close it had gotten with Xavier. I couldn't help but feel defeated in some ways. Like all of our hard work, trying to find the other half of the incantation, was for nothing. The guys did the morning chores while the girls relaxed and made plans for a visit from Sky and Xavier to Oak Creek in the near future. We left for home right after lunch, taking precaution to ensure that we weren't being followed. I could tell Lucas didn't want to leave. He tried to hide it; however, I could easily see how much he missed his home.

I woke up as we pulled into our driveway just after eight. Aunt Marie and Sara made dinner plans tonight at our house; however, Sara and Matt needed to go home first. Graham rode with us just in case anything should happen. My back was stiff from leaning on Lucas for the past two hours as I slept; it felt good to get out and stretch. With bags in hand, Lucas and I followed Aunt Marie up the walk to the porch.

Lucas stopped suddenly, dropping the bags to the ground and pulled me closer to him. I could tell that there was something wrong. I looked around; however, I couldn't see anything, just the night around us. Then, a figure stepped out from behind the bushes, the same bushes that someone was hiding in months ago. Without hesitation, Lucas threw his hand out. We heard a thud, the figure no longer standing. Lucas and Graham rushed over, picked up the person by the arms, and dragged him closer. In the light, I could see it was a man probably in his thirty's. He didn't struggle he just let them pull him to the porch light.

"I'm not here to harm anyone. I came to see Marie," he said.

Aunt Marie stepped into his line of view, "Drew?" Uncertainty rang in her voice, "Drew Evens?"

I could see him smile, "Yes, it's me."

Graham studied Drew for a moment longer and then let go of his arm, "He's telling the truth. He's not going to hurt anyone."

Lucas looked at me before letting go of the other arm. Aunt Marie gestured for the man named Drew, to come inside the house. The rest of us followed them in. Now that we were in better light, I could see Drew better; he's on the handsome side, strong features, green eyes, and sandy colored hair.

"What are you doing here?" she asked in a curious tone.

"I'm just passing through, I heard you were living here, so I thought I would come see how you were doing," he answered. He looked at Lucas, rubbing the back of his head, "You are good, you must be a Protector."

Lucas nodded without saying a word. He was still in Protector mode.

"Who is your Natural?"

Lucas tightened his arm around me.

"Ah I see," he eyed me suspiciously. "I see a resemblance, is she yours?" Drew asked Aunt Marie.

"No. Where did you say you were heading?"

It seemed like she was trying to change the subject.

"East; I need a change of scenery."

Aunt Marie introduced us as Lucas, Kendall, and Graham, not disclosing that I was her niece. I found it to be very strange. Graham hasn't taken his eyes of Drew since he arrived except when Lucas would look at him. If I had to guess, he was continuously reading Drew.

Aunt Marie asked Drew if he wanted to stay for dinner and if he needed a place to stay. Lucas gave her a disapproving look; however, she ignored him. After comparing Aunt Marie's hopeful expression to Lucas's disapproving one, Drew wound up declining both invitations. Aunt Marie knew that Drew based his decision on Lucas's uninviting glare and looked at Lucas firmly.

After checking Graham's expression to see what he thought, Lucas sighed, "Fine."

Even though this was Aunt Marie's house and I was her niece, Lucas pretty much had control over my safety.

Nineteen
Truth

The tension had eased some. The guys sat around the kitchen table while Aunt Marie and I begun to prepare dinner. Drew was asking random questions about Aunt Marie's life. I thought I saw a yearning expression sometimes as they talked. It made me wonder just how well they did know each other.

"So, how is your sister?" he asked.

Aunt Marie looked at me; her eyes were full of the panic that she was trying to hide in her expression. I looked away and concentrated on my work.

"Oh, I see," he cleared his throat and changed the subject. "I felt the change. It was strong; I think the True Natural must be close."

I looked up at Lucas as Drew spoke. Lucas watched him intently.

"Where do you think it came from?" Drew asked.

Unwillingly, everyone's eyes, except for Drew's, turned to me. It only took a moment for Drew to realize that I was the True Natural.

"Oh!" Drew's eyes widened slightly and were full of questions.

Lucas stood up quickly, knocking the chair over backwards to the floor, his eyes narrowing. Graham stood up with him and put his hand on Lucas's shoulder.

"Easy," Graham warned.

"I think you should leave," Lucas said through his teeth.
Aunt Marie turned the burner off and rushed to the table.

"Just hold on a minute," she said. "Graham, is he going to hurt anyone?"

Graham looked at Drew, reading him; his gaze lingered only for a few moments, and then he turned it to Lucas. Lucas sighed heavily, picked up his chair, and then sat back down.

"Not that I can tell. He's more curious than anything."

I heard the front door opened and closed; Matt and Sara had arrived, maybe the tension would ease up some. After taking off their coat, they entered into the kitchen smiling; it faded once they saw that we had company. Drew looked confused; He looked from Aunt Marie, to me, then to Matt and Sara.

"Well isn't this a surprise," he looked back at Aunt Marie. "The way you two were acting I thought your sister was dead."

I immediately froze at his words, the knife in mid cut. I looked up in confusion. What was he saying? At first, I couldn't grasp the expression everyone was wearing. Images and memories began to flash through my mind and slowly the pieces started to come together. I felt the blood draining from my face. I opened my mouth in shock as I realized the meaning of his words. I looked from Matt to Sara; I now understood that it was shame and guilt that they wore on their faces. My chest felt heavy as I tried to breathe. With every breath drawn, it felt as if it were get tighter and tighter.

I shook my head in disbelief, "No."

This can't be. They can't be my, my...parents. Their motionless expression told me otherwise.

"Kendall," Sara said as she took a step towards me.

Anger quickly replaced my shock and confusion. I hastily stepped back, jaw clenched. I shifted my gaze away from them to Aunt Marie saving Lucas for last.

"Did you have anything to do with this?" I asked him in a low angry tone.

He stared at me with saddened, guilty eyes. Feeling betrayed and humiliated, I left the room without another word.

"Kendall, wait!" Lucas called after me.

"Leave. Me. Alone!" Each word roared with as much volume as I could muster.

I was angry with everyone; however, I never thought that Lucas, my Protector, would lie to me. I made it up the stairs and in to my room before I heard anyone follow me. I felt so betrayed. How could they do this, lie to me for all these years? I slammed my door shut with a wave of my hand and threw myself face down into my pillow. The tears flowed uncontrollably.

I stayed in my room away from everyone for the night. The last conversation was with Aunt Marie with a feeble attempt to calm me down and get me to come downstairs. My side of the conversation was to tell her to go away. After that, I would hear someone come up the stairs every now and then; probably checking on me to make sure I was still in my room.

I woke with my shoes and light off, which neither I had done myself. I had no recollection of falling asleep. The pain in my chest was still there like an undercurrent, as though it was dragging me under water and I was unable to swim to the surface. I rolled off my stomach and sat up. My back ached from the way I had slept. I rubbed my swollen eyes and read the clock, twelve twenty four. I grabbed my stomach as it rumbled; it was empty. I hadn't eaten anything since lunch in Wyoming. I climbed out of bed and opened my half-opened door, which I'm sure Lucas had done. I almost expected to see him sleeping on the floor outside my door. Even more, I expected to see someone up; however, I was alone downstairs. After eating leftovers straight from the fridge, I went back to bed and cried myself to sleep.

Not wanting to face the miserable day ahead of me, I forced my eyes open and got out of bed. I was still upset this morning and it showed. The mirror reflected that I look terrible; my blue eyes were circled and red from crying for…who knows how long last night.

As I got ready for school, I thought about Matt and Sara; even in my thoughts, I wasn't ready to say who they really were. I have always wondered what my parents would be like; I guess I already knew. The truth is I think I have known since that first day I met Matt. I thought about how familiar his eyes were, how he had immediately come across as a father figure to me. I thought about Sara and how her features were so familiar; I should have seen it then how much Aunt Marie and Sara resemble each other. I never dreamed that they were still alive to put it together. My stomach groaned in that uncomfortable pain, the kind you get when you are about to be sick. Knowing I wasn't going to eat anything, I brushed my teeth and hair, and went downstairs to get something to drink hoping that would help.

Just like every other morning, Aunt Marie was already up and ready for work. She was drinking her coffee at the kitchen table. She set the paper down as I walked in.

"Hi," Aunt Marie sounded remorseful.

I didn't respond to her, I was still angry.

"Kendall we need to talk."

I continued to ignore her while I got the carton of juice from the refrigerator and poured myself a glass.

"I know you are upset and hurt, but if you would just let us explain_"

"I don't want to hear it right now," I said.

I guzzled my juice and headed for the living room to wait for Lucas. I thought about sneaking out and driving myself to school; however, before I could make a decision I saw him sitting on the couch waiting for me.

"Good morning," he said in the same tone as Aunt Marie.

"What's so good about it?"

He sighed, "Kendall I_"

"Can we just go?" I cut him off and headed for the closet to get my coat.

When he parked the truck, I opened my door and got out. Before he cut the engine off, I was already walking across the parking lot; he had to run to catch up. Sam was in our usual meeting spot. She looked back and forth from me to Lucas and immediately knew that something was wrong.

"Are you okay?" she asked.

I clenched my teeth, "Let's just get to class."

The morning seemed to drag on. My pain and anger was getting worse by the minute. I told Sam that my parents were still alive, who they were, and how everyone had lied to me my entire life. She was shocked, and of course took my side. She asked how I felt about it. I told her I didn't know yet; this is one hundred percent the truth. I have been thinking about that since the night before. I had mixed emotions. I was angry from being lied to, I felt betrayed of the secrets, happy because my parents were alive, sad because they've missed so much of my life, and now nervous to see them again.

At lunch, Lucas tried talking to me; however, I was still too angry with him to participate in the conversation he was trying to start. Actually, it was more like reasoning and apologies. We were on our way home when he tried again.

"Will you please just let me explain?"

"Why, so you can lie to me some more? No thanks."

"I never lied to you Kendall."

"Really? Then what would you call it?"

He didn't have an answer. He sighed and continued to drive in silence. He pulled up in front of my house before I spoke.

"I just can't believe you didn't tell me. We shouldn't have

secrets. How can you protect me if there are secrets like this?" I asked.

That struck a nerve. The muscles in his jaw tightened and he looked at me with eyes slightly narrowed, "That has nothing to do with nor has gotten in the way of me protecting you."

I glared right back at him, "Fine, I just can't stand being lied to. I didn't think you of all people would."

His expression softened a little, mine remained hard with anger. I could feel the stinging in my eyes as they welled up with tears. I had to get my next words out before my tears spilt.

"I don't think I can be with someone who lies to me."

Without waiting for a response, I got out and went inside.

Days had gone by; the only real change was that Drew was gone; however, I suspected that when things settled down he would be back. I also suspected that there was something there between Aunt Marie and Drew.

I spent the afternoons in my room until dinner; however, as soon as I was done eating and dishes were done, I was back upstairs. Several times during those days, Lucas and Aunt Marie had teamed up and tried to reason with me; however, I wasn't ready to talk, I was still much too angry.

Since Lucas and I had broken up Graham has driven me to school. Lucas of course, was right behind me in his truck. Normally he would not agree to the separation; however, given the circumstance, he went along with it; for now, as he put it. He put up a brave front; however, behind his eyes, I could tell I had hurt him when I broke up with him. We agreed that some space was needed to let me think things through for a while. Space is what I got; however, Lucas was always near, in the shadow protecting me.

The only one I could talk to beside Sam, without getting angry, was Graham. I had asked him Monday why I never felt this was coming. He confirmed what I already knew; that I knew all along that I just needed to put it together. Graham also told me that he didn't believe in coincidences, that things happen for a reason and it will get better. At this point, I am not certain that things will ever get better; however, I didn't say that to him.

By Thursday, I was getting tired of looking at the four walls of my room. My chest remained heavy with heartache and I was still upset; however, I decided to take my homework to the living room. Once I got downstairs, I realized that we had company, Matt, Sara, and Graham. These days I never knew what was going on downstairs. Every head turned as I walked into the room, their faces shown no trace of shock or surprise. Not speaking to anyone and feeling like a display item, I lay down on the floor and opened my books.

Dinner was just as awkward. I was nervous, this was the first time I had seen Matt and Sara since I had found out that they were my parents. Like Lucas, they were giving me some space to let the information sink it; they appeared just as nervous as I did. It was a very quiet evening. Through out dinner the only noise there was, was that of forks scrapping across plates; every once in awhile someone's eyes would flash to me. I felt like I was a bomb that they had to tip toe around for fear that I would detonate at any time. I sighed and put my fork down; I couldn't take it any longer.

"Okay fine. I am still really angry with most of you, but I am ready to listen to what you have to say."

I saw Aunt Marie and Sara smile a little while flashing their eyes to Graham. I now understood the gathering; he was the reason why everyone was here. He must be exceptionally well at reading people to know that I was giving in soon, pinpointing it to tonight. I shouldn't have been surprised. Sara started.

"We didn't want you to find out like this," her voice was low as she spoke.

"Why didn't you tell me?" I didn't ask angrily, only pointedly.

"We asked Marie and Lucas not to say anything. We wanted to tell you ourselves," Matt replied.

"We have been waiting for the right time, but it just seemed to never show up," Sara added. She looked into my eyes, "I am so sorry."

I sighed and looked down at my hands, picking at my nails.

"So I guess you have a few questions for us?" Sara asked after a few moments of awkward silence.

Questions? I have been so consumed with anger that I haven't even thought about what to say or ask them. I quickly thought of a couple questions before the silence made the situation too awkward again.

"You really are my mother," I looked from Sara to Matt, "and father?"

An obvious question, yet I felt as though I needed confirmation for it to seem real.

"Yes." they both answered.

I took a deep breath. It was actually easier to hear than I thought it would be. The answer to my next question probably wouldn't.

"Why did you give me away?"

Sara sighed. I could see pain and sadness in her eyes as she spoke, "Isaac had been gone for a couple of months when I found out I was pregnant with you. We didn't think then that you were next in line to be the True Natural, yet we couldn't take any chances." She looked at Matt for him to continue with the story.

"It was rumored that Malik was looking for the next True Natural to raise as his own and do his bidding until there was no more use for him or her."

"Why did you think it was me? What if someone else was

pregnant?" I asked confused.

"That's where I come in to the story," Lucas answered. "I sought them out a few months after Isaac's death. After doing research, I found only one Natural pregnant. Sara." He reached for my hand; however, pulled it away when he saw my disapproving glance.

I was beginning to understand; however, understanding didn't rid me of the anger I had.

"Lucas and Matt protected us both until we were certain. We knew what you were as soon as you were born. Well, Lucas knew and I could just feel it."

"We were very proud, yet also very scared," Matt said. "Malik figured out who the next True Natural might be."

"We couldn't let anything happen to you. We thought separating might be safest for you, but I couldn't bear the thought of leaving you for one minute, let alone until you came into your powers," Sara paused for a moment and sighed. "However, eight months and several attacks later, we decided it was the only option," she paused again fidgeting with her hands. "We picked a small town far from where we were living at the time to meet up when we felt it was safe again. When the coast was clear we secretly handed you to Marie." She wasn't looking at me anymore as she spoke. She was looking down, staring at nothing, "You just looked at me with those big blue eyes, smiling, not knowing that it was the last time we would see each other for a very long time. I kissed you one last time on the cheek, before I put a hidden spell on the two of you and then you vanished into the night."

Matt put his arm around her as she wiped the tears from her eyes. I felt my own tears overflow and stream down my cheeks. I couldn't help but to feel sad for her. I could see how much it hurt her to let me go. Matt continued to hold her with eyes unfocused like hers, probably replaying the moment.

Sara finally took a deep breath and continued, "Oak Creek

was the small town we had picked." She waved her hand out and around her.

"Why hasn't Malik tried to find me before now? I mean if he knew who I was then I should have seen him before."

"Well, after we gave you to Marie we told everyone that you had died," Matt replied.

"I didn't have to pretend to grieve, that was what it felt like for me," Sara added. I could see the hurt deepen in her eyes.

"About a year later we contacted Marie," Matt continued.

"How?" I asked

"After we were settled, I called them from a payphone in a different city with our phone number and P.O. box," Aunt Marie replied.

"We sent money each month and gifts sometimes," Sara added.

Something clicked with what she had said, "Secret stash."

I didn't ask it; however, Aunt Marie had answered anyway, "Yes."

I looked up to see a smile playing on the corners of her mouth.

"Lucas bought the house we are living in now about a year ago, we moved in with him to help get things in order," Matt continued. "We started watching out for you even more than before as summer was coming to an end."

"Even more?" I asked.

"I was never too far away for any length of time," Lucas answered. "I have always protected you."

I could see the emotion flooding in his eyes. I had to look away. I hated to see the sadness there; however, anger and emotional turmoil prevented me from doing anything about it right now. This was so hard; I was still confused, hurt, and angry, although now that I had heard the story, I understood that all of them were only protecting me.

It was getting late and I had school the next day. After

saying goodnight to everyone and promising that we would talk more, I went to my room. Sleep came a lot easier than the previous night; however, I still tossed and turned as I rethought the story of my life.

The next day I felt better. The weight of my chest had lightened. I descended the stairs to meet Graham for a ride to school; however, he wasn't there. Instead, Lucas was waiting for me.
"Where is Graham?" I asked stiffly.
Even though I understood the situation better, I was still upset with him.
"He and Matt left early this morning to check the towns south of here. I am taking you to school today," he answered.
I started to get nervous, ignoring the fact that the ride would be awkward, "What happened?"
"Nothing; Matt just wants to make sure Malik or anyone else is not anywhere near here."
Good, I don't think I could handle Malik at the moment.
"I'm just going to grab breakfast to go and I'll be ready."
With my uncooked pop tart in hand, I followed Lucas out to the already running truck.
It was sunny, yet cold. The prior snow had melted; however, more was expected soon. We were supposed to get three to six inches at some point this evening. I noticed that Lucas kept watching me from the corner of his eye. I knew that he wanted to talk; however, I wasn't ready yet.
We were two of the last few people to arrive for school. He parked the truck in one of the only few spaces left in the back of the school parking lot. All of the closer ones had already been taken.
"About last night," he started to say, but I cut him off.
"I don't want to talk about it right now. I just want to go to school."
He sighed and shut the truck engine off. Sam pulled in and

parked a few spots down from us. I could hear her footsteps as she ran to catch up with us. She noticed the distress on my face and walked quietly beside me. She had been a good friend through out this mess and it made me respect her even more.

I couldn't concentrate in any of my classes, all I could think about was Matt and Sara and the conversation we had last night. I was very happy that my parents were alive; however, I was still angry and emotional that they didn't tell me who they were after we met. I couldn't get the pain and suffering I saw in Sara's eyes out of my mind.
"Kendall…Kendall?" Mrs. Blake called to me bringing me back from my inner thoughts.
I heard giggles coming from around the room. Mrs. Blake had her arms folded and was looking straight at me, with a not-so-happy look on her face.
"I'm sorry, what?"
Before she had time to answer me, the bell rang. I took a deep breath and let it out in relief. To be in trouble with a teacher is not what I needed right now.
"Five hundred word essay due on Monday; Title it Citizenship Civic Values and make it about the role played by the United States in securing peace," Mrs. Blake reminded us as we gathered our things.
"Wow five hundred words! At least we have two days to get it done," Sam commented.
"Yeah, but we have that English paper due too," I added.
"And the Spanish letter from Mr. Pierce. Homework is going to take all weekend," Sam used her whiny voice.
That was good in my opinion. I needed something to keep my mind busy.
I walked with Sam to her locker while she grabbed her book bag, "Are you coming over tonight?"
We didn't get a chance to talk today and I really needed to

have some one-on-one girl time.

"Yes, but I have to go home first, then I can come over and you can tell me what's on your mind," she smiled weakly.

I couldn't help but smile back. No matter how bad I was feeling my best friend could always make me feel better.

The sun was hidden behind clouds and snow had begun to fall. The storm had come in sometime after lunch. It looked like it could be worse than what was predicted. I pulled my winter hat down farther as I walked with Lucas to the truck. It was already covered with a thin layer of snow.

Just like this morning, the ride home was awkward with silence and distance between Lucas and I; and, just like this morning, he kept glancing at me from the corner of his eye. I knew he was going to try to talk to me again about last night. Sure enough as we turned onto my street, he started the conversation.

"Kendall, we should talk about last night."

"I don't want to talk right now."

That wasn't true; however, I didn't want to talk to him while I was upset. Lucas pulled up to the curb. I got out before he had a chance to say anything more and quickly walked towards the house. He had the ignition turned off and had caught up with me before I had the door unlocked.

"I want to explain_"

"I said I don't want to talk about it right now!" I raised my voice to a near shout.

I unzipped my coat and opened the closet door.

"Why won't you talk to me?" he raised his voice to match mine.

I turned to face him; his expression was a mixture of sadness and anger.

"Because I am still angry!" I shouted.

"Why is it you can forgive Matt and Sara, but you can't forgive me?"

"I haven't forgiven anyone for lying to me!" I zipped my

coat back up and stomped my way passed Lucas out into the snowstorm.

I didn't plan to walk far; I just needed some air and space to clear my head, so I was shocked when I looked up. All I could see was a white curtain all around me. It was snowing so hard I couldn't tell how far I had walked. I sighed heavily. I wasn't ready to go back; however, I decided it was probably the smartest thing to do. I heard a sound to my right, like snow crunching under the weight of feet. I looked around at an attempt to find the source; however, I was blinded from the snow and wind. Panic began to set in as I turned around and headed back in the direction I had come from. I know I'm not too far from home.

The snow-crunching noise moved along with me and now it was on both sides of me. I didn't dare use my magic blindly. Panic completely took over and I started to run. I hadn't gotten very far, a few yards maybe when I slam into him. Hands grab both of my arms; however, I didn't look to see who grabbed them. The familiar face and the wicked grin the man in front of me was wearing preoccupied me. My heart started racing as he placed his hand on my forehead. I managed to let out a high-pitched scream just before everything went dark.

Twenty
Betrayed

Cold and shivering, I opened my eyes to complete darkness. I couldn't see; however, my other senses kicked in. It smelled musty and I could hear footsteps above me, nothing else. I lay on something hard and cold that felt like concrete. I couldn't remember how I had gotten here. I tried to think; however, it just made the throbbing in my head worse. My hands were tied behind me. I struggled, yet I managed to roll on my back and sit up. Dizziness and nausea instantly hit me. I closed my eyes and took a few deep breaths to ease my queasiness. When they subsided enough I reopened my eyes. It was too dark to see my surroundings. I could hear more than one set of footsteps along with voices that appear to be arguing; however, I couldn't make out what they were saying.

Time escaped me; I don't know how long I had sat there on the cold concrete floor when I saw a crack of light. It shone in the darkness ahead of me. The high position of the light confused me. The room brightened as the crack got bigger. I saw a shadow and heard footsteps coming from it. As the sound got closer, I realized it was someone descending a flight of stairs. From the light, I could see dusty old boxes and other clutter lying around; I realized then that I was in a basement.

"You're awake," said a familiar scruffy voice. I couldn't place where I had heard it from though.

I could see the silhouette of a person at the bottom of the stairs. Without speaking further, he walked over and helped me up off the cold floor by my arm. He led me sideways up the stairs, keeping my hands away from him. By his actions, I knew that he knew who I was and what I could do.

I had to blink a few times to clear the blurred vision for my eyes to adjust to the blinding light. We were standing in an old-styled out of date kitchen. The wallpaper was peeled halfway off some of the walls. Bare wire from the light fixture dangled over my head. The floor in the kitchen was torn and littered with outdoor debris; I knew where we were, the old Emerson house. Sam and I use to play here as kids, until it was condemned a few years ago. It has been empty for almost fifteen years, ever since Mr. and Mrs. Emerson died.

I was led to the next room that held a moth-eaten sofa and a fireplace that was blazing with a recently lit fire. It warmed the outer layer of my skin. It felt good after being down in the freezing cold basement. With my hands still tied behind my back, he led me to the sofa and pushed me down. There was no other light than from the fire in this room; however, it was enough to see the man's face who had gotten me from the basement. The instant I saw his face, the memories flashed in my head; the fight with Lucas, the curtain of white, the crunching sounds in the snow, the wicked grin, and finally the darkness.

"Mr. Pierce?"

"Yes Kendall, it is me," he said. He stared at me with the same grin as before. "You like my little snow storm? Of course I had to wait until it snowed and luckily for me a storm showed up."

I only felt confusion as he continued to look at me.

"What do you want?" I asked, feeling nervous and panicky.

"It's simple, you. You see, my job was to keep an eye on you, to monitor your every move, to wait for that perfect moment."

My heart was still racing, I knew what he was about to say.

"Malik will be very pleased that I have you."

I was prepared for this part when I woke up in the basement; however, it still hit me like a ton of bricks.

"He's on his way you know," he was nonchalant as he spoke. I was frightened.

He put some more wood on the fire; it stirred sending embers into the air above it, "It is too bad about your old Spanish teacher though. I'm sure she will be missed."

Shock ran though my body as I realized what he was implying.

"You killed her?" I shouted at him.

"I did what had to be done to get you inconspicuously," his grin was gone and his expression turned serious and mean.

"You won't get away with this. Lucas is looking for me."

As I said these words, I felt this deep connection with Lucas and I knew that what I was saying was true.

"That may be true; however, he doesn't know where you are and I made damn sure I stayed away from Graham."

He saw the surprised look on my face.

"Yes I know Graham, at least know of him. I listened to your conversations all these months."

Two men came in from outside and in to the room. They looked nothing like Mr. Pierce; these men were scraggily and dirty.

"Malik will be here in an hour." One of them reported.

"What do we do with her?" The other one asked jabbing his thumb in the air in my direction. "Kill her?"

A chill crawled up my spine driven by his words.

"No you idiot! Malik wants her alive."

All three of them looked at me. Their gazes were filled with hunger, a hunger for power. My instincts were trying to take over. I could feel the warmth spread through me; however, with my hands tied behind my back there was nothing I could do. I took a few deep breaths to calm down and tried to work my hands free.

I listened to the men's petty argument about who's turn it was to get more firewood when the door slammed open and then closed with the same force. I heard the sounds of heavy footsteps echo off the wooden floor. The three men stood as a figure of a man stood in the doorway between the foyer and the room I was kept. I could see smiles spreading on each of their faces and I knew that Malik had just arrived. I couldn't see him very well until he stepped into the light of the fire. His appearance startled me, although it shouldn't have. I wasn't expecting him to be so young. All this time I imagined an older creepy guy from one of those thrasher movies; however, of course, he would be young, using his powers all these years he wouldn't age. He looked strong and fit and I noticed there was a triumphed smile on his strong featured handsome face. His hair was chin length and dark, as well as his eyes, not the pleasing dark of Lucas's eyes, but something more sinister. He wore jeans and I could see a dark shirt under his open coat.

"Kendall, it's so nice to finally meet you," his voice was smooth and excited.

I glared at him and didn't respond as he stared at me.

"Very good Andrew," Malik complimented Mr. Pierce. He turned and faced the other the two men, "One of you go get some more firewood." He looked at me and smiled, "These things take time."

The man who spoke first earlier, went out the door.

"So," Malik said as he paced around the room. "You have reached full maturity with your powers." He didn't look up as he paced. "I also hear that you are what we expected you to be, very powerful, which is one of the reasons why you are tied up." He smiled deviously, "We wouldn't want you to do anything stupid now would we?"

Uh oh, did he know what I was doing? When I didn't respond to him, he stopped right in front of me. He put his hand under my chin to force me to look at him.

"Just as stubborn as I suspected too." After a moment, he let go of my face and continued pacing.

As I struggled to free my hands, I felt a sudden jolt of relief. I sensed that Lucas was near. I forced myself to hide my smile. I wondered what was taking the man who had gone after the firewood so long. I wasn't the only one who noticed that something was off.

"What is taking Ren so long? He only had to go around back," the other man asked whose name I didn't know.

"You two go check."

"What about her?" Mr. Pierce asked.

"I think I can handle her just fine without you. Now go!" Malik commanded.

The two men obeyed him; they walked out of the room and then through the front door leaving Malik and I alone. Before Malik turned back to me, I wriggled one of my hands free, but kept it hidden behind me.

"Now, there are two ways that this could be worked out," there was a smile on his face. "The first is for your benefit as well as mine; you can join me and work alongside me. Together we could be great."

His smile and voice was alluring. If I was a stranger as to who he was, hadn't know what he has done and was willing to do, I could have easily fallen for his charm.

"And the second?" I asked.

His alluring smile turned devious, "Well, that doesn't go very well for you."

He stopped pacing and stood in front of me again, waiting for me to answer. I couldn't help but think about what would happen if he killed me and took my powers. Would he go and leave my family unharmed? Or, would he kill everyone that I loved? Just before I was able to answer him the front door slammed open; I knew immediately that it was Lucas. Malik turned his back to me at the sound of the slamming door; that's when I took my chance. I jumped up from the couch and threw my hands out.

"How about neither!" I shouted as he flew forward towards the fireplace and into the bricks.

I ran as fast as I could into the foyer where Lucas was and into his arms. I had never been happier to see him in all the months I had known him. He squeezed me tight for just a moment before letting go of me and taking my hand, leading me out the door. I knew it wouldn't be long before Malik would follow. We had made it off the porch and halfway across the yard towards the woods, when I felt like someone had pushed me forward. Lucas and I both lost our balance and fell to the ground.

"I'll hold them off; you get away from here as fast as you can," Lucas said as he stood up.

I quickly rose to my feet and saw that Malik and Mr. Pierce were already heading in our direction; they looked angry. I used all of my strength and threw a wave of magic towards them; however, they didn't fall. Instead, Malik blocked my magic with his and then he sent another wave of force towards me. It hit me hard enough to knock me into the air. I landed about ten feet backwards from where I stood. I landed with a thud, hitting my head hard on the ground. My body ached and my head spun; however, I stood back up quickly ready to fight.

"I underestimated you, but it will never happen again."

I backed up towards the woods as Malik slowly closed in on me; they were still too far away for cover. I glanced to Lucas and Mr. Pierce fighting. Lucas was better than Mr. Pierce was which meant that Lucas was winning. Malik followed my line of view and quickly changed direction from me to the two men fighting. I played the command of Lucas telling me to run in my head; however, I couldn't leave him here with two against one. Lucas was losing now that someone as powerful as Malik was fighting against him. I ran forward throwing a wave of magic towards them when all of a sudden pain overcomes me. My hair was tangled into something and I couldn't go any further. I turned myself just far enough to realize that it was a hand that my hair was tangled into; it was the man who had left with Mr. Pierce. He yanked me back making me slam into him. I struggled and elbowed him in the stomach in an attempt to get away; however, his grip was too tight. He quickly recovered the blow and pulled my arms behind my back. He edged me forward to the fight before me. The fight instantly stopped. I could see the horror on Lucas's face when he looked at me. Mr. Pierce grabbed Lucas while he was distracted, yanking his arms behind his back and trudged him forward. Lucas had cuts on his face and he was bleeding from his lips and nose. Mr. Pierce looked just as bad. A pleased look spread across Malik's face as he analyzed the situation.

"Well, well, well, looks like I have won," he said slowly. "So now," he looked back at me. "The choice is up to you. Do you join me or do you die?"

I wasn't doing either of those; somehow, we would get out of this. I glared at him without answering.

"Hmm, no answer; I am very disappointed."

He turned from me to Lucas. I saw Malik straighten his arm out in front of him just before I heard Lucas's yell. My eyes widened with horror and I struggled to break free as Lucas was being tortured. It lasted only a few moments; however, it seemed to go on forever.

"Stop! Please stop!" I cried out.

I couldn't stand this. I tried to break free from the strong hold the man had on me. All I managed to do was hurt my arms even more. I stopped struggling when Lucas was quiet. Malik changed his pleased expression to an annoyed angry one.

"I will only ask you one more time," his voice was filled with menace.

"Kendall, no!" Lucas shouted.

Mr. Pierce kicked the side of Lucas's knee so hard that I could hear the crack over his scream. There was no doubt in my mind that it was broken. Lucas fell towards the ground; however, before he landed, Mr. Pierce stood him back up.

"Please stop!" I begged.

"Your answer."

I couldn't take this. I couldn't let Lucas be tortured any longer. I stared into Lucas's eyes as I made my decision. I would never give Malik what he desired most, I would not be responsible for so many innocent deaths. What I was about to do would hurt Lucas tremendously; however, he would survive. His eyes were filled with hurt and tears, he knew what I was about to do. I tore my eyes away from his and locked them on Malik.

"If, I give you what you want, will you let Lucas go?"

"No Kendall!" I heard Lucas say, yet my eyes remained on Malik.

Malik didn't even think about it before he answered. A slow wicked smiled spread across his face, "Yes, I have done it before."

I exhaled with relief that Lucas would be saved. Even though I had never told him, I loved Lucas with all of my heart and soul; nevertheless, if I had to join Malik or die to save him, then that was *exactly* what I was going to do. I looked at Lucas to see his face once more. I didn't want to say goodbye, but I wasn't going to let him die when I could save him by joining Malik. Lucas's eyes were angry and sad at the same time; looking at them hurt every ounce of me.

"Please don't do this!" Lucas shouted.

"There is no other way," I simply said. Then I tuned my attention back to Malik. I lifted my head and squared my shoulders, he would not see me weak, "I will join you, *if* I have your word that you will let Lucas go." I glared at Malik as I awaited his answer.

"I give you my word that I will let go," his wicked smile returned, "of his life!" Malik turned around to Mr. Pierce and Lucas. "Andrew now!" he commanded.

Mr. Pierce put his hand on Lucas's chest. Lucas's eyes never moved from mine, they said a million words as the light that I loved so much dimmed and then went out.

"Lucas!" I screamed as he fell to the ground.

Emotions ran through me as I saw him lying on the ground. My body was on fire, a heat that I have never felt before. The wind started to blow all around me and the earth shook so hard that everyone fell to the ground except Malik; he stood smiling happily, which fueled my anger perfectly. I threw both of my hands out towards him and released my powers with such force that I knocked him to the ground as well. The smile was gone when he stood back up. He sent his own powers towards me; however, I pushed it back on him making him fall to his knees. Mr. Pierce and the other man gathered their bearings, stood back up, and began to move towards me. I picked up the man and threw him into Mr. Pierce knocking them back to the ground. I turned my attention back to Malik as he was standing up. I wasn't having that. I kept sending pain, after pain, just as he did to Lucas, keeping him down. With each surge sent, I would move closer, until finally I was close enough to touch him. My instincts were telling me to touch him. Now would be a good time to listen to myself. Without thinking, I knew what I had to do. I placed my right hand on Malik's chest, while my other hand was still sending crippling pain to him. His eyes rolled back in his head as I felt his body heat start to leave him. Some of my anger was going with it. Before he died he disappeared, completely vanished underneath me.

Only a moment had gone by since I touched Malik and he

disappeared. I looked around; there was no trace that Malik was here or of what he had done until I saw Lucas. His body lay motionless on the ground. I snapped out of my trance-like state and rushed to his side.

"Lucas. Oh God, I'm so sorry. Please no!"
My whole body begun to hurt, my heart hurt the worst. Tears started to flow down my cheeks as I knelt down beside him. His eyes were closed; he looked like he was asleep. I shook him, not wanting to believe it was too late.

"Lucas please, don't leave me, I need you! Somebody please help me!" I screamed in to the night.
I looked around in the darkness in hopes that someone would be there to help me; however, no one was there. I was alone in the cold winter night. I could feel the last of Lucas's heat completely leave his body. It was too late to save him; I knew he was gone.

"No!" I cried out.
I couldn't let go. I sat there with him as I cried, looking at him as I caressed his face and lips. I held him close as I bent down to his ear and said my last words to him.

"Lucas, I love you."
I kissed his lips one last time and then I lay my head on his chest and cried. My heart shattered into pieces and a piece of my soul dies as I say my goodbyes.

Twenty One
Souls

I knew I probably should go call for help; however, I wasn't ready to leave his side. I lay over him in pain of his lose, with one hand on his chest and the one draped over his lifeless body. I've only known him a few months; however, I just couldn't imagine my life without him. I was going to miss him so much. I would miss the way his eyes lit up every time I came in the room and how he looked at me just before he kissed me. I would miss his arms around me, holding me tight to make me feel better. I felt guilty; the last words I had said to him before all of this had happened were of anger. Now I would never be able to make it right. I broke his heart. If I could take it all back, I would.

A sudden new feeling took over me; I had no control over it, yet it was okay, I felt wonderful and warm. I let it consume me, smothering my pain and me. As I felt the last of his heat leave his body and the cold settle in, I now felt the warmth start to return to it spreading at a tremendous speed. I could hear a thud-thud, thud-thud, thud-thud, and then I felt arms go around me. I was disoriented and confused. Instead of arms pulling me up and away from Lucas, they were pulling me tighter to him. Was it possible? Or, was I delusional? Even at that thought, my heart began to race with hope. I pulled away from him as much as was allowed, to see his beautiful brown eyes open and looking up at me. They were full of life and that wonderful light again.

"Where do you think you are going?" he asked. Lucas's voice was rough and strained, yet he smiled.

"Oh Lucas!" I hugged him tightly.

He winced in pain; nevertheless, he hugged me just as tight.

I pulled back quickly, "Don't you ever do that to me again!"

He chuckled my favorite little laugh and then winced once again. I sat up so I wasn't crushing and causing him unnecessary pain anymore.

"You are hurt," I looked him over. "Badly."

His leg was broken for sure and by the way he winced when he laughed, probably some ribs too. I thought back to me almost killing Malik and now bringing Lucas back to life. I was hoping I would be able to heal him as well. I placed my hands over Lucas's ribs and tried to concentrate. I focused with all I had; however, nothing happened. After a few moments, I relaxed my arms and hung my head. Lucas took my hand and squeezed it weakly.

I smiled a little at the comfort he always provided, "Come on, let's get you home."

He shook his head, "No, I don't think I can walk very far, I'm pretty banged up."

"Then I'm going to get help."

As much as I hated to leave his side, he needed help. I started to stand; however, he grabbed my arm pulling me back down to him.

"No stay with me. I brought my cell we can call the others to us."

I patted his jeans pockets for his phone (mine was lost or stolen when Mr. Pierce kidnapped me), pulled it from his left pocket, and called Matt. After explaining that Lucas was hurt, but we were okay and briefly what had happened, I told him where to find us.

"They're on their way," I reported to Lucas and put the phone in my pocket.

Lucas took my hand. "There is something I have been wanting to say to you and before anything else happens again I want you to know…" he paused and looked into my eyes.

They were full of the kind of emotion I liked to see, the kind that speeds my heart rate.

"I love you."

I instantly burst into tears. Lucas looked scared and wounded, as if he had made a terrible mistake in telling me that he loved me.

"I'm sorry," he whispered. His voice was rough and sad.

I looked at him through my tears, "Don't be. That is what I said to you before you woke up."

A smile spread slowly across his face, as well as mine.

It was getting colder and I started to shiver; however, I didn't care. I could have gone inside out of the storm, but I still couldn't leave him. The snow was piling up on Lucas's jacket as he lay on the ground. I couldn't do anything about the cold, though I at least could keep the snow off him. I waved my hand around us, making a dry bubble to keep the snow off us.

We sat there minutes, maybe hours before we were found. I saw the lights before I heard the vehicle approach. Aunt Marie got out and rushed to us, while the others checked the surrounding area.

She knelt down on the side of Lucas opposite from me, "You're hurt." She looked up at me, "Are you?"

"I'm fine, please just help him."

Quickly, but gently -most of the time- she worked and healed Lucas; his knee was first. I could see the pain on his face as she realigned it, causing a sick popping noise. If I never hear that noise again, it would be too soon. His ribs were next and finally the cuts he had on his face and hands. Aunt Marie brushed them away as if they were dirt.

Lucas sat up and took a deep breath, "Thank you Marie." I instantly felt better and even relaxed a little. He stood up and held his hand out to help me up. As he pulled, I felt pain and I realized then that I *was* hurt; my body ached and my head throbbed from being knocked out and thrown to the ground a couple of times. I groaned as he pulled. When Lucas eased up, I started to fall back to the snow-covered ground; Lucas and Aunt Marie instantly caught me.

"Marie," Lucas said.

I shook my head, "I'm fine until we get home."

"You are hurt let me heal you now."

"But, I'm cold," I whined.

Lucas chuckled and carried me to the vehicle.

Lucas climbed in beside me, "You need to text Sam."

Inside the house, I lay on the couch with a blanket over me to keep me warm. I let Aunt Marie heal the parts that hurt the worst first, mostly my head and back. There were rope burns around my wrists that didn't really hurt they just looked horrible. Once Aunt Marie healed everything on me, I used Lucas's phone to text Sam and tell her I was all right. She was worried of course, and wanted to come over. I told her that I didn't think her braving the storm was a good idea when I was fine. She reluctantly agreed.

Sara was hovering over me behind the couch, watching me closely as Lucas started telling everyone what had happened. Even though I was safe, I could tell that she was still concerned. She had lost me once so to speak.

"Malik sent people to watch Kendall after so many failed attempts. That's why we haven't seen or been attacked, they were waiting for the perfect moment. The cop we knew about; however the teacher…" he shook his head in disbelief.

He continued to tell the story when it dawned on me that

Lucas knew where I was. It baffled me.

"How did you find me?" I asked him.

He stopped in mid sentence. He looked as though he didn't understand it either.

"I...felt you," he answered with all eyes on him now. "I heard you scream and rushed out, but you were already gone. I wanted to run after you, I just didn't know which way you went. Instead of running aimlessly, I closed my eyes and pictured you in my head. It felt like the right thing to do. All I could see was darkness; however, I knew you were close. Sam called just then to tell you that she wasn't coming because of the storm. I told her you were taken. After calming her down to get an answer, I asked what was familiar on the west side of town to her. She told me a few places; however, only one stood out to me, the Emerson house. I approached the clearing near the house and saw a man outside. I took him out easily and came to find you."

He told the rest of the story up until he died. Even though I could see and hear him, I could still feel the emptiness and heartache of losing him. I could still see him lying dead on the ground in front of me even if it was briefly. I had to fill in the rest of the story up until Lucas woke up. Once I had finished it was quiet, everyone was looking at me with an expression I considered as awe.

"What?" I simply asked.

"You brought Lucas back to life?" Aunt Marie asked me.

I glanced at Lucas and smiled.

"Yeah, how did I do that?" I asked her.

She shook her head, "I'm a healer and I can't even do that."

I felt my forehead crinkle and my eyebrows pull together as I really thought about it.

"How *did* I do that?" I looked at Lucas for an answer; however, he just shrugged his shoulders.

"It's very, very rare," Graham said.

"What do you mean?" I asked him.

"Didn't you say you knew that Kendall wasn't far?" he asked Lucas.

"Yes. Somehow I knew that all I had to do was focus and I would be able to sense her."

"Did this happen with Isaac?" he was smiling.

I had a feeling that Graham already knew the answer. Lucas thought for a moment and then shook his head to indicate that it had not.

"I felt him as well, just before he came inside to rescue me," I added.

Graham's smile got even bigger.

"What are we missing?" Matt asked.

"You see, souls have many different patterns so to speak. Some are very close; however, there are only two exactly the same. If they find each other it's a miracle, a very rare one."

"So what you are saying is that Lucas is my soul mate?" I smiled inside as I asked the question.

"Exactly; however, it's more than just that. You'll be connected in a way that no one else is. You'll be able to feel each other in special situations as in tonight. I actually had a feeling shortly after I saw the two of you together; however, you never showed the signs until now."

I looked at Lucas just as he looked at me, we both smiled at each other.

"Just how rare is this?" Sara asked.

"It happens once in a few million to the normal humans and the chances of a Natural and their Protector having a matching soul is remarkable," Graham answered.

Something else dawned on me. Actually, I'm surprised Aunt Marie didn't think of it.

"I almost killed Malik and I brought Lucas back to life, why couldn't I heal him?" I asked her.

"I think that you have a special power, unlike anything we have ever come across."

"I've never heard of it either," Matt added, "but she's right, you are something special."

Everyone had decided it would be best to stay the night because of the storm; it was much worse than they anticipated. Beside, I felt safer with everyone here. Tonight had taken a lot out of me and I was exhausted. I was wobbly when I stood up, so Lucas helped me up stairs.

I looked in the mirror; the person reflecting back at me looked as tired as I felt. I took a nice long hot shower until the water turned cold and then dressed into my pajamas. I opened the bathroom door and shut the light off. It was dark, only a crack of light shown through from my room down the hall. I imagined myself back in the basement of the Emerson house. My heart began to race and I started to panic. I flicked the light back on and immediately started to calm down. Wonderful, this would be just what I need, to be afraid of the dark on top of everything else. I left the bathroom light on and walked down the hall to my room.

Lucas was sitting on the edge of my bed waiting for me. He was smiling until he saw my face. He immediately jumped up and rushed to me.

"What's wrong?" he asked.

I shook my head, walking across the room and sitting on the bed, "I'm okay, it's just the darkness reminded me of the basement."

Lucas walked around to the other side of the bed; he laid down, pulled me close, and wrapped his arms around me. Immediately the scared feeling started to fade.

"Any better?"

I nodded. A few moments pass by as I lay in his arms letting him comfort me, before either of us spoke.

"I didn't get a chance to say thank you for saving my life," he said. He trailed his fingers along the length of my arm.

"You're welcome."

I was half laying on him. When he sat up, I was forced to go with him.

He moved the hair from my face, "No, I really mean it. Thank you."

I put my hand on his face and looked into his eyes, "I would do anything for you." We both smiled.

"As I would for you."
His smile faded.

"What's wrong?"

He didn't answer me right away; however, I could see the pain in his eyes.

He sighed, "I should have been able to protect you better. I shouldn't have let you walk away in the first place. Tonight is all my fault."

I couldn't believe what I was hearing. I shook my head, "Don't say that. Malik would have found a way. He has been watching us for months maybe longer. You died trying to protect me. I'm the one who should say thank you."

He entwined his fingers with mine and then smiled, "Why don't we call it even?"

"Fine, although I think I'm right."
Lucas chuckled at my stubbornness and lay back down on the bed pulling me to his side. He wrapped his arms around me once again. The warmth of him comforted my deepest fears, all but the heartache I caused. I sat up turning around to face him, half-lying on his chest.

"I'm sorry."

He looked confused. His eyebrows pulled together, "For what?"

"For everything," my eyes welled up with tears. "For being so upset that I broke up with you and broke your heart." The tears spilled down my cheeks.

"Shh," he wiped the tears from my face. His touch was warm and gentle. "Don't apologize. I'm the one who is sorry," he moved the hair from my face again. "I should have insisted that they tell you from the start. Can *you* ever forgive *me*?"

I looked in to his eyes and smiled, and then I leaned in and kissed him. I pulled back after a moment. "Does that answer your question?"

He smiled mischievously, "I don't know. I don't think I heard you."

I laughed out loud. After the night we have had, full of pain and sadness, it felt good to laugh.

"I love you."

"I love you too," he pulled me to him and kissed me once more.

Epilogue

It has been a week since I was abducted and Lucas died. We haven't seen Malik or his people since then. Even though it has settled down a bit, the protection for me hasn't let up. Lucas is just as protective as ever. It was snowing again; it hasn't stopped since Friday. The storm from the night of my kidnapping turned into a blizzard, thanks to Andrew, or I should say Mr. Pierce; Andrew could manipulate the element of water. School had been canceled until Tuesday because of the storm, which I was grateful for. For one thing, I needed some time after everything that had happened, and for another, I wouldn't have had my homework done for Monday.

Karman has completely ignored us. Sam realized what had happened that day I pinned Karman against the wall. She was happy that I had finally gotten the best of her. Like Lucas, she was worried if Karman could keep her mouth shut. I, on the other hand, had no worries about that. I saw Karman in the bathroom yesterday. As I walked in, she cowered against the wall and edged her way out, her eyes never meeting mine. We also got a new substitute Spanish teacher; Lucas made sure that he and Graham met her.

With Grahams help, Lucas and I have been working on our new power; we are not getting very far though. Graham said that we might only be able to "feel" each other during special situations, but he also said that it just might take awhile to get the hang of it.

We have talked about the 'parents' situation some more. I haven't completely forgiven them for lying to me for so long. It isn't going to be easy; however, we are on the long road to recovery.

Everyone, including Sam, was at my house tonight. Dinner, dishes, and homework were done. Now we were sitting in the living room talking about the coming months. We think Malik has disappeared for a little while, until he hatches a new plan. As to him disappearing…I had no idea how he had accomplished that. Lucas said that he was teleported from there; Malik, Mr. Pierce, or the other guy had that power. The state that Malik was in, suggested that one of the others had it. I still didn't understand how I had almost killed Malik and how I had brought Lucas back to life. Aunt Marie and I had practiced healing plants; however, I just couldn't do it. Graham had said that it was the same kind of energy and power that I had used during the battle in Matt and Sara's yard. Looking back on it now, I had to agree. It felt the same way, that same uncontrolled feeling. I don't like it; it scares me. Like always, Lucas could tell when I was worried or thinking about something too hard.

He reached for my hand, "You okay?"

I gave him a reassuring smile, "I'm fine."

He kissed the top of my forehead. I caught Sam watching us, she was grinning. She was happy that we were back together.

"What do we do now?" I asked him.

"What do you mean?"

Our conversation attracted the others' attention.

"Well, Malik isn't dead, he will be back, and probably soon," I looked around to the others. "What happens now? Do we keep trying to get the incantation?"

I felt disappointed and hopeless. How were we supposed to get the incantation when it was in the tight clutches of Malik?

"The incantation isn't the only way to kill Malik

anymore," Lucas said.

I knew what Lucas meant, I was just hopping it wasn't true, "I have the power within".

Those words scared me more than anything has so far. As always, Lucas's words comforted me and helped my worries and fears.

"We will never stop. I will protect you. You will be safe."

Made in the USA
Middletown, DE
25 September 2016